l,
bu safety as
ack
makes his move against Jungor Stonespringer,
and all of Thorbardin pays the price.

Kayolin is guarded by different dwarves now,
these the supporters of Regar Smashfingers's rule,
as Brandon and Gretchan find when they return
to Garnet Thax. After years of no contact with
Thorbardin, Regar has grown impatient and declared
himself king, supported by the Torc of the Forge,
an artifact crafted by Reorx himself and showing
the god's favor. No longer will Kayolin bow to
Thorbardin's will. They have heard nothing from
Thorbardin, and have asked nothing.

The signs of war hang over both cities as
Brandon and Gretchan carefully maneuver
through the frightening politics of Garnet Thax,
trying to stay out of the way long enough
to be sure the Bluestone family is safe,
but after hundreds of years of isolation,
there are still secrets for those
who dare to question.

The ones who dare have come.

DWARF HOME

The Secret of Pax Tharkas

The Heir of Kayolin

The Fate of Thorbardin
September 2009

DOUGLAS NILES

Dwarf Home • Volume Two

The Heir of Kayolin

Dwarf Home, Volume Two
THE HEIR OF KAYOLIN

Published by Wizards of the Coast, Inc. DRAGONLANCE, WIZARDS OF THE COAST, and their respective logos are trademarks of Wizards of the Coast, Inc., in the U.S.A. and other countries.

Printed in the U.S.A.

Cover art by Matt Stawicki
First Printing: October 2008

9 8 7 6 5 4 3 2 1

ISBN: 978-0-7869-5003-4
620-21894740-001-EN

U.S., CANADA,
ASIA, PACIFIC, & LATIN AMERICA
Wizards of the Coast, Inc.
P.O. Box 707
Renton, WA 98057-0707
+1-800-324-6496

EUROPEAN HEADQUARTERS
Hasbro UK Ltd
Caswell Way
Newport, Gwent NP9 0YH
GREAT BRITAIN
Save this address for your records.

Visit our web site at www.wizards.com

To Alaina, and her
Brave New World

PROLOGUE

The Journal of Gretchan Pax: Being the Complete History of the Dwarf Peoples of Krynn, Entailing the Rise and Fall of Great Nations, the Legacy of the God Reorx—He Who Is Master of Every Forge—and the Future that Still Awaits Our Indefatigable People.

The following is an excerpt therefrom:

The dwarves of Krynn, my people, have endured thousands of years of violence, strife, brutality, treachery, and cruelty. Sadly, much of this torment has been self-inflicted. Too often one clan, city, or band of dwarves has wreaked villainy upon another for shortsighted reasons of avarice, vengeance, or simple blockheaded intransigence. After long and thoughtful consideration, I have come to realize there is a single explanation, a sole source to this eternal problem:

Men!

I refer, of course, to the impossibly stubborn, pin-headed, narrow-minded, eternally complaining male members of the dwarf race. In a broader sense, my assessment perhaps might be expanded to extend to the masculine gender of other peoples, such as humans, ogres, or elves, but, given the scope of my writing, it is my intent to focus upon my own race.

So, I write again: Men!

They are impossible to reason with, to understand, to inspire, or to motivate. As evidence, I have my own experience to serve as solid proof. I have been exposed to an array of male stubborn mulishness during the past year, a year during which I have had the rare opportunity to dwell in the fabled fortress of Pax Tharkas. Here I saw and even influenced great events and witnessed the beginning and end of a potentially disastrous internecine war, one of so many in our history. I have come to understand that our people stand perpetually at the brink of great opportunities, a grand future, and yet at every turn our destiny is thwarted by the shortsighted, timid, and just plain stubborn *men* whom Reorx, for reasons beyond my understanding, has chosen to lead us.

My arrival in this hallowed place preceded only by a short time the violent clash between two very different factions of dwarves, groups separated by more than a thousand years of deep-seated antipathy. The Neidar hill dwarves inhabit the many towns scattered across the rugged countryside surrounding this fortress. The ancient rivals of the Neidar are the mountain dwarves who now hold Pax Tharkas. These mountain dwarves, now dwelling on the surface of the world, are refugees from the great underground nation of Thorbardin, a place currently controlled by a violent cult of religious fanatics, I am told by credible sources. The mountain dwarves of Thorbardin have sealed that vast and ancient kingdom against the outside world, but a small portion of the population escaped to claim this ancient home on the surface.

A year ago the hill dwarves, deceived into serving a minion of dark magic, attacked Pax Tharkas in a frenzy, and it was only the intervention of Reorx—through the humble person of myself, his loyal priestess—that unmasked the black fiend. He was vanquished, and the shamed hill dwarves hastened back to their homes.

I remained here, in the fortress, and saw the victorious mountain dwarves stand at the brink of greatness. It was here that I met my father, General Otaxx Shortbeard, a venerable warrior whom I had never known. He is the strong right arm of the exiled monarch, Tarn Bellowgranite. It was my good fortune to come to know King Bellowgranite, former ruler of Thorbardin, now the leader of the refugees who fled that kingdom for Pax Tharkas. And I felt my affection grow for a heroic warrior, Brandon Bluestone—the fighter who wielded his Reorx-blessed axe and played a crucial role in the mountain dwarf victory. In the daze of triumph, I envisioned an even greater potential before us, a historic opportunity to change the dwarf race forever.

Yet in the end, each of these males has balked at any of my suggestions, any move to consolidate our victory, and to move toward a golden future. Sad to say, I have had more encouraging conversations with the wretched gully dwarf, Gus Fishbiter, than with my father, with the king, or with Brandon. My dog and I are proud to have helped Gus following his magical escape from Thorbardin. I consider him to be "less male" than the others, yet now, even Gus languishes without purpose, dwelling among the others of his kind in the filthy, lightless tunnels beneath this fortress.

My goal, my life's work, remains as it has ever been: to study, to witness, to observe the varied dwarves of Krynn. As my mother's daughter, I was raised among the Daewar refugees who followed Severus Stonehand to the east, seeking the original dwarf home. As an adult, a sturdy dwarf maid and priestess of Reorx, I set out to return to the modern lands of my people, visiting and observing and writing about my travels. I was determined to visit fabled Thorbardin and, eventually, the northern nation of Kayolin.

Naturally, a number of men conspired to keep me from achieving that goal. To be sure, Thorbardin remains closed against any approach, sealed by its fanatical king to ensure it remains "pure," untainted by external forces. Tarn and Otaxx seemed uninterested in even *trying* to change this state of affairs. I have told them of the legendary artifact, the Tricolor Hammerhead, a tool capable of smashing any fortification. The hammer consists of three wedges of magical stone. Though fate has placed two of the three stones—the blue and green—into Tarn Bellowgranite's hands, he remains utterly, pigheadedly unwilling to pursue any kind of search for the third, the Redstone. It is as if, even if he had the means to breach Thorbardin's gates, he would not attempt to do so.

With Thorbardin beyond my reach, at least for the time being, I have repeatedly, although gently, expressed my desire to visit the other great dwarf nation, Kayolin. Brandon Bluestone calls that fair place home and could take me there; it lies but a month or two's travel to the north. But he left there as a fugitive, apparently—unjustly accused of a crime—and remains unwilling to return. In Brandon I have seen flashes of greatness, and in fact, he has roused in my heart passions I have never before known. But his obsession over his family's bad fortune—the Bluestone Luck, they call it—prevents him from acting decisively to improve his circumstances. Though his family was once rich, powerful, and influential in Kayolin, his father's position is now tenuous because of the hostility of the ruler and his powerful minions, and Brandon dares not challenge the status quo.

Until now I despaired of him, believing he would simply remain here, allowing another year to slip past without any forceful action. For all the previous months here, there has been no word from his home—until today. A package, long on the trail, dispatched from Kayolin to the Neidar town of Hillhome, then begrudgingly forwarded by the hill dwarves to the lofty fortress where he has been temporarily residing, finally reached him here in Pax Tharkas. Even as I write these pages, he is reading an extensive missive dispatched by his father.

Whether the news therein will spur him to some sort of decision, only time will tell.

Part I

Thorbardin

ONE

TWO GUILDERS

The old dwarf muttered to himself and stomped his cane against the stones of First Street, in the great city of Norbardin. It was a relatively new city, excavated under the mountains following the Chaos War, and the road was wide and straight. The stones underfoot were set so smoothly that there was barely a crack between them to be seen or felt, and that was a good thing for the elderly pedestrian, since he could barely see.

Still, using his cane to probe before him, he hobbled along at a fair clip, despite the wear and tear of a life that had bent his backbone and forced a permanent stoop onto his once-broad shoulders. He was a Theiwar, with the distinguishing pale skin and light, almost fawn-colored, irises in his sensitive eyes that mark so many of that breed. His beard was long, but thin, the wispy hairs a universal slate gray in color, and his balding pate was fringed by only a meager few strands of the same colorless gray.

He glanced around and squinted nervously as other dwarves, hustling and bustling, stepped around him and hurried on their way. The old dwarf veered to the other side of the street so he didn't have to meet approaching pedestrians face-to-face. At one point he paused to glare at the outside of a shuttered shop, the little store displaying the *Abercrumb's Fine Silverwerks* sign. Satisfied that the interior was dark, devoid of customers, he continued on another dozen paces and turned in at a door on the other side of the street. He entered the little shop and slammed the door hard enough to start the overhead sign, *Two Guilders Novelty and Pharmology Emporium,* swinging violently.

He stood in front of the counter of a small store. Every bit of the wall space, except for the front door and another door leading into the interior, was lined by shelving—smooth stones of slate that rested in precise grooves cut into the rock walls. Those shelves, in turn, were covered almost to overflowing with bottles and tins, small boxes and casks, ceramic mortars and glass beakers, and an array of even-harder-to-identify materials. One jar held preserved eyeballs, which seemed to stare nosily in every direction. Other containers held more mysterious objects, such as worms or entrails coiling in viscous liquid. Something that looked like a pile of dead, dry bats— which, in fact, it was—rose in moldy chaos in one dark corner.

Other rows of merchandise were more practical and immediately useful in nature, such as the cabinets of clothing that included exotic items like boots that made the wearer tread utterly silently and cloaks that camouflaged one into matching almost perfectly the surroundings of stone or water. All the goods were for sale, at prices that could be negotiated but that were invariably high. The products were many and varied; customers, however, were few.

Peat and Sadie Guilder were both accomplished Theiwar magic-users, belonging to the order of the red robes, and for decades they had made a decent living sharing the fruits of their magical skills with those dwarves who could overcome their inherent distrust of magic enough to spend hard-earned steel on one or another of the unique products that the Two Guilders Emporium offered. Unfortunately, such dwarves had proved to be very rare indeed.

"I'm here!" the old Theiwar called loudly. "I'm home!"

"Who's there?" came the query from the back room. "Is someone there?" The voice was female, raspy with age, and tart with determined curiosity.

"It's your husband!" the Theiwar snapped. "Who else would it be? You didn't exactly expect a customer, did you?"

The crone of a dwarf woman who emerged through the interior door gave no response to his question. She was stooped and aged like her husband, with a wrinkled face and tiny, glittering eyes. Her white hair was tied in a thin braid that trailed down her back. She wore a shapeless dress, and when she momentarily glared at Peat, she smacked her lips to reveal a precious few yellowed teeth standing sentinel on her gums. She stepped past him and went to the front door. Pulling it open, she glared up and down the street before she flipped the sign on the outside of the door from *Open* to *Closed.* Shutting the door, she carefully made sure it was locked. Only then did she turn and look at the dwarf who was her husband of more than one hundred years.

"You could at least tell me you're home!" she declared querulously. "And what took you so long?"

she demanded. "I've been about stewing in my lizard broth waiting for you!"

"Well, Sadie, I don't exactly move like I used to," Peat replied patiently. "But I circled the whole square, stopped to get the gossip, and even had a beer with a sergeant of the palace guard. All in all, a good day's work—though I could use another beer, now that I think of it."

"There'll be time for that later!" Sadie snapped, still glaring. "Didn't you think of me back here worrying about you?"

Peat shrugged, squinting nearsightedly at the blurry features of his wife's face. Doggedly he continued his report. "Then old Abercrumb caught up with me in the middle of the square—there was no way I could dodge him. I had to listen to him go on for an hour about the state of business along First Street. Couldn't hardly disagree with him, but I just wanted to be out of there. He finally left, told me he had to get back to his shop."

"Well, at least you didn't meet old Abercrumb," she muttered vaguely. "That nosy Hylar would have wasted even more of your time! Did you get to the square?"

"I *told* you—ah, never mind," Peat said, rolling his eyes. He held up a small piece of parchment that was marked with some arcane symbols, hastily scratched with the piece of graphite Peat carried in his belt pocket.

Sadie smacked her lips around her few remaining teeth and studied the sheet. She huffed and muttered indecipherably, but her anger had passed. "Well, come in the back, then," she said at last. "And tell me what you learned."

The back room of the Two Guilders shop was as crowded and messy as the front. The notable difference was that the rear chamber was larger. Two very big desks occupied one wall, while a hard sleeping pallet took up the far corner. A magical light, feeble and flickering as the power of the incantation waned, glowed from an unburned candle mounted on the wall. The desktops were strewn with parchments, and an array of quills and inkwells were scattered around the papers.

"What are you working on?" Peat asked, glancing at the fresh ink on one of the parchments.

"I was doing some work to pass the time," Sadie admitted, waving at the desk.

"I can see that much!" Peat replied. "Answer me straight for once. What were you *doing?"*

"Yes—I was stewing!" she barked. "I told you that! Don't tell me you're going deaf as well as blind!"

Peat merely sighed and followed her past the desk.

She shook her head impatiently. "So what's going on in the city? Did you get the information the Master requested?"

Peat instinctively ducked and glanced over his shoulder, though the two elderly dwarves were alone in the shop's workroom. Even so, he lowered his voice to a whisper.

"The king is going to cancel the Festival of the Forge—claims it's heretical and obscene, of course, just like everything else he doesn't like. And when he makes the announcement, he wants his troops in position to squelch any uprising in the city. So he'll keep most of his men-at-arms in the palace garrison and the Midfort to keep order. All four of the city gates will be lightly manned, so that Jungor Stonespringer can divert the number of soldiers he needs to watch his own people in the heart of Norbardin."

"As if he doesn't have the city cowed like a whipped rat," Sadie said scornfully. "He'll never be overthrown from within anyway!"

Peat continued as if he hadn't heard. "I spoke to some of the gatehouse captains—bribed them with a bottle of dwarf spirits. Enhanced, of course." He glanced nervously at one of the potion bottles on a nearby shelf. "The officers were quite specific in their deployments. I wrote the numbers down as soon as I could get away."

Sadie nodded. She knew that a tiny dose of charm potion, mixed with potent alcohol, was the method preferred by both of them when their master needed information about the royal garrison—or about anything else happening within Norbardin. She hadn't heard the details of Peat's report, but her husband's notes were precise, inscribed in a code that only the two Guilders—and their master—could unravel.

"It took you long enough. I'm still surprised you got any information before the potion wore off!" she snapped.

He bit his tongue, staring at her irritably. Rather than reply directly, he put down the scrap of parchment upon which he had made his notes. They consisted of some abstract symbols, with a number beside each symbol. The note marked the locations of Norbardin's key defensive positions, including the main gate, the two side gates, and the large ramp, currently raised, which blocked direct access to the city from the Urkhan Sea.

Sadie looked over the notes and nodded, satisfied. "They'll be at half strength during the festival, then, the fools!"

"Do you think the Master will make his move then?"

She shrugged but then nodded thoughtfully. "I'd say the signs are right." She handed the note back to her husband, and nodded to a bell jar on a corner table. "You send the message. I want to keep working on that scroll."

"What scroll is it anyway?" he repeated, but her back was already turned and she either didn't hear him or chose again to ignore his question.

Peat sighed long-sufferingly and went over the jar, using his cane to tap through the many obstacles littering the shadowy floor of the workshop. He sidestepped a pile of dusty books and, with a snap of his fingers, kindled a fire on the burner nearby. Gingerly he set the bottle and its stone base on top of the burner.

Sadie returned to her desk. The soft blue glow of magic surrounded her, and Peat watched her, still entranced after all those years, until finally the odor of baking stone reminded him that the Sender was ready.

He wheeled around to face the table and put a heavy leather glove on his left hand. Holding the note in his right, he lifted the hot bell jar and smoothly placed the note on the stone beneath it. That circle of slate was already glowing red from the steady heat. He murmured a single word of magic as he set the jar down then blinked—surprised in spite of himself—as the spell of sending took the missive and bore it away.

—DH—

In an enclosed cavern, deep beneath Norbardin, a similar bell jar flashed a blue glow. The stone base, empty moments before, held a sheet of shimmering parchment—or, at least, a magical approximation of such a page. A short, black-robed wizard had been working at a nearby table. Though the jar was behind him, he immediately sensed the message's arrival and turned to raise the glass with a gloved hand. With the other hand he picked up the illusionary sheet. He read it quickly and nodded in satisfaction as the magical missive dissolved into a shower of tiny sparks, embers drifting gently to the smooth stone floor.

"The time has come," announced the powerful wizard, addressing the rank of attentive apprentices standing nearby awaiting his orders. His voice was soft, but the words seemed to linger in the air, each one fully absorbed by the intent listeners.

Willim the Black took a deep breath, and for a time stood stock still, relishing the moment. The missive was a significant document, and as he reflected on its importance, he understood that his life, his circumstances, were about to change dramatically. He knew beyond all doubt that the throne of Thorbardin, the leadership of that great dwarf nation, finally lay within his grasp. He wanted to savor the occasion.

Finally he would break out of the lair that had been his fortress, his prison, for the past decade. In many ways the great chamber was perfect, blocked as it was from the rest of Thorbardin by solid and impenetrable walls of stone. It had been carved from the bedrock of the mountain range on the orders of the previous king, Tarn Bellowgranite, but the chamber had been abandoned when a fearful menace had been discovered there.

That menace had become Willim's tool, as were the young, potent Theiwar dwarves he had brought there to train. Fifteen young magic-users, out of the original forty, had survived a year of especially grueling apprenticeship. They stood before their master, each wearing the plain black robe of the wizardly order. Beards combed, chests thrust forward with justifiable pride, they awaited his inspection, his approval, his command.

Willim the Black, the most powerful wizard of Thorbardin, an ally of Dalamar the Dark himself, strutted back and forth before the row of magic-users, appraising them. The powerful master knew he was grotesque in his physical appearance, but the well-trained apprentices did not react to his terrifying visage. Willim's eyeless face, lids sewn shut with gruesome stitches, swept back and forth across the pale, serious faces of his assistants. Through the power of the spell of true-seeing, the enchantment that permanently enhanced all of his senses, he perceived each steady gaze, beheld the tension in legs and arms, absorbed the purposeful determination behind each bearded face.

And on a lone nonbearded face as well.

Willim the Black felt pleased. Fifteen of the sixteen were young Theiwar males, pale skinned and bushy bearded, strapping and strong. The oldest, Gypsum, had proved to be exceptionally able with a variety of lethal magics, potions, and charms—as well as quick and deadly with his keen knife. Two others, Shale and Petro, had excelled in displays of reckless courage, deceit, treachery, and disguise. Like all of their comrades, they possessed cruelty and sadism in abundance in their characters and undying loyalty to Willim above all.

Almost against his will, the wizard felt his attention drawn to the sixteent apprentice, the lone female in the group—indeed, the only one of her gender Willim had ever accepted into his circle. Perhaps she, too, felt the attention of his seeing spell, for her own eyes—pale and wide—virtually glowed in response to the pleasure of his inspection.

Facet Anvilmaster would have been worthy of closer inspection to any male dwarf, of any age. She had long dark hair, in contrast to her alabaster skin, and unlike most dwarf maids, she did not constrain it in braids or tails. Instead, it flowed past her shoulders, shimmering down, far down her body, becoming virtually indistinguishable from the silken darkness of her wizard's robe. Her breasts swelled that robe most attractively, and the pronounced curve of her hips and thighs was suggested by the ripples in the garment every time she moved. Her full lips were a bright crimson, a shocking contrast to her pale skin, suggesting nothing so much as the color of fresh blood.

Willim shook his head, startled by his own thoughts—it was no time to be so distracted. Female flesh had never held any appeal for him. Why should that change in her presence?

It was a time for action, not idle thoughts! He inspected his apprentices again, stalking along their file, knowing that none of them had failed in the tests he had presented, yet fully realizing they also needed one more crucial lesson. It would be the ultimate lesson on the subject of loyalty and, to Willim, the most important lesson that his underlings could learn. His attentions passed over a few of the most accomplished apprentices—Gypsum, Facet, Shale, a couple more—knowing they were too valuable to be wasted. Of the others, it didn't much matter which one he picked, and he quickly settled upon a candidate.

"Krave!" he snapped, and the black-bearded dwarf in the middle of the row snapped to an even more rigid state of attention.

"Yes, Master!" replied that worthy student, honored to be singled out. He was clearly unaware of the wizard's grim intent.

"How long have you been in communication with King Stonespringer, the false monarch? He who would weaken our nation with his foolish superstitions, with his fanatical devotion to ancient mythology?"

Immediately Krave's already pale skin blanched to a snowy white. "No, Master! I swear—not I—I never—"

"Liar!" snapped Willim the Black, pointing a stubby, black-gloved finger at the cringing dwarf. The apprentices to either side of Krave took quick sidesteps away from their accused comrade even as that pathetic, young Theiwar raised his hands before his face.

"Master, I promise—"

Those were his last words. Willim snapped his fingers and uttered a guttural, deadly word. Blue magic flashed in the air, leaving a lingering stench of brimstone as a jagged bolt of light struck Krave in the chest. Blasting his black robes out of the way, the lethal spell churned through his skin, his ribs, tearing into his heart. The deadly enchantment squeezed that organ until it burst with a wet *splat.*

Krave fell, instantly dead, but before the body hit the floor, Willim was already stalking back up and down the rank of survivors. He knew that his visage, with the stitched eye sockets and scarred face, was abominable to them, and he let their gaze linger on him as, one at a time, he took their measure. Many were shaken; a few, like Gypsum and Shale, remained utterly impassive, though the former had been spattered by no small amount of blood. But all of them had seen and would forever remember the price of betrayal.

The lone female, he was intrigued to note, had licked her red lips until they glowed like enchanted rubies. Her eyes were alight, and she quivered with something very much like exhilaration.

"Facet!" he snapped, relishing the sudden fear that tightened her mouth, rendered her face even more pale.

"You and Gypsum will remain behind. The rest of you, step forward and take your potions."

She relaxed then, smiling slightly at his words. Gypsum remained impassive as the other black-robed dwarves advanced, each grabbing one of the bottles of elixir their master had arrayed on the stone tabletop. The Theiwar apprentices unstoppered their vials then turned to look at Willim expectantly.

"You know your assignments," the powerful wizard began. "For more than a year, you have all been preparing for this day. But that preparation is nothing compared what lies ahead!" He nodded in satisfaction as the looks of surprise and unease flickered across the bearded visages. "I have been waiting for this moment for decades, for more than a century! I have chosen you, trained you, taught you so that you could help me attain my goal. I expect, from each of you, success or death. Remember that: Success, or death. Now, drink your potions, and go to your stations. You will know when it is time to strike."

The thirteen young Theiwar nodded nervously, their bearded faces betraying a mix of eagerness and resolve. Gypsum remained rigidly at attention. Alone among the group, Facet offered that thin, suggestive smile, a slight pressing together of her lips that, Willim sensed, was an expression she reserved for him alone.

Each of the thirteen tipped the small bottle to his lips and sipped half the contents, reserving the rest for their return to the lair. One by one they blinked out of sight as the potion of teleportation sent them instantaneously through the darkness of Thorbardin to the positions Willim had assigned them. Only Gypsum and Facet remained behind, both standing expressionless and attentive before their master.

"I have decided that Facet will accompany you," Willim told Gypsum, watching him carefully. The wizard was neither surprised nor displeased to see an expression of resentment flicker briefly across the young male's face.

"As you wish, my master," Gypsum replied briskly.

"The two of you have the most important task of all," the supreme magic-user continued. "Just as the attack commences, the king will have emerged from his chambers to address the people of Norbardin from his prayer tower. You will be waiting for him, and you must strike as soon he appears. When he is dead, we can expect that the rest of the royal troops will fall into disarray. Our success will be assured."

"Aye, Master," Gypsum declared, his hand caressing the ivory hilt of his silver-bladed dagger.

"Thank you for this honor, my master!" Facet declared breathlessly, that strange, alluring expression once again brightening her eyes as she stared at him, touching the long, keen knife she wore at her belt. She shivered again, and he felt the thrill of that unusual power she possessed inside of her. It was alluring, yet dangerous. Should he fear it?

No, he told himself. He should *use* it.

"Now, drink your potions and go!" barked Willim. "I still have much to do!"

Gypsum and Facet each took up two bottles that their master had placed before them. The first, an elixir of invisibility, would mask them from discovery. The second, the potion of teleportation, would carry them to their objective.

Moments later, the two apprentices had vanished, and the black robe was alone in his lair. He stared at the place where Facet had stood moments before, his spell of vision playing tricks with his mind. It was as though her robe had teleported before her flesh did, leaving a momentary, and tantalizing, image of her naked body lingering in the air.

Why was he having such feelings? What purpose could lust serve him when his life's goal was so nearly complete? He didn't know why it was happening, but he couldn't deny the quickening of desire, the heat that flowed, all unbidden, through his body.

Then he remembered that he was not quite alone.

He strode across the floor, ignoring the lofty alcoves and the wide ramp leading up and away from the great chamber. That ramp ended in a solid wall, for the room had no physical connection to the rest of Thorbardin. It had once been excavated to serve as a new council hall for the thanes, except that a chilling discovery—Gorathian—had caused the dwarves to abandon the place, to seal it off from the nation forever.

Or so they had hoped.

Willim stopped at the edge of a deep crack that spread in a jagged streak across the stone floor. Heat welled from that chasm, and a dim redness glowed in the depths. The wizard could feel the heat against his skin, and with the power of his seeing spell, he could perceive the creature lurking in the depths, radiating fire, and yearning with hunger.

"Soon, Gorathian, my pet," he whispered.

Fire surged from the deep gap, flames licking into the air, crackling and swirling. If Willim was not protected by powerful magic, his flesh would be charred by such infernal heat. Because of those spells, however, the fiery explosion was a mere balm to his skin, inflaming his own will, strength, and determination.

He sensed the monster rising from the depths of the cavern, its great wings spreading and vast claws tearing at the foundation of the rock. Hatred and hunger fueled its ascent, and Willim could discern the mighty jaws as they spread wide, flames surging forth. Gorathian would have killed him, consumed him, if it could but reach him.

"Remember!" he cautioned sternly. "I am your master. You answer to my control; you remain here by my will. And soon, also by my will, you shall fly free, be released by my will," he promised with an edge of steel to his voice. "But not yet! Not yet!"

With a single gesture, he slashed his hand before his chest, and Gorathian fell back precipitously, restrained by a spell of such mastery that even an immortal being of raw chaos could not overcome it. And so Gorathian plunged back down to the prison in the deep bedrock below Thorbardin, fuming and frustrated, but thoroughly bound and trapped.

Willim turned his eyeless face toward the ceiling. He muttered a single word—no potion for him!—and vanished, leaving the lair to the smoke and the heat and the churning protection of the imprisoned monster.

Two

Uneasy Crown

The high Kharolis was the greatest mountain range on the continent, a soaring realm of rocky summits, frigid glaciers, and sheer cliffs. The inhospitable terrain was not conducive to human habitation, nor was it inviting to the cities and towns of any civilized, nor even uncivilized, folk. It was a realm of precipice and rocky crag, of ice and storm, fit only for the wild beasts and, perhaps, the occasional hill giant. Even the Neidar hill dwarves disdained the rugged heights, preferring instead to live in the more temperate and fertile valleys that surrounded the great range on all sides.

Underneath those mountains, however, lay a different reality: a mighty kingdom, carved into the bedrock of the mountain range, including a subterranean sea, one great city, many warrens and mines wherefrom the inhabitants drew sustenance and mineral wealth. The teeming city of Norbardin and the deep, still sea were flanked by vast, ruined cities, proof of an even greater might in a time not so long past. It was Thorbardin, the ancient and greatest home of the dwarf race upon all the world of Krynn.

Much of Thorbardin's population, wealth, and industry were centered around the great metropolis of Norbardin, a relatively new city. Norbardin had been created by the decree of the former king, Tarn Bellowgranite, as a matter of necessity. Throughout most of the nation's history, five great cities had thrived around the shores and in the environs of the Urkhan Sea, the great subterranean waterway of dwarfkind. A sixth city, called the Life-Tree, was the home of the Hylar clan, traditional leaders of Thorbardin. The Life-Tree had been excavated in the massive pillar of living stone that rose from an island in the middle of the sea, extending all the way to the ceiling of the vast, watery cavern. For more than a thousand years, the cities had been the homes of the five clans: Hylar, Daewar, Daergar, Theiwar, and Klar. Each group of dwarves dwelled for the most part in insular, segregated communities, Hylar living beside Hylar, Daergar among Daergar, and so forth.

Decades earlier, when the Chaos War had wracked the world of Krynn, the ancient capitals of the clans had been weakened and scarred by the onslaught of horrible beings, legions of deadly warriors and their greatest allies, the fire dragons. The invading forces had been destroyed, but at great cost, leaving the legendary cities of Thorbardin weakened and ruined. The Life-Tree had collapsed upon itself, leaving only a few broken ruins as remembrance of that great city. A stubby, huge stalactite marked its place on the cavern's ceiling, while a shattered island rose from the middle of the sea to mark the Life-Tree's tomb. The great delvings along the shore of the lake had been scattered and broken, gouged and ravaged by the forces of Chaos until ceilings collapsed, columns fell, and the great, cavernous spaces were rendered too treacherous for continued settlement.

Thus had commenced the migration and creation of Norbardin, constructed around the great fortress that had once been Thorbardin's North Gate. Most of the dwarves had abandoned their ancient cities and moved en masse to Norbardin. The most numerous clans—the Theiwar, Daergar, and Hylar—established flourishing districts in the steadily expanding cities. The miserable Aghar, the gully dwarves, trooped along behind—until Tarn Bellowgranite, the king of Thorbardin, was dethroned. Some time after his coronation, the new monarch, Jungor Stonespringer, offered a bounty for every Aghar killed. The gully dwarves who survived lived in fear, cowering in deep warrens, risking life and limb whenever they ventured forth to raid for garbage or scraps.

Another populous clan, the Klar, found themselves—or, more accurately, were deemed to be—unfit to dwell cheek by jowl with their fellow dwarves. Wild-eyed and unstable, the Klar were quick to anger, enthusiastic in violence, frenzied in celebration, and altogether unpleasant as neighbors. Though a few Klar lived in the underbelly of Norbardin, most of the clan wandered like savages through the backwaters and byways of the great kingdom. Called the "feral" Klar, they remained as unpredictable and maddened as ever.

Tyrannical and fanatical, King Stonespringer instituted a harsh and repressive regime. Claiming that he drew his power directly from the father god of dwarfkind, Reorx the Forge, the king banished females from all manner of commerce and public life; he executed criminals and foes with quick and ruthless violence; he demanded complete obedience—and significant tribute—from all who would call themselves his followers.

Despite the reign of King Stonespringer, Thorbardin remained the greatest nation of dwarves on all the world of Krynn. More than two thousand years in the making, the vast realm was recognized by most dwarves as the only true seat of the dwarf high king—the monarch recognized by the greatest number of the stubborn and tradition-bound peoples. All clans in every dwarven city were led by the clan thane, and in other, smaller nations such as Kayolin, the rank of "governor" was the commonly accepted title of leadership.

Frequently during the long age of those fractious peoples, the claimant of the throne was a controversial choice, and more often than not, he ascended to the lofty seat over the bleeding and broken bodies of his enemies. Indeed, fight by single combat—usually a mortal duel—was the time-accepted method of determining the worthiness of any prospective king. So it could be said Jungor Stonespringer was part of dwarf tradition.

However, he had carried the trend to an extreme of cruelty and violence that was unprecedented. He had gained the throne through victory in the Arena of Death, and many times had defended that throne, always dispatching the challenger in cunning combat. Though in recent years he had become physically thin and frail in appearance, his wiry strength was, if anything, more legendary. He had never met a quicker opponent, and he specialized in the fatal blow—to belly, throat, or lung—that allowed the victim to fully comprehend his defeat as his blood and wind slowly slipped from his flesh.

He had lost one eye in the arena, but his enemies, and even his friends, whispered that the golden orb he had placed in the empty socket could sense treachery in every unseen corner and every lightless alcove within the great city of Thorbardin. The golden orb carried no such power, of course, but Jungor Stonespringer encouraged the rumors and the silent fears. And, indeed, it seemed to his few friends and many enemies alike that he had a unique ability that allowed him to smell the slightest treachery, to anticipate actions, and to prepare his own defenses to meet a foe's best-laid schemes. Jungor Stonespringer was not only alert, paranoid, and careful; he invariably proved to be very lucky as well.

Beyond the confines of the arena, King Stonespringer had arranged for the mutilations, disappearances, or murders of countless enemies. His decrees had forced the kingdom's female citizens into the status of virtual chattel, enriched his friends, and impoverished his foes. Above all, he was admired and hated for the fact that he had forced the former king into exile and, following Tarn Bellowgranite's departure, had ordered the great gates of Thorbardin sealed against the dangers—some real, many imagined—presented by the world beyond the mountain.

Jealous and suspicious, unpredictable and insecure, quick to anger and ruthless in revenge, Stonespringer had steadily tightened his grip upon the crown through edict and action. No enemy survived his wrath, no friend was fully trusted. The king prayed to his god, and his god must have been listening, for in all things the king's will was—had to be—obeyed.

Unpleasant realities did not trouble King Stonespringer's dreams. If anything, they eased his path into slumber, for Jungor Stonespringer, thane of the Hylar clan, high king of Thorbardin and all dwarfkind, was not susceptible to doubt. A true believer, he *knew* that his accomplishments were the will of Reorx. If anyone doubted that the Master of the Forge had chosen a humble, one-eyed dwarf as his messenger, let them step forward and speak out—and then see what would happen!

Soothed by his certainty, the king rolled over on his hard bed and pulled the single coarse blanket over his shoulders. He was skinny, almost frail—a physique that was unusual for any male dwarf, let alone a powerful ruler—but then, he was a dwarf who had long turned his back on crude, mortal concerns. Food and drink were bare sustenance to him. The comfort of female flesh was utterly unnecessary. He lived for the righteousness of his rule, the punishment of his enemies, and the aggrandizement of his power.

Thus, it was not hunger, nor thirst, nor lust that disturbed his slumber in the great chamber of his palace. There was no daytime, no night, in Thorbardin, but like most subterranean dwarves, the king was a creature of habit and schedule. He was amid the depths of his sleeping interval when he started awake, suddenly aware that something was very wrong.

Immediately, he sat upright. His lone eye flashed as he glared around his cold, barren chamber.

"What is it, my lord Reorx?" Jungor Stonespringer whispered into the darkness.

He addressed his god aloud, though he didn't expect a verbal response. But he listened with his ears, with his heart, with every fiber of his being. And he heard the following truth:

Danger walked the streets of Thorbardin, reported his god. It came in the guise of bloodshed, treachery, and violence, and his own people were the source of the threat.

He had taken the step of canceling the obscene, disgraceful Festival of the Forge, and there were many who were not happy with their king's absolute sense of morality. There were stirrings of unrest. As always, those who disagreed with Jungor Stonespringer would have a simple choice: they would modify their thinking, or they would die.

Stonespringer's agents and spies provided a steady, if not entirely comprehensive, window into the schemes and activities of his many citizens. His most trusted general, Ragat Kingsaver, had a smaller network—just a few watchful regulars—but over the past years, they had proven even more reliable as monitors of subversive activities. It was one of Ragat's best agents, a Hylar silversmith, who had recently reported strange behavior among some Theiwar residents. Ragat, ever an independent thinker, had suggested the rumors might indicate a rebellion developing outside the city of Norbardin. Jungor Stonespringer had listened well but disagreed, suspecting that the most likely source of trouble lay within the crowded neighborhoods and slums of the great capital city.

In preparation, the king had posted his numerous garrison troops accordingly, ready to respond to any provocation in the city's great square, teeming streets, or—the most likely source of unruly behavior—the squalid slum called Anvil's Echo, lowest of Norbardin's many low neighborhoods.

The king was certain the attack, when it came, would come from within. He had only one known enemy in Thorbardin who was based beyond the city's walls, and that was the mad wizard Willim the Black. But Willim was isolated in his deep laboratory, and the king was certain the wizard lacked the capacity for anything more than a brief, bothersome raid. Stonespringer's spies, who lurked everywhere, in every inhabited city and town, reported no evidence of any substantial rebel force about to gather.

No, the danger Jungor Stonespringer perceived, the trouble that had disrupted his sleep, must certainly come from within his own populace. Knowing he had little to fear, he laid his head back on his thin pillow, closed his eyes, and once again slept untroubled.

—DH—

It was called the Isle of the Dead, but once it had been known as the Life-Tree, the great column-city of the Hylar dwarves and the greatest of the many wonders of Thorbardin. Critically weakened during the savage depredations of the Chaos War, the great pillar had finally collapsed, leaving a massive stalactite hanging from the ceiling of the Urkhan Sea and a rubble-strewn island rising in a jagged cone from those still, black waters.

For many years that island had been abandoned, left to the ghosts of the thousands who had perished there. It was menaced by frequent collapses as loose rocks broke free from the suspending pinnacle above to shatter on the broken terrain below. The regular bombardment was utterly lethal to anyone who dared to dwell upon the island's surface. All who traveled the environs of the sea became familiar with the sounds of crashing stone; the impact caused an echo to reverberate for many minutes—seemingly permanently—as the sound lingered, repeating back and forth over the stillness of the sea.

The great cities that had once lined the shores of the sea were for the most part abandoned, left to become bleak ghettos and slums, barely supporting the few refugees who eked out survival in the deepest cellars and dungeons of those once-populous places. Teams of feral Klar dwarves also still roamed the perimeter of the lake, but even those impetuous, wild savages avoided the Isle of the Dead.

Willim the Black, however, had visited the island many times during the past decade, usually in a guise such as a gaseous form that rendered him invulnerable to the pummeling of an unfortunately timed rock collapse. His inspections had revealed a vital truth to him: in recent years, the number of rocks plunging from the lofty stalactite had slowed and virtually ceased. Most likely, the loose rocks had all broken free and fallen, while the inverted pillar that remained was solid and securely held to the vast cavern's ceiling. In any event, though the dwarves remained superstitiously fearful of the island, it was no longer the killing zone it had been twenty or even ten years earlier.

Thus the abandoned island was the perfect place for a secret army to gather and drill, and for months Willim had been using it for just that purpose. His teleporting spell brought him to the very summit of the cone-shaped island's central mountain, and there, as he had expected, he found his top commanders waiting for him.

"Greetings, my master," said General Blade Darkstone. The Daergar warrior, with his braided beard tucked into his steel-linked belt, towered over the black-robed wizard, and the breadth of his shoulders was at least twice that of Willim's. Nevertheless, the commander bowed most humbly as the black robe mage popped into view.

"Greetings, General," Willim replied. Using the unmasking power of his magic vision, he inspected his military leader and was pleased with what he saw.

General Darkstone was a dwarf who craved vengeance, desiring to strike out at King Stonespringer with every fiber of his being. Willim knew that the general's family had been taken by the monarch in the early years of his reign; his wife and children had been killed—all except for a lovely daughter, who had been claimed by the king and offered to one of his lackeys, Ragat Kingsaver, as a trinket for his pleasure. Darkstone's beautiful young daughter had killed herself before Ragat had been able to take her to his bed. In their rebellion, the grieving father would at last have his vengeance.

"Soon his blood will wet your sword," the wizard said softly, clapping the burly Daergar on the shoulder with an almost gentle touch.

"May Reorx make it so," the general replied, his voice thick with emotion. "And I thank you, Master," he added, once again bowing very low.

So, too, did the others on the flattened hilltop. Even in the absolute darkness of the vast Urkhan cavern, Willim could see and relish the size and quality, the utter obeisance, of his army.

General Darkstone's Theiwar lieutenants, commanders of heavy infantry, crossbow, and scout companies, stood behind the general with clenched fists and wide, warlike grins, already imbibing the fierce joy of the imminent battle. Nearby, Captain Forelock, leader of the Klar berserkers, stared so wildly around that it looked as though his eyes were darting in two different directions. He all but drooled at the prospect of the coming conflict, caressing the long haft of his warhammer as if it were an object of love—which, no doubt, it was. Captain Veinslitter, leader of the Black Cross Regiment of Daergar heavy infantry, clapped his brawny fist to his chest, while Captain Harlan, keen-eyed leader of the Hylar skirmishers, merely greeted his master with a studied bow.

One other warrior, not a dwarf but an ally of the dwarf army, lurked at the fringe of the circle and waited to catch the eye of his master. The other dwarves could not see that other one, but they sensed its sinister presence and gave it a wide berth.

To Willim, the creature was clear and manifest. Real and powerful, it stood beyond the fierce dwarf warriors, looming at the back of the circle, black-winged and crimson-eyed, and eager to get started. The black wizard's minion was a creature of an alien and terrible realm, summoned to Krynn to do Willim's bidding. Its black wings, jagged as a bat's, trembled in anticipation. Waves of power emanated from the huge monster. When Willim nodded in its direction, the creature quickened and growled, and the dwarves gave the minion an even wider berth. The being rattled its claws and breathed its steamy breath, trying to stay patient.

"The time has come, my bold warriors," the wizard declared at last, pleased at the vast power arrayed before him. He turned and paced across the flat hilltop, noting the ranks of the captains' companies waiting around the shore of the island. Hundreds of boats had been assembled, their prows resting against the Isle of the Dead. Each was captained by an experienced Theiwar helmsman; each would be propelled by its passengers, a dozen of whom would man oars in each boat.

"The king sleeps and dreams his misguided dreams," Willim proclaimed. "Tomorrow, we will awaken him from his last slumber!"

The men stiffened and saluted; only the need for stealth held them back from a lusty cheer.

"Now, cross the lake!" Willim the Black ordered. "The attack on Norbardin begins in twelve hours!"

The plans had been established, rehearsed, memorized,

modified, and refined over the past year. There was no need for any more talking. Each of the commanders gestured in the darkness; their sergeants barked marching orders to the men. The dwarves tromped steadily down the steep grade of the cone's slope, breaking into the sections, twenty-four dwarves strong, that would cross in each individual boat. At the water's edge, they filed smoothly into the flat-bottomed crafts, and in a matter of minutes, the small vessels were pressing through the still, dark sea, propelled by the soft splash of hundreds of bone-handled oars.

Only Willim and his chief minion remained on the hilltop. For a long time they watched as the boats sliced through the water. They did not move yet, but neither were they going to lag far behind the army.

For when they moved, they would travel in the blink of an eye.

—DH—

The blue jar pulsed with light, filling the small room at the back of the Two Guilders Novelty and Pharmology Emporium with a lingering glow. Peat Guilder, who had been sleeping with his wife on their pallet in the corner, immediately sat upright. His nerves tingled with alarm. In his twenty years of service to the Master, that light had flashed three times, and each occasion had brought mortal danger to Sadie and him.

Urgently he nudged his wife, who was a deeper sleeper than Peat. By the time she stirred, he was up and moving, making his way across the workshop, stepping around the piles of books, wedging his way between two overflowing trunks, stretching to reach the bell jar. The vessel still glowed with that lingering blue aura, a magical light originating from the frail-looking sheet of parchment that reposed within the jar.

"What is it?" Sadie asked, rubbing her eyes as she stiffly climbed to her feet.

Peat donned a glove and lifted the hot jar. He squinted, but couldn't make out the intricate details on the note so he handed it to Sadie as she limped over to him. She read swiftly as the magical paper turned to smoke in her hand.

"Climb the Cloudseeker," she said aloud.

Peat nodded in resignation. "So the Master's war begins," he said. "We'd better get ready."

"Yes," his wife agreed. Her hand, in the midst of the smoke cloud, was trembling. "Yes," she repeated. "The Master needs us . . . must get ready."

"I'm ready right now!" he said defiantly as though she had challenged him.

"You don't have to do anything but look foolish and be ready to cast a spell!" Sadie snapped in reply. She rummaged in a trunk and pulled out a large woolen cloak that she wrapped around her shoulders. A smaller kerchief covered her hair, and when she pulled the hood of the robe up, her face was deeply cast in shadow. She murmured a spell, and her nose grew long and hooked, while her chin sprouted a few bristling hairs.

"Can you tell that it's me?" she asked a tad vainly.

"I wouldn't know you if I was standing right in front of you," Peat replied, blinking. He was certain that even someone with decent vision would not recognize her.

"Good. Now get out of here. Remember, we can't be seen together."

"I remember," Peat retorted, though in fact he had momentarily forgotten that crucial part of the plan. He took hold of his cane and quickly left the store, tapping up the street toward the great market square at the city's center. The place, as usual, was crowded but quiet—the king didn't tolerate rowdiness or unruliness among his subjects. Once there, he mingled with a crowd of old dwarves at an ale wagon, paying a copper coin and helping himself to a glass in order to blend in. He kept his eye on the street, and soon Sadie—looking a hundred years older, more stooped and withered even than her real self—emerged and made her way through the aisle between the stalls in the big plaza. Even with his blurry vision, Peat could follow the disguised crone's progress.

Finishing his beer, he was about to order another when he recognized Abercrumb pushing his way up to the cart. Ducking his head and turning away, Peat regretfully decided he had better not have a second ale. Instead, he followed quickly behind Sadie as she moved on.

The market square of Norbardin was crowded, a teeming maze of aisles, stalls, plazas, and shops. But the dwarf citizens moved in small groups, making way for each other with undwarflike politeness and with little conversation or eye contact.

The wide plaza covered a vast area of flat pavement, terraced into several levels, sprawling out for nearly a mile behind the great central gate of the dwarves' city. Stalls and carts covered much of the space, lined up in orderly ranks, creating roads and alleys between the vendors. The whole place, as with the rest of Thorbardin, lay under a vast, overhanging roof, studded with spearlike stalactites. The only illumination came from the oil lamps burning here and there, each at the expense of one of the merchants so as to better illuminate that seller's wares and to draw attention to that particular location in the midst of the hundreds of similar booths.

A hubbub of commotion up ahead caught Peat's attention, and he saw that Sadie had turned toward the noise as well. Still keeping a safe distance from each other, they drew up to the back of a crowd that had gathered around a royal herald. The speaker was flanked by twenty armed dwarves of the palace guard, and the warriors of the escort glowered so fiercely that the citizens averted their eyes as they listened abjectly.

"The Festival of the Forge has become a bacchanalia of depraved behavior and dishonors the dignity of the very god is purports to exalt!" cried the herald. "It is the word of Reorx, relayed through his loyal servant King Stonespringer, that the festival is heretofore canceled. Normal schedules of industry and mercantilism will continue to apply!"

The herald continued his spiel, outlining the harsh punishments promised to any citizens who dared to flaunt the king's decree. A few of the listeners exchanged furtive glances, but no one dared murmur a single word of objection. After all, the beloved Festival of the Forge was simply joining a long list of celebrations and rituals, long held as tradition but banned because of Stonespringer's strict interpretation of Reorx's will. They were almost getting used to it.

In another minute the herald finished and, still guarded by his escort, moved on to exhort another part of the great merchant square.

Even as he had departed out of earshot, no one raised a murmur of protest. Nervously eyeing nearby strangers, the citizens of Norbardin went about their business. Hunched, cloaked dwarves moved everywhere, weaving back and forth on the tangled and winding roadways, clustering around the booths and carts, examining goods and quietly quibbling about prices. Despite the throngs of customers and the hundreds of transactions in progress at any given moment, the bargaining consisted of only whispers, furtive exchanges of steel, and quick, stealthy departures. Rarely did voices rise above the background hum, and when they did, it was invariably a brief argument between two males, each short-tempered dwarf displaying his stubbornness and tenacity in the time-honored fashion. Everywhere the mood was somber, with no one daring to display anything approximating insubordination—or joy.

The females among the dwarves were especially muted, speaking, dressing, and moving so as to avoid drawing the least attention to themselves. They were cloaked from head to foot and always were escorted by a watchful male—by decree of the king, a male who was a relative or some other legal protector. Stern, frowning enforcers—a special and particularly intolerant breed of the monarch's royal guards—stalked among the crowds, ready to club or arrest any female they discovered to be in breach of the royal decrees.

Peat followed a group of those royal guards, but broke off when he sensed that his wife was ready to act. He stood a dozen paces away, waiting, watching her.

"Did you hear?" whispered Sadie, an anonymous shape distinguished only by the fact that she was unaccompanied, as she glided among the groups of dwarf shoppers. Her masking robe suggested she was slender, even frail, but there was nothing weak about her voice or her words. "The mountain is going to fall!"

"What do you mean?" asked another dwarf maid who overheard, her tone hushed but urgent. Nearby other shoppers ceased their bargaining, shuffling closer to listen, glancing nervously around to make sure there were no enforcers nearby.

"It is in the auguries!" insisted Sadie. "Doom will rain upon the highest of the high. Thorbardin's mighty will fall, and the meek will perish in the same storm."

"Horrible!" gasped another listener, clasping a gloved hand to her veiled face. "But are you sure?"

"I tell you, the auguries of the Forgemaster do not lie! Take good care—hold your dear ones close! Bar your doors, and make your offerings to Reorx! The storm will come very soon."

"How soon?" asked another breathless shopper.

"This might be the day! It will be upon us before the turning of the next interval. Beware!"

"But you cannot know for certain, surely?" protested an elderly matron, her voice rising slightly to penetrate the growing buzz of excitement and alarm. "What auguries are these?"

"The Master of the Forge—Reorx himself!—told me in a dream and confirmed it in the ashes and leaves of my morning rituals," retorted Sadie, hunching lower, letting the cowl of her hood droop open to reveal her exaggerated features. "I consulted the priests, and they tell me there is no denying the truth! The stones are loose; the mountain is cracking. The fall is coming soon!"

Dwarves are far from the most superstitious of peoples, but something in the conviction of Sadie's voice gave her listeners pause. By speaking of the mountain falling, Sadie made them think about an earthquake, and there was nothing more terrifying, more deadly, no menace more conceivable to the subterranean-dwelling mountain dwarves. The females looked around nervously, heads bobbing as, one after the other, they seemed to accept the grim truth of the old woman's statement.

"What's going on here?" demanded a burly Hylar swordsman, roughly pushing his way through a trio of female shoppers. He wore the red badge of the king's enforcers, and he glowered with the stern, suspicious expression that seemed to be required, almost part of the uniform, of that elite and hated company.

"What did she say?" he demanded when no one answered immediately.

"It's a warning from Reorx!" one of the citizens barked. "The mountain will fall!"

"Nonsense!" declared the Hylar. Despite his confident reply, he glanced nervously upward at the shadowed ceiling lofting far over the city's streets.

"You there!" the guard demanded, addressing Sadie. "Is this true? You are spreading these tales?"

"The mountain will fall!" Sadie crowed fearlessly. She spoke loudly, her harsh voice spearing the darkness, carrying across the square with its brazen and shocking assertion.

"How dare you speak thus? You spread false rumors!" retorted the enforcer, eyes bulging. Certainly he had never encountered such insolence in all his years on the job. His hand went to the hilt of his sword as he glared at the old woman. "You can be whipped for that, you know."

"I speak the truth!" she said. "The king is a fool if he doesn't see it!"

The man's eyes widened. "Now you speak sedition!" he growled. "You're coming with me!"

Sadie straightened up, looking at him boldly. Something in her expression held him back as he blustered and glared at the old dwarf woman.

He didn't see Peat gesturing, subtly flicking his finger upward, muttering the single word to a simple spell. But he heard the *crack* as a piece of stone, one of the slender, spearlike stalactites far overhead, broke free from the looming mantel. Many dwarves in the crowd cried out in alarm, scattering as fast as they could.

The burly enforcer didn't hear the warning in time. His last breath was an explosive curse as the pointed shaft of stone struck him on the head. The sharp, slender stone smashed the dwarf to the ground and shattered in an explosion of smaller chips.

The king's man lay dead in a steadily expanding pool of crimson.

By then the panicked shoppers had fled, shouting the alarm, in every direction. Their words—"The mountain is falling! Reorx is angry!"—echoed through the vast space as they stumbled over each other and crashed into carts and stalls, spilling goods and breaking bottles, their fear swelling.

The chaos rippled through the great plaza and into the streets that fanned out through the whole city. Each fleeing dwarf frightened ten more, and those ten spread out to further fan the flames of panic.

The shouts grew wilder:

"Death comes!"

"The fury of Reorx is upon us!"

"Run for your lives!"

It seemed that the terror only grew in strength as it spread, and within another two minutes, the tidal wave of fear was surging unstoppably toward even the far corners of Norbardin.

—DH—

Gypsum and Facet were teleported to the highest edifice of Jungor Stonespringer's royal palace, the king's prayer tower. It was a lofty structure, a spire that rose almost to the ceiling of the great cavern over Norbardin.

Emerging from the side of the ruler's personal quarters, it held a lofty vantage over the royal fortress, the great square, and all of the city center. A rimmed parapet circled the shaft just below the top, while, a mile away, the city's main gate loomed above the other side of the great market square.

The two black-robed Theiwar arrived unseen, having cast their spells of invisibility before they drank the elixir of teleportation. They could lurk there, unseen, for many hours while they awaited their opportunity. Knowing the Master's plan, they realized they probably would not even need that much time. They could hear the sounds of excitement and fear from the city streets and understood that events were already in motion.

Facet, however, had provided herself with an additional edge. Back in the laboratory, unknown to her partner, nor even to Willim himself, she had cast a spell that allowed her to detect invisible objects. So though both aspiring assassins were invisible to normal view, Facet remained invisible to her companion, while Gypsum, crouching nearby, revealed himself as a shadowy outline to the female Theiwar.

"Do you hear that?" Gypsum whispered as a rumble of crowd noises billowed from the vast square. Someone shouted commands in a vain attempt to restore order, but from the screams and shouts, it sounded as though a large mob had been seized by panic. Dwarves could be heard scrambling through the square, knocking over tables, jostling and fighting each other as they all tried to flee some unseen disturbance.

"It begins," Facet replied quietly.

"Be ready to strike at once!" Gypsum ordered haughtily.

"Fear not," the female wizard replied. "I will be—I *am*—ready."

She sat there, still and silent, observing her partner. At the same time, she held the hilt of her knife, gently rubbing her fingers up and down the flat of the silver steel blade.

THREE

A WIZARD'S WAR

Though the metropolis of Norbardin lay some six or seven miles from the lake, several winding tunnels and one wide, smooth roadway connected the city to the shore of the Urkhan Sea. Each of the routes was guarded by a small garrison, but the two flanking tunnels lacked any kind of defensive fortifications. Instead, they terminated simply in stone wharves at the shore of the Urkhan Sea. The landings were manned typically by two dozen guards, but the number had been cut in half because of the king's decision to reinforce his troops in the inner city. Wharf-watching was boring duty, and the sentries at those outposts spent most of their time sleeping, gambling, and drinking; only rarely did one even bother to look out across the dark lake that never changed appearance.

The wide central road had a sturdier protection against attack from the sea. A vast ramp, constructed of timbers brought into the dwarf nation a century earlier, when commerce between the surface and underground worlds was routine, stood like a wall against the shore of the great body of water. Controlled by winches and levers on the landward side, it presented a solid barrier to anyone trying to reach the city from the water.

It was to that ramp that five of Willim's apprentices had teleported themselves.

Unlike the two side tunnels, the barrier was not garrisoned by the king's guards, for it was believed that any attempt to breach the ramp would have to be so loud and destructive that a company of defenders from the main gateway, just a few miles away, would have plenty of time to reach the platform before it could be destroyed.

Quickly the Theiwar magic-users went to work, deploying a mixture of spells, magically silenced hammers, and brute strength. They released the locks holding the ramp in place, activated the winches, and, using the weight of the ramp itself to assist them, lowered the huge barrier until the edge dropped right to the surface of the water.

The five apprentices gathered on that ramp, gazing across the Urkhan Sea, straining for a glimpse of movement. Finally they discerned what they were looking for: white wakes trailing away from the bows of a dozen, a score, a hundred boats, all churning toward the city under the power of expertly coordinated oarsmen.

"Here they come," said the tallest of the magic-users, nodding in satisfaction. The apprentices stood aside and waited for their master's army to arrive for the assault against Norbardin.

—DH—

Three Theiwar magic-users, more of Willim's apprentices, teleported into the middle of the great gatehouse that, after the Urkhan Ramp, was Norbardin's second line of defense against the potential rampages of a band of feral Klar or any other threat that advanced against the city from the direction of the Urkhan Sea. The displacement of air caused a slight pop of sound, quiet enough that even those guards who were awake didn't notice anything. Quickly the young wizards-in-training went to work.

One of them descended the long stairway into the largest storage locker, near the front rank of the ramparts. There he found thousands of arrows and crossbow quarrels, casks of oil, bales of tinder to be ignited and tossed from the walls upon enemies, as well as a host of spare armor and weapons. With instant determination, the dark wizard picked out the oil casks and quickly tumbled some of the bales around the large, greasy kegs. When he judged the pile sufficient, he backed off a dozen steps and pointed his finger.

"Igniti!" he hissed, the single magic word bringing a spark to his fingertip. The glowing ember that had materialized drifted through the air and came to rest among the pile of dry tinder. A tiny flame erupted immediately, quickly consuming the fuel, growing in brightness and warmth as it embraced the heavy, flammable casks.

By then, the arsonist was out of the storeroom, scrambling back up the stairs as fast as his short legs could carry him. He met one of his Theiwar companions on top of the ramparts just as a trio of royal guards on routine patrol emerged from a nearby doorway. They gaped in momentary astonishment, startled by the presence of the black-robed dwarves who were lurking just a few paces away.

The second apprentice raised a hand. *"Slumbris!"* was all he said. The spell of sleep went to work immediately; the guards staggered and dropped to their knees. One was carrying a shield, and the first apprentice leaped forward and caught the metal disk before it could clang onto the floor.

By then, the third of their companions, also operating according to Willim's instructions, had arrived at the lofty arch over the high gate leading into the city. That gate was currently open, but it pivoted on a pair of massive stone hinges, and could be slammed shut with only brief seconds' notice.

The last of the apprentices glanced at the hinge and saw that the massive stone slab was poised to turn. He extended a hand and touched the stone.

"Decripis," he whispered, and immediately that stone began to crumble. As it rotted away, the ten-ton slab of the gate settled onto the ground. It did not move appreciably, but no longer was it ready to be moved easily. Rather, when the gate crew tried to close the gate, they would discover that the entire massive weight of the barrier was resting very comfortably on the ground. It would take about a hundred ogres or a thousand dwarves to budge the gate.

Well satisfied with their work, the apprentice wizards took up their daggers and retired to the shadows of the great gatehouse. They knew that they wouldn't have long to wait.

—DH—

The shore of the Urkhan Sea, in most places, rose as a steep slope of rock directly from the waterline toward the looming ceiling above the vast subterranean space. In several places, however, caverns and excavated passages reached the lakeshore and provided access to the large network of tunnels, cities, and food warrens—the living space of Thorbardin's dwarves. As the fleet of boats approached the shore, General Blade Darkstone divided his army into three groups directed toward three landing sites.

"Row, you worms!" hissed the helmsmen, beating a stealthy rhythm on muted, leather-topped drums. The sound whispered across the lake, almost inaudible beyond a few hundred paces, but the drumbeat kept the boats moving at a steady speed even as the three detachments slowly diverged toward their beachheads.

To the left and right, the landing sites were the small tunnel mouths terminating in docks and wharves; each was the objective of a small force, numbering some fifty boats. It was the center, where the broad ramp had been lowered, that the main portion of the attacking force, numbering more than two hundred boats, would come ashore.

General Darkstone, in the lead boat, could see the ramp had been lowered precisely as the wizard had planned. The commander was the first dwarf ashore, and he was met by two black-robed apprentices.

"We have not been discovered," one of them informed him.

"Good." Darkstone turned back to the boats, which were drawing up to the ramp as close together as their many oars would allow. "Debark and form up," he said in a hushed voice. The word swiftly passed from boat to boat: the main route to the city was open.

He watched the veteran troops splash onto the ramp and move rapidly forward to clear the way for the next arrivals. When he turned to look along the dark road leading toward Norbardin, he didn't see his army; instead, he saw his daughter's face in his mind's eye. She was beautiful and young, as he remembered her—before she had been captured by the king's agents and given away like some sacred token to Ragat Kingsaver. When she had killed herself, she had salvaged her honor and signed a death sentence for the king and his commanding general.

"Rest well, my child," Darkstone whispered to himself.

Then his brow knitted and he pictured Jungor Stonespringer, General Ragat, and the task ahead.

"Your hour of judgment is near," he promised his enemies, who remained unseen in the darkness. But surely they must know he was coming.

—DH—

"Hey! Who goes there?"

The first challenge came from the leftmost of the landing sites, where one of the royal garrison had taken note of the disturbance on the water. The reply came in the form of a hundred crossbow bolts, loosed by archers standing in the prows of the approaching boats. The sentry fell into the water with a gurgling splash, and the panicked cries of his comrades receded quickly, as the small garrison fled precipitously toward Norbardin.

The garrison at the right tunnel similarly bolted, and the flotillas reached dry land at the same time. The dwarves wasted no time in scrambling out of their boats. The flanking forces charged, shoulder to shoulder, along the two narrow tunnels leading into Norbardin. Veinslitter's Daergar, a disciplined formation bearing swords and axes while protected by shields and plate armor, marched in tight ranks along the road to the left. To the right, Captain Forelock's Klar advanced in a swarm, jogging along the smooth pavement, grunting and shouting as they picked up the pace of their advance.

General Darkstone himself led the main body of his force, the Theiwar regiments with Hylar skirmishers in the lead. As they were the largest of the army's elements, the general took extra time to organize and form up his units as boat after boat debarked, depositing its complement of the army onto the sloping shore formed by the lowered ramp. Eight boats could pull up at a time, and the empty crafts were quickly shuttled out of the way so the next wave could beach and make ready. The dwarves of William's army had drilled the procedure many times on the similar shores of the Isle of the Dead, and the practice paid off as the whole operation of emptying the many boats took less than fifteen minutes.

When the whole force, several thousand strong, had landed, Darkstone supervised organizing them into ranks, and finally they all started marching toward the city. They moved at a measured pace, for it was Willim's plan that the two flanks would be engaged before the powerful knockout punch was delivered by the center.

The right wing advanced first, with General Forelock's Klar charging at an enthusiastic trot, whooping and shouting as they swept around the bends of the narrow tunnel—stealth being not much valued by the impetuous Klar. As the right formation spread out, the dwarves of that undisciplined clan raced each other toward the nearest enemy positions. Barely a mile from the lake, the Klar berserkers encountered the first guard posts of the king's royal garrison. Because of the inevitable noise they had made during their advance, they found the defenders stoutly waiting for them—but the fanatical attackers would not have had it any other way.

The first guard posts were blockhouses carved into the walls on both sides of the roadway. They had stout metal gates, usually left open, ready to block any undesirables. The guards, alerted brief moments earlier by the sound of the wild-eyed Klar's advance, had already started to swing that gate shut when the attackers burst into a mad sprint. Howling wildly, the Klar hit the moving barrier at full tilt, the weight of the onslaught slamming the gate back against the defenders.

Swinging axes and swords with mad glee, the berserkers hurled themselves at the doors and the shuttered windows of the two blockhouses, quickly forcing their way inside. The outnumbered defenders had been expecting a small raiding party at best and were stunned by the onslaught of a full regiment. The king's defenders were quickly slaughtered while the rest of the Klar spilled through the barricade and down down the tunnel in a mad rush toward the streets of lower Norbardin, some three miles away.

To the left, the Daergar also had taken out their first guard post in a sudden, silent rush, approaching the city gates with more stealth. There, the last of Willim's apprentices had worked their sleep spells on the advance guard posts, and as a result the first company rushed through the entryway before the guards even knew what was happening. As some of Willim's warriors took control of the wide plaza just inside the gate, the follow-up ranks swarmed over the defensive positions, killing the royal guards in their barracks, often before the startled dwarves had time to get out of bed.

In the center, finally, the Hylar skirmishers took the main gates of Norbardin in a whirlwind of fighting. The ruined hinge of the massive gate was discovered too late, and the great barrier stood useless as the attackers stormed past. Many of the garrison dwarves were distracted, having been called to fight the fire that had erupted in the gatehouse's main storeroom. Using grappling hooks and ropes to scramble up the steep walls, Willim's attackers carried the upper ramparts in the first few intense minutes of combat. The main bulk of Darkstone's force, the Theiwar regiments in their tight, disciplined formations, marched through the gate and broke into a double-time march.

The first goals, all three of them, had been achieved by surprise and ferocity. Across a wide plaza, protected by a series of moats and walls, loomed the next, the main objective: the royal palace of Jungor Stonespringer, High King of Thorbardin.

—DH—

The king of Thorbardin was jolted awake, wrested from a dream wherein he was being tended, most gently, by a harem's worth of beautiful dwarf maids. The dream was exceedingly pleasant, and his initial reaction was outrage that someone would have dared to interrupt his reverie. Almost immediately, however, he realized that something was gravely wrong.

First, a dwarf—one of his guards or household members, almost certainly—had the audacity to pound loudly at the door that led into the king's sleeping chamber.

"Your Majesty!" came the urgent cry, and Stonespringer recognized the voice of his chamberlain, Robards. "Please get up! We are attacked!"

Shaking his head, the king sat up in bed and swung his short, skinny legs over the edge of his hard mattress. Even above the clamor of Robards's shouts of alarm, he could hear screams and battle cries, all close enough to indicate the enemy was already in the city. Even as he digested that shock, he heard the resounding clash of steel against steel, a nightmarish clanging that seemed to fill the whole of the great plaza beyond his palace walls.

His good eye flashed wildly as Jungor Stonespringer stared around his barren sleeping chamber. One object compelled his attention: the gleaming golden orb of his artificial eye. He snatched it up and pressed it into the empty socket, trying to process all the commotion.

"It is a test!" he croaked, understanding immediately. Reorx was displeased with the people of Thorbardin, and in his wisdom, the Master of the Forge had chosen to test their devotion, their strength, their faith.

"It is a test of faith!" he repeated, much more loudly, crowing his realization to Robards, to anyone else who could hear. "Reorx is testing us!"

"Yes, Majesty!" the chamberlain replied. "He tests us most assuredly! You must take up the reins of rule and prove to him our worthiness!"

Ignoring the aide—the king had no need of such advice—Jungor stood up and crossed the room, snatching his thin robe from its hanger and shrugging the plain garment over his thin shoulders. Like the rest of his lack of adornment, like the frail physique that attested that he did not overindulge in food and drink, the simple robe was intended to serve as an example for his people. They would behold their ruler in such minimalist attire and strive to emulate his disdain for riches and ostentation.

But those concerns were far from his churning mind at the moment. The king threw open the door to his chamber to confront Robards. The chamberlain's face was flushed above the bush of his braided, oiled beard, and sweat beaded generously across his brow. "Sire, they have attacked from three directions and breached the great gates. Already the attackers swarm into Anvil's Echo and across the great plaza!"

"Who dares attack us?" demanded the monarch.

"We don't know," stammered the aide. "Dwarves, to be sure—it seems there are Klar and Theiwar among them. They came at us so quickly that we have not yet divined their purpose or their lord. Could it be the Failed King, come to reclaim his throne?"

"No, no. It cannot be Tarn Bellowgranite," Stonespringer replied, thinking aloud. "Thorbardin itself remains sealed against the outer world, and he cannot reach us from his bastion in Pax Tharkas."

"No, indeed, lord. It cannot be Bellowgranite," Robards agreed.

"Willim the Black!" snapped the king, fastening onto the identity of the one rebel who was known to dwell deep within the mountain fastness of the dwarven nation. "It must be him. But he has no army!"

"Perhaps he does now," the chamberlain replied hesitantly. "There have been reports of sorcerers among the first wave of attacks. Some guards were enchanted into sleep, and it seems that magic might have been used to disable the city's main gate."

"Impossible!" insisted Stonespringer, even as the thought sent a stab of worry through his bowels. Sorcerers attacking! At the same time, he had been warned by General Ragat, and apparently Ragat had been right: the menace to his kingdom lay beyond, not within, the city. The king had guessed wrong, and his troops were beleaguered inside the gates of Norbardin. With the aid of his sorcerers, Willim the Black's forces had gained access to the city and brought the war right to the gates of the royal palace.

An insurrection led by the wicked black-robed wizard was the worst nightmare King Stonespringer could imagine. Indeed, the monarch had ordered the wizard slain more than a year before, had even—at considerable expense—procured potions of teleportation to allow his assassins to magically transport themselves into the wizard's otherwise impenetrable lair. Too late, he realized that he had not obtained enough teleport potion for his successful assassins to return and report upon their mission. He had counted on their success. Though none of them had in fact returned, he had been lulled into thinking that the wizard had been removed as a threat. Even as rumors had surfaced in the past months that talented young Theiwar were again being recruited by a mysterious magic-user, that mercenary dwarf warriors were slowly sneaking away from Norbardin and gathering at some unknown location, the monarch had convinced himself that Willim was no threat and that no one would dare to challenge his complete mastery of Thorbardin.

It seemed his mistakes would be tested by Reorx.

The sounds of battle echoed through the great plaza of Norbardin, the tide of combat threatening to wash up against the walls of the royal palace itself.

"Call up the constables and reserves!" Stonespringer barked loudly. "Get a message to General Ragat—tell him to use every available dwarf in the city's defense."

"It shall be done, sire!" Robards declared, frantically waving at a signalman who was standing in the doorway of the king's chamber, hastily writing notes. "But, Your Majesty, nothing would help so much as a public appearance by yourself as soon as possible. I beg you—go forth onto your prayer tower and rally the city with your own words!"

"Yes, I shall," Stonespringer agreed. He snatched up the royal scepter, a tall staff tipped with a large, spherical ruby. Stamping the butt of the pole on the floor, he stalked across the floor of his chamber, pushed open the outer door, and marched boldly onto his balcony.

—DH—

"It's started!" Peat shouted, closing the door behind himself and clapping the lock.

"Who farted?" Sadie demanded crossly, emerging from the shop's back room.

"No, not farted! The war, the war! The war has started!" the male Guilder replied in exasperation. "I can hear the battle going on in the square—right at the end of the street!"

"Eh?" His wife blinked, smacking her lips as she digested the news. "So it's started, then."

"I guess you could say that," Peat agreed with a silent groan.

"I don't like it much," Sadie warned. "Bad for business, for one thing. And if the Master needs us again . . ." She let the foreboding idea drift, unfinished.

"Do you think he will?" Peat asked worriedly. "I'm not as young as I used to be." In fact, even their simple mission, the task of spreading fear and confusion in the great square, had caused his heart to flutter dangerously. He didn't even want to think about the chance that Willim the Black would find fault in their performance, be stymied in his own endeavors, and call upon them to perform even more arduous, dangerous activities.

Their musings were interrupted by the sound of a persistent pounding on the outer door, the entry to the shop. The two Guilders hobbled out of the back, Sadie leaning on her cane while Peat squinted at the door as if trying to see right through it. The knocking was repeated, even more insistently, so finally, with some prodding from Sadie, he released the latch and pushed it open.

"Abercrumb!" he exclaimed, feigning pleasure as he recognized their neighbor, a merchant who ran a silver shop on the other side of the street. Peat pointed at the sign beside the door. "I'd love to chat—but, you see, we're closed now."

"We're *all* closed," muttered Abercrumb, pushing open the door and brazening his way inside. "That's what I need to see you about. Business has come to a complete halt. I expect this, whatever it is, this war, to come spilling down First Street at any minute. Why, some dwarves are talking about the end of the world! How can I sell my silver plates to folks who are worried about the end of the world?"

Abercrumb was a Hylar, unusually slender for a dwarf. He had a nervous habit of playing with the straggling ends of his long beard while he was thinking, or listening. He was doing that as he looked worriedly from Peat to Sadie and back again.

Sadie clucked in sympathy. "True, we haven't had a customer in days," she said, nodding. "Business has been terrible for a long time. And now no one will buy novelties and tokens when they're wondering if an army of rebels is going to come smashing down their door!"

"These new rebels—do you know who they are?" Abercrumb asked, looking slyly out of the corner of his eye. "That is, are they Theiwar—you know, of your clan?"

Peat chuffed irritably and straightened himself. "I'm sure I don't know anything about it! Certainly there's a wizard behind some of this mischief, but don't make the mistake of thinking all the Theiwar are in some kind of league against the king!"

"Oh, no, I'd never make that mistake," Abercrumb responded smoothly. "It's just that, well, business has been so terrible, and I wondered if you have any ideas about what is happening all of a sudden. When things might get better or blow over."

"Well, if we hear anything, we'll let you know!" Sadie declared. "Not that we are getting any information that you couldn't get yourself. Just keep your eyes open!"

"Oh, I'll keep my eyes open. You can count on that!" Then Abercrumb departed with his words—he was known to be a curious, even nosy, fellow—hanging in the air.

"I don't like it," Peat groused. "For all we know, *he* could be spying on *us* while we're spying on the king."

"I don't like it either," Sadie replied in disgust. "But what are we going to do about it?"

That was a question with no good answer. Peat shook his head, discouraged. "I wish we could just get out of here, out of Thorbardin altogether," he said morosely. He gestured at the jumbled mess of their shop. "Even if we had to leave all this behind!"

He didn't notice his wife scratching her chin as his words plunged her deep into thought.

—DH—

Gypsum and Facet saw the initial rank of the attackers burst through the gates of Norbardin, and heard the trumpets and drums sound with alarm. They remained magically concealed, poised on the parapet atop the king's prayer tower. Each young wizard clutched a long dagger; both silently watched the door below them. Facet, still enhanced by her spell of invisibility detection, also watched her companion, stealing frequent glances at him to make certain he was following the plan; she smiled thinly to think he could no more see her than he could see the air between them.

They listened to all the clamor, the shrieks of alarm from the dying defenders, the cries of the many dwarves fleeing from the violence that stalked through the streets and square, and the curses of the many more who milled about in fear, shaken and unsettled by the old crone's dire prophecies of earthquake and doom. The city was in panic, and if the king still slept, the two Theiwar knew that it must be a very unsettled slumber.

"Summon the king!" called one nearby officer. "Sound the alarm—we're under attack!"

The time was soon. Gypsum raised his knife and reached out to touch Facet's shoulder, feeling her nod in response. She gripped her own blade, staring down, intently watching the door leading to the king's chambers. The two dwarves would have been in plain sight to any nearby observer except for the spell of invisibility that masked them from detection, so long as they stood still and made no sudden gesture or move.

Soon the king's portal burst open, and royal guards charged out to gawk over the ramparts, witnessing the size of the attack with shock and horror.

"It's civil war!" one cried, turning back to the doorway. "Alert the king!"

More cries of alarm and death were ringing throughout the city, and still the two assassins waited and watched, prepared for their victim to emerge. Once again the door burst open, and two armed guards charged out to flank the entrance. The two guards were followed at once by a gaunt, robed figure carrying a ruby-tipped scepter.

"Now!" Gypsum spat as the robed king raced through the doorway underneath the two Theiwar assassins. He sprang outward, dagger extended. His abrupt movements broke the thrall of the invisibility spell, but that was no hindrance, for Gypsum was on target, plunging toward the dwarf monarch's unprotected back.

"Sire!" One of the guards at the parapet, turning to gesture his king forward, had spotted the flash of movement. With surprising quickness, the dwarf dived at his king, tackling the ruler to the ground.

The Theiwar assassin could not alter the path of his dive. Gypsum stabbed as he smashed into the floor, but his blade sliced through the back of the foolish guardsman. Even as that soldier died, King Stonespringer wriggled away, shrieking in fury and terror.

"Kill him!" gasped the king. "It is the will of Reorx that he die in my presence!"

Gypsum rolled to one side, wrenching his knife free from the soldier's fatal wound and bouncing to his feet. He spotted the king, but already a half dozen burly Hylar had grouped themselves before the monarch and the erstwhile assassin. The Black Robe looked upward, seeking Facet where she had lurked beside him on the mantel. Nothing moved there; if she was still in place, she was still immobile and invisible.

Yet she *must* be there! He had touched her arm, felt her presence just moments earlier. Why did she not attack? The opportunity was golden.

"Strike now!" Gypsum called out to her, urging Facet to strike the king's unprotected back from her vantage overhead. Certainly she, like he, would gladly sacrifice her life in the Master's cause! The apprentice wizard feinted a charge and danced away from the guards' swords, making sure that their attention remained focused on him, not the unseen danger. He parried a defender's slice with his dagger, fanatical determination allowing him to smash the larger weapon aside with his slender blade.

Why did she still not attack? Retreating, he cast an urgent spell, using his left hand to aim a stream of magic missiles at the king. The sparking, hissing darts struck the chest of a guard who bravely stepped into their path, and Gypsum cursed aloud as the last of the magic missiles killed the soldier but failed to strike the monarch.

The Theiwar mage had to defend himself in earnest, swords coming at him from all sides. He couldn't sidestep as the tip of a weapon plunged in to tear the flesh of his biceps. Cursing in pain, he spun, backing all the way to the edge of the rampart.

Blood trickled down his arm, and he grunted as another sword tip cut him, gouging his left hip. He recoiled from the blow, but there was nowhere else he could retreat. He stared into the one good eye of Jungor Stonespringer, saw the king's face distorted by rage and fear, heard his shrill voice calling for the guards to slay the would-be assassin.

"Facet!" he cried, a desperate last croak as more blades struck home, including one that plunged into his belly. Flailing, Gypsum sliced the sword hand of that attacker, but his mind, his reflexes, failed as the blood drained out of him in too many places.

Once more he peered up at the balcony, and at last he saw his fellow apprentice crouching there. Facet had moved, shrugging away the spell of invisibility, but she stared down on him with a thinly smiling face that was cold, cruel. Her blood red lips were curled mockingly.

Gypsum's dagger fell from nerveless fingers, and he raised his hand in a mute plea. The king, his back unprotected, stood directly below the female; she could launch herself at him at any time, landing on him for a certain kill.

Gypsum dropped to his knees, not even feeling the rain of blows that continued to cut him, to kill him. His vision grew foggy, and his last glimpse of Facet was of his fellow conspirator mockingly blowing him a kiss before she spoke a magic word and blinked away, alive and treacherous, ready to fight again on another day.

FOUR

STORM UNDER THE MOUNTAIN

Willim the Black teleported to the commanding rampart in the city's main gate and quickly located General Darkstone. The wizard simply watched as his commander ordered his companies through the gate and had them form up within the city for the next phase of the attack, the charge toward the palace across the great square.

Only when the troops were well organized, moving smoothly into position, did the wizard summon his general with a curt gesture.

"Yes, my master?" asked Darkstone, hurrying to kneel before the magic-user.

"Have your men bring me the hearts of two slain enemies. They must be warm and freshly bleeding. Then proceed with your attack."

"Yes, my lord," promised the general. He quickly dispatched a pair of aides to perform the task before returning to his regiment on the square. Less than a minute later, the aides returned with the grisly trophies.

Willim dismissed the dwarves but clasped the two hearts, one in each hand. Closing his eyes, he squeezed the organs, silently casting his powerful spell of summoning. Blood dripped from his fingers, but it was consumed by magic before it could strike the ground.

Soon the wizard felt the embrace of black wings and noted the looming presence of his minion, an even blacker shade against the darkness of the sunless world. The monster rose before him, maw gaping, eyes flaring with crimson hunger.

"Go!" commanded Willim the Black. "Strike at the very bottom of the city! Spread terror there, and bring that fear back to me!"

With no sound, the minion bowed, flapping its huge bat wings and flexing its sharp, hooked claws. The magic user could sense its pleasure at the command, and Willim watched, breathing hard from the exertion of the summoning—and from his own excitement—as the minion sank through the stone floor of the city.

He knew that it understood the command, and that it would obey.

—DH—

The streets of Anvil's Echo, the lowest levels of Norbardin, were crowded with the wretched and the poor. Narrow passages twisted between looming, sediment-stained walls, as water—and less identifiable liquids—sluiced through gutters. Dark, shadowy holes lined the walls, in most cases without any doors. A stink of rot and effluence pervaded the air in those close confines, but thousands of residents bustled their way around the "Echo" with no apparent difficulty.

For they were—except for the all-but-exterminated gully dwarves—the lowest of Thorbardin's low. They scraped and scrimped, working as coal-haulers and boiler-scrapers, street-sweepers and debris-rakers, earning but a few miserable coppers a day if they were lucky. They dwelled, often two or three families at a time, in tiny, cramped, poorly ventilated hovels that were little more than caves.

But there were advantages to being so far away from the attentions of the powerful. For one thing, the king's enforcers didn't spend much time among the miserable poor of Anvil's Echo. Perhaps it was because there was so little wealth to be mined from those hapless folk. Or maybe the rich and powerful avoided the shadowy, sewage-stinking alleys because of the miasma that seeped through the air. No doubt, at least part of the guard's aversion to the Echo was the fact that more than one of the bearded fanatics who so readily enforced the regime's repressive policies had been found with his throat slit, lying in one of those back alleys. Invariably, by the time the body was discovered by another party of guards, the slain enforcer's belongings, including weapons, boots, and clothing, had all been claimed by one or another of the thieving dwellers of that most miserable of Norbardin's neighborhoods.

There, unlike the rest of the great city, some female dwarves dared to challenge the monarch's repressive rules. The bold dwarf maids, though few in number, operated their own stalls and stores, always in darkened alcoves off the main roads of Anvil's Echo. On those streets, some of the women of Norbardin went about uncloaked, faces bare in proud defiance of the king's harsh decrees. They walked without escort, talked loudly, even dared to argue with those males who were foolish enough to challenge them. In fact, Anvil's Echo, though filthy and poverty stricken, was closer in nature to the dwarf cities of the past than were any of Norbardin's higher and more prosperous neighborhoods.

And there, as elsewhere in the city, the population was purely dwarf, so the inhabitants worked hard, drank even harder, and took their frustrations out upon each other. Brawling and thuggery were common in Anvil's Echo, and the strong routinely lorded it over the weak. Rough overseers, sometimes wielding whips or cudgels, held their laborers to their looms or forges or stitching, while those suffering workers cowered and cringed and sought to earn a few lousy coppers for a hard day's work.

The outbreak of civil war, as Willim's rebel forces swarmed over the three main gates leading into Norbardin, was barely noticed there in the deepest depths of the city. The sound of the violence was a distant distraction, and the dwellers of Anvil's Echo had little care for who won or lost. One thing was for sure: whichever side prevailed, their miserable lot and their endless work would go on.

But all that labor came to a halt, along both sides of one narrow street, when the stones of the pavement began to shift and shimmer, as though a puddle of black oil leaked up from below. Passersby gasped and sprang away from the fast-growing murk, their cries of alarm bringing people out of the shops and down from both ends of the long roadway. Dwarves gathered in a circle, whispering and muttering then edging backward as the darkness coalesced into something very solid. Like a pillar of shifting black smoke, it rose from the ground, climbing and writhing until it was taller than any dwarf.

And it continued to grow and climb and writhe.

"What is it?" called one foreman, pushing his way through the throng.

"It ain't natural, that's for sure," one old fellow retorted, taking another step backward.

"It's some kind of creature!" warned a dwarf maid, an edge of hysteria to her voice.

"Ah, calm yerself," barked the foreman. He took another step forward but, despite his bravado, couldn't bring himself to draw any closer to the black form.

That black shape of murk loomed high above the damp rock of the Echo's nearby main thoroughfare, and even the largest and most brash of the bullies quailed.

The minion of Willim the Black was a bat-winged monster, with embers like Abyssal fires for eyes. Those fiery coals glowed with an infernal light.

The circle of dwarves widened and edged back.

Finally, when the creature spread its black wings and uttered an otherworldly roar, panic seized the crowd of dwarves. They turned as one and started to run, tripping and falling over each other. The weak and the slow screamed and fell as the stronger and faster elbowed them out of the way. The minion struck, stomping among the fleeing dwarves, slaying randomly right and left with slashing blows of its taloned hands. Terrified dwarves fled both ways along the narrow street, crying out in terror, spilling onto the main thoroughfare and gathering more and more of the population into their flight.

And the panic spread, and the people screamed, fleeing.

—DH—

Peat Guilder could hear the commotion of war from the front room of his shop. The clash of steel against steel, the shouts of battle cries, the wailing and screaming of the grievously wounded—they echoed down the street from the great plaza. Even with the front door closed tight, he couldn't drown out the din. Every once in a while, he felt certain that the fighting was getting closer to the shop, but then it would recede again.

Sadie was in the back room, still laboring over the tricky scribing of the mysterious scroll she had been working on. A few hours earlier, Peat had asked her how the work was coming, and she'd just about bitten his head off. No fool, he had left her alone since then. Finally he couldn't take it anymore and went to the door to the back room.

"What are you working on there, anyway?" he demanded.

Somewhat surprisingly, she looked up at him without her usual angry or irritable expression. "Remember what you said?" she asked.

"What? I say lots of things—most of which you don't even hear," he replied.

She ignored the barb. "You said you'd like for us to get out of here, even if it meant leaving this shop, all our possessions, behind."

"So? I was thinking out loud. What of it? I think out loud all the time."

"Did you mean it? Would you be willing to live in poverty, start over again, if we could get away?"

He was startled by the question and still trying to formulate a sensible reply when he heard the loud clank of the shop's front door opening.

"Hello? Is anyone here?"

The voice came from the front of the Two Guilders Novelty and Pharmology Emporium. Peat bustled out of the back room, leaning on his cane, squinting at a prosperous-looking Hylar, stout and middle-aged, accompanied by a frumpy dwarf maid, with two young ones peering from behind their mother's skirt. The shopkeeper cleared his throat and overcame his surprise—they were the first potential customers he'd seen in several weeks. Even before the war, the king's stern disapproval of magic had served to keep dwarves away from the shop that specialized in that unsavory field. Those of the Hylar clan, in particular, tended to look askance at the two Guilders.

"Um, yes," he said. "Welcome to Two Guilders. How can I help you?" He gestured to a row of vials and bottles. "A potion to help with sleeping, perhaps, in these troubled times? Or something of a more exotic nature?"

The Hylar family advanced into the shop, allowing the door to slam behind them.

"What is it?" Sadie demanded crossly from the storeroom. "Are you talking to yourself again?"

She, too, hobbled into the shop and gawked in surprise at the sight of the Hylar family standing there. "What do you want?" she demanded as Peat winced at her harsh tone.

"They're *customers!*" he hissed. "You do remember customers, don't you?" He offered a thin smile to the Hylar father, whose gold belt buckle, fine vest, and fur-lined boots were apparent even to Peat's feeble eyes. The woman wore several diamond bracelets, a glittering necklace, and a pair of gemstone earrings. The customers were clearly well to do.

"I apologize for my wife's ill manners," Peat said, glaring at Sadie—who was still staring open mouthed at the Hylar family. "But please," he said, turning his gaze back to the Hylar, "how can we help you? Perhaps you know that we have an impressive assortment of charms and trinkets, as well as the potions that you see before you."

Indeed, he felt justifiably proud as he indicated the well-stocked shelves with their array of contents. "We have a number of unique items here—many of them unavailable in any other shop in all Thorbardin," he said, trying not to sound boastful. "We have elixirs that will ease the temperaments of contentious adversaries and others that will allow you to vanish from sight in a moment, should an unwelcome visitor present himself at your door. With such a potion, I assure you, you won't be seen unless you *want* to be seen."

"Er, yes," said the Hylar, who Peat felt virtually certain was a fellow businessman, perhaps a vendor of exotic fabrics or rare gems. "Truth is, we've never really come in here before—"

"We've known about you, of course," gushed the dwarf maid. "But, well, you know how people talk. We'd never really felt right about all the magic and—"

"Now, hush, dear," said the Hylar patriarch sternly. "These nice Theiwar don't need to hear our life story!"

"Well, what would you like to see now that you are here?" Peat said, gritting his teeth impatiently. "In these troubled times, there must be something we can offer."

"Well, it's because of the magic, you see," said the Hylar, introducing himself as a merchant whose name was Horth Dunstone. "That's why we came to you."

"There's no other way to do it, only magic," said his wife. "Only magic can help us."

"Help you to do what?" asked Peat gently.

"Well, there's the war. Times are hard. My business has already suffered. My children, well, all of us, our lives are in danger. As is everyone else's of course. But we really hoped you could help."

"Again, help you in what fashion?" Peat felt his fixed smile starting to slip. "Do you need to hide, to protect yourselves?" His voice dropped conspiratorially. "Do you have an enemy you want to hex? To sicken, perhaps, or to blind—temporarily, of course."

The Hylar's eyes widened at the litany of possibilities, and he gulped nervously. Finally, he seemed to shake off his fears, clearing his throat as he recovered his nerve. "Well, it's just this. Can you help us to get out of Thorbardin?" the merchant asked bluntly. "Just get us, our whole family, as far away from here as possible?"

Taken aback, Peat blinked. "Well, I'm afraid not," he said with a shrug of genuine disappointment. "I mean, we could help you conceal yourselves, and if the gates were open, you might be able to slip through. But as I'm sure you know, the king has sealed us against the world. There's no way to—"

"Wait!" It was Sadie, cutting him off with a sharp word. Peat was too puzzled to be annoyed, which would have been his usual reaction to such an interruption from his wife. He looked at her curiously, wondering what she had in mind.

"It might be possible," Sadie said. "It would be complicated . . . it would be very, very expensive—"

"Oh, that's quite all right. I can afford to pay!" Horth Dunstone offered quickly.

"Then come back tomorrow," Sadie said. "We'll have an answer for you then."

Peat was staring at his wife, so utterly astounded that he didn't even say farewell to his precious customers as they bowed politely and made their way out the door.

—DH—

"The king has spoken! Rally to me, brave Hylar! Hold the wall!"

Ragat Kingsaver, General Commander of the First Division of the Royal Guard, shouted the commands from the roof of his barracks, a fortified structure just inside the main gate of the king's fortress. After scrambling around for several hours in the initial confusion of the attack, he was fully girded for battle: his armor vest protecting him, his boots buckled securely. He slapped the hilt of his sword as he stalked back and forth, looking around coolly, making the best plan possible for the defense of Norbardin.

Ragat's bald head was unadorned by a helmet, as was his custom, and his beardless face—almost unique in all the king's army—made sure that he stood out prominently on any battlefield. Beyond that, the gleaming silver circlet of his shield formed a bright focal point that caught the eye of enemy and ally alike. The Kingsaver Shield, bestowed upon Ragat by the king himself, was one of the most fabled artifacts in Norbardin, and his loyal troops believed the legend whispered about it: that his army could not be defeated, so long as the general still possessed his enchanted shield.

The general had been a warrior all of his adult life. In his younger years, he had been a drunken, even dissolute, bully, ever willing to shed blood, to meet violence with violence, to take that which he desired by the dint of his will or, when necessary, the point of his blade. He had been an outlaw, had been sought for punishment by the agents of the former king, Tarn Bellowgranite, when the great civil war erupted in Thorbardin so many years earlier. Naturally, Ragat had joined the side of

Jungor Stonespringer . . . not because of any fondness for the upstart, but simply because he was the enemy of Ragat's enemy.

Yet a strange thing had happened to him during that war. The words of Stonespringer, emerging from the dwarf's mouth as if they were drops of gold spraying from Reorx's own forge, had touched Ragat deeply, inspiring a new seriousness, which, matched by his well-known combat skills, had helped him become a sergeant. He easily made captain not long thereafter. Listening to the aspiring ruler's wise words, his entreaties toward faith and discipline in the name of Reorx, Ragat had found himself moved and ashamed of his own past, his weaknesses. In the wake of hearing that first speech, Ragat had resolved to cast aside his wicked ways and meet his new ruler's high expectations.

His skills as a fighter had propelled him upward through the ranks of the new king's army. During a crucial battle, all of Jungor's bodyguards had been injured or slain, and Ragat himself had stood before his commander, killing any who dared approach.

For his stand, he had been awarded the title of "General Ragat Kingsaver," and he had fought at his lord's side for the rest of the short, violent war. When Jungor Stonespringer won the throne of Thorbardin, he rewarded Ragat with command of all the royal troops. He had even offered him a woman as a prize, the beautiful daughter of one of the king's enemies. Ragat hadn't been particularly interested in the woman, and when she had taken her own life, Stonespringer had been more distressed than his loyal subordinate.

Finally, the king had ordered a special talisman forged for his loyal general, a shield made from platinum and steel, blessed by all the priests of Reorx. It was unbreakable and shone like a beacon of righteousness whenever danger threatened the throne.

The fiery blessing of Reorx was strong in the king, and it gave to Ragat a sense of purpose that had been lacking in his earlier campaigns. A member of a gruff race of tough individuals who placed little weight on sentiment, Ragat Kingsaver had embraced his monarch's values, his creed, and his personality with all of his warlike heart. His shield was the physical proof of that loyalty, that love. He would gladly lay his life down for his king.

The general's troops were garrisoned on the lower level of the royal palace itself. His two thousand dwarves were the elite of Jungor Stonespringer's army, veterans of the battles that had brought the king to power; rewarded well for their service; loyal, like him, to the last drop of blood to the king and his noble, god-blessed cause. Right at that moment they were proving their mettle—rallying, arming themselves, pouring from their barracks, forming into companies and regiments under prodding by sergeants and captains.

Ragat could see from his vantage that the three main gates on the south side of the city, the portals connecting Norbardin to the environs of the Urkhan Sea, had all been breached by a swift and aggressive attack. He was at a loss to understand how all three bastions could have fallen so quickly and simultaneously. He wondered what had happened, and though he suspected sorcery he knew that there was nothing he could do about that, not anymore. Instead, he had to act fast and contain the damage.

"Sergeant Major!" he barked as the dwarves of his division formed up before the royal palace.

"Yes, General!" said Barx Standfist, the veteran centurion who had served with Ragat on every campaign over the past three decades. Standfist, already wearing his plate armor, with his mustache and beard waxed stiffly, stood at attention just a few steps away. The general couldn't repress a smile at the display of his old sergeant's readiness.

"I want every reserve company in Norbardin mustered at once. Have them report to the training yard on the other side of the palace. Then put out the word to the quartermasters. We will need a new draft of recruits; have them start the processing immediately."

"Aye, sir. At once," replied the veteran sergeant major. Instead of starting away at once, however, he cleared his throat, shuffling his feet.

"Yes?" asked the general, knowing from experience that the old veteran wouldn't waste time with delay or idle conversation.

"Every one of the south gates fell," Standfist said. "Do you think . . . well, might it have been treachery?" he growled.

Ragat could only shrug. "Either that or wizardry. No, I can't think of any other explanation. But now is not the time to worry about spilled milk. Go!"

"Aye, sir. I'll start the mustering right away."

With that, the loyal subcommander departed. Ragat turned to study the battle that was spreading across the terraces of the great plaza.

Clearly, the unknown enemy was attacking with three distinct columns. One of the formations seemed to be made up of Klar berserkers. Their whooping and howling, the gleeful, almost musical, sounds of their wild fighting carried clearly to Ragat's ears. The Klar were advancing rapidly into the plaza, but already some of the impetus of their charge was seeping away as the notoriously unreliable troops stopped to loot the shops and stalls or wandered into the side streets and alleys leading to the taverns of one of Norbardin's seedier neighborhoods. Ragat knew the Klar would not be the worst threat, at least not right then.

The force to the right was coming up against a solid formation of the royal guard. The guard formed a line of shields linked together almost like a wall. Ragat suspected that the surviving troops of the initial garrisons had banded together under an intrepid captain and, rather than dispersing themselves against the great numbers of the enemy, had concentrated their strength in that fashion. To Ragat's practiced eye, the shield wall looked like a good tactic, and the garrison dwarves seemed to have a reasonable chance of holding firm.

That left the middle prong of the enemy attack as the main threat. Ragat could see that it was the most numerous of the three columns and included a mix of several troop types: he noted crossbows launching lethal volleys of missiles, burly axemen charging in a wedge, and infantry advancing in a line, also with linked shields.

By the time he concluded his survey of the battlefield, the front rank of the royal force was already advancing, lightly armed skirmishers forming a line that bristled with the steel tips of short, deadly spears. Ragat raced down the stairs and out the palace gate, where he found the company commander. The general waved him forward, using both hands to signal the charge. Immediately, the spearmen charged into the square, their battle cry—"For Reorx and Stonespringer!"—roaring from five hundred throats.

Even as the first rank charged, the other regiments of the division tightened behind the spearmen. One by one, they girded themselves, standing shoulder to shoulder, and they started across the plaza. In a matter of a few minutes, Ragat could see the front rank of the attackers brace and halt, staggered by the sudden counterattack.

As the rest of the division marched forward, the momentum of the battle shifted, and the attack was broken.

Then the rest of the royal garrison spilled out of the palace. When Ragat sent those fresh troops surging into the fight, he knew that the city of Norbardin would not fall, not on that day.

FIVE

THE CHARGE OF THE BLACK CROSS

Willim looked over the battlefield with steadily mounting frustration. The Theiwar commander stood atop a captured gate tower, a vantage with a view across the entire Center Gate of the city's main defensive line. The troops of the rebel forces held the gate, the towers to either side of that wide portal, and the minifortresses carved into the bedrock of the cavern in support of those gate towers. From each fortress, a narrow, lofty bridge arched toward Norbardin's wealthiest districts. Below, the wide plaza, usually a scene of vigorous commerce, spread out as a ravaged battlefield, marked by upturned carts, wrecked stalls, and many dying and dead dwarves.

For hours that fight had raged back and forth across the square. The energy of the Klar charge had been dispersed on the right flank as the undisciplined troops had broken away from their companies to plunder and drink. Roaring laughter and bawdy songs rose, incongruously, from many of the taverns and ale stalls on the fringe of the square.

Willim knew there was no point in even trying to

rally those troops until the plundering and the carousing and their aftereffects had passed.

In the center and to the right, the more disciplined formations of Hylar, Theiwar, and Daergar troops had battled themselves to exhaustion against the firm stand of the Royal Division. Casualties had been heavy on both sides, and a lull had settled over that area as both offensive and defensive troops sought the rest, water, and food that was necessary before they could resume the fighting.

With a muttered curse, Willim teleported to General Darkstone's headquarters, hastily established on the second floor of a masonry shop at the edge of the square. From there, the veteran commander could observe the royal palace nearly a mile away.

"Why aren't you pressing the attack?" demanded the black wizard, materializing next to the general, who didn't flinch at his sudden appearance.

"We carried the outer defenses in the first rush, my lord," General Darkstone reported stolidly. "But the city defenders rallied surprisingly well. They have met each of our probes with fierce counterattacks. We cut them down by the dozens, but they bring up replacements by the hundreds. Now, in the center, we have two full divisions standing against us."

"Then kill them by the hundreds or the thousands!" Willim snapped, gesturing irritably.

Darkstone, no fool, bit his tongue rather than make an impertinent reply. Instead, he stared as though thinking before nodding tersely." He cleared his throat awkwardly. "We hear them still invoking the king's name, Master. It would seem that the assassination attempt was not successful."

"No!" barked the wizard, though it was news to him—bad news. Gypsum and Facet had failed? How could that have happened? Even as he pondered the prospect, he pictured Facet slain, maybe captured, and felt a surprising pang of heartache at the thought she might be dead. Why did she affect him so? What sort of bewitchment did she possess?

"What about the Black Cross?" Willim pointed at the deadly regiment of Daergar heavy infantry, currently idle in the rear ranks of the center column.

"Yes, I'm holding them in reserve, sir. In the event of an enemy breakthrough, we'll need them to plug the gap."

"An *enemy* breakthrough?" snapped the black robe wizard. "It is we who will do the breaking through! Send them now to the attack. And that's an order!"

"Aye, aye, sir," replied Blade Darkstone evenly. Though he disagreed with the command, he knew it would be unwise to say so. Instead, he ordered a signal flag raised, and the Black Cross regiment started moving forward.

"What about the heavy infantry?" muttered Willim darkly.

The old commander repressed a sigh, saluting firmly. "Master, that part of the Black Cross I was also holding in reserve. However, they are ready," he reported.

Willim gestured impatiently at the tight, neat ranks of the Daergar heavy infantry unit. They covered a front some two hundred yards wide, with sword- and shield-bearing heavy troops in the front, a rank of spearmen behind, another line of heavy troops in the third rank, and the elite crossbow teams in the very back of the formation. "Send them in!"

General Darkstone gave the signal.

The main complex of fortifications was firmly in the control of General Darkstone's forces, and the other gatehouses were also in the hands of the attackers, who blocked all routes of access between Norbardin and the Urkhan Sea. But the royal garrison troops of the First Division had marched into the middle of the great square and formed a line that the rebels had not been able to crack.

Willim cast a fireball to open the attack, sending the churning sphere of flame through the very center of the royal ranks. A hundred dwarves died on the spot, but before Darkstone's skirmishers could rush into the gap, a full complement of reinforcements charged up and over the still-smoldering bodies of their slain comrades to again tighten the formation and hold the line.

Willim and his general watched as the Black Cross and the heavy infantry moved into position for a full-on assault against the royal defenders.

"Those are General Ragat's men," Darkstone declared, watching the royal troops as they stoically prepared their defenses. "I'd know that drill anywhere."

"What does it matter who commands them?" snapped Willim. "I want them pushed out of the way!"

"It's the commander what makes all the difference," Darkstone retorted, in a tone that sounded very much like insolence to the short-tempered wizard. "Any other general, and they'd have routed away when that fire blew out their center."

Willim stared at the flanks of the Royal Division, where a motley lot of citizens, no doubt the king's pathetic conscripts, were rushing forward to support the veteran troops. The recent arrivals, a veritable mob, were armed with pitchforks, hammers, picks, and a few swords and spears. If anything, they would weaken the defense.

Willim spotted Captain Veinslitter in the middle of the Black Cross regiment. The Daergar leader wore a silver helm that was festooned with a crimson plume, and he was looking up at the rampart, toward his general and the wizard. Feeling those eyes upon him, Willim nodded, and General Darkstone ordered the climactic attack forward.

With a roar of battle lust, the Daergar attacked. They advanced in a rush, sword tips extended past the line of shields. Even at full speed, their discipline held—there was no wavering in the straightness of the line, no gap opening between one fleet dwarf and his slower comrade. Like an advancing wall of steel, the Black Cross bore down on the ill-equipped and virtually unarmored troops of the king's militia.

The roar of the charge swelled into a thunder as a thousand throats chanted "Black—Black—Black!" in steadily hastening cadence. They were calling out the name of their own unit, but Willim the Black allowed himself to reflect on the irony that it was his name as well. Plus it was the stark and chilling color of the order of magic he had cherished all his life. The power of the Black Robes: soon it would rule Thorbardin!

Shortly, the rebels' shield wall smashed into the first of the defending troops. The hammers and pitchforks of the royal contingent broke against the steel shields, and the untrained troops dropped by the score. Yet they showed a fanatical willingness to die and fell back only when the Black Cross veterans put their shoulders down and pressed ahead in murderous fashion. The line of battle surged, shouts and screams rising from the wounded, and finally the irregulars started to roll back, pushed and trampled.

The line of the Daergar veterans wavered once or twice as some pockets of resistance proved more stubborn than others, but it made a steady advance. The hobnailed boots of the heavy infantry stomped over the bleeding bodies of the enemy wounded and slain, and the dwarves put their weight against the heavy steel shields, pressing ahead. Their swords, every blade streaked with blood, hacked and gouged at the mass of defenders.

"They show some courage, Master," General Darkstone allowed as more and more of the militia troops hurled themselves into the fray to assist the royal guards.

"Then let them be courageous fools!" snapped Willim. "I want their blood to flow like a river down the streets!"

Moments after the first impact, the second rank of the Black Cross halted, dwarves cocking back their arms, holding their short, stout javelins at shoulder height. At a command from Veinslitter, they launched the weapons in a dense volley. Each spear was tipped with a razor-sharp, barbed tip of the strongest steel, backed by the weight of a heavy shaft, and when the rain of missiles came down, the lethal points tore through whatever paltry shield or armor lay in its path and the flesh, bones, and bodies beneath.

Hundreds of the defenders fell, pierced through, many writhing in agony amid spreading pools of blood. Others, stabbed in the heart or the skull, lay still, killed instantly. Some twisted the weapons free from gory wounds, even as the cruel barbs tore painfully at the victims' flesh. A very bold and lucky few, having eluded the barrage, picked up the javelins and tried to hurl them back at the attackers. But most of the return missiles missed their marks, bouncing off the armor and shields of the regulars, clattering to the ground with more noise than effect.

Still the shield wall pressed forward, advancing steadily over the bodies of the hapless defenders. Captain Veinslitter strode forward step by step with the first rank, shouting exhortations, clapping his men on the shoulders as he stalked behind the line, wielding his own blade whenever a tiny niche allowed him to lunge directly at a foe.

The royal guards and the undisciplined, conscripted citizens were undeniably outmatched by the steady, well-equipped veterans of the Black Cross. But for some reason that Willim didn't readily understand, the defenders refused to break, to surrender, or to flee.

He watched as one white-bearded old fellow charged forward with a pitchfork, jabbing it futilely against the shield wall until he was cut down by a stab to the abdomen. As he fell, he thrust his weapon one more time, and one of the Black Cross dwarves stumbled, taking a tine in the hinge gap of his armor around his knee.

At the same time, another pair of dwarves, wearing only stiff leather smithy tunics, raised hammers and hurled themselves against the shield wall. Even from his lofty vantage, Willim could hear the resounding bang of the heavy mallets against the metal shields. One of the smiths went down, cut almost in two by a sideways slash, but the other brought his hammer down heavily on the swordsman's wrist, breaking bone and forcing the veteran to drop his sword. The injured infantryman backed out of the line, his place quickly taken by a comrade, but too many Black Cross dwarves were being similarly attacked and forced to yield their positions on the shield wall.

"Why do they stand?" he demanded of General Darkstone. "We're killing a score of them for every one of our men wounded!"

"I know," growled the commander unhelpfully. "But our numbers are limited. Look."

He pointed toward the wall around King Stonespringer's fortified palace. Willim saw the gate open, spilling hundreds more irregulars onto the plaza. Some of them weren't even armed, but still they howled and charged, hurling themselves with suicidal frenzy into the mass of dwarves battling the Black Cross. They picked up weapons from the dead and wounded, eagerly surging forward to join the battle against the rebels.

At the same time, more of the irregulars were advancing from the side streets, swarming into the square with little semblance of order or formation. Some came at the Black Cross ranks from the side or even from behind.

Fortunately, the veteran Captain Veinslitter recognized the fresh threat, pivoting his troops on the right flank to meet the new danger. At the same time his crossbowmen fired at the dwarves surging toward the rear of the Black Cross. So effective was that volley that a hundred of the enemy fell, and the few survivors among them were so intimidated by the deadly crossbows that they pulled back. Under their captain's steady, shouted orders, the Black Cross resumed its slow, deliberate advance.

"They are penetrating too far," Darkstone declared grimly. "They're in danger of getting cut off."

"No!" retorted Willim. "Keep charging—break them! Smash through to the palace!"

The general nodded and, when Veinslitter looked up, simply gestured the captain to continue pressing the attack. The Daergar captain touched his silver helm and cheered the Black Cross regiment forward with renewed determination. Every few steps they had to pause and launch a volley of crossbow bolts against the militiamen who were milling around near the streets that spilled onto the plaza from nearby neighborhoods.

More and more citizens attacked from the side, rushing out of the alleys and streets, carrying makeshift weapons or picking them up from beside the bodies of the slain. It was a floodtide more than a thousand strong, a relentless force of nature.

"There—a breach!" called Willim, spotting a gap in the defenders.

No sooner had he spoken than a hundred howling irregulars filled the gap, threatening to sweep around the exposed flank of the outnumbered veterans. Veinslitter reacted by pulling his right flank back, thinning out his ranks to extend the length of his line. Even so, there were too many of the militia, too few of the Black Cross. The king's loyalists started to spill around both sides of the Daergar heavy infantry, and there were no longer enough troops to extend the line. The Black Cross curled back to the right and the left until it resembled a horseshoe, fighting countless foes to the left, ahead, and to the right.

And still more of the king's troops and volunteers, ill-trained and poorly armed but seemingly infinite in number, charged into the square toward the beleaguered Daergar.

At last even Willim recognized the grim reality.

"Sound the retreat!" he barked tersely, and Darkstone immediately passed the command to his trumpeter. The brass call finally signaled the dwarves of Veinslitter's elite company to back away from the grip of the frenzied mob.

But already it might be too late. The possessed defenders followed the thinning lines of the Black

Cross as the veteran Daergar tried to fight their way free of what was becoming a deathtrap. At the same time, organized ranks of the Royal Division advanced against Veinslitter's left flank, nearly surrounding the formation. The line fractured, the Daergar on both flanks fighting as islands of resistance in an enemy sea, while the remnant of the center struggled back toward the gate. Willim grimaced in anger as more and more of his veterans fell, vanishing under the press of the enemy's rabble.

The few surviving Daergar finally made it to the gatehouse, where the rest of the rebel army stood ready to support them. Even so, Willim could see that his elite company had been decimated; only about a quarter of those veteran warriors had made it back to his own position. The wizard ground his teeth, knowing that his best regiment had been squandered, without a single foot of ground gained to show for the sacrifice.

Beside Willim, Blade Darkstone covered his eyes with his gloved hand and uttered a sob of despair. The wizard grimaced and turned away.

—DH—

"What did you mean, telling them there might be a way to get them out of Thorbardin?" Peat demanded soon after the Hylar family, buttressed by sudden hope, had departed with the promise to return in twenty-four hours. "Surely you're not thinking of our ring?"

The two Guilders had several very precious treasures that were definitely not for sale. One of those was a ring of teleportation, a device that would allow the wearer to magically travel to another destination. Only a few were said to exist on all of Krynn.

"Of course not!" Sadie retorted. "There's only the one ring, and therefore only one person could use it. It wouldn't be much good to those four Hylar!"

"Well, I know that," replied her husband, peering at her with his watery, nearsighted eyes. "But what in Reorx's name are you talking about then?"

"That spell!" Sadie replied, a wide grin brightening her nearly toothless mouth. "The spell on the scroll, the one that I've been saving for a very long time."

Peat harrumphed. "I know what's in the scroll cabinet. There's nothing in there that will get a blind rat out of Thorbardin, much less a family of Hylar."

"Ah," Sadie said, her eyes gleaming in her wrinkled face. "But this is a special scroll! I have been trying to copy it for a while now, and I am almost done."

With her husband tottering along behind, she led him into the storeroom at the back of the shop. With considerable effort, she bent down and tapped several times at a piece of rock that looked like the foundation of the bottom shelf. To Peat's immense surprise, the rock swiveled away to reveal a dark aperture—the entrance to a secret compartment.

"Eh?" he said. "How'd that get there?"

"I made it myself," his wife said smugly as she reached inside to pull out a long tube. She handed it to him and stood up with surprising alacrity, given her age and arthritic limbs. "Now take it over here to the worktable!" she instructed.

Peat, speechless for once, did as he was told. He unscrewed the cap on the end of the tube and pulled out a roll of parchment while Sadie muttered a quick spell, igniting the candle that rested in a wall sconce above the table. Under the bright yellow glow, Peat could make out the words at the top of the piece of parchment.

"A dimension door?" he asked in surprise. "You want to conjure a *dimension* door?" He had intended to ask how she had gained access to such a powerful spell, why she had hidden it from him, what she had planned to do with it. Instead, he just gaped at her, amazed at the idea and imagining the possibilities.

Sadie smiled so wide that her toothless gums were exposed. "Just imagine how much we could charge to use it," she said.

"Aye," he said, nodding thoughtfully. "Pretty much whatever we want to for someone who really wanted to get out of here. And who had the money to pay."

"Darn tootin'!" his wife rejoined, cackling gleefully. "Now get out of my way. I need to finish the copy so we can save the original. We've got a lot of work to do!"

He looked over her shoulder at the complicated magical scribing. It was a spell far beyond his ability, and he was slightly awed by the knowledge that his wife had kept the scroll a secret from him. But mainly he felt proud that she was capable of such magic.

"So . . . tell me again how it works," he finally asked.

"It's a dimension door," she snapped, though a measure of pride softened her tone. "When I read the spell, the door will open—one portal here, wherever I cast the spell. We can step through the door and come out at the other end, which will be wherever I want it to be. Or we could let somebody else go through—somebody who could pay. And then I would have to make another copy for us to use later."

"So we could actually leave, escape Thorbardin," Peat said, scarcely daring to believe it. "Even the Master couldn't—" He bit his tongue, unwilling to finish the thought. Yet even his partial admission scared his wife, who clocked him over the head.

"Don't even *think* such things!" she hissed. "Think about the Hylar and how much they will pay."

Only then did another, eminently logical, question occur to him. "But where would we send them?" he asked.

"I've been thinking about that," Sadie replied. "We don't want them to end up in the wilderness somewhere or in some den of humans or draconians. That would be bad for business. I think the safest thing would be to send them to some mountain dwarf holding outside. I was thinking of Pax Tharkas."

"Yes," he agreed thoughtfully. "Pax Tharkas might work. There won't be any war going on there, not now. We could even go there ourselves!" he added, surprised at how tempting the notion was.

"There won't be many customers for us in Pax Tharkas either," Sadie said tartly. "And we can't exactly take our inventory through the door, in any event. We would hardly have enough steel to live there. We'd be paupers!"

Peat nodded, crestfallen.

His wife had started another scroll, copying the first one she had so laboriously created. He frowned and cleared his throat, looking at her questioningly.

"Think about it!" she barked at him. "These Hylar are not the only dwarves who want to get out of Thorbardin," she said. "I'm going to make another copy of the scroll. It'll take me a day or more to rewrite the scroll, but then we'll use it for their escape, and they'll pay us very well for the privilege. And they might not be the only ones willing to pay a hefty sum of steel to get out of here before the war sweeps his whole world away."

"And we . . . we could charge them all to use the door?" Peat said. "How much could we ask?"

"How much is a rich dwarf's life worth?" Sadie asked.

SIX

STANCHING THE FLOW

Willim snarled out loud as the remnants of the Black Cross regiment streamed away from the palace, fleeing across the great plaza, limping through the gaps that opened in the rebel line. His initial estimate was accurate: far more than half of the elite, highly trained troops remained where they had fallen. Those not already dead were dying or were quickly slain by the impetuous militia who raced forward to capitalize on the enemy's sudden collapse. A few knots still held out, veterans battling back-to-back, but one by one, those stalwarts vanished under the relentless onslaught.

The survivors, the wizard saw with his magical gaze, bled from multiple wounds. Many of them limped, and the few able-bodied ones were trying to help their injured companions escape from the debacle.

The black wizard turned his back on the disaster, thinking furiously. With his eyes turned toward the plaza, he studied the rank of royal dwarves that extended all the way across the plaza. The troops of the Royal Division formed a solid wall, an obstacle blocking the rebel army from reaching Jungor Stone-springer's palace.

"Master, I have returned."

Willim heard the voice and recognized the speaker as his female apprentice, Facet. He spun around. She was kneeling on the floor at his feet, and her face was turned downward. He could see her black hair, shiny with a wetness that looked too much like blood.

"Facet! Look at me!" he commanded.

She raised her eyes, and he was stunned to see the blood smeared across her face. Her forehead was gashed, with a piece of skin hanging down over one of her eyes. The crimson liquid was everywhere, garish on her ice-white skin. He saw that she cradled one of her hands, also bloody, against her breasts, pressing it there with her other hand.

"What happened?" the wizard demanded vehemently. Facet's beauty was marred, and he wanted nothing so much as vengeance against the ones who had done such a thing.

"Gypsum and I reached our position on the king's balcony. But, Master, we were betrayed. Even before the king showed himself, we were set upon by guards. I wanted to teleport away, but Gypsum was caught in the grasp of the royal sentries. I tried to save him, my lord, I really did, but when I fought them, the guards struck me with their swords. I saw Gypsum fall, dead, and only then did I magic myself away."

"Thank all the gods you're alive!" Willim said sincerely, kneeling down and taking her good hand. His eyeless face, the stitched lids blank and scarred, was turned toward her, and the spell of true-seeing allowed him to study all of her wounds. She had been cut in several places, deep and bloody wounds, though fortunately none likely to prove fatal. He could sense the grief, sadness, and shame that burned within her beautiful flesh.

"But, Master, I failed you!" Facet declared with a sob. "Punish me! I do not deserve to live!"

"Hush, my maid," Willim said soothingly, feeling a rush of tenderness for Facet, for her devotion and her undeniable skill. He would find who had betrayed her—and himself!—and that treacherous dwarf would suffer. But for the moment . . . "You are injured," he said, touching the flap of skin on her forehead, feeling her flinch away from the pain. "Go to the healers at once; tell them that it is my personal command that your flesh be fully restored at once."

"Thank you, my lord. But surely there are others who need the healing magic worse than I?"

So tender, so thoughtful was she! Willim felt a rush of affection for his apprentice, an emotion he had never felt before, not in all of his adult life. "You know my command. I would like to see you well, whole, and unscarred again as soon as possible." He stood and helped her to her feet. She clung to him, and he relished her touch until, finally, he disengaged from her embrace. "Now go," he said gently.

She departed slowly, yet too fast for the Black Robe, who already regretted her absence.

Willim saw Captain Veinslitter, commander of the Black Cross, approaching. Good, the wizard thought. I need to punish somebody. He stood stiffly, his eyeless face turned away as he magically observed the loyal captain, a warrior whose bravery and competence had been demonstrated a dozen times or more, approach. The Daergar knelt on the rampart platform before Willim the Black and bowed his head abjectly.

"I offer you my life, Master," declared Captain Veinslitter. "My regiment failed you. I have no excuse."

He removed his red-plumed helmet with a flourish and even pulled his black hair aside so that the wizard could plainly see his pale, defenseless neck.

And Willim sorely would have preferred to kill him right then and there.

The failure of the Black Cross attack and the loss of so many of those steadfast, veteran troops was a bitter blow to his long-planned campaign. The death of the lackey who had failed to carry the day would have been deeply gratifying.

The logical part of the wizard's mind, however, argued that vengeful punishment would accomplish less than nothing. Willim was an emotional firebrand, but he was also a pragmatist. He had prepared too long, fought too hard, to accept failure at that juncture. He wouldn't allow his temper, his thirst for momentary satisfaction, to distract him from his larger goal.

"Get up," he said, his voice dripping with disgust. "Yes, you failed. But you will have a chance to redeem yourself. See to your troops. I want them rested, their wounds healed insofar as that is possible. I will have another task for them . . . and very soon."

"Thank you, Master," declared Veinslitter tightly. If he was relieved to have his life spared, he gave no sign. Indeed, though the concept was foreign to Willim himself, he sensed that the captain was deeply saddened by the loss of so many of his loyal soldiers. Fool, Willim thought, marking it down as a lesson about the Daergar's character. Your troops are only so much ammunition, to be used up as the commander desires!

The rage swelled up again. Veinslitter *was* a fool, undeserving of his master's mercy.

Then he had another thought.

I know how Facet can redeem herself.

—DH—

"Hey, Oldar," General Ragat Kingsaver said, clasping the shoulder of the veteran soldier sitting on the stone ground outside the palace. He nodded at the bloody bandages wrapped around Oldar's knee. "How's the leg?"

"Ah, it's a bother, sir," replied the battered dwarf. His eyes lit up at the sight of the bald-headed general and his gleaming silver shield. "But I reckon it'll hold me up if the bastards come back for more."

"Good man," Ragat said. "We gave them a real bloody nose; let's hope our own bleeding stops before they come at us again."

Oldar nodded and closed his eyes as he leaned his head against the wall. A soft smile creased his bearded lips, and Ragat knew that his brief words had done the man a world of good. He sighed as he straightened and started along the rest of the line.

There were more than a hundred wounded dwarves lined up behind the front line, and though he recognized each face, the general was ashamed to realize that he could place a name to only a dozen or so of the brave dwarves. They had limped there or been carried on the backs of others after the battle, and the priests were working among them, healing as many as their limited powers would allow, bandaging and encouraging the rest.

By Reorx, he was proud of them all! Ragat felt the emotion well up inside of him and blinked his eyes to clear away the telltale tears. He cleared his throat gruffly and looked out across the square for a moment while he recovered his composure. Thus, he didn't see his monarch approaching but heard the whispers as they spread along the line.

"The king is coming! It's King Stonespringer!"

"My liege!" Ragat declared, spinning on his heel to observe the stern, forbidding visage of Jungor Stonespringer as the ascetic dwarf made his way down the list of wounded. Overcome by emotion, the general dropped to his knees then pressed his face to the paving stones. He would have reached out to kiss the hem of the king's dirty robe, but he feared that would be too forward.

"Rise, my general," Stonespringer said gently. He reached down to touch Ragat's shoulder, and the general shivered with a pleasure that was almost ecstasy. "You and your men did very well."

The words sang in the Ragat's ears. "Your leadership, sire, is like the meat of strength to your men. All would have been willing to die in your service; any of them would have felt such a sacrifice to be an honor!"

Neither the general nor the king saw the subtle looks of skepticism that passed between several of the men who overheard. But then, neither of them really cared what those minions felt; the issue of war was far too important to be left to the opinions of the ordinary fighting men.

"Get some rest, my brave general," the king said and again his touch on Ragat's shoulder felt like the personal blessing of Reorx. "This war is far from over, and it is my wish that you be well prepared for our enemy's next gambit."

"Sire, your presence, the blessing of your praise, restores my spirits better than a month of resting. When the enemy comes, we will be ready for him!"

"Good, my general. I know you will. But, even so," Jungor chided gently. "Go to your quarters and get some sleep."

Ragat bowed his head, overcome with pride. "As you command, my liege," he pledged.

The king moved on, stalking among the men who had shed their blood in his service. Ragat watched him go until the shadows swallowed him, and only then did he turn to step through the ranks of the wounded, starting back to his quarters. Two bleeding dwarves shifted on the ground to let him pass through the door. One had a plaster cast wrapped around his chest; the other was missing an arm.

Neither met the general's eyes as Ragat passed by. Nor did the commander pay them any notice: instead, his eyes fixed on a cloaked figure standing in an alcove at the base of the castle wall. As soon as Ragat caught the dwarf's eye, the fellow ducked back into the shadows. With a glance around to make sure he was not being observed, the old warrior followed the figure into the dark niche.

"Greetings, great General," whispered the dwarf. Even though the fellow was masked by a hooded robe, Ragat recognized the voice of his trustworthy spy.

"What do you have for me?" Ragat asked, knowing that the agent wouldn't have come to him there, in such a risky place, if he didn't have some urgent matter to report.

"Just this, lord. I think the black wizard retains an active spy in the mercantile district. Two of them, actually—partners in a business. I have watched their comings and goings and feel certain that they are serving as a direct conduit to our enemy."

"Good work," Ragat said. "Keep an eye on them

for now. I'll see about them for myself as soon as the fighting is over."

"As you command, lord," said the spy, bowing deeply. Ragat nodded in dismissal, and the robed fellow left through a hidden door in the back of the alcove. Soon, the general knew, his spy would be back in his silversmith's shop.

—DH—

Captain Veinslitter lay on the platform of Willim's command tower. The loyal warrior's blood leaked profusely from the garish slash across his belly, but he had not so much as cried out in pain when the keen knife had suddenly, surprisingly, plunged into him. His eyes had widened in sudden understanding; then he had fallen. He twitched slightly in the widening pool of blood. He lived for the moment, but he would soon be dead, and he knew it.

Standing over the commander who had failed to carry home his attack, Facet wiped the blood from her blade and slipped the clean weapon back into her sheath. Her face was again clean and unscarred, healed by the wizard's most potent priests. Her black hair was neatly combed, sweeping back from her white skin like a sheen of smoky strands. Her crimson lips, moist and full, pursed in cruel satisfaction as she watched the life drain from her victim.

Willim stood nearby, half turned away but studying the scene nonetheless with the full glare of his spell of true-seeing. He had seen Facet's eyes flash excitedly as she had stabbed the captain, whose only mistakes had been preordained by the enemy's superior defensive position. No matter to the black wizard; Veinslitter had disappointed him, he had been punished, and the rest of the rebel army would soon know what happened to those who failed.

The wizard struggled to mask his emotions, but he felt a rush of affection and admiration for the dwarf maid who was becoming his most treasured apprentice. How strong she was! How ruthless! How loyal!

"I am very proud of you," he said, pleased to see the flush of exultation that spread across her porcelain features.

"Come," Willim said as Veinslitter's feeble twitching finally settled into the stillness of death. "I have other officers who have failed me as well."

Facet nodded, her lush lips compressed into a tight smile. When Willim started to walk away, she followed him. He didn't face her, but with the gift of his magical sight he watched her . . .

And he desired her.

—DH—

Peat and Sadie worked through the night. He organized the chaotic mess in the shop while she labored over completing her copy of the scroll. Peat heard the steady *scritch scritch scritch* of her quill against the parchment but forced himself to stay away from her and let her work uninterrupted. Tempted though he was, he didn't even try to peer over her shoulder.

The sounds of battle had, at last, faded away. Peeking out the door, he saw the streets were quiet; the fighting seemed to have ground to a halt. No one was walking around.

However, Horth Dunstone with his wife and two children returned to the Two Guilders Emporium promptly at the appointed hour. Peat, still wondering about his wife's surprising possession of the powerful scroll, led them inside. He made sure that the *Closed* sign hung in the doorway and followed the customers toward the back of the shop.

The chubby merchant turned to him with an expression of almost pathetic hopefulness on his face. As his wife and children continued on inside, he whispered to Peat. "Do you have good news for me?"

"I believe we might be able to help you," the Theiwar answered. He cleared his throat. "But, as I warned you, it will be expensive."

"Oh, of course, of course!" the customer said. He pulled a fat purse from his belt and eagerly extended it to Peat. "I trust this will be sufficient. Mostly diamonds, of course, though there are some exceptional emeralds, sapphires, and rubies in there as well. It's, well, it's basically my life's fortune, with only a few stones left to help us get established on the outside."

"I see," said Peat. "Please wait here."

He left the fidgeting Hylar in the shop and went into the back area, where Sadie was just inscribing the last symbols on the copy of the spell scroll she had been laboring over for the previous sixteen hours. Beside her, illuminated by the same lamp brightening her worktable, was a smooth steel tray with raised edges. Barely able to breathe, Peat turned the purse upside down, and they both gawked in astonishment as a dazzling array of stones spilled onto the metallic surface. True to Horth Dunstone's word, most were glittering diamonds, though a few red, blue, and green gems also glimmered in the midst of the crystalline treasure.

Peat immediately snatched up one of the largest diamonds, while Sadie picked through the stones to find a large emerald and another gem, a ruby of crimson red. Each of the Guilders held their stones up to the light, examining them critically.

"A bit crude in the carving but genuine," pronounced Peat, setting the diamond down and picking up several more with shaking fingers. He quickly confirmed that they, too, were real.

"These are brilliant. This is a fortune right here!" Sadie declared, breathing hard. "More than we've ever held in our hands!"

"I take it the services we promised," Peat asked hesitantly, "are ready?"

His wife nodded. "Bring them in here; we don't dare do this out in the front room."

Moments later the four refugees, each clutching a small bag of belongings, had gathered in the back of the shop. Sadie closed and locked the door behind them before picking up the copied scroll. She would read the spell from the copy, which would cause the magic to consume the writing, while preserving the original for future profit—as well as an eventual path of escape for themselves, if the time came for the two Guilders to leave.

"Where are we going to go?" the Hylar girl asked a little plaintively.

"Yes, where?" asked Horth Dunstone as if the thought were just occurring to him.

"Pax Tharkas," Sadie declared, looking at the scroll. "There are dwarves there, refugees of Thorbardin from before the gates were sealed. They will make you welcome."

Of course, there was no way she, nor anyone else, could predict what kind of reception the new refugees would find, but that wasn't her problem.

That was enough for the Hylar. They were anxious to leave. "Let's go, then!" urged the mother.

Sadie began to read the incantation on the scroll. The blue glow of arcane power emanated from the page, spilling through the small room. The thrum of magic pulsed through the air, and the family of refugees seemed to shrink together, each leaning upon the others for support. With each word spoken, the ink of that symbol burst into flame, chewing through the parchment so, as she reached the end of the spell, she was holding only a thin strip of charred material.

When she was done with the casting, a shimmering blue pattern began to appear on the wall of the shop's back room. It pulsed and glowed with an eerie light, and all six dwarves couldn't help but shrink away from it. Slowly the image expanded until it was a circle more than six feet in diameter. The glowing azure ring surrounded the vortex at its center, the true heart of the dimension door spell. It began to appear as a dark hole in the wall, a mysterious portal offering passage to an unseen destination.

"Now, now," Sadie said, recovering to address the Hylar parents. "It won't last long. I'd suggest each of you take one of the children by the hand and step through."

With a last, frightened look at the two Theiwar, the Hylar couple did as Sadie suggested. With their children's hands firmly clutched in their own, first Horst then his wife edged closer and finally stepped through the magical blue surface. The dimension door swallowed them quickly and silently took them away.

Not daring to believe what they had just witnessed, the two Guilders stared at the shimmering image in shock and disbelief. After a few moments, they shook themselves free of the trancelike fascination and went back to the worktable where they began to count their gems.

It was some minutes later before Peat, wealthier than he had ever been in his life, thought to look up at the place where the spell had glimmered on the wall.

The blue door was gone, the stone so cold and dark that it looked as if nothing had disturbed it at all.

SEVEN

BLOOD ON THE STONES

The rebel army faced the royal troops across the wide swath of Norbardin's plaza. For a number of hours, the two forces had remained frozen, two gigantic entities that had fought to exhaustion and could no longer move. Yet each understood that the battle was far from over and would resume when both were refreshed.

The king's troops had spent the interval eating, repairing broken weapons, sharpening dulled blades, and strengthening defensive positions. They had piled makeshift ramparts along their front, forming barricades from the detritus of the stands and stalls that had once occupied so much of the square. The building materials of the stalls—usually stone slabs occasionally mixed with fibrous fungi-boards and rare planks of real wood imported, long before, from the surface world—formed walls and platforms.

With the notable exception of the ale vendors, whose goods had been confiscated by the combatants and quickly consumed, even the products of the sellers had been used in the manufacture of the barricades. The stock of the stonemasons had been hastily organized into solid walls; the finished products of the metal-workers were converted to use as weapons; even the raw ingots of iron and tin were stacked by the catapults to serve as ammunition in the face of the next enemy charge.

The rebel forces, alternatively, had spent little time picking over the battlefield except to clear paths and evacuate the wounded. The wounded warriors had been dragged back to Willim's lines. Those with only minor hurts were bandaged and returned to their companies; the more grievously injured would be left to their own devices on the tables and floors of several inns that had been commandeered as infirmaries. Those who could recover were expected to do so; those who could not were left to die.

Willim's troops, too, needed food and were given sustenance in the form of dried meat and mushroom bread. After the dwarf warriors ate, the black wizard ordered the rebel troops to assemble on the plaza in front of the city's main gate. He, Facet, General Darkstone, and two other captains who had failed in their jobs mounted the steps to the highest platform, where the five dwarves stood in plain view of the assembled troops.

At a nod from the wizard, Facet stepped up behind one of the officers.

His eyeless face expressionless, Willim addressed his voice to the throng of troops while directing his words at the first doomed soldier.

"Captain Balfour. Your axemen failed to carry the corner redoubt. Do you deny this charge?"

"No, Master. I failed, and I deserve to be punished." Balfour's voice was steady, dispassionate.

Willim nodded at Facet, and her hand moved swiftly, the keen blade slicing through Balfour's thick beard and the equally thick neck underneath. With the wet gurgle of air and blood mixing in his slashed windpipe, the captain pitched forward and lay still in the midst of a puddle of blood.

Facet's black eyes gleamed and she licked her crimson lips as she took up position behind the next officer.

"Captain De'Range. Your pikemen broke and fled in the face of an enemy counterattack. Do you deny this charge?"

"No, Master!" croaked De'Range, his eyes wide with terror as Facet stepped up to him. The veteran dwarf's legs shook, and General Darkstone, one step to his left, flashed him a scornful look. Again the wizard nodded; again the keen dagger slashed, and the captain fell beside his fellow officer. Facet took a step to her left, blood still streaming from the knife blade as her eyes came to rest, almost affectionately, upon the general.

"General Darkstone!" Willim barked. The sturdy Daergar veteran stood at attention, eyes front. "You are my army commander. Yet your army failed to win the battle. Do you accept responsibility for your abject performance?"

"Master, I can only offer my worthless life as penance," Darkstone said stiffly. Despite himself, his eyes shifted warily to Facet. The female wizard was stroking her bloody blade, careless of the sticky liquid covering her fingers. She seemed nonchalant, even bored. Her alabaster features, chiseled and beautiful and as cold as marble, were a warning to the troops who stood rapt below.

Willim nodded. "That is the honorable answer I expected. Therefore, I decline the offer of your life and instead give you this charge: you will lead the next attack, and you will carry the battle into the king's palace. Do you accept this task?"

"Yes! Thank you! With all my heart and soul, Master—with all my sinew and steel! I shall prove myself worthy of your trust or die in the attempt."

"Yes," declared the wizard loudly. "I believe you will." Willim stepped close to his general and lowered his voice, speaking into Blade Darkstone's ear. "And when you enter the palace, you may take revenge for your family, for your daughter. You may take the one called Ragat Kingsaver and exact payment in flesh. But the king you shall save for me."

"Yes, Master. As you command," Darkstone pledged grimly.

Willim stalked to the very edge of the platform, stepping up onto the knee-high rampart so his assembled troops could see him from his boots to the top of his head. He turned his eyeless face upward and raised his voice to a shrill yell.

"My brave warriors!" he cried. "We will attack again, and this time, I will send a leader before you, one who will sweep the enemy from his entrenchments and pave the stones with his blood. Facet! Bring me the hearts!"

Immediately the female dwarf bent down over the slain captains. With a word of magic, she touched their metal armor, and the breastplates broke open to reveal the lifeless chests underneath. With quick slices of her keen blade, she cut out first Balfour's then De'Range's heart. Reverently she carried the still warm organs to the wall, where she knelt and placed them at her master's feet.

"Thank you, my dear one," the wizard said, surprising all the dwarves—none so much as Facet herself—with his tender tone and unusual words of endearment. Then he touched her chin, lifted her face toward his, and absorbed the beauty of her perfect features, her blood red lips, the swelling wonder of her magnificent breasts.

He barked loudly again, his words cutting through the vast cavern like a crack of thunder.

"Now, my warriors. Watch and take courage! I shall summon the one who will lead your attack!"

He shouted words of pure magic, and the two hearts swelled and began to spew black smoke.

—DH—

Meanwhile, far away and blissfully unaware of all that . . .

Gus Fishbiter, Highbulp of all the Aghar in Pax Tharkas, was living the good life. He had shelter from the weather, food when he needed it, and affectionate female companionship. Furthermore, no one had tried to kill him for as long as he could remember, a span of at least two days. He tried to count the days: one, two, one two. Yes, two.

He reflected on his wonderful fortune as he leaned back on his mattress—packed with real straw!—and watched Berta massage his large and exceptionally filthy feet.

"You miss that one," he said, wiggling the large toe on his left foot. "Needs a good rub."

"All right, Highbulp," Berta said with a sigh. "But how 'bout then you rub my feet?" she asked hopefully.

Gus snorted and chortled. That was one thing he really liked about her: how funny she was. In truth, he was a pretty lucky gully dwarf.

"Finish two feet; then get highbulp some food," he declared, stretching out and loudly cracking his joints. He yawned, smacked his lips, and indulged in a long, slow, luxurious excavation of his left nostril. His efforts were so productive that he was about to repeat the procedure on the other side when he was distracted by something.

"What that?" he said, his sparsely whiskered chin dropping in astonishment. Something was happening to his wall!

He stared at the side of his throne room—the throne room that was, in fact, merely an unused cellar chamber in the great fortress of Pax Tharkas. Many Aghar—more, even, than two, which was the highest he could count—lived in that cellar and the surrounding, moldy dungeons. They grubbed and rooted and scavenged, as did gully dwarves everywhere on Krynn, surviving on garbage, bugs, rats, blindfish, and whatever scraps they could steal from the other clans of dwarves who occupied the higher reaches of their ancient fortress. They stayed out of Gus's way, and he, in turn, didn't try to give them any orders since that would have tested his authority.

It was a nice, quiet, stinky place to live, lacking the hostile Klar and Theiwar that had made Gus's former life, in Thorbardin, such a trial. In Agharhome, he had lived with his family, each member of which was larger and meaner than Gus and regularly tried to steal his food. Whenever he had ventured out of the den, he had to worry about feral Klar hunters and Theiwar bunty hunters.

Of course, he would have lived his whole life in that great underground nation except for the unfortunate encounter that had led him into the clutches of a nasty Theiwar black-robed wizard. He never failed to shudder when he remembered that mage's eyeless face as his captor had studied the hapless gully dwarf in his steel-barred cage. Gus still didn't understand how he had escaped from that horrible wizard's lair, but he knew that it had something to do with a strange drink he'd snatched off the wizard's table. He could still remember the mad dwarf's rage as Gus had swilled the liquid and suddenly found himself outside of Thorbardin, on a mountaintop, standing in a deep drift of what he had later learned was called "snow."

And Gus had benefited from more than few lucky breaks since then.

He'd met the most beautiful dwarf maid in the world, the priestess of Reorx called Gretchan, and accompanied her to that wonderful place. He'd eaten fabulous and tasty foods, witnessed majestic objects—most notably the sun—that he would have never seen in Thorbardin, and he'd even learned to value the smell of clean, fresh air.

In his earlier life, Gus could never have imagined an existence as pleasant, as luxurious, as comfortable as the one he had created for himself there in the Agharhome of Pax Tharkas. Berta—it was she who had recognized his greatness and proclaimed him highbulp—was a wonderful consort and saw to his needs with selfless devotion. The other Aghar around there more or less left him alone, which is all any oft-persecuted gully dwarf could ask for. If they didn't seem to recognize him as their lord and master, neither did they try to beat him up or kill him. There was usually enough food to eat and never any Theiwar bunty hunters trying to cut his head off.

Still, in a quiet corner of his mind (actually, all the corners were pretty quiet, but anyway, when he stopped to think about it) Gus had to admit that, sometimes, it was kind of boring in Pax Tharkas. Yes, boring. Things were getting boring.

A fellow could eat only so often and get so many foot rubs or back rubs or whatever else rubbed without feeling like he needed to go and do something else. Sometimes he missed Thorbardin's fabulous lake, the miles and miles of tunnels that he could explore, the massive caves of the food warrens that he could enter if he could manage to sneak past the jealous guards. Pax Tharkas, in contrast, was just, well, there.

So when the wall of his throne room started to glow with a blue light that was almost certainly magical, Gus was not so much frightened as intrigued and yes, thrilled—though he did take the altogether sensible precaution of pulling Berta in front of him so, if something horrible emerged from the blue light, it would have to eat through her before it got to him. He gaped at the swirling azure image, saw a dark spot, like a deep hole, appear in the middle of the bizarre light, and yelped out loud when he saw something moving around in there.

A big, fat dwarf appeared in the midst of the swirling blue image, lunging from the wall directly into the highbulp's throne room with a wild-eyed stare. He was pulling a smaller dwarf by the hand, and almost immediately after that came a dwarf maid, also holding the hand of a child. She looked at Gus and screamed.

Gus and Berta screamed too.

Four new dwarves stood in the Aghar throne room, huddled together in a knot, gaping in shock at their surroundings.

"Where are we?" demanded the fat dwarf, reaching out a hand to try and calm the still screaming dwarf maid.

"Who you?" demanded Gus, clutching the quivering Berta to his chest as he stared over her shoulder.

"Agharhome!" Berta screamed, apparently deciding to answer the fat dwarf's question in a selfish attempt to preserve her own life.

"Agharhome Pax Tharkas!" Gus shot back. "Where from, you?"

"Why, we come from Thorbardin," said the fat traveler smoothly, apparently calmed by the information. "So this is Pax Tharkas, eh? The old crone was telling the truth, it would appear. Where are the other dwarves? The Hylar and such?"

"Up there," Gus replied, pointing at the ceiling. Deciding that he was in no immediate danger of assassination, he released Berta, who scrambled away and, for some reason, shot him a hurt look. "Up those steps," the highbulp added, helpfully pointing to the throne room door and the stairwell leading up to the fortress proper. "This way."

"Er, yes," said the traveler, clearing his throat. "Um, thank you, and sorry to startle you."

Gus simply shrugged. He was watching the wall where the blue circle with its black hole—a dark passage that looked like a tunnel—was slowly disappearing. The four surprise visitors, who appeared to be normal, if affluent, Hylar, quickly departed through the door, starting up the stairs. It was a minute later that Gus made the connection.

"Huh," he said to the still-sulking Berta. He pointed at the place where the magic blue portal had faded.

"That wall go to Thorbardin!"

—DH—

"What is that thing?" demanded King Stonespringer. He and General Ragat stood atop the wall of the royal palace, staring across the wreckage of what had once been the great market plaza of Norbardin. The rebel force, nearly a mile away, had started to advance. At first, it looked as though only the left flank was moving, while the right flank remained in place; there seemed to be a big gap in the center of Willim the Black's formation, with something unusual filling the gap.

"I don't know, sire," Ragat Kingsaver replied, hoisting his silver shield. He set his feet and braced himself. "It's certainly no dwarf. I suspect the wizard's power at work."

Indeed, as the enemy swept closer, the unnatural shape that strode at the head of the rebel army came into all too clear a view. It was three or four times taller than any dwarf, twice as tall as a large man. But no part of it was humanoid.

It was a being of pure black, except for the burning red coals that gleamed like eyes from its face. A pair of jagged wings, like a bat's, spread behind its shoulders, waving sedately with an air of sinister power, deep and abiding menace. It strode upon taloned feet, and similarly clawed hands curled into fists at its sides. As it walked, it kicked through the debris of crushed benches and stalls, even smashed through an intact herbalist's shop that had somehow survived the first round of battle.

To the left of the monster marched one great part of the rebel army. The Black Cross regiment, those of its members who still survived, formed the nearest flank, with its tattered battle pennant proudly raised above the two or three hundred remaining troops of that veteran company. Other units, Hylar and Theiwar and Daergar, spread out to the side of the Black Cross and advanced with the same measured tread as their fellows.

On the other side of the rebel army, the Klar, marked by their characteristic shouts and blood-curdling whoops, massed and seethed and gestured, shouting challenges and brandishing fists and weapons. Still, even as the main army advanced, the impetuous Klar curiously held their ground, for the time being holding back from the attack.

"Huh! Why is Willim holding his Klar in reserve?" asked the king skeptically. He doubted there was any way a commander could hold the berserkers back from a good fight for very long.

"I am puzzled by it," Ragat replied evenly. "Likely, he doesn't want them to get too far ahead of the rest of his force, so he's biding his time before releasing them."

"Should we pull the royal army back to the palace?" wondered the king. Mutely he pleaded with his god for wisdom. Why didn't Reorx show him what to do?

"There's no room for them all within the palace grounds, sire. No, we have a good formation here. My advice is to meet them where we stand."

As if to prove the truth of his general's surmise, the enemy commander chose that moment to release the Klar. With an unworldly howl, the mob swept forward in a rush, quickly catching up to the great army that had been marching forward for the past few minutes. At the same time, that army picked up its own pace.

King Stonespringer clenched his jaw, physically bracing himself for the imminent onslaught. The king saw swords, shields, pikes, and crossbows, all poised for battle as the two lines, each thousands of dwarves strong, swept toward a violent clash.

Yet it was the black creature at the center of the rebel army that riveted the king's attention, and it was that monster that started the battle. Those ragged wings spread wide as it took to the air, swooping low above the plaza, straight at the middle of the Royal Division. Those brave and loyal dwarves didn't waver; instead, they launched a volley of crossbow missiles as soon as the beast approached close enough. Jungor gaped in shock as he saw the bolts pass without effect right through the hulking black body.

"Is it a ghost?" he asked in mute horror.

But the monster immediately proved itself all too tangible as it came to ground in the midst of the Royal Division's first line. It picked up a dwarf in each of its taloned hands and tossed the heavy, armored fighters through the air as though they were children's toys. The bodies tumbled through the ranks of their comrades like rolling stones, shattering the neat ranks even as their bones were crushed and their flesh bruised into pulp.

Disciplined veterans formed the front of the division's line, and many stood fast in the face of the horror, while others, in displays of exceptional courage, rushed forward to strike at the unholy monster. Dwarves stabbed and slashed with their keen steel blades, but the swords merely bounced off the creature's sinuous black flesh. The minion swept to the right, kicking with a powerful, taloned foot, and those wicked claws raked through the line, leaving three or four dwarves ripped and bleeding in the wake of the strike.

The dwarves hurled more missiles—arrows and heavy spears—at the creature, but like the first volley, the flying weapons simply soared through the black creature's body as if the minion were nothing more than smoke. It whirled and charged to the left, clearing out more of Ragat's frontline warriors and driving the rest of the division back in chaos.

The rebel dwarves wasted no time in exploiting the breach. Charging Hylar, sprinting on the heels of the minion, slammed hard into the broken line, thrusting and sweeping with long swords. Some of the king's troops tried to rally, only to be smashed by the minion as it pounced, catlike, right into the midst of the knot of brave fighters. The dwarves tried to stumble away from the lethal swiping talons and snapping jaws, only to fall victim to the Hylar skirmishers who relentlessly continued to press forward.

The rest of the rebel force came on quickly, snapping the cohesion of the royal line in many places. The heavy infantry of the Black Cross regiment, clearly desiring to avenge so many fallen comrades, smashed into the line with such momentum that the defending dwarves could only stagger backward in a daze. Here and there the shield line broke, and hulking Daergar axemen thrust themselves into any fresh gap. They hacked and chopped in every direction, splitting shields and smashing helmets, acting with such fury that the king's troops had no choice but to mount constant counterattacks—and each new gap or melee pulled more strength from the once-impenetrable shield wall.

Then the howling Klar struck the juncture of the regular and militia lines, doing so with such force and frenzy that the defenders, those who didn't instantly flee headlong from the maniacal berserkers, were simply cut down on the spot. Whooping with shrill cries of triumph, the Klar sprang after the fleeing dwarves, leaping on their backs and bearing them to the ground, where they were summarily dispatched with bloody hacks and crushing blows. The surge of battle was a continuous thunder.

"You men of the Echo company, stand firm there!" shouted the general to one group. General Ragat marched back and forth on the wall above and behind his troops, exhorting them to greater courage, challenging them when they began to waver. "Hold, dwarves! Gainer, look to your left!"

The king watched it all, clutching his scepter, feeling his heart pounding against his ribs. Ragat's movements had become more urgent, his voice cracking and hoarse as the pressure swelled. A company of young spearmen suddenly broke and ran; another formation of axemen was overwhelmed by the intensity of the enemy attack.

The monster seemed to be everywhere, pouncing upon helpless dwarves, using its wings to carry it along the line, rending with talons, and biting with its terrible jaws. Trailing blood from every limb, it flew up, threw back its horrid head, and uttered an earthshaking howl.

Even the most steadfast of the king's troops quailed in the face of the unnatural horror. Ragat shouted in vain, trying to stem the growing tide of fear, but even to Jungor Stonespringer it was obvious that his royal troops were breaking in too many places to reverse the tide. Frenzied Klar scrambled over the dead bodies of their foes. The Black Cross survivors, seeking vengeance, burst through a narrow gap in the defense, and a hundred Hylar skirmishers spilled after them, savagely expanding the breach.

"Fall back! Retreat to the palace!" General Ragat finally ordered when the line had been shattered in too many places to count.

The troops of the Royal Division and the hordes of

loyal militia dwarves started running for the open gates. A great throng backed up at the entry as the panicked dwarves struggled to get through, to enter the imagined safety of the palace. Others, seeing the bottleneck, turned and fled from the plaza into other escape routes, running down the many streets that led into the crowded quarters of Norbardin.

And the rebel wave came on.

—DH—

"So when can we do it again?" Peat asked, scooping the diamonds he had just counted—for about the twentieth time—off the worktable and into a small, sturdy lockbox. He turned the key to secure the little chest and muttered a spell of sealing as he touched the lid. That secured the gems against any lock-picking thief, and the box would stay that way until he got the urge to count the stones again.

"I thought you couldn't wait until we got out of here ourselves," his wife replied tartly.

"What? Now? No! This is the business chance of our lifetime. Why, we made more steel from that Hylar than we have in twenty years of peddling potions and gadgets!" Peat beamed, thinking of all that treasure in gemstones; he knew there was more, much more, to be made. "So when can we do it again?" he repeated.

Sadie frowned. "I've been thinking about that." She glanced around, confirming that they were alone—a rather extreme precaution since they were in the back room of the shop and the front door was locked with the *Closed* sign prominently displayed. "We better make sure the king's men don't find out that we've opened up a magic way out of Thorbardin."

"Of course I know that!" Peat retorted. "It's got to remain a secret from the king, sure. But you have made one copy of the spell; make another one, and then you can cast it again as soon as we find another dwarf or two willing to pay for the dimension door."

"So," Sadie challenged him. "That's what's troubling me. How do we get more customers when we can't let anyone know what we're doing? Not the king, and certainly not the Master; you can imagine what he'd do if he found out we're freelancing!"

Peat frowned, scratching his balding head. "That's a problem," he admitted. "We've gotta be careful, so we can't advertise. And those Hylar came right to us. We were just lucky the first time, I guess."

A loud knock banged against the front door, and both Guilders looked at each other, wide eyed and trembling. Moving toward the front of the shop, Peat was startled to hear a great commotion, shouting and crying and the trampling of many feet, coming from out in the street.

"Well, go see who it is!" Sadie demanded, collecting her wits.

The old dwarf clumped to the front door and opened it a crack. He saw dwarves running past, fleeing from the square, screaming in panic—something about a monster and rebel butchers running wild. Right in front of him stood Abercrumb, his fist raised for another knock on the door. He wasted no time in pushing his way into the shop.

"You know we're closed!" the Theiwar merchant protested feebly, still gawking at the chaos in the street.

"Who isn't?" the silversmith replied. "I mean, I was keeping my own place locked and my sword handy, just in case things got worse. And they have! Now look what's happening!"

"What's going on?" demanded Sadie, hobbling out of the back room.

"The rebels are storming the palace!" Abercrumb replied indignantly. "There's some monster afoot too. Those folks out there are lucky to have gotten out of the square with their lives! As for me, I'm just trying to avoid ruin and thought we should stick together in these dangerous times."

"Yes, stick together," Peat repeated unenthusiastically. He added rather pointedly, "You're right about how close we all are to ruin. Why, we haven't had a customer in weeks!"

"Oh?" Abercrumb said, raising his eyebrows. "I thought I saw a rather prosperous-looking fellow—Hylar, if I guess correctly—coming in here just yesterday. Looked like he brought his whole family with him. Had the look of real wealth about him too. So he wasn't a customer?"

"No!" Peat said, feeling a knot grow in his stomach. "He was—was lost! Very lost. Was looking for directions to—to—"

"He couldn't remember where, that's where," Sadie interjected. "And he left a few minutes later. I hope the poor fellow found his way."

"Oh, I see. Well, thank you," said Abercrumb, shifting his penetrating glance from one Guilder to the other. "Though, funny thing. I was sitting by my front window all night, yesterday. Nothing else to do, you know. And I could swear I never saw that Hylar leave. Never saw *any* of 'em leave."

"Oh," Sadie said quickly. "Most likely, you drifted off to sleep and didn't see him leave. Let me guess—did you have a bottle of dwarf spirits near at hand?"

Abercrumb flushed. "Well, there's no call for that sort of remark!" he huffed before stiffly turning and stomping out the door. Peat noticed that the crowd in the street had thinned to a few stragglers, though sounds of battle still rang from the direction of the square.

Sadie wasted no time in slamming the door shut behind him, while Peat swiftly refastened the lock. "So the Master's forces are storming the palace!" he croaked.

"Good," she said. "He'll have other things on his mind until the battle is through."

Still, the elderly Theiwar were trembling as they made their way into the back room, looking at each other's wide eyes and ashen faces.

"Do you think Abercrumb suspects anything?" asked Peat, his voice tremulous.

"Of course not!" Sadie snapped. "How could he have the slightest idea what we are up to? I don't think there's a Hylar in Thorbardin who even imagines that a dimension door is possible, much less than I am able to cast one. Still, I don't like him visiting all the time. I think he has friends in the court. He's too nosy—and too close—for comfort."

"What are we going to do about this? About him? About everything?" moaned Peat, sitting on a work stool and wringing his hands.

"Well, we're not going to panic, for one thing," Sadie said firmly. "Now, stop groaning and let's talk this over."

Peat drew a ragged breath, and they began to talk. Had anyone else seen the refugees coming through the shop? They hoped not. Did anyone else suspect they had a fortune in gems in a secret lockbox? They really hoped not. Had they attracted the attention of the king or, even more terrifying, Willim the Black? They really, really hoped not. Sadie reassured Peat, and Peat reassured Sadie, and they started to make a plan.

All the same, they were both startled when, a few hours later, another knock sounded from the front door. It was much quieter than Abercrumb's, but both Guilders just about jumped out of their skin when they heard the tapping. Still, Peat made his way to the door, opened it, and found another dwarf standing there. He was dressed in a fine silk cloak, and he looked surreptitiously up and down the street, which was at last empty and quiet.

"Hurry—come in!" said Sadie, following her husband closely and all but yanking the dwarf into the shop. "What do you want?"

"Well, I . . . it's kind of a secret," the dwarf said. He appeared to be a swarthy Daergar, but the gold chains adorning his neck and the sparkling buttons and cufflinks on his tunic suggested a personage who was very well off financially. "I have, that is, I had a neighbor, Horth Dunstone. A Hylar merchant. Perhaps you know him?"

The two Theiwar looked at each other, eyes wide. "You *had* a neighbor, you said," Sadie repeated. "What happened to him?"

"Well, I know he was anxious, desperate even, to get himself and his family out of Thorbardin. He told me, in the strictest confidence, that you were going to help him." The Daergar looked at them imploringly, but neither of the Guilders made any reply.

"So now, well, I was wondering . . . do you think you could do the same thing for me?"

EIGHT

THE FIRE OF THE FORGE

Jungor Stonespringer stood on the highest rampart of his palace's prayer tower—the same platform where the Theiwar assassin had tried to kill him, and where the assassin had paid for the treacherous attack with his own life. It was while examining the body of the foiled murderer that the king had first realized the truth about his enemy. Not just the fact that the assassin had been a Theiwar, but that he wore the garment of a black-robed mage.

The king knew beyond any doubt that it was Willim the Black who had created, who led the rebellion. Beyond the identity of his slain agent, the proof could be found in the spells used against the royal troops, including the violent explosions of fire and lightning, the lethal blasts of thunderous meteor showers, and the searing magic missiles that had scourged the ranks of his loyal soldiers. No other but the eyeless Theiwar wizard was capable of such powerful enchantments, of dispatching such magically skilled agents.

Not to mention the foul black minion.

The king had been driven to his lofty redoubt, a

platform carved around the circumference of a stout stone pillar that extended all the way to the ceiling dome over Norbardin. Indeed, the elevation was such that he was poised more than a hundred feet above the level of the great plaza, while the ceiling of the top of the cavernous chamber was only twenty or thirty feet higher than his head. The pillar itself was hollow, with the prayer platform and other ramparts lower on the shaft accessible by a wide, spiraling stairway. Firing platforms stood at many levels within the tower walls. Narrow slits in the thick stone walls allowed defenders to shoot from those platforms in all directions, while offering good protection to any return fire from attackers below.

It was clear to Jungor that his forces were losing the battle, even though fighting still raged around all of the palace environs. The royal troops were trying to enter the palace, but many—perhaps a thousand—remained trapped outside the main gate, where they fought with the desperation of cornered animals against the rebels that closed in from three sides. With commendable courage, General Ragat was trying to organize the defenders, brandishing his own silver shield as a proud badge of his status, his courage.

"Shields out!" he barked to those on the left. "Raise your pikes!" he commanded the spear-carrying dwarves on the right. "Stand fast there," he encouraged the swordsmen in the middle.

For some minutes, it looked as if they might be able to hold the gate. While the line was stabilized, General Ragat came through a portal and scrambled up a stairway to a higher platform, where he could benefit from a better view of the frenzied fighting. Even more of the king's troops surged across the courtyard and out the gates, reinforcing the brave pocket of defenders and blocking the retreat of those with faltering courage.

Then: butchery and disaster! Willim the Black was there, standing on a broken cart behind the rank of his troops. The Black Robe pointed at the knot of defenders and cast a terrible spell. Even from on high, the king could see the tiny pebble of brightness, like a marble of pure, hot flame, that floated in almost leisurely fashion toward the heart of the battle, past the rebel troops and into the middle of the defending ranks.

The king could only watch with horror as a searing, brilliant fireball exploded in the middle of that tightly packed mass of his loyalists. He heard the screams and, in moments, smelled the seared flesh as the powerful wizard urged his rebels forward into the charred and blackened swath where so many of Stonespringer's soldiers had died.

Led by the few survivors of the Black Cross company, the attackers pushed through the gate, carrying the battle into the courtyards directly below the prayer tower. A desultory volley of crossbow bolts flew from the arrow slits on the walls of that tower, the missiles plunging haphazardly into the throng of dwarves fighting their way through the palace gates. More of the king's troops lined the outer walls, but there, too, the rebels scrambled upward. Magical fireballs—not so terrible as Willim the Black's apocalyptic incineration, but still deadly—blossomed here and there as nimble Klar and Hylar climbed ropes and lifted ladders, allowing them to seize the positions scoured by fire.

The king could see that the most deadly threat to the defenders was the hulking black minion, the magical creature summoned by the enemy wizard. The evil being seemed to be impervious to normal weapons, and its talons and fists punched through the royal troops wherever they dared to stand and face it down. Brave dwarves were smashed to the ground, their armored helmets, breastplates, and shields crushed and deformed by the marauding beast. Others were cast into the air, their torn and bleeding bodies becoming missiles in their own right, smashing into their former comrades, disrupting ranks, and terrorizing those troops who were already starting to waver in the face of the horror.

Everywhere across the half mile of plaza he could see, deep into the streets of Norbardin where they led way from the great square, and around the palace walls, dead and dying dwarves sprawled. It was a panorama of blood and severed limbs, and above it all could be heard the pathetic moaning of those warriors too badly injured to crawl away to safety, though unable, at least yet, to escape into the stillness of death. The battle seemed to have no form or focus anymore: it was just random groups of dwarves trying to slaughter other scattered dwarves. One pocket of rebels was surrounded inside the wall, but they cut down every one of the king's soldiers who tried to approach them. Beyond the palace, loyal warriors fought individually and in pairs, often taking on ten or twenty of the attackers, fighting on long after any hope of victory, or survival, was gone.

The king groaned in despair. He saw General Ragat mustering some of the elite Royal Division at the gates to the keep, within the palace walls. The loyal dwarves were fighting furiously, with the rebels inching closer on all sides. It seemed only a matter of moments before they'd be overwhelmed and the attackers would surge into the palace proper.

Then everything Jungor Stonespringer had worked for, the purity of the dwarf peoples, the restoration of the true law of Reorx, his own primacy, would end.

The king's heart was proud almost to bursting at the valiant courage of his loyal troops. The dwarves of Norbardin stood bravely in the face of the horrific onslaught, but they had insufficient weapons and inadequate tactics to counter the threat of such powerful spells. They had no solution to the depredations of the black minion. How had Reorx failed him when the nation was so nearly cleansed of unholy influence? When righteousness, as decreed by Jungor Stonespringer, was so close to prevailing?

"My master! My lord! Strike them all down!" the monarch screamed from his prayer tower. "Slay them! Kill them! Let the stones feast on their blood!"

But the stones, the mountain, the world itself gave no reply.

Jungor wept as he beheld the fate of the loyal dwarves who served him, but it was starkly, appallingly clear that such bravery by trained and untrained alike would be no match for the lethally armed and thoroughly obsessed mercenaries of the rebel armies.

He spotted good Ragat Kingsaver stalking among his men, exhorting the defenders to greater efforts, and the monarch watched in awe as a few dozen wounded garrison troops stood shoulder to shoulder to try to halt the attack of one hundred Klar berserkers. For the moment the keep would hold, but a whole company of Hylar spilled over the palace wall and burst into the main storerooms. Within minutes smoke billowed from the smashed doorways as a year's worth of food supplies were ignited.

"Ragat, my general," the king said softly, his voice

more of a moan than a cry. "Would that you could save me again!"

—DH—

Ragat Kingsaver's arm felt as heavy as lead. His vision was blurred, obscured by his own sweat and by the spattered blood of the many dwarves he had slain during the endless battle. Still, he pressed forward to take his place in the line, cutting down a leering Klar that charged toward him with an upraised axe. The royal soldiers took heart from their leader's example, and in a frenzy of swordplay, they drove back the latest press of attackers. For a moment, the skirmish settled into almost a lull as the nearby rebels fell back from the courageous veterans guarding the door of the royal keep.

It was then that Ragat felt the prickling of alarm in his scalp and spun away from the line of battle, staring upward. He spotted Jungor Stonespringer high above and met his king's eye for a moment. He sensed the despair, the need in that desperate gaze and suddenly knew that he was in the wrong place. The gates would stand without him.

The king himself was endangered

"Hold courage, sire!" he called. "I'm coming to you!"

The loyal general darted into the palace and raced up the spiraling stairs, past the royal quarters, all the way up to the prayer tower. He passed the archers who were steadfastly shooting and reloading at the arrow slits along the tower walls, quickly bursting onto the rampart.

King Stonespringer gazed at him, the golden orb of his artificial eye gleaming incongruously against the sooty, sweat-stained parchment of his skin. Ragat wanted to embrace his liege, to offer him comfort, support, and love—but he remembered himself and his place, so he threw himself to the floor before his despairing lord.

"Sire!" he cried. "Take heart! The enemy grows weary, and we may yet prevail!"

"Rise, my general," said the king with a strange calm. "Come with me to the edge of the rampart. Join me in prayer."

"Yes, my liege, of course," the loyal warrior, his heart breaking, replied. He was no stranger to prayer, but he didn't believe it would help them in their hour of desperation. He followed his king to the edge of the tower's platform but then couldn't keep himself from gesturing mutely at the scene of violence and chaos reigning below. Hylar skirmishers charged from the burning storehouses, carrying the fight into the very barracks of the First Division's quarters. Everywhere the attackers were making headway, charging through the chambers and courtyards of the royal palace.

"But, perhaps, my lord, your own prayers may prove sufficient. I might suggest that I should be better employed trying to command the troops?"

Stonespringer shook his head. "There is no victory for us in this battle, not by force of arms. But pray with me, as I beseech the Master of the Forge. It may be that we will find our best hope with him."

"As you wish, my lord," said Ragat Kingsaver resignedly. He felt a terrible sadness as he rose to his feet, hoisted his silver shield to his shoulder, and followed the king to the rampart at the edge of the prayer tower.

He could not stop himself from glancing down from the great height, and his eyes were inexorably drawn to the sight of the black minion as the monster came to rest upon the rampart above the palace gates. That was when the creature itself looked up, its red eyes flaring as they seemed to lock on the two dwarf leaders on the lofty platform.

"O Master! Lord of the Forge, Fire of the Hearth—Great God of Thorbardin and of all faithful dwarves!" beseeched the king, his voice a shrill wail that somehow carried over the crashing din of battle. "Show us thy will! Strike down our enemies, for they are thine own enemies as well! They are faithless dwarves, full of wickedness and bile!"

The minion launched itself into flight, black wings pushing through the air. Jaws gaping, it soared upward, over the battle and the palace, climbing higher and higher as it swept toward the lofty prayer tower. The monster extended its taloned hands, reaching out toward the small, unprotected figure that was the king of Thorbardin, whose sole eye had been momentarily closed in prayer. But as the words to his prayer died on his lips, Jungor Stonespringer opened that lone seeing orb and froze in terror.

"Run, sire—to the tower!" cried Ragat next to him, already full of fear but bravely stepping in front of his liege. With rising panic, he realized that Jungor Stonespringer couldn't seem to budge. His feet might as well have been nailed to the floor as he stared into the gaping maw of the wizard's black minion. The creature's vast, batlike wings pulsed with almost contemptuous ease as it rose from the square, soaring higher and higher toward the king. The monarch struggled to open his mouth, to flex a muscle, to say something, but he was paralyzed by the approaching image of his own death.

Fortunately for the ruler, his commanding general still had his wits and his courage. Ragat Kingsaver, his bald head gleaming with a sheen of sweat, stood in front of his liege on the high platform, blocking him from the coming threat. He held his gleaming shield—the Kingsaver Shield—up so high that he could barely see over it.

Knees flexed for balance, the loyal warrior leaned forward with a fierce look, bracing himself to take the brunt of the minion's attack. The winged creature flew closer, climbing higher so he was above the prayer platform. The beast was nearly scraping the ceiling dome over the city's cavern. Then, jaws gaping, it dived toward the tower, uttering a ground-shaking, bellowing roar from its widespread maw.

The monster struck the magical shield, the silver barrier that had been blessed by Reorx himself, and Ragat met that charge with the full strength of his body, knowing full well that it was the last act of his life.

But the clash didn't knock him backward, didn't even upset his footing. The minion smashed against the shield and, shockingly, was jarred backward. Howling, the monster rebounded and hovered in the air, reaching around the barrier, trying to slash with claws that couldn't quite reach the courageous Kingsaver.

The minion howled and tore at the shield, and Ragat, feeling a surge of bravado, charged forward, slamming the silvery disk against the black torso. The Kingsaver Shield struck the black minion full in the chest, and the monster flew backward, shrieking a deafening cry. The result was a searing flash of light, a silent blast of brilliance so intense that the king himself howled in horror, clasping his hands over his one good eye. The whole of underground Norbardin was illuminated, outlined like a city on the surface of the world under a bright, noonday sun.

Ragat sensed it then: The light was Reorx, and the god finally had made his displeasure known!

The flash of light shimmered through the cavern, an electrical blast so brilliant that every dwarf who was in the great chamber was effectively blinded. Those who happened to be looking right at the blast would need days to recover their vision; even those who simply saw the reflection were stunned and reeling, unable to see normally.

The light washed over the city, silent and irresistible, pulsing under doors, through shutters, and into trenches and battle redoubts. It seared into the eyes of the warriors and frightened the cowering citizenry with its power. Children cried out in terror, and their parents could only clasp them to their breasts and try to still their own trembling limbs.

Smoke erupted from the minion's charred, black skin where the shield had struck it. The creature writhed and shivered, still shrieking. Its body seemed to be consumed, blackness turning to brilliant light that was not obscured even by the smoke churning upward from its chest. Its limbs shriveled, its wings dissolved, and its body fell away from the high tower.

In the very middle of the battle, the minion quickly faded away, leaving only a smudge of black smoke lingering in the air. Dumbfounded, Ragat watched the thing fall, peering over the rim of the shield—for he, almost alone in all the city, had been spared the brilliant light since his face had been hidden behind the barrier of the Kingsaver Shield.

—DH—

Sadie and Peat were apprehensive about activating the dimension door again, but the wealthy-looking

Daergar, Inkar Dale, had promised to bring them a chest full of platinum coins and a necklace of perfect—and in underground Thorbardin, exceptionally rare—pearls. In the end, their avarice had overcome their caution, and they had instructed Inkar to return as soon as he could gather suitable payment.

The old Theiwar crone had barely completed recopying the scroll for the spell—which was a very complicated incantation, no matter how often or fast it was done—before Inkar returned to the shop. He brought with him a companion, a much younger female dwarf who regarded Peat with wide, innocent-looking eyes, as he opened the door and quickly ushered the two into the shop. The Theiwar leaned out to glance up the street, looking particularly in the direction of Abercrumb's shop. But he was relieved to see that his nosy neighbor's windows were darkened, the shades drawn.

Inkar shucked off a backpack that was obviously very heavy and reached in to pull out a sturdy chest. He flipped it open to reveal a dazzling array of platinum coins, all stamped with the image of Tarn Bellowgranite. "These are original royals," he said, indicating the treasure. "The most valuable coin ever minted in Thorbardin."

"I recognize them!" Peat said, all but drooling at the sight. Only after a moment did he remember they were still in the main room of the shop. "Quickly, come this way," he said, bringing the two Daergar into the back where Sadie was just bottling her ink and cleaning her quill.

"They're here," he said quite unnecessarily. "And he brought a chest of platinum coins!"

"What about the pearls?" Sadie demanded greedily.

"Oh, yes, of course," Inkar said, reaching into a pocket of his fine tunic. He pulled out a strand of alabaster stones, more than two dozen of them. Sadie snatched them out of his hand, holding them up to the light and passing them through her wrinkled, bony fingers. The other three dwarves seemed to hold their breath, none speaking or moving until the Theiwar crone completed her inspection.

"They'll do," she said, nodding curtly.

"Do?" Inkar was offended. "Why, they're a treasure the likes of which this kingdom has never seen! How dare you—"

"Do you want to get out of here or not?" Sadie demanded curtly. "And I assume your wife is going with you?" she added with an arch look at the young maid, causing the timid female to blush furiously.

"Ah, yes. That is, she's not my wife, but yes," Inkar stammered, the previous insult apparently forgotten. "Um, my wife is . . . that is, she doesn't exactly . . . she doesn't want . . . er . . . she's not coming on this trip. But Sellen here, she will accompany me."

Peat raised an eyebrow. He couldn't help but admire the shapely young dwarf maid and realized that Inkar probably had several reasons for wanting to get out of Thorbardin.

"All right, then. Come over here," he said, indicating the floor beside the blank stretch of wall.

The two dwarves complied, and once again Sadie, squinting and speaking very slowly, very carefully, cast the spell of the dimension door, using the same terminus—Pax Tharkas—that she had devised for Horth Dunstone and his family. Soon the shimmering blue circle formed on the wall, and shortly thereafter, as Peat gestured them forward, the two refugees stepped into the dimension door and disappeared.

—DH—

"Master, I can't see!" cried Facet, her hands pressed to her face.

The chaos of battle had ceased almost at once as all of the dwarves in sight of the prayer tower, and many who were out of sight as well, recoiled in the shock of the sudden, impossibly bright flash of light. Some moaned and cried out, others sobbed in fear or awe or despair. Many on both sides dropped to their knees, wailing, calling out the name of their god, and pleading for his mercy.

None tried to use their weapons or to continue the attack.

"It's the king," Willim hissed. His own eyeless vision, because it originated in the magical spell of true-seeing, remained unaffected by the brilliant flash. So he easily saw Jungor Stonespringer crouching atop the prayer tower, hiding behind the silver shield held by his general. That shield was blazing with an otherworldly light, too bright for any normal dwarf to view.

But no doubt about it, the minion was gone, vanished in the blast of what could only be deemed godly magic. A cloud of smoke was lingering in the air, all that was left of the mighty being. The wizard could scarcely believe that his most potent ally, his most powerful tool, his secret weapon, had been blasted into nothingness, just like that.

"It was the king, damn him!" he repeated. "And he will be mine!"

He took Facet by the hand and muttered a word of command. Immediately the two wizards took to the air, Willim guiding his blinded apprentice in flight as they soared toward the prayer platform, zeroing in on Ragat Kingsaver and the kneeling form of Jungor Stonespringer.

—DH—

Slumping to his knees, blinded by the godly light, stunned by the vision of his lord's power, King Stonespringer reached out to touch and reassure his loyal commander. He could barely see, but he could feel Ragat standing there, trembling.

"What happened?" asked the monarch.

"Your prayer was answered, sire," said the general reverently. "Reorx made his will known. In the blast of his light, the battle has ceased. The dwarves of both armies are stunned, unmoving."

"Then order them to attack!" the king urged. "Now is the time!"

"I cannot, my lord," Ragat replied humbly. Still himself unaffected by the brilliance, Ragat could see the stunned soldiers on the square and in the palace. Most knelt or lay flat. The few that tried to move did so haltingly, stumbling over obstacles, groping with their hands. "They are blinded . . . as are their enemies. None can see who to slay."

The king raised his arms in supplication, his blinded eye staring upward toward the looming stalactites, the jagged stone ceiling looming so close to his head.

"O Master of the Forge!" he cried abjectly. "You forsake us! Why do you leave us to wander in the darkness? I beg you, upon my life and my faith and my fear, if you would destroy us, then smite me now! Bring stone to crash down upon my head, to crush my skull, to spatter my brains!"

"Sire, it was the god's light that did this!" Ragat argued feverishly. "It was Reorx's will that the battle come to a halt!"

The king paid him no heed. Instead, he continued his frantic prayer. "But if you indeed favor us, if you would give us victory, then again show us your power! Wield your might against the foe! Bring destruction down upon him!"

"You ask for too much, fool!"

The threatening voice came from Willim the Black, who was soaring like a bird through the air and just coming to rest on the platform nearby. Ragat recognized the hideous, scarred, eyeless face, and he knew from the wizard's confident movements that he, like the general, had escaped the blinding force of the light. Willim was flying hand in hand with another black-robed wizard, a beautiful female with white skin and red, shining lips. She stumbled a little as they came to rest on the parapet and reached out to grope, unseeing, for her master's arm. Unlike her master, she seemed unsteady, even frightened.

"It is the black wizard, sire. He is here," Ragat said in a low voice.

"You're mad, you magic-deceived fool!" spit the king, rising to his feet and gesturing blindly in the wizard's direction with his scepter. "It is Reorx's will that your army be defeated and now that you too shall die!"

"Do not offer me your childish your words of empty faith!" snapped Willim. "My magic is as mighty as your god's! Did you not see your army falling back, your soldiers dying under the weapons of my own troops? Do you think I have given up?"

"You will bring nothing but your own destruction!" retorted the king. "All you offer is doom—and in that doom you shall find your own death! Reorx so wills it!"

The king waved his scepter again but could only sob in frustration when the god failed to respond, to act, to smite his enemy. Ragat stared at Jungor, uncertain what to do. At the same time, the female wizard, moving unsteadily, clutched at Willim's arm even as the wizard yanked away from her. Her pale features were locked in an expression of horror.

"You will die, now, King Stonespringer!" taunted Willim, edging forward. "You have fought the wrong fight, against the wrong enemies—and you have only weakened Thorbardin. Under my reign, the grandeur of our nation will be restored."

"You speak words of falsehood," the king replied, his arrogance reviving. "I have dethroned one false king, and I shall not yield to another."

"You need not yield," Willim said with a cold laugh. "You need only die."

He raised a hand and pointed a stubby finger at Jungor Stonespringer. His scarred, eyeless face twisted into a leer of pleasure as his lips parted and he began to chant a spell.

Ragat did the only thing he could think to do: he lifted the Kingsaver Shield and charged directly at the wizard. Willim barked in surprise but dodged out of the way before Ragat was able to strike him; his blinded apprentice was too slow to react, however. The shining metal disk of the shield, blessed by all the priests of Reorx, struck the coldly beautiful Facet in the face, and she screamed as she toppled backward, over the lip of the prayer tower, leaving Ragat staggering at the brink of the precipice.

"No!" shrieked Willim the Black.

The king and the shield were both forgotten as Willim took to the air, magically flying to rescue the falling female. In a swish of movement and a flash of his black cloak, he was gone, crying out for the apprentice, diving through the air to snatch her in his arms before she smashed into the pavement a hundred feet below.

At the same time, Stonespringer's voice rose from a throaty bellow to a shrill, penetrating cry. The king had not seen his general's attack, nor the wizard's fall. He only knew his rage and frustration as his will was thwarted and Willim escaped. He screamed at the roof over his head, and his words bounced from the stone, echoing over the battle. He called down the vengeance of his god, he shrieked his hatred for all that was unholy, he demanded that his enemies be slain—horribly and at once.

Perhaps it was some trick of acoustics, the shape of the stone amplifying and expanding the sound of his voice. Or perhaps, indeed, it was the power of the god himself. In any event, as the words were enhanced, as the force of Stonespringer's voice spread across the field of battle, the ground began to shake, the tower to sway sickeningly, like a tall tree in a strong wind. Several chunks of stone broke from the ceiling, raining destruction upon those dwarves who were out in the open plaza below.

Then, after the initial worrying tremor, the ground began to rumble more violently. More stones broke from the ceiling, plunging onto the plaza, crashing explosively among the cowering, blinded dwarves. Ripples of movement caused the plaza to buckle and flex, here rising, there plunging away into darkness. Jagged cracks appeared in the ground, and some of them swallowed dwarves who were too slow—or too blind—to escape.

The screams of the doomed added to the rumbling, thunderous groaning that wracked the air.

Nothing so inspires terror in the subterranean-dwelling dwarves as an earthquake, and that temblor was enough to send every warrior of every army, even blinded as they were, fleeing for cover. The waves of destruction swept through the city, knocking over towers, bringing walls and ceilings tumbling down, knocking the wounded from their beds.

Shaken to the core, the bravest fighters took shelter under roofs, tables, shelves, anything they could find. Weapons fell from nerveless hands, friends and enemies sought shelter in the same protection—even the fires of the battle were doused as dust and debris tumbled downward and smothered the flames.

The war was forgotten, and miserable dwarves who still lived prayed for their lives . . . and all of them prayed to the same god.

Part II

Kayolin

Nine

The New King

A proclamation to the dwarf citizens of Garnet Thax:

This is the word of Regar Smashfingers, once Governor and soon-to-be King of Kayolin:

My brave and intrepid dwarves, we know that our nation has faced a multitude of challenges arising from the current state of the world—challenges that require swift and decisive action. As your leader, we publicly resolve to face these obstacles with determination. So long as our people, the dwarves of Kayolin, remain united and resolute, we shall know triumph and prosperity, and we will deliver to our enemies an unending diet of defeat, devastation, and destruction.

Good citizens of Kayolin, you are loyal dwarves, steadfast strivers in the mines and warrens of our great nation. Likewise, we on the throne steadfastly strive to rule you with a gentle hand and a visionary heart. For the better part of two decades, our appointed role, traditional through the long centuries of our history, has been that of your Governor, with authority drawn from the

High King on his throne in distant Thorbardin. This is a legacy dating back to our founding as a colony of that great nation, when we were dependent upon Thorbardin for support, for military protection, and for a steady maintenance of trade.

However, it has become apparent to us, and to all perceptive citizens of our nation, that two Great Truths have emerged over the last centuries. In conjunction, these Truths require a new approach to Kayolin's government and, indeed, to our relations with the rest of Krynn.

The **First Great Truth** has been long in the making, but it can no longer be denied. We are forced to conclude that the dwarves of Kayolin stand alone as the representatives of our race, the mountain dwarves, in our large and significant corner of Krynn. We must face the determination that the other lands of our kinfolk, our brave cousins who dwell under all the great mountains of Ansalon, have been subjugated, conquered, or even quite possibly exterminated by threats that remain as yet unknown to us. Be the enemy elves or dragons, men or minotaurs, ogres or giants, we know not. But we must acknowledge that those other nations of dwarfkind have been silenced, and it is quite likely that we in Kayolin stand alone as survivors among the mountain dwarves.

Consider that communication from the nation of our One True King, the High Thane of Thorbardin, on his throne beneath Cloudseeker Peak in the Kharolis Mountains, has utterly ceased. No word, no message of any kind, has been received from Thorbardin in more than ten years. Because we knew that Thorbardin, as indeed all of the lands around the High Kharolis, was wracked terribly by the onslaught of Chaos and subsequently endured a violent and consuming civil war, it is clear that we can no longer rely upon any rulership, or governance, from that once mighty realm.

It is a melancholy fact but true: We in Kayolin must accept the possibility that we stand alone. There can be no expectation of guidance, solace, aid, or alliance with the ancient home of our ancestors. This First Truth does not mean our doom, not in any sense, but it presents a challenge to our heritage and demands a new way of ruling ourselves and of seeking solutions to our problems.

The **Second Great Truth** has also been long in the making, though the current dire situation is a more recent development. By its nature, this Truth is a direct threat to our prosperity, our happiness, and indeed, to our very survival. It is a Truth understood, to some extent, by every child of Kayolin, for it ties into the ancestral enemy of our homeland. But now, my loyal citizens, that enemy presents a menace to our prosperity, our safety, and even our very survival.

Every child of Kayolin learns of the horax at a very young age. No horror is so pervasive, so relentless, and so long standing as this scourge that dates to the earliest days of our nation's founding. The voracious bugs, each two or three times the size of a full-grown dwarf, number in their teeming thousands and form a horde that dwells in the very depths of the world, far beneath our deepest delvings. Ever hungry, soulless, and aggressive, they have been a menace to Kayolin since our nation's establishment, more than a thousand years ago. All know that, throughout most of that time, the horax have been held at bay by dwarven ingenuity, engineering, and courage. Some eight hundred years ago, our ancestors took it upon themselves to insulate dwarfkind from the horax. Our predecessors built a series of walls, barricades, and traps, ensuring that the horax could not penetrate into the city proper, walling them off and securing them in their fetid, deeply buried hives.

For hundreds of years, those measures have been successful, and long was the menace held at bay. As your ruler, however, it is our sad duty to report that in recent years the horax have again emerged from their dark lairs to raid aggressively into the under-levels of Kayolin. No more do these lethal arachnids hide in the dark recesses, fearing dwarf steel and dwarf courage. Whether they are driven by hunger, wickedness, or some inherent hive-lust, that we do not know and will not ever comprehend; they have begun to swarm from their dens to raid our stores and warrens, attack our delvings, and to capture and slay our miners.

In the last two years, these attacks have progressed to an unprecedented level. More than a hundred Kayolin dwarves have been dragged into horax lairs, wrapped in webbing, poisoned with lethal venom, and consumed to fuel the swarm's insatiable appetites. Purely villainous, eternally hungry, the giant bugs form a threat to the survival of our nation equal to any menace in the history of dwarfkind.

Throughout our existence, of course, we dwarves have faced a multitude of enemies. Be they dragons or giants, ogres or goblins, we have battled for our place in the world. Usually we have been aided in these fights by steadfast allies, such as the hill dwarves or humans—even, during moments of great desperation, by the elves or the metallic dragons. We have prevailed in great wars, epic conflicts that have shaped the very history of Krynn.

Yet unlike such previous threats, the horax are a threat to our nation alone. Their dens lie beneath

Kayolin, offering neither access nor egress to any other part of the world. Thus, we cannot request, nor should we expect, the warriors of any other land to come to our aid in this contest.

In the face of the **Two Great Truths**, we hereby decree the following steps, to be carved upon the scroll-stones as law from this day forward:

I) We dwarves of Kayolin withdraw our fealty from the unknown, possibly nonexsistent, monarch in distant Thorbardin. No longer am I, henceforth known as 'we,' Regar Smashfingers, a Governor, in service to that king. From this moment on, we who rule Kayolin shall be called King in our own right.

Indeed, my loyal dwarves, it is time for Kayolin to stand as a kingdom upon its own, centered around our great capital of Garnet Thax, secure in our mountain fastness against the schemes and encroachments of human, elf, goblin, and ogre. In the person of ourself, Regar Smashfingers, we humbly accept this historical burden, and pledge to strive with never-ending diligence and perseverance to see that the honor, prosperity, and safety of Kayolin is upheld.

The governorship has been a long tradition, an indelible part of our nation's history, but it is time for that tradition to be relegated to the past, where it belongs. New times call for new measures, and the most important new measure is the coronation of our own King. Reorx himself wills that Kayolin be subject to no foreign lord, no external master. We are a kingdom, and we desire—we need!—a King.

The tradition of Kayolin's rulership is deeply seated, of course, ingrained into our history. We may recall tales told by our elders, learned by them as youngsters:

when the first settlers established our home in Garnet Thax, under these mountains of Kharolis, they brought with them a legendary artifact. This was a silver torc, emblazoned with fabulous gems. The Torc of the Forge, the great talisman of Dwarf Kings, was created by Reorx himself as a sign of his favor, and it was brought to Kayolin in the early days of our nation.

And then, tragically and mysteriously, it was lost into the depths of the world. All of Kayolin's dwarves have learned that for more than a thousand years this torc, this symbol of a king's throne, remained missing. Without the great talisman, Kayolin survived as a governor's seat, lacking the need—and the symbol—of kingship. But now, in the hour of our greatest need, the artifact of our ancient regime would prove to be a timely and propitious find.

And indeed, this is such a moment in our history, for it is our great pleasure to announce that the Torc of the Forge has been located at last, discovered by Lord Alakar Heelspur's eldest son, Baracan, in the depths of the world. The torc came to Kayolin with the first wave of migrations and was lost when the deep delvings of our city were excavated. As was foretold in the first of the atrium, the torc has come forth when most needed, to signal the regal blessings of our god.

Baracan Heelspur has returned the torc to its rightful place in Garnet Thax. As proof of our god's blessing, the stones that encrust the ring of the torc are even now being incorporated into a splendid crown, a symbolic headpiece that will serve as visual proof of our reign's rightful status.

It is our expectation that the citizens of Kayolin will react to our ascendancy with joy, with celebration, and a continuation of the steadfast loyalty that is such a treasured component of the dwarf character. A series of banquets, culminating in the coronation itself, shall mark the first full month of the new year as a period of unprecedented celebration in our long history.

Of course, we must acknowledge the existence of certain reactionary and criminal elements, wretched dwarves who will stand in the way of progress and act only to obstruct at every turn. It is because of this danger that we shall have the second decree inscribed upon the scrollstones:

II) From this day forward, until such time as the king declares the crisis to be past, a state of emergency shall exist in Kayolin. This unique and dangerous time requires firm steps and resolute determination to overcome the many perils before us. Specifically, the emergency condition shall result in the following procedures:

1. Lord Alakar Heelspur is appointed to a new position: Director of Loyalty and Enforcement. He shall be empowered to recruit honorable dwarves into his ranks and shall be awarded with a large scope of powers. His League of Enforcers shall act as his agents and have the authority vested in our own royal name. Furthermore, he shall be tasked with identifying the aforementioned reactionary and criminal elements within the kingdom, arresting those undesirables, and obtaining confessions from same. Suitable punishment for malfeasance shall be determined on a case-by-case basis; these disciplinary decisions remain the provenance of ourself, the king.

2. The full might of Kayolin shall be mobilized to counter the threat of the vicious horax. All members of militia companies shall assemble under their local officers and stand by for orders. Operations against the horrible bug creatures shall commence at the earliest

opportunity. Recalcitrant citizens who attempt to shirk their military duties will be conscripted and will form the first rank of the battle formations.

3. The activities of the New Regime, including the celebrations associated with the coronation, and the imminent campaign against the horax shall be funded through a selective tax. A one-hundred-steel surcharge is hereby established on the activities of any hill dwarf seeking to do business in Kayolin. Any dwarf of any race who desires to conduct business beyond the gates of our nation shall pay a ten percent tariff, with value to be established by the Director of Loyalty and Enforcement, on any goods transported into or out of Kayolin. Finally, the small communities of Theiwar, Klar, and Daewar who live comfortably with the safety of our mountain fastness, shall each furnish one thousand steel from each neighborhood quarter as a small token of gratitude for the protection provided them by the Hylar and Daergar might that is the backbone of Kayolin's greatness.

Let the words of the king be inscribed into the scrollstones! From this day forth, the decree of Regar Smashfingers is the law of Kayolin!

TEN

HOMECOMING

"So your father's letter warned you not to come home, which is why you're going home?" Gretchan Pax said.

Brandon Bluestone, walking along at her side, merely grunted in acknowledgment. An eagle screeched overhead, banking across the valley, soaring between the mountain peaks. The sun shone brightly, penetrating even the dense canopy of the pine forest. Yet the stubborn dwarf plodded along in a cloud of gloom, glowering as if he were marching toward a battle or some other dolorous occasion.

"I just want to make sure I understand your logic—or should I say, lack thereof," she continued as if she didn't mind talking to herself. "I mean, so that I can write it down accurately the next time I have a chance to work on my journals."

"You don't have to understand it!" Brandon Bluestone retorted. "And while we're reminding ourselves of things we already know, you didn't have to come along with me either."

"Oh, but I did," she replied with that cheerfulness

that Brandon could find so Reorx-cursed annoying. "You know I've wanted to see Kayolin all my life. I spent a year with you in Pax Tharkas asking you to take me there. Which you wouldn't do until you got a message from your father warning you to stay away from the place. So now you're taking me to Kayolin."

"I'm going to Kayolin," he growled. "You happen to be tagging along."

"Call it what you will," she said, unabashed. "Anyway, we should get our first view of the gate today, don't you think?"

He growled in exasperation. "Look, you read my father's letter as well as I did. Not only does the governor plan to crown himself a king, but he's created a League of Enforcers to impose his will on the people of Kayolin. Knowing Regar Smashfingers like I do, I'm certain that he's using those agents to go after those who disapprove of him. And chief among those people will be my father. I won't be surprised to find that he's already been thrown into some royal dungeon . . . or worse," he concluded grimly.

She reached out and took his hand, squeezing it affectionately. Again, he grunted, somewhat more pleasantly. For some time they simply walked together, striding upward along the winding mountain road. Gretchan's large black dog, Kondike, padded eagerly at her side. In her other hand she held the long, smooth staff, capped with the tiny anvil, that was her most prized possession. She was a very beautiful dwarf maid, with hair falling in long blonde curls around her shoulders and upper back. Her blue eyes sparkled with vitality, and her full form curved the front of her tunic in a way that still caught Brandon's eye whenever he looked at her, which he did very frequently.

But for the time being, he was lost in his own thoughts, worries, and fears.

Brandon was a handsome and strapping dwarf with broad shoulders, and flowing brown hair and beard. He was dressed in sturdy workman's clothes, leather trousers and boots that were worn from long use but still served to protect his feet. A large backpack straddled his shoulders, and a keen, silver-bladed axe swung from a strap at his belt.

The scent of the pines surrounded them, brushing their skin in the cool breeze that blew down from the heights of the Garnet Mountains. The smell brought a strong wave of nostalgic memories to Brandon, who had spent much of his life hunting, prospecting, and exploring the peaks and valleys of that majestic range.

Yet as he walked, every one of those memories seemed imperiled by the present, and he felt himself borne down again by the weight of the responsibility that had compelled him to return.

"You're thinking about that proclamation that your father included with his letter again, aren't you?" Gretchan asked softly.

Brandon nodded. He had shown her the letter, which included a copy of Regar Smashfingers's proclamation of kingship. "I don't know if the king is behind my exile, but the fact that he promoted Lord Heelspur to head of his League of Enforcers makes me think so. It was Heelspur who was behind my brother's murder, and I had to leave Kayolin because I accused him of the crime, remember? It's pretty clear which side the king came down on."

"What about all that stuff about the horax? Do you think the king is making it up?"

"Who knows? I mean, every Kayolin dwarf knows about the horax. Even with the walls and barricades and such, one or two of the bugs still make their way into the sublevels once in a while. They're damned nasty, and if there ever was to be a real infestation of them, I think it could be pretty bad. But it just seems convenient to have them turning into a widespread menace all of a sudden, just when Regar Smashfingers is looking for an excuse to seize even more power than he already had."

She let go of his hand and almost skipped as they came around a bend in the winding road. A tall mountain came into view again, its sturdy shoulders mantled in white snow. The gentle, rocky ridges, far about the timberline, stood out in such crystalline relief that it seemed as though they could see every rock, niche, and snowdrift. The summit had been part of their horizon for several days, but their new vantage proved that they were getting very close indeed.

"I can't believe we're almost there!" Gretchan said breathlessly. It was several moments before she realized that her companion had fallen a number of paces behind. "Brandon!" she called, turning and waving to the bearded, plodding dwarf. "Come on!"

"What's your hurry?" the big dwarf demanded sourly. His sturdy legs chugged along, and the large backpack looming higher than his head didn't affect his balance or bearing. Even so, he moved more slowly than he had on any day during the long trek northward. "We'll get there when we get there," he added.

"But—there's Garnet Peak, right there!" she said, her cheeks flushed, eyes bright with excitement. She turned and pointed to the lofty, snowcapped mountain that had dominated their view for the past few days. "Your homeland is right underneath it!"

"Don't you think I know that? After all, I was born there!" Brandon snapped.

"Well, you sure don't sound like someone who's going home for the first time in more than a year!" Gretchan retorted. "If you were walking any slower, a glacier would beat you!"

"Glaciers move down mountains. We're climbing up," he shot back, allowing a smug smile to gleam through his beard.

His companion sighed, her shoulders slumping as she shook her head and looked at him. Her excitement and enthusiasm seemed to all drain away in that look, and he felt a stab of guilt.

"You're really worried about what you're going to find in Kayolin, aren't you?" she asked sympathetically. "Look, if you really want to stop here, to turn around, we can. We don't have to go there if you don't want to, you know. We really don't."

"I suppose not. It's only the one thing you've been talking about since we met—the chance to see Kayolin with your own eyes. But we don't *have* to go there." A look of hurt flashed in her eyes, and he immediately regretted his sarcasm.

"Look," he added hastily. "I'm sorry. I'm worried about my father. And . . . it's just . . . you know I left under some rather stressful circumstances. I'm also worried about what we're going to find in Kayolin in general, the whole city and nation. And if something's happened to my parents . . . You know, the Bluestone Luck—"

"You *changed* the Bluestone Luck! Did you forget that already?" She pointed to the shiny weapon at his belt. "It was you who saved Pax Tharkas with Balric Bluestone's axe! You fought that black minion; that is still the bravest thing I've ever seen!"

Her words make him look up at the snowy massif of Garnet Peak, the mountain where Balric Bluestone had disappeared—during the Cataclysm—leaving his axe to be recovered by his son, Brandon's ancestor, immediately after the destruction had ceased to rain down upon Krynn. Legend had it that the weapon had been blessed by Reorx himself, and most assuredly, it was a mighty blade, keen and enchanted.

But the descendents of Balric Bluestone had not prospered from that blessing. Catastrophe had piled upon misfortune and mingled with tragedy through the more than four hundred years since that singular event. House Bluestone's fortunes had waned, a series of business setbacks had taken their toll, and the family members had a way of finding disgrace or meeting up with untimely death. Brandon's father, Garren, had struggled to survive as a moderately successful businessman, and his brother, Nailer, had been murdered by assassins that, Brandon had learned, were sent by the most ruthless and richest lord in Kayolin: Alakar Heelspur.

It had been that murder, and Brandon's own life threatened, that had led the younger Bluestone to flee the land of his ancestors. A year earlier he had made his way south, across the Newsea. He'd been ambushed and betrayed by hill dwarves, sentenced to death, then thrown into the dungeon of his own mountain dwarf cousins when they had mistaken him for a hill dwarf spy.

Of course, all those adventures had also led to meeting Gretchan. She had rescued him from that dungeon, and together they had turned back the hill dwarf attack. Yes, he and Gretchan were not a bad team. He hung his head, forced to admit to himself that his luck hadn't been all that bad.

"Well," he admitted, blushing. "It was really you who banished the minion back to—well, to wherever it came from."

"I could only do that through the will of Reorx," the dwarf priestess replied cheerily. "And because you had the courage to stand up to the creature."

As they hiked steadily higher into the mountains, Brandon smelled the pine forest with new delight, heard the brooks and waterfalls of the Garnet range, and was reminded of all the good things about the place that had been his home for all of his fifty years—excepting the past eighteen months. And he finally felt that it was good to be going home again.

He had spent the past peaceful year in Pax Tharkas with Gretchan and the dwarves of Tarn Bellowgranite's Thorbardin refugees. He had shared Gretchan's joy at the discovery that Tarn's old general, Otaxx Shortbeard, was in fact the father she had never known.

Throughout the year, Gretchan had yearned to continue her explorations, wishing to travel to the one great dwarf nation of which, as yet, she had no first-hand knowledge. Brandon had consistently refused to take her to Kayolin—until the letter from his father had arrived. For more than a month they had been journeying northward. They had trekked across the plains south of the Newsea, booked passage on a ship to Caergoth, and even purchased horses that had carried them all the way to the city of Garnet, gateway to the mountain range of the same name. They had sold their horses in that city two days before and were completing the journey on foot, following the smooth, paved road high into the mountains.

The slopes to either side of the valley grew steadily steeper, and they came into view of some small glaciers, permanent sheets of ice clinging to the creases and couloirs in the shady recesses of the upper reaches. The Garnet range was much smaller, the cliff faces more gentle, the crests more rolling, than the lofty realm of the Kharolis. But from down here on the valley road, the mountains looked plenty big.

Brandon took comfort from that familiar, pastoral vista. It wasn't until they came around the last bend in the road and he saw the massive gate itself that he again thought about the realities of his homecoming. Would he be welcome in Kayolin? What was the fate of his father? What business was it of his that Regar Smashfingers had crowned himself king?

Kayolin's main gate barred entry to a lofty tunnel at the base of one of Garnet Peak's true precipices, a soaring cliff rising some two thousand feet to a shoulder of the massive summit. In times of war, the entry was sealed by a massive stone plug, but at the moment, as usual during times of peace, that gate was retracted far into the mountain, leaving the tunnel mouth gaping as a black hole in the rock wall. The road led directly to that entrance.

It was midday, so there was no other traffic in view as the pair of dwarves strolled up to the looming entry. "In morning, it's crowded with hunters and lumberjacks heading out," Brandon explained. "And the same thing is usually true in reverse at night. But most of the time it's just a few travelers coming and going, maybe some merchants from Solamnia or dwarves carrying their own goods down to the humans."

"My skin is tingling!" Gretchan said, looking up in awe as they moved into the shadows of the tunnel. The roof towered some fifty or sixty feet over head, and the gateway was a similar length wide.

"Well, just remember. Act like you've been here before when we walk in. There'll be some redcoats, soldiers of the Garnet Guards, watching the gate. We'll have to nod politely at the guards so they can make sure we're not goblins or ogres, and then we'll get lost in some of the midlevels. I know a few nice taverns where we can catch our breath and I can maybe send word to my dad."

"You don't think the king or his men will be looking for you?" Gretchan asked as the coolness of the shady cavern enclosed them. Their dwarf eyes quickly adjusted to the low illumination.

"Don't see why," Brandon replied. "I've been gone long enough that I suspect he's forgotten all about me. Probably doesn't ever expect me to come home."

They grew silent as they advanced into the tunnel of the nation's main gate.

Brandon nodded casually to an axe-bearing guard in black metal plate armor as they started on past the guard post. He could smell the hops from a nearby brewery, and his mouth watered at the familiar, evocative scent.

"Just a minute there, fellow," said the guard, stepping forward and, surprisingly, placing his hand on Brandon's arm. Three more armed and armored dwarves, also garbed in black, emerged from a small alcove in the side of the cavern to back up their comrade.

"What is it?" Brand asked, puzzled.

"You can't just walk in here!" the sentry declared. "I order you to stop, in the name of the Enforcers!"

Brandon bit back a sharp retort. "Sorry," he said. "I've been traveling for . . . for a while. What do I need to do?"

"Give us your name!" snapped the guard. "Who are you?" Another stepped out to further block their retreat.

Caught by surprise, Brandon didn't even think of lying. "Brandon Bluestone," he said stiffly. "Of Kayolin. This is my home!"

"Check the list," said the first guard.

"And what's your name?" another dwarf-at-arms demanded of Gretchan. "Are you a native of Kayolin also?"

"I'm Gretchan Pax, from Pax Tharkas," she replied. "Just visiting here."

"Bluestone!" snapped an unseen guard in the alcove who was presumably consulting the afore-mentioned list. "Take him! Lord Heelspur has his name down here!"

"What?" Brandon declared, starting to step back as two guards seized his arms. His gut wrenched in sudden panic. He had read about the League of Enforcers in the king's proclamation, but he didn't expect his own name to be on their lists. Reflexively he put his hand around the hilt of his axe.

"Oh, he's not *that* Bluestone," Gretchan said breezily. She laughed, a musical, trilling sound, and waved her staff gently before the faces of the sentries. The top of that shaft, the small anvil that was the symbol of Reorx, glowed slightly, and Brandon realized that she was casting one of her priestess spells.

"He's the Bluestone you've been waiting for. Aren't you glad he's come home?" she asked sweetly.

"Oh, Bluestone!" said one of the guards, his face breaking into a broad smile. "Yes! Welcome back! It's been too long!"

"Yeah, it's great to see you!" said the first guard, releasing his arm to clap him on the back.

"Uh, yes. Sure. Thanks," Brandon said as Gretchan took him by the arm. Kondike trotted along behind him as they swept out of the gateway and into a Kayolin that Brandon was not sure he would recognize.

ELEVEN

THE DEEPSHELF INN AND THE ATRIUM

Brandon led Gretchan by the hand into Kayolin, walking as briskly as he thought he could without attracting any undue attention. He was still shaken by the discovery that his name was on a list held by the guards at the gate.

The two passed the Gateway Brewery and its public room without entering that classic watering hole. Instead, Brandon followed the long entrance tunnel for perhaps a quarter of a mile then turned into one of the passages leading into the lower levels of the city of Garnet Thax. The route had at one time been a mine tunnel, but it had been widened and supported with the installation of stone archways every fifty feet or so. It was mostly empty; the few dwarves they met were miners bearing wheelbarrows, tools, and other objects from one work site to another.

The most direct route from the main gate of Kayolin into the city of Garnet Thax was a wide thoroughfare, a ramp lined with inns and plazas as well as numerous shops, leading directly into the main residential zones of the city, the midlevels. Spooked by the fact that his name was known, and that the Enforcers might be searching for him, Brandon elected to lead Gretchan on a more circuitous route into the city proper. They made their way into the deep-levels, a district of smelting and forging plants, passing along narrow, darkened streets, moving quickly amid the infrequent pedestrians in that industrial locale.

Kondike, who seemed completely comfortable in the underground setting, paced easily along behind them. The dog drew more interest from passersby than did the two dwarves.

"Those sentries—they wore black, not red," Brandon noted. "They must be a new outfit. The Garnet Guards are well known for their scarlet tunics."

"Have things changed very much otherwise—at least, that you can see?" Gretchan asked as they strode along past a row of smithy stalls, where the clang of hammers striking steel made a rhythmic cadence and created enough of a din that they could be certain they wouldn't be overheard.

"It looks pretty much the same as before," the Kayolin dwarf admitted. He gestured as they passed a large chamber, visible through a series of arched openings off of the road. Massive piles of coal filled one side of the room, while dwarves chopped with picks to reduce the fuel to small chunks and cart it into the interior of the factory. They could hear the sound of roaring furnaces and feel the waves of heat emanating as far as the passing tunnel. "I mean, work is getting done. From the look of those coal supplies, the foundries are as productive as ever—maybe more."

"Why don't we just go to your parents' house?" his companion asked. "You'll be able to learn a lot from them, I'm sure."

Brandon nodded. "We'll end up there, yes. But I don't want to just march down the street and go in the front door. Who knows who might be watching? What if the League of Enforcers has a spy there . . . or if my father has already been arrested?"

She grimaced. "I didn't think of that. You're right to be careful. Then where are we going?"

"To a tavern I know. It's called the Deepshelf Inn, and we're not likely to bump into friends of the king there."

They turned onto a wider road, one that curved gradually as they walked along. Sooty smiths pounded their hammers against red steel anvils in several shops to the left, and they passed another foundry where they could see red-hot metal being poured from a great bucket into a series of molds, sparks trailing from the liquid. The workers all wore heavy leather aprons, hoods, and gauntlets with slit faceplates to protect themselves from the searing heat.

Gretchan looked around wide-eyed and would have stopped to investigate if Brandon had let her. Instead, he continued to lead her along until they came to a wide cave mouth on the side of the road. The establishment's name, Deepshelf Inn, was carved into the mantel above the entrance. From within came sounds of laughter and genial argument, as well as smells of roasting meat, burning tobacco, and yeasty beer.

They stepped through the door into the crowded interior. The entryway was fairly dark, but the rear of the room was much brighter. As they advanced, Gretchan saw that the inn's great room ended in a broad, curved balcony that was open to the air on the far side. The vast space was illuminated from above by a diffuse glow that, while it wasn't as bright as daylight, suggested the pale glow of sunset or dawn.

"It looks like a view of the outside world!" she exclaimed.

"That's the Atrium," Brandon explained. "It's a shaft that runs up and down through the center of Garnet Thax. The palace stands at the very top. All of the city's levels have a view of the Atrium at some point—I guess you could say it's Kayolin's most significant feature."

"Like the Urkhan Sea in Thorbardin," she suggested in a tone of wonder.

"Maybe," he replied with a shrug. He'd never thought of it like that before; as a Kayolin dwarf, the Atrium was just another part of ordinary life.

"What's at the bottom?" Gretchan asked.

"Nobody knows. The horax have their dens far down there, somewhere. Lower than that, you'd probably come to the middle of the world; if you look down there, you can see the faint glow of lava and even feel the heat." That vista had never failed to impress him as a boy, first, then as an adult.

"Can we sit next to it?" she asked, as if reading his mind. At first he was reluctant because there seemed no place more likely for him to be noticed. The balcony at the outer rim of the inn was visible to observers on the various levels above. But since they were in the deep-levels, it would be hard to pick them out on the crowded terrace. In fact, it would be pleasant to sit near the Atrium. Gretchan's questions made him feel fond of it.

They made their way between the crowded tables, past the bar, and finally found themselves on the balcony, with the Atrium yawning before them. Gretchan gave a little gasp of surprise and stepped right up to the low stone railing that prevented an accidental fall. After glancing around for any signs of overly curious dwarves—though the bar, including the balcony, was crowded, all the customers and servers seemed to be occupied with their own business—Brandon stepped up to join her.

He felt, again, the dizzying sense of space that the Atrium provided, and he instinctively understood why the nation's ancestors had chosen to build Garnet Thax around the vast, airy shaft. The deep well plummeted below them. They were near the bottom of the city, so most of the view downward was simply barren stone walls, cliffs that were pocked with ledges and the occasional crack, chimney, or cave mouth. The shaft here was perhaps a hundred and fifty feet across, and if they looked directly ahead, they saw a balcony similar to theirs, though not as large or as crowded, on the other side.

A few more of those vantages marked the presence of the city's very deepest levels, below, until the gradually narrowing shaft vanished into a blue mist. Far below, a faint crimson glow, like the embers in a dying fire, suggested the deep fires at the heart of Krynn.

"You're right; I do feel the warmth," Gretchan said, leaning over so precipitously that Brandon grabbed her shoulder. "It's rising like a breeze."

"Yep," Brand agreed, not releasing his grip. "It warms the whole city."

They turned their eyes upward and beheld a dazzling array of lights where lanterns marked the more prosperous parts of the city. A series of shelves jutted from the cliff as it ascended toward the heights. There were dozens of levels to Garnet Thax, each of them centered around that deep shaft. They could pinpoint numerous other balconies, and many dwarves were leaning against the railings just as they were, taking in the sights. The Atrium was the focal point for all the dwarves of Kayolin, and many innkeepers exploited that fact by establishing patios and tables with a view.

Hundreds of dwarves were visible all around them, leaning on balconies like theirs, talking, drinking, or just staring thoughtfully. Looking around, Brandon hoped no one would notice them and recognize him.

From the great room of the Deepshelf Inn, they could hear sounds of raucous laughter, mugs clinking in a steady round of toasts. "The Deepshelf is one of the lowest social establishments in the city—in elevation, as well as class. The folks in here are mostly miners and laborers." He gestured toward the higher reaches of the great shaft. "Up there, you'll find a lot of prosperous merchants, with the wealthiest—and the nobility—sticking to the very top levels. The midlevels have a lot more inns and cafés right on the Atrium," he explained. "It's always been a popular spot for Kayolin's dwarves to congregate. On the highest levels, those just below the governor's palace, there are private manors with their own balconies looking out onto the shaft. Those are generally considered the most desirable homes in all Garnet Thax. The Heelspur clan owns one that circles halfway around the shaft at one of its widest points."

"It looks like it gets wider the higher you go," Gretchan observed.

"Yes, that's right. It's about three hundred feet across at the palace level, and gradually narrows as it descends. Some say it's only ten or twenty feet wide down below, but it's been a long time since anyone went down to look."

They found a small table near the edge and took their seats. A few minutes later, a serving maid came by to ask for their order; she returned with their drinks, but the priestess ignored hers; she was still gawking at the vast shaft of the Atrium. Brandon also wasn't ready to dive into his tall mug of bitter beer. He sat morosely, alternately watching Gretchan, peering around, and staring at the black slate table.

"How did you do what you did back there?" Brandon asked. "How did you get me past those guards who were going to arrest me?"

"Well, it was a simple charm spell," she replied modestly. "Pretty useful on dimwits like those four. They probably still think you're a long-lost buddy. And when the effect wears off, I hope they'll be too embarrassed to tell anyone what happened."

"But to think of my name on some kind of list!" Brandon declared, still trying to wrap his head around the idea. "Things are worse here than I imagined."

"They mentioned the League of Enforcers," Gretchan said. "I take it there was no such vigilance at the checkpoints when you left here?"

He shook his head. "No. But times have changed—and fast. I've got to find my parents and hear about what's going on here!"

"I'm sure they'll be happy to see you," the priestess returned mildly.

"But if my name is on a list of undesirables," he replied, "who knows? Their house may be watched. My father helped me get out of here when the governor and Lord Heelspur wanted my head."

"What about friends?" Gretchan asked sensibly. "Some of the people you know, who you trusted—and could still trust. Why don't we seek one of them out, find out what's going on, maybe see if they'll get in touch with your father for us so you don't walk straight into a trap."

"That's a good idea," he answered. "I have friends here, and they'd probably be glad to see me. Two of them were real good friends, as a matter of fact. I'd trust them with my life." He felt a twinge of embarrassment, and shook his head ruefully. "It's just . . ." His voice trailed off.

"It's just what?" Gretchan pressed.

He grimaced. "Well, they're both female, and, um, I was kind of close to them. They'll be glad to see me, I'm sure.

"But I'm not sure they'll be too happy about you," he concluded glumly.

—DH—

The monster inched along, clawed talons scrabbling at the stone floor. Though it had large, multifaceted eyes, it was not hampered by the lightless surroundings. A pair of antennae quivered from the crown of its bulbous head, touching, smelling, and tasting the moldy air. Its legs, all eight of them, stiffened in preparation for a charge as those extra-acute senses told the being that prey was near.

Behind the creature came another, and another, and still more. The column of huge bugs moved with arachnoid stealth, joined legs smoothly propelling the long, segmented bodies, scuttling steadily forward. Each of them was protected by the armored carapace that was the monster's natural shield. Despite their insectoid appearance, they moved in unison, like a well-trained company of soldiers.

They were similar but not entirely identical insofar as the last of the creatures in the file was a bright red in color, while most of the others were pale gray, almost white. Furthermore, while all of the others possessed wide, sharp mandibles, the red one had a smaller pair. That unimpressive weaponry was perhaps balanced by the presence of a bulbous mass underneath the creature's head. The mass throbbed and wobbled like a living thing and was tipped with a moist knob, almost like a nozzle, which twitched and wiggled hungrily.

The heads of the monsters bulged grotesquely. The wicked pincers at their mouths were sideways-snapping jaws, and they flexed eagerly on the first of the beasts in the file. That one abruptly stiffened, bringing the column of its fellows to an abrupt halt.

The monster quivered, sensing, tasting, hungering. It was in a new place, a fresh hunting ground for the creature. It was blessed with the hive memory of all of its kind, and for thousands of years it had dwelled in those deep caverns, far below the surface of the world—a surface that the monster and its fellows had never experienced and would not have tolerated if, by some miracle, they were exposed to the brightness of the sun. But it and its race knew the deep caverns very, very well. For all those centuries, throughout the passing of millennia, it had made the caves its own.

Until, only lately, new paths had been discovered. Places where there had once been solid stone barriers were exposed as tunnels, new routes through the underground world. The monsters had crept into those new places, exploring, tasting, touching, smelling, and bringing the new knowledge back to the hive. Often those new pathways had yielded prey, and the monsters had carried much fresh meat back to the queen, allowing her to feast on dwarf blood, to grow fat and fertile, and to lay many more eggs.

The numbers of the monsters had grown great, their teeming masses crawling and clacking and clawing throughout the vast dens of the underworld. Sometimes they ventured too deep into the bedrock, to the realms where subterranean fires heated the rock, so the creatures were forced into retreat, lest they be roasted alive.

But more often they probed upward, where the new tunnels were being opened, where the dwarves lived. There were many routes to pick from, and all were explored by the aggressive, hungry beasts. They always traveled in groups, and as the queen dispatched them in every direction, the terrain known to the hive steadily expanded. Some of the explorations ended in dead ends or fiery fountains of lava, but many others moved onward and up, probing farther and higher into the realms of the dwarves.

It was such an expedition that was exploring yet another newly discovered route. The lead monster's antennae quivered with excitement. It could hear the sounds of laughter and argument and dwarves feasting very nearby. Abruptly those twin sensors stiffened, fully erect, a clear signal to the file behind it.

Then it charged, numerous feet scrabbling across the stone floor, mandibles clacking aggressively at the forefront of its bulbous, hideous head. It rushed from the narrow tunnel into a larger, circular cavern. More than a dozen filthy dwarves sat there, bickering amiably over the flesh of a large cave slug that they were attempting to divide.

The gully dwarves shrieked and bounced to their feet as the clacking monster burst from concealment, but the creature moved too fast for the hapless fellows. It seized the nearest gully dwarf with its four front legs, pulling the wriggling fellow up to its head. The sharp mandibles sliced though soft flesh, driving the Aghar into a frenzy of struggling. Blood spilled from the deep wounds, but the dwarf's frantic squirming only made the monster squeeze harder and cut deeper into the captive's flesh.

Holding its still-living prize aloft, the monster backed away from the band of dwarves to allow its kin-bugs to attack. The rest of them spilled out of the narrow tunnel one at a time, the whole file following their leader. Each of the giant bugs pounced on a gully dwarf, even as the panic-stricken wretches tried to flee. A few reached the exit, sprinting into the dark tunnel. But their stubby legs were no match for the speeding monsters, and most of the Aghar, when they ran, were caught in the monster's sharp jaws before they had covered fifty feet.

In seconds there were only three dwarves still free of the clutching mandibles: a female and two youngsters. With the little ones clutching her grubby hands, she darted away from the obvious exits, sprinting toward a small crack in the cave wall. She had almost reached the safety of that refuge when the last of the monsters, the red one, came into the filthy cavern.

That crimson arachnid reared upward. The bulbous lump tilted, wet nozzle quivering as it spewed forth a long, sticky strand of webbing. The gooey material shot across the cave and blocked the entrance to the narrow crack. The female Aghar tried to claw it away with her hands, but her limbs quickly stuck in the web. The young gully dwarves shrieked as another strand of sticky web shot from the creature's throbbing organ. That one struck all three Aghar, wrapping itself across their heads, and though they struggled frantically, their twisting and grappling only further ensnared them.

The red bug dropped its forequarters so all eight feet rested on the floor, and slowly the web, still attached to the bulbous organ, began to retract. It seemed to suck the strands back into the bulking grotesqueness on its throat, and as it reeled the sticky web strands in, it brought the three gully dwarves, all of them sobbing and shrieking pathetically, right up to its narrow, pinching jaws. With a toss of its head, it wrapped the Aghar even more securely in the gooey web and casually threw the bundle onto its segmented back.

Finally, with twelve of the monsters each holding a wounded, bleeding, but still living dwarf in its crushing mandibles—and the red one bearing the trio of webbed Aghar—the file of horax started back into the darkness, through the narrow tunnel, toward the hive.

They would bear their prizes to the queen.

TWELVE

TO THE OLD HEARTH AGAIN

All right. I guess we should head up to my old neighborhood. There's an inn there where one of my old friends works," Brandon replied. "Um, they might be able to help."

"Don't you mean *'she'* might be able to help?" Gretchan, with a twinkle in her eye, asked.

"Well, yes I do!" Brandon snapped, dropping a steel coin on the table to pay for their drinks. He stomped toward the entryway, hastened along by her laughter. His ears burned, and he could *feel* them turning red.

He wasn't sure why his face felt flushed, but he was suddenly terribly chagrined about all the carousing and womanizing he'd done in the city, back when life had seemed so much simpler. He and his brother, Nailer, had cut a wide, if shallow, swath through the maids of Kayolin, and truth to tell, they'd enjoyed every minute of it. He tried to console himself with the thought that, for the most part, the maids of Kayolin hadn't seemed to mind much either. With his brother slain, he realized that the women he had, sometimes, treated rather shabbily were still likely to be his best allies in the city.

Gretchan seemed in a good mood regardless, humming to herself as they weaved their way through the crowd and left the Deepshelf Inn. She took in the scenery and chattered cheerfully. She remarked about the intricacies of iron tools in one shop and about the orderliness of a clean, bustling factory, glimpsed through a large door, as they made their way down the narrow street and around first one, then another, tight corner.

"They can't be much different from similar kinds of places where you came from," Brandon suggested, exasperated by her positive attitude.

She shook her head. "The delvings in the east, where I grew up among Severus Stonehand's Daergar, are a lot more primitive than this. And remember, I've never had the chance to see Thorbardin."

"Yeah, I guess I see your point," he admitted. For the first time, it occurred to him that Garnet Thax was certainly the most spectacular dwarf delving that Gretchan had ever seen. Once more, he felt guilty about having taken that unique place for granted in the past.

"Let's avoid the main road," he suggested as they passed one of the great, spiraling ramps that connected the many levels of the city. "We can take some of the smaller stairwells that lead up through the city. They're steeper to climb but a lot more private. I'd hate to run into Heelspur's Enforcers."

They followed a straight and relatively wide avenue away from the central shaft of the Atrium. To either side the smithies and manufacturing centers had given way to small residences, apartments stacked two or three high with small, round doors and, only rarely, a window looking out onto the street. Stone steps led to the higher entrances, which were recessed from the street. The flat ceiling over the roadway tended to be about twenty feet overhead, providing many shadowy alcoves, especially along the top layer of dwellings to each side.

There were a few dwarves coming and going along the street. Doors opened here and there, and a few young fellows simply sat outside of their apartments and watched the street with hopeless eyes. The dwarves were dressed if not in rags, then in relatively poor and careworn garments. The occasional lamp in the street was dark, as if no one wanted to spend the steel to refresh it with oil. Brandon couldn't help thinking that the area was a perfect place for spies to lurk or ambushers to hide, and he constantly looked over his shoulder. But honestly, he told himself, it didn't seem like the kind of neighborhood where they'd run into any Enforcers.

They came to an arched alcove at the side of the street. Illuminated by low-wick oil lamps, they could see that it entered onto a landing and was connected to a tightly spiraling series of stone steps leading up to the right and down to the left.

"Here's one of the stairwells," he said. "Let's head up."

They entered and climbed for a long time, ascending several hundred feet as they moved from the deep-levels into the city's midlevels. The stairwell itself was cloaked in shadows except where dim lamps illuminated each of the landings, which provided access to streets, once every thirty or so vertical feet. As Brandon had predicted, fewer dwarves were out and about up there. The ones they met didn't give them a second glance, though several children gawked as Kondike, eye to eye with them, trotted by.

"Here we are," Brandon said finally. Kondike still padded along behind as they emerged into a street and turned toward the Bluestones' neighborhood. Brandon felt a strange mix of emotions as he noted the familiar locales, the shops and inns he had frequented during most of the years in his life. The streets were lit more consistently there, and they heard loud laughter and crude boasting as they passed one open doorway. Even so, the pedestrians tended to walk with their heads down, avoiding strangers' eyes. Even if Gretchan didn't notice anything amiss, Brandon knew the neighborhood, and it seemed a good deal less neighborly than when he had departed the city a year and half before.

The Cracked Mug was a small and prosperous establishment, offering good food and very good beer at reasonable prices. It was only a few blocks away from the Bluestone family home, occupying a strategic position right at the level's exit to the main ramp spiraling up from the deep-levels. The two travelers approached it from a back alley.

Brandon had spent many hours in that place, partaking of the fine fare and pleasantly flirting with the lovely barmaid Bondall Fairmont, who had been one of his first and longest-lasting lovers. As he and Gretchan stood outside the Mug's open front door, and he smelled the familiar, tantalizing aroma of roasting meat, he felt as though he were a far-ranging traveler who had finally come home.

"This is a good place to stop and see what I can find out," Brandon said. Still, some unspoken hesitation held him back, and for a long time he stood on the street, looking at the faded sign depicting a stout beer stein with a jagged break running through it.

"Hey, daydreamer," Gretchan whispered, prodding him. "I think you'll attract more attention standing here in the street than you would if we went inside."

"Yep, you're right," he agreed, opening the door and holding it so Gretchan could enter first. He took a deep breath and forced himself to pick up his feet, moving through the doorway into the smoky, crowded great room. The ceiling was low, supported by arches carved from the bedrock of the mountain. Most of the tables were occupied, but he spotted a small one in back and ushered Gretchan in that direction. As usual, the dog stayed close to his mistress's heel, moving nimbly through the crowd.

They sat down with their backs to the others in the room, though Brand kept his head cocked, looking over his shoulder. He spotted a barmaid—sure enough, it was Bondall—coming toward him and, catching her eye, surreptitiously raised a finger to his lips.

The pretty maid's eyes widened momentarily, but she held her tongue as she bustled over to them. She cracked a sly, teasing smile as she spotted Gretchan, while the priestess, for all her bravado, blushed a pale pink.

"So, stranger, what'll it be?" Bondall asked before leaning down to rest her elbows on the table. "You do know there are bad ones looking for you, don't you?" she asked in a quiet voice. Then she winked at Gretchan. "And who's your friend?"

"Uh, this is Gretchan Pax. Gretchan, Bondall Fairmont . . . an old friend," he growled. "And yes, I do know they're looking for me. They had my name on a list at the outer gate."

"Yep. I guess old Heelspur would really like to put the screws to you. Just when he was claiming his son discovered that vein of gold, you put him on the spot by blaming him for your brother's murder. Mind you, most of Kayolin believes your version of events—that Heelspur boy doesn't have the gumption to search the deep delvings, let alone face a cave troll. Everybody knows that he was lazy and a coward to boot."

"A lot of good it did me to tell the truth," Brandon said bitterly.

Bondall shrugged. "What else were you going to do? Now, do your mum and dad know you're here yet?" she asked.

Brandon shook his head. "I was afraid the place might be watched. I didn't want to go up to the front door without some kind of disguise, and also I thought I should give my folks a bit of warning that I'm here."

"Well, let me take care of that warning part," Bondall said with a grin. But immediately she turned serious. "And hey, it's good to see you, but be careful."

"I will," he replied, but she was already bustling back to the bar. Gretchan took his hand and they watched Bondall speak to another dwarf maid, one who was sitting on the customer side of the bar. That female got up to step behind the counter while Bondall bustled out the front door without a backward glance. The fill-in barmaid brought a couple of mugs over to Brandon and Gretchan, plopped them on the table, and went back to the bar without a word or a glance.

"How'd she know we wanted these?" the priestess asked.

Brandon, already taking a deep draught of the cold, hop-flavored brew, simply shrugged. "Good camouflage," he suggested, wiping the foam from his mustache with the back of his hand. "Everyone in here is drinking their fill. We'd look silly sitting here just twiddling our thumbs."

Gretchan allowed as how that made sense, though she sipped at her beer with a little more gentility than her companion did. They sat in silence for a half hour, nursing their drinks, until Bondall returned and came straight over to the table. She carried a woolen cloak with a deep, cowled hood.

"They're thrilled and can't wait to see you," she said. "Not that they aren't worried for you as well. But here, put this on, and cover your head. Go right to your house, and they'll let you in."

"Thanks, Bondy," Brand said gratefully, standing.

"Yes—thank you so much," Gretchan agreed sincerely.

"You'd do the same for me," she replied, speaking to Brandon. Then she touched Gretchan on the shoulder and looked her straight in the eyes. "And you take care of him; he's a fair catch."

"I—I know he is," Gretchan replied, embarrassed again. "But I don't think I've, um, caught him yet."

Bondall merely smiled, a knowing, sympathetic gesture. "Good luck," she whispered as the couple started toward the door.

—DH—

The queen horax lay atop of a vast mountain of eggs, sensing the stirrings of life beneath her. Many of the shiny orbs had already hatched, sending slick neophytes oozing toward the exits from the cavern. They twisted and thrashed, working free of the thick membranes still coating them as they emerged from the eggs, using nascent mandibles to chew a hole through which they could break free from the gummy wrap.

At first the neophytes wriggled like snakes or slugs, but by the time they reached the connecting tunnels, they had stretched their legs away from their segmented bodies, standing shakily and starting to crawl.

The massive, bloated shape of the queen occupied her place in the center of the hive, and she steadily created more eggs, spewing them from her swollen abdomen onto the ever-growing pile. Resting atop the eggs, she had been steadily lifted over the recent years, until her bulbous body lay very near the ceiling of the large chamber. But still she ate, and still she produced many eggs.

Her soldiers had been feeding her well, lately, bringing warm, bloody morsels of dwarf meat that the queen greedily consumed. She was not introspective, probably not even capable of that which is called "reflection," but she perceived that the space around the hive was expanding and that her soldiers were venturing farther and farther afield, finding new sources of food, bringing that food to her so she could birth more soldiers.

The horax were timeless beings; they had dwelled in that cavern since the Age of Dreams. Once they had been small in number, the offspring of the very first queen, until the dwarves had come there. Then began the reign of the second queen, and the horax had swarmed steadily upward, feasting, thriving, growing, until the dwarves had blocked them off and sealed the tunnels, preventing the hive from spreading.

But at this moment, in the reign of the third queen, some of those tunnels had been opened again—not by the horax, who could not dig through solid rock, but by some other unknown force. The bugs had been quick to exploit those openings, and her soldiers roamed and explored, claiming unprecedented prey, bringing to themselves and to their queen a greater supply of food. They were horax; they did not question the nature or motives of their benefactor, one that clearly wanted the swarm to expand, to reach out . . .

To kill and eat more dwarves.

—DH—

Outside of the Cracked Mug, the street seemed much busier than it had when they'd first arrived. "Changing shifts at the mill, I think," Brandon guessed, judging from the dusty cloaks on many of the dwarves moving to and fro. He pulled his robe over his shoulders, using the hood to conceal his face, and led Gretchan and Kondike down the street and around the corner. He felt a lump in his throat as he approached the front door of his beloved house, from which he had fled a year and a half earlier.

Before he could knock, however, the portal opened and he stepped inside into the frantic embrace of his mother, Karine Bluestone. Gretchan and the dog quickly followed, and his father, after a nervous glance up and down the street, quickly shut the door.

Brandon extricated himself from his mother's embrace to introduce his companion. He noted at once the expression of concern, even anger, on Garren Bluestone's face.

"Why did you come back here?" his father asked finally. "Do you know what they want to do to you?"

"I got some idea at the outer gate!" Brandon retorted. "If Gretchan hadn't worked her magic, I'd be in chains already."

"Magic?" Karine asked, wide eyed. She took in Gretchan's ruddy skin, her golden hair, and the tall staff she held in her hand. "You don't *look* like a Theiwar . . ."

"I'm Daewar," Gretchan replied smoothly. "And I'm a priestess of Reorx. Not a wizard."

"Oh, well, yes, of course," stammered Brandon's mother, unclear about the distinction. "But you saved my son from the guards. We owe you quite a bit."

"That's not the half of it," Brand said. "She broke me out of a dungeon in Pax Tharkas and won a war against the hill dwarves after Harn Poleaxe tried to kill me." He shot his father an accusing look.

"Harn? My old friend?" gasped Garren Bluestone.

"I think we have a lot of catching up to do," Karine interjected smoothly. "Why don't you all sit down, and I'll pour us some drinks. And, um, Gretchan: it's terribly nice to meet you."

"And you both as well," she replied, the warmth of her smile even soothing Garren's bristling nerves.

Karine went into the kitchen while Brandon met his father's disbelieving gaze. "Harn betrayed you?" Garren asked, shaking his head. "He was only after steel after all, huh?" The old dwarf's face suddenly blanched. "What about thc Bluestone?"

"It's safe," Brandon said. "That's what Harn was after, and he stole it for a time—but I got it back. Now it's in Tarn Bellowgranite's hands—he's the former king of Thorbardin, living in exile in Pax Tharkas."

"King of Thorbardin? Pax Tharkas?" Brandon's father was stunned as he mouthed the legendary names. He shook his head again, trying to digest the stunning news. Gretchan escorted him to a seat while Karine returned with a tray that was weighted down with four heavy mugs.

Soon they were all seated around the hearth, sipping warm mead from a fresh keg Karine had just tapped. Brandon sensed his father's edginess—both of the men cast frequent glances at the front door—but Gretchan calmed them a bit by doing most of the talking. She told Garren and Karine all about the hill dwarf war against Pax Tharkas, exaggerating Brandon's heroic role and downplaying her own contribution. Garren and his wife were caught up in her story, and Brandon was surprised—and more than a little pleased—to see his father looking at him with an expression of unrestrained pride. Responding to Karine's questions, Gretchan talked a little about her own family and background and told them of the great history she hoped, one day, to write.

But finally they had caught up with the past, and the present worries that had been gnawing away at Brandon burst to the surface.

"What about what's going on here in Kayolin?" Brandon asked anxiously. "Your letter finally caught up to me in Pax Tharkas. So now, I understand, Regar Smashfingers has created his own League of Enforcers? And the horax are on the march again, so much that the king has mustered troops and is making war on them?"

"Aye, to the first, anyway," Garren said. "Lord Heelspur's son, the same one who stole the claim you and Nailer found, leads that nasty bunch of rascals, the so-called League of Enforcers. They are the king's eyes and ears, everywhere in the city."

"And the war against the horax?"

"That's been more talk than action, to tell you the truth. I've heard of a few companies being mustered but not of anyone moving out to fight the danged things. They do seem to be creeping about more than usual. We hear mostly rumors, though."

"But Smashfingers is making no pretense anymore about his status? He's claiming the throne of a king?"

Both Bluestone elders nodded. "He claims his people—his Enforcers, really—have discovered the Torc of the Forge, down in the delvings under the city," Karine explained. "Do you remember the story of the torc?"

"I know it from my own readings," Gretchan said when Brandon shook his head. "It was a silver collar, surrounded by a ring of blue sapphires, that was supposedly forged by the god himself during the Age of Light. For years it was handed down from one dwarf king to another, but it was lost more than a thousand years ago, when the dwarves—and their king—marched out of Thorbardin to join Huma's war against the Dark Queen."

"Yes," Karine said. "And as the king reminds us, when it was lost, the legend arose that it would be discovered when dwarfkind was in dire need of a new king. Now he's claiming the torc is proof that the time is right for his coronation."

"Has he let a priest of Reorx examine the artifact?" Gretchan asked. "To make sure it's authentic?"

Karine sighed. "That would be a good idea. Unfortunately the priesthood of our god has not exactly flourished in Kayolin during the last . . . oh, since the time of the Chaos War. I doubt if the king would agree to such an inspection, even if a priest could be found. Most of the worshiping done in Garnet Thax now, I fear to say, is done at the altars of power and steel."

"That part hasn't changed, then," Brandon agreed. "Then what can we—?"

The door smashed in without warning, and two burly dwarves, dressed in black leather tunics, charged into the room. One flourished a large hammer—the tool that he had obviously used to smash in the door—while the other pointed a sword at Brandon's face. Two more similarly clad dwarves, swords drawn, swaggered into the room behind them.

"Brandon Bluestone, I arrest you in the name of the League of Enforcers!" cried the swordsman. His attention quickly shifted. "And Garren Bluestone, you're coming along too this time. You'll be charged, I daresay, with harboring a fugitive!"

Kondike leaped to his feet, barking and hurling himself at the hammer-wielding dwarf. That fellow, caught by surprise, took a wild swing at the dog. He missed and went down screaming, dropping his hammer as he struggled to hold the snapping jaws at bay.

Brandon instinctively leaped to his feet, snatching up his axe, as two more of the black-clad Enforcers rushed through the door with their short swords drawn. Gretchan scooted to the side, clutching her staff, and Brandon's father stepped in front of his wife. As Brandon unveiled his legendary weapon, the Enforcers hesitated, eyeing the keen, shiny blade.

He was vaguely aware that the priestess was chanting something.

Then the room filled with smoke, a churning mist so thick, he couldn't see. He heard a loud thump, and one of the Enforcers cursed and toppled with a crash. Then someone—Gretchan, he realized—took him by the hand and jerked him toward the front door. He bumped into a dwarf—from the feel of the leather tunic, he knew it was one of the king's men—and put down his shoulder, driving the Enforcer, hard, into the wall. Still holding onto the cleric's hand, Brandon waved his axe, hearing the blade clash into a sword.

Somewhere nearby, his mother screamed.

THIRTEEN

A FLIGHT AND A FALL

Run!” Gretchan insisted in a hoarse whisper, still pulling on Brandon’s hand as they stumbled into a murky fog so thick that the dwarf couldn’t see his axe blade, which he was holding up in front of his face. Kondike barked and growled frantically, and he heard an Enforcer cry out somewhere behind them. His shoulder had slammed into the doorframe as the priestess pulled him outside; then they were in the street, boots scuffing on the cobblestones.

That thick murk still surrounded them, more like fog or smoke, but lacking any smell or sense of wetness.

“Kondike!” Gretchan snapped, before jerking Brandon’s hand, pulling him away from the uproar at the Bluestone home.

He hated the thought of fleeing his house when he knew that the Enforcers were confronting his parents. And how had they found him so quickly? Had Bondall betrayed him? Even as he entertained the thought, he rejected the notion. Apparently Heelspur was concerned enough about Brandon to make sure his home was constantly watched.

They ran a few more steps, still blinded by the fog. "What is this damn murk?" he demanded through clenched teeth. "Why can't we see?"

"It's just a little spell, dearie," the priestess replied, grunting as they bumped into some hapless pedestrian and bowled the cursing dwarf over. "It will give us a few moments to conceal ourselves, hopefully escape. But not for long, so hurry!"

"But my father!" Brandon protested even as they broke out of the cloud to find themselves on the street a short distance away from the Bluestone home. Kondike raced at their heels, his hackles high, mouth hanging open to reveal his tongue and long teeth. "They've got my parents now!" He glanced back and saw that the obscuring cloud still churned in front of the Bluestone domicile. But the vapor seemed to be thinning, and his companion pulled hard on his hand.

"And they'll have you in their clutches too if you want to go back there and act the hero," Gretchan insisted sharply. "Do you think your father wants that?"

"No," he admitted, once more following along.

"If we're free," she added, "we might be able to help them more."

Even as she spoke, he saw three more big dwarves, wearing the black leather tunics he'd already come to despise, moving into the street before them to block their path of escape. The two on the flanks each drew a sword, while the third, weapon sheathed, advanced between them and held up a hand.

"Halt in the name of the League of Enforcers!" demanded that one.

Kondike lowered his head and put on an explosive burst of speed. He sprang into the air and smashed the unarmed dwarf in the chest, snarling jaws snapping at the flailing Enforcer's beard. Brandon raised his axe and charged at one of the swordsmen.

As the other moved to help his comrade, Gretchan shouted one word at him: "Stop!"

Immediately the dwarf froze in his tracks, his body contorting as he tried to move feet that had apparently been cemented to the street. "What in Reorx's name . . . ?" he demanded.

Brandon slashed his axe at the third Enforcer and knocked the dwarf's sword free, the weapon clanging and spinning across the stones of the roadway. He lowered his shoulder and barreled into the disarmed dwarf, sending the fellow tumbling backward. He and Gretchan plunged past and raced away, the priestess again calling back to Kondike. With a last snap of his powerful jaws, the big animal bounded after his companions.

"This way," Brandon urged, giving Gretchan's hand a tug. They raced down the street, past the Cracked Mug. A crowd, attracted by the commotion, was gathering outside the bar. Brandon was gratified as the dwarf citizens parted for them then closed in behind, providing another few seconds' gap between the fleeing fugitives and Lord Heelspur's Enforcers.

Brandon aimed for the nearest of the connecting stairwells, reasoning that they would have a better chance of losing their pursuers if they could escape from that level of the city. But as soon as they veered around another corner, he saw more of the black-garbed agents standing guard before the landing leading into the stairwell. There were something like a dozen of the dwarves in that detachment, and seeing Brandon and Gretchan, half of them charged while the others held their position at the stairwell.

"How many of those bastards *are* there?" Brandon wondered out loud, looking back to see more of their pursuers emerging from the crowd outside the Cracked Mug. He spun around, momentarily at a loss for direction, and was startled again when Gretchan barked an order and took off running. "Follow me!"

He was swept along, quickly sprinting up to her side. "You should let *me* lead!" he insisted. "I know this city!"

"I have a plan!" she shot back. More of the Enforcers appeared in front of them, so detachments were closing in from three sides. Gretchan startled him by tugging him around another corner.

"Not this way; we're going to be trapped!" he cried out.

She plunged on, while he felt he had no choice but to follow. They ran down a narrow lane between bustling shops selling food, fabrics, drinks, and tools. Dwarf merchants and customers dodged out of their way, cursing. Kondike's sudden appearance caused a young dwarf maid to scream, and Brandon knocked over the handcart of a vendor selling savory mushroom tarts.

"Sorry!" he called over his shoulder, still plunging onward behind Gretchan.

The fugitives approached one last intersection, beyond which loomed a wide plaza and the lip of the great Atrium of Garnet Thax.

Brandon was momentarily relieved as Gretchan skidded to a halt at the last side street before the Atrium. They could turn right or left and keep running; if they continued straight ahead, they'd be trapped at the lip of the sheer cliff wall. She whistled sharply, and Kondike stood rigid, staring at her with upraised ears.

"Kondike—go!" she commanded, pointing down the

side street. "Run!"

Immediately the big dog spun about and sprang away, his long legs carrying him quickly along the lane, parallel to the edge of the Atrium. Crouching low above the street, the dog stretched out and sprinted in a blur of speed, dashing among the startled dwarves to all sides. In a flash he was gone from view, though Brandon could track his swift progress by the startled reactions of dwarf pedestrians who scrambled to get out of his way as the dog ran farther and farther away from his two companions.

They heard shouts from up the street and saw a whole company of the black-clad Enforcers, more than a dozen of them, charging in their direction.

"Halt!" cried the one in the lead, brandishing a short sword. "Stop them!" he exhorted the crowd. "They're under arrest!"

As happened with the crowd outside the Cracked Mug, the pedestrians showed no inclination to tackle the wild and dangerous-looking fugitives, though neither were they so rash as to try to obstruct the large group of weapon-brandishing Enforcers. Once again Gretchan pulled Brandon along, running right onto the plaza beside the Atrium until finally they halted, facing their pursuers, with the stone railing, barely thigh-high, crowding their backs. Brandon was acutely aware of the treacherous plunge, the shaft leading into the very center of the world, yawning a mere step or two behind him.

"Now what?" he demanded, raising his axe, holding the haft across his chest as he prepared to make a last stand. As the dozen or more agents closed in, he remembered Gretchan's stories to his parents, in which she had inflated his battle prowess. He glanced at her in exasperation. "Just how good of a fighter do you think I *am?*"

He was startled to see that she still carried the large cloak he had used as a disguise, apparently having tucked it under her arm as they had fled the Bluestone house. She extended it toward him. "Trust me," she barked as she sat down on the stone railing that marked the edge of the bottomless pit. "Here, tuck that axe in your belt, take two corners of this cloak, one in each hand, and hold on tight!"

Every instinct in his body urged him to confront her, to refuse her mad plan—whatever it was. The shouts of the pursuing Enforcers rang in his ears as the king's men warily started to close in.

"Get down from there! Come away from that edge!" snapped an officious dwarf with a neatly trimmed black beard. His voice was shrill, nearly cracking from the high excitement as he gestured to the dwarves of his company, pointing at the two fugitives.

"Take him, men! Surrender, you!" he squawked, waving his arms wildly.

The pursuing Enforcers didn't exactly rush to obey, for they had slowed their charge and spread out to form a semicircle, blocking any path of retreat Brandon or Gretchan might have chosen.

Instead of running or fighting, however, Brandon did as Gretchan commanded, stowing his axe and hastily taking the corners of the piece of rough cloth. He saw that she held the other two corners of the square fabric. Looking into her eyes as he sat down on the railing beside her, he was startled to see a flash of amusement in her expression. Then her face grew deadly serious and she quickly swung about on the stone railing at the edge of the Atrium, extending her legs so they were dangling dangerously over the edge.

"What in Reorx's name . . . ?" he muttered even as he imitated her actions. The Enforcers, only a dozen steps away, watched them skeptically; none of them seemed willing to charge toward the edge of the pit.

Somehow Brandon wasn't surprised when she gave him her next command:

"Jump!"

What else was he going to do as he saw her start to slide off the railing?

He jumped.

—DH—

Meanwhile, back in Pax Tharkas—well, actually deep below Pax Tharkas . . .

Gus had been spending a lot of time in his throne room—the throne being the large, flat rock upon which he sat when he was pondering the heavy responsibilities that were incumbent upon him by virtue of his exalted status as highbulp of Pax Tharkas. His prime task on that day was to determine what manner of food he would send Berta out to fetch. She had a keen eye and a steady hand when it came to bonking rats over the head with a well-aimed stone, and she invariably gave the meatiest, most tender morsels to her lord and master, the highbulp. But in point of fact, Gus was getting a little tired of rat meat.

Of course, if he had been an introspective fellow, it would have dawned on him that never before, in his life or any imagined Aghar existence, would he ever have imagined that he could get tired of any kind of food, much less good old reliable rat meat, so long as said food wasn't actively poisoning him. (Even gully dwarves tended not to favor foods guaranteed to make them sick, though in a pinch such sustenance would do.)

Berta, as usual, was sitting attentively at his feet, waiting for him to make his wishes known so she could serve him. For a long, long time—during the first two days of his reign at least—she had assumed that posture with a beaming smile, knowing that merely to serve the highbulp was an honor beyond comprehension. Lately, Gus had noticed—for the past two days at least—she had not been smiling so much. Again, if he had been one to think carefully about things, he might have noticed that the expression on her face was actually closer to a scowl than a cheerful smile. But, of course, he didn't notice.

"I think big dwarf food be nice, for change," he said finally in a proclaiming voice. "You know, you steal meat and cheese and stuff from Hylar kitchens." He breezily pointed toward the ceiling. "Up there, two times up from here."

Shockingly, the usually obedient Berta leaped to her feet and planted her filthy fists on her hips, glaring indignantly at the highbulp. "How I get big dwarf food? Huh? What kind of bluphsplunging idea you think, anyway? Big dwarves kick Aghar right back down stairs! They watch food, not share with Berta! They beat Berta!"

She drew a deep breath while Gus blinked in astonishment. "Me think highbulp should go get *Berta* food!"

Gus popped to his feet, spluttering indignantly, glowering at his rebellious subject. She merely glowered back. "What kind of doofus-stoop idea be that?" the highbulp demanded of Berta when he could finally articulate. He grasped at the thin hair to either side of his scalp and pulled in exasperation. How could a lowly female speak to a highbulp like that? What kind of bluphsplunging place was Pax Tharkas, anyway?

"Me highbulp!" he croaked in a vain attempt to assert his lord-and-master-ship.

"Me Berta!" she retorted with her maddening obtuseness. "Berta sick of highbulp! You no boss no more!"

With that, she sat back down, her back straight, her chin—what there was of it—jutting stubbornly into the air. She crossed her arms over her scrawny chest and made a point of looking away from her astounded lord and master.

Gus could only stare at her in dismay.

Berta's attention was directed toward the dungeon wall, so by chance she noticed the distortion, the haze of blue magic appearing there, before Gus did.

"Huh?" she blurted. "Here come Thorbardin again!"

"What? Where?" demanded the highbulp, following Berta's gaze. He saw the shimmering blue image appear on the wall, right where the four travelers, the Hylar family, had stepped into the room before. He remembered that they had told him that they came from Thorbardin, a fact that made him think, longingly, of his once-beloved home.

Perhaps it was just the growling of his stomach or his shock at Berta's sudden rebelliousness or maybe the boredom that had descended on him over the past few months had taken a deeper hold than he understood. But as he spotted that shimmering magical gateway make its appearance and discerned the figures of dwarves, two of them, lurking about somewhere inside there, he was seized with inspiration.

In that flash of insight, he realized something: Thorbardin was a world of plentiful, wonderful food, especially the sumptuous cave carp that were unknown in Pax Tharkas and abundant under the mountain. Blissfully he recalled the great Urkhan Sea, the huge caverns that he had grown up exploring, the multitude of abandoned cities and deep, fungus-laden warrens. In his nostalgia-tinted memory, even the Theiwar bunty hunters who had tried to cut his head off seemed like more of an amusing highlight than any real threat.

The blue circle glowed brightly on the wall, establishing that clear ring of color with the dark hole, snaking away like the mouth of a narrow tunnel, at its center. Almost immediately the two dwarves stepped through the wall. One was an old male; the other, a much younger female, and they both recoiled when Gus bounced to his feet and came striding forward.

"Hi," he said. "This Pax Tharkas. That Thorbardin, right?" he asked, pointing at the glowing blue door.

"Er, yes," stammered the male dwarf, ignoring Gus's outstretched hand. He edged away from the magical aperture.

"Hey, wait for me!" Berta called, bouncing to her feet, stomping after Gus. "You go to Thorbardin? I go too!"

"All right!" beamed the highbulp of Pax Tharkas, once more in command. "Come now!"

The magic opening still shimmered in the wall. Berta drew a deep breath and put her stubby little fingers into Gus's outstretched hand. Together they stepped into the blue doorway, Berta cringing while Gus blinked slightly, briefly wondering—it was a very deep thought for him—if he was really doing a smart thing.

But then it was too late to change their minds. The blue light grew very bright and warm around them as they seemed to be drawn along and inside and up and whirling through the winding tunnel. Gus took one step, which seemed to travel a very long way. Then, suddenly, they tumbled through another round hole and found themselves in an underground room, some kind of workshop crowded with shelves and benches, with boxes and barrels lining the walls. The blue circle, which they could see lingering on the wall behind them, quickly faded away.

The chests on the floor, many with lids open because they were overflowing with interesting objects, seemed rather promising to Gus—even though nothing exactly looked like food. Still, he was in Thorbardin, and plenty of food was lying around somewhere. Before he could saunter over for a look, however, he heard a strangled, gagging sound.

He turned and looked up to see a pair of elderly Theiwar dwarves, staring at them in horror. The old woman was making the noise, her eyes bulging out and her nearly toothless gums smacking and flexing as she tried to talk. The old male had swooned into a faint, collapsing on the floor. Recovering her wits, the female glowered and pointed a bony finger while she started chanting something that sounded very much like a spell.

Gus knew spells were bad things, to be avoided at all costs. "Come on!" Gus said, tugging on Berta's hand, sprinting toward the door that led out of the room. A magic missile zinged into the stone floor behind them, sending up a spray of sparks, but by then they were into the next room and moving fast. A few seconds later, Gus had found his way out onto the street and was swaggering along the walkway with Berta beside him, gawking this way and that while the female Theiwar's shrieks and curses echoed behind him.

"Ah," Gus sighed, all regrets behind him. It was

Thorbardin, all right.

Home sweet home.

—DH—

Brandon felt a dizzying sensation of weightlessness as he and Gretchan plunged into the Atrium of Garnet Thax. The walls of the massive shaft seemed to fly upward, and his stomach surged with disorienting nausea. He wondered, for the briefest of moments, if the shaft really was bottomless since it seemed the only way they might survive the ultimate plunge would be if they could keep falling and never smash into the ground.

But that was a hopeless notion: the glowing crimson lava down below pretty much guaranteed that they'd burn up even if they somehow managed to survive the long fall. The wind stung his eyes as they dropped and dropped through space. Brandon kicked and thrashed helplessly, barely sensing the levels of the city flying past.

Still, he clung to the two corners of the cloak as the priestess had instructed him. He stared at her, noting that she was holding tightly to the square of fabric. At some point she had thrust her staff through her belt. She wasn't looking at him, or anything, it seemed, for her eyes were tightly closed. Her lips were moving, however; she was casting a spell. After she quickly chanted a short phrase, Brandon felt a tug from above.

He looked up in surprise to see that the cape had somehow expanded in size so that it was eight or ten times larger than it had been a moment before. Not only that, but the supple fabric had inflated from the pressure of the air they fell through. As he tightened his grip on the corners of the magically enhanced cloak, he could tell that it was dramatically slowing their descent—an impression that was confirmed when he glanced at the nearby wall and saw that, while they were still falling, they were descending slowly enough that he could watch the startled expressions on the faces of the dwarves who happened to be looking into the Atrium from the balconies on the deep-levels as the fugitives floated past.

"Stop them! Arrest them, in the name of Lord Heelspur!" came frantic commands from far above, the Enforcer captain's squeaky voice echoing through the deep shaft.

Brandon couldn't see the fellow because the large cloak blocked his upward view, but he wasn't surprised that none of the Enforcers plunged after the pair, who continued to float down deeper and deeper into the stone-walled chimney. Brandon was surprised at how warm it was getting; the temperature seemed to be climbing rapidly as they descended.

They drifted past a wide gap in the wall, and he saw a number of dwarves shoveling coal from large piles into the metal carts that carried the fuel to the smelters and smithies in the lowest levels of the city. One of the diggers dropped his shovel in startlement as he happened to look out and catch a glimpse of the two dwarves riding their makeshift parachute down the Atrium. By the time he shouted to attract the attention of his coworkers, Brandon and Gretchan had passed from sight, but they heard a clatter and scramble as the entire workforce raced to the edge of the pit to gawk.

He spotted the Deepshelf Inn as it swept up from below; then they passed by it too. He met the eyes of a waitress who was carrying a tray crowded with full mugs; by the time he heard her scream, followed by the loud crash of crockery, they were already gone.

"Um, this was a pretty good idea," Brandon admitted, relaxing a little and twisting to try to look around. "But that was the last of the deep-levels we just passed. Do you have any idea how to stop us before we get down to the fires of the Abyss?"

"I have a sort of idea, but I'm not sure how it will work. Look, can you swing your legs like this? Let's try to shift ourselves closer to the wall."

Following her lead, he kicked his feet at the same time as Gretchan, starting a pendulum motion toward the cliff then back to the middle of the shaft—which was growing steadily narrower as they continued their rapid descent. They swung sideways again, and he felt a sickening dizziness, momentarily wondering if they would tip the cloak so much that they would lose buoyancy and plummet into the fiery depths. Instead, he found that they were indeed edging closer and closer to the rough stone wall.

Here and there the precipice was scarred by cave mouths and broad, shelflike ledges. All of a sudden Brandon realized her plan: if they could swing into one of those openings or land on a ledge, they might have a chance to arrest their fall. He didn't even begin to think about their prospects of climbing back up to Garnet Thax undetected.

"Look, there's a spot!" the priestess said, pointing with her toe. Brandon saw it too: a wide cave hole, gaping like a mouth in the cliff wall. A narrow ledge jutted from the floor of the cave out and into the Atrium. "Let's swing and drop . . . on 'three!' "

Trying not to think about the seemingly bottomless drop off the edge of the shelf, Brandon followed her count, swinging his legs over in the steady "one," "two," "three" count she barked out. On the last, their feet swung over the ledge, and they both let go of the cape, tumbling onto the shelf. Brandon landed on his feet, flexing his knees, but Gretchan stumbled and slipped, rolling to her side and starting to slide over the edge.

Diving toward her, Brandon reached out a hand, and Gretchan caught it with both of her own. The force of landing on the ground nearly wrenched his shoulder out of the socket, but he pulled her away from the ledge, rolling onto his back and holding her on top of him.

"Well, that wasn't so bad," he said, grinning into her face.

But she wasn't looking back at him. Instead, her eyes were trained on the dark cave just behind the ledge. Whatever she saw there caused her to draw a deep breath and scream.

FOURTEEN

INTO THE UNDERDARK

Where's my wife?" Garren Bluestone demanded. "Where's Karine? What did you do to her?"

The dwarf struggled against the ropes that bound his arms tightly behind his back. He twisted in the muscular grip of at least two captors. He couldn't see anything because the Enforcers had placed a dark hood over his head before they'd even removed him from his house. He'd heard his wife screaming for help but had been powerless to intervene as his captors dragged him into the street.

She had been pulled out the door with him, but Karine's voice had faded into the distance as they forced him to march along, leaving her and his home behind. Whether she had been taken in a different direction or perhaps returned to the house, he didn't know. He'd felt miserably helpless and terribly frightened for his family as the king's Enforcers pushed Garren toward the nearest stairway. With swords poking his back and buttocks, the prisoner had been marched up a long series of steps. He'd been too distraught to count them but estimated that he'd climbed some six or eight of the city's levels. His best guess was that he was in the League of Enforcer's headquarters, which he knew to be on the level directly below the palace—the very highest level of all Garnet Thax.

After hearing several doors clank open then slam shut behind him, Garren was pushed down into a hard wooden chair. One more door slammed, very nearby, and he heard several other dwarves moving around him and chairs scraping on the floor. Someone with a big chest and a deep voice coughed harshly.

Abruptly the hood was pulled from his head. Garren was seated at a small table, his arms still bound behind him. Two black-clad Enforcers stood flanking him; one of them had removed his hood.

But the captive dwarf's eyes immediately went to the fellow sitting across the table from him, a villain regarding him with flat, emotionless eyes. Garren recognized Baracan Heelspur: the son of Lord Heelspur had his father's large, hooked nose, and a thick head of dark hair that sprouted so low on his forehead it almost merged with his black, shaggy eyebrows. His eyes receded far into his head and were shaded by a blunt, protruding brow. They might have been black cave mouths, dark spots underneath a shelf of cliff.

"I'm so happy that you could join us," Baracan said, his sneering tone unmatched by any expression of delight or even interest in those black eyes. "I've wanted to have the pleasure of your company for some time now. I was just waiting for the proper occasion."

"Where's my wife?" demanded Garren. "What have you done with her, you butcher?"

One of the guards smacked Bluestone, hard, on the ear. "Don't insult the captain," snarled the dwarf.

Wincing, his head ringing, Garren drew a breath.

"Where is she?" he repeated.

"Don't worry about her," Baracan Heelspur said with an easy chuckle. "It's you we're interested in. If you tell us what we need to know, nothing . . . untoward . . . will happen to your lovely wife."

"Is she here? Did you lock her up too?"

"I told you," Baracan said with just a hint of annoyance. "Stop worrying about her. It's *you* we're interested in."

"All right." Garren forced himself to breathe deeply, to remain calm. "Why are you interested in me? What do you think I've done?"

"Obviously, for one, you were harboring a fugitive. Your son is a renegade dwarf, I'm certain you understand. Not only did he defame me, personally, in the presence of the king, but he sought to deny my father's rightful claim to a new, and very valuable, vein of gold ore. You'll be flattered to know that he was one of the first outlaws to be placed on the list; you might even say his name was noted before there even *was* a list."

Garren seethed. He knew the real story: his two sons, Nailer and Brandon, had discovered the ore on a daring expedition. They had battled and slain a fearsome cave troll in the process. Then, as they had made their way back to the city, they had been ambushed by masked assassins. Nailer had died; Brandon had been fortunate to escape with his life. The purpose behind the assassination had become clear when Garren and his surviving son had heard Lord Alakar Heelspur loudly claim the ore in the name of his clan, crediting his son with both the discovery and the slaying of the cave troll. Brandon's appearance in the royal court—and his strenuous objection to Heelspur's claim—had badly embarrassed the lord. Lord Heelspur hadn't forgotten that humiliation.

But Garren knew better than to try to make Brandon's case then and there. Perhaps the contemptible dwarf sitting across the table from him had even been one of Nailer's killers. That possibility caused Garren's pulse to pound in his temples, and he strained against his bonds with all his strength. But the ropes were thick and the knots secure; he could only glare at the captain of the Enforcers and imagine his vengeance.

"He slipped into the city rather cleverly; my guards at the Kayolin gate have since been reassigned to gully dwarf surveillance. But how did he escape from your house? My men claim they were mysteriously blinded when they tried to arrest him."

"How should I know?" Garren spat. "I couldn't see anything either."

"It smacks of sorcery, if you ask me," the captain of the Enforcers said.

Garren shrugged. "Is that against the law now too?" he asked.

"No . . . not yet. So do you deny that your son was in your home when my men raided your cozy little domicile?" probed Baracan.

"My son was visiting my wife and I," Garren said stiffly. "I was not aware that you consider him a fugitive or that his name was on any 'list.' He's been traveling for more than a year, and we were naturally delighted that he had finally returned home."

"Do you deny that you, yourself, secreted him out of the city immediately after he slandered my father in the king's court?"

"You and I both know that he told the truth," Garren said levelly. "And the truth cannot be called slander. The rest I neither deny nor affirm."

"He slandered my father!" declared Baracan, pounding

wildly on the table. For the first time his eyes flashed with emotion: they burned with a plainly murderous rage. Garren felt more certain than ever that Baracan Heelspur, personally, had taken part in Nailer's murder. He met the captain's gaze with a level look, while in the deepest depth of his soul he harbored murderous thoughts of his own. Perhaps some of that hatred showed in his eyes since, for just a moment, the Captain of the Enforcers averted his eyes and blinked nervously.

Abruptly he turned back to the prisoner and pointed an accusing finger. "And don't think we don't know about the rest of your nefarious schemes. We've been watching those who follow the Bluestone faction for a good long time now."

"Bluestone faction? Nefarious?" Garren had never heard his family referred to as a 'faction' before. "What in Reorx's name are you talking about?"

"Don't play dumb." Baracan sneered. "When there's a band of rebels in the city and they use your name to identify their group, you can be pretty sure my Enforcers are going to take action."

"I tell you, I don't know anything about any so-called Bluestone faction!"

The head of the king's secret police force just laughed. "Apparently there are still some Kayolin dwarves who don't understand that the Bluestone Luck is a genuine curse. They don't recognize that the misfortune that has befallen your once illustrious line only proves that you are not fit to rule this city—and you never were!"

"Who claims I want to rule Garnet Thax?" Garren snapped angrily. "That's preposterous!"

Baracan shrugged. "Deny it all you like. In any event, you have now been caught committing a clear, undeniable crime."

"What crime, damn you?"

"You were hiding a fugitive, your son, from the king's duly appointed authorities! Do you dare to deny your treason?"

"Yes!" shouted Garren, forgetting all thoughts of restraint. He struggled against his bonds, glaring at the secret police captain. "And I accuse you and your father of murdering my oldest son and conspiring to steal my family's lawfully discovered vein!"

"Well, that simplifies matter, then," Baracan said coldly, "since you have proved your treason here, now, in front of witnesses. You will sign a confession, and then the matter will be referred to the king for adjudication."

"I'll sign nothing, you criminal!" spit Garren. "What makes you think I will?"

Baracan turned those coal black eyes toward one of his assistants. "Bring in the prisoner's wife," he ordered. "And summon the Interrogator."

Garren stared in horror as Karine was pushed through the door. She was gagged, her hands tied behind her, but his heart broke to see the terror in her eyes as she looked at him. The captive dwarf strained against his own bonds as his wife was roughly pushed into a chair. When he thrashed futilely, someone bashed him over the head, and when he cursed, a dirty gag was stuffed into his mouth.

The next dwarf to arrive was the Interrogator. He wore a black leather mask over his face, and his hands were clad in supple gloves of the same material. An array of knives, hooks, pincers, and shackles dangled from his belt. With great, almost loving care, he began to lay out his tools. Some of them were barbed; others had narrow, serrated edges. All of them looked very sharp. Only when the whole collection lay spread on the table, within easy reach, did he turn his masked face toward Baracan Heelspur.

"Would you like me to start with the bitch, my lord?" he asked in a smooth, oily voice.

It was Garren who replied, groaning through his gag and slumping in his seat. He moaned through his gag, shaking his head, while his wife struggled to protest.

"You're a little hard to understand right now, but I take it you will sign?" the captain of Enforcers asked Garren.

The prisoner nodded weakly, looking at his wife with a beseeching expression, seeing her eyes fill with tears.

Baracan snapped his fingers at the Interrogator and waved him away. With a heavy sigh of disappointment, the masked dwarf packed up his tools. Karine was taken from the room while another Enforcer removed the male prisoner's gag.

Two minutes later, Garren Bluestone had signed and sealed a confession, admitting that he was treasonously planning to hide his fugitive son from the king's authorities. Karine Bluestone was allowed to leave, while Garren was taken away to a dark cell somewhere in the middle of the secret Enforcer headquarters. For the second time during the interview, Baracan allowed himself a flash of emotion, emitting a tight smile as Garren was dragged away. He was obviously pleased as he reflected that the king would review the confession and would almost certainly pronounce a sentence of death.

—DH—

Even as she screamed, Gretchan pushed herself off of Brandon, struggling to pull free the staff she had thrust through her belt before their hasty descent into the Atrium. Brandon, reacting by instinct, rolled from his back and bounced to his feet, pulling the Bluestone Axe from his own belt and staring into the darkened cave.

He found himself face-to-face with an arachnoid horror, a monster that reared upward, segmented body lifting its ghastly head high. Two solid mandibles clacked audibly in front of its thin, slicing mouth, while four legs thrust menacingly forward. Four more supported the back half of the body, which reminded Brandon of a horrible snake, head raised, poised to strike. The monster was huge, the multiple segments of its body forming a whole that was at least twelve feet long. The portion that reared above the floor was higher than Brandon, who was a very tall dwarf in his own right.

The monster's body was the same gray-white as the stone walls of the cavern. But its eyes chilled him the most. They were multifaceted and seemed to reflect Brandon's horror-stricken image in at least a dozen different planes. They bulged obscenely, shifting and glittering, clearly focused on the crouching, trembling dwarf. Some of those facets seemed to blink, while others simply stared. The huge eyes were cold and emotionless, yet somehow Brandon sensed in them a profound, almost insatiable, hunger.

The creature was a horax, Brandon realized at once. He had never seen one of the creatures—indeed, few dwarves had encountered the arachnoid monsters and lived to tell about it—but the realization set off an instinctive fury, an inherent hatred within him. The traditional enemies of the Kayolin dwarves were such a visceral, long-standing foe that he was almost compelled to hurl himself at the creature, driven by a battle fury that settled like a red cloud over his vision. He growled deep in his chest, like some savage animal, raising his axe over his head. His beard and face tingled as strength and tension thrummed in his veins, and he felt an almost irresistible compulsion to attack.

But some voice of reason held him back. He saw more of the long, segmented bodies creeping along the floor of the cavern behind the first one, and—almost too late—realized that at least two horax were clinging to the ceiling of the tunnel. They were all of that same pale gray color, and when they were still, they blended very well into the stone of their surroundings. If he had tried to attack, those overhead would have dropped onto his head and back, and he would have been devoured at once. He was chilled by the thought.

So he forced himself to stay calm, standing protectively in front of the priestess, axe lowered to chest height. He warily regarded the looming monsters. Gretchan's hand pressed against his shoulder, and he heard her murmuring a prayer to the Master of the Forge. A sense of keen readiness flowed into his body, as if the blessing of the god were being transferred directly through his cleric into the flesh of the warrior dwarf.

For long seconds the ancient, hereditary foes stood staring at each other, two dwarves confronted by ten or twelve of the giant bugs. Suddenly the first horax acted, the forefront of its body lashing out with whiplike speed. Two vicious mandibles clicked loudly, the sound a loud, startling *snap* as they flashed toward Brandon's face. But the dwarf was ready, raising his axe in a single smooth movement, then driving the enchanted blade down in a slashing blow. Gretchan's prayer calmed and focused his aim. The keen edge struck the monster right between its bulging eyes, splitting the hard carapace of the head almost as though he were chopping into a piece of firewood.

A spray of disgusting, greenish ichor burst from the wound, and the monster, twitching and thrashing, fell dead. But the next one sprang forward in the same instant, clawing and scratching on the stone surface as it charged over its slain fellow, making the same loud clicking with its wicked jaws. Brandon brought his axe around in a sideways slash, and the second creature recoiled, then snapped its head forward with lightning quickness. The dwarf used the side of his axe as a shield, blocking the lunging strike. He took a step to the side and chopped again, slicing deep into one bulging eye.

The horax pulled back, uttering an ear-splitting squeal and flailing. Brandon didn't give it a chance to recover; instead, he stepped into his swing and brought the axe down in a crushing, overhand blow against the crown of its bulging head. That horax, too, fell dead.

But more of the giant bugs were approaching, apparently undeterred by the loss of their two mates. A trio of them advanced side by side, clawing over the bodies, rearing high to lunge down at Brandon. Still steadied and strengthened by Gretchan's hand on his shoulder—and her words, as she continued to chant her ritual prayer—the steel-wielding dwarf didn't allow the monsters to get too close. The evil heads lunged and struck, but he rushed to meet them with the blade of the Bluestone Axe. He gashed one so deeply the monster went into a frenzy of thrashing and twisted itself right off the ledge, into the depths of the Atrium. When two others pulled back, he struck again, gouging a deep gash into the belly of another horax. He grimaced as he wrenched his weapon free, realizing that the abdomen of its segmented body was just as heavily armored as its head.

Still, the injured horax, dripped fluids, backed away, clearly weakened. Brand followed up the strike with a charge, stepping onto the body of one of the slain monsters, scrambling up to slash his axe against another. The keen blade sliced through the connecting tissue, and its entire head tumbled free and rolled off the precipice.

The other wounded monster collapsed, legs splayed, mandibles silent. Behind it, Brandon could see at least two more of the horax, tentatively scuttling forward out of the cave. He angled to parry their attack, positioning himself to shield Gretchan if the creatures charged in tandem.

But, just then, the wounded horax snapped upward and sideways, the sharp pincers of its jaws biting into Brandon's thigh with crushing force. Brandon couldn't suppress a cry of pain, even as he reflexively twisted around to bring his axe against the creature's head, crushing the carapace and killing it at once.

Gasping in pain, blinking away the tears that swam in his eyes, he felt himself swaying, the injured leg threatening to collapse beneath him. The two horax in the cavern lunged ahead together, climbing over the bodies of their slain hive-mates, rearing high and snapping forward. Brandon tumbled away from one pair of snapping jaws, swinging his axe around and cutting off one foreleg. Two more limbs reached for him, gouging his arms with what he realized were sharp, curving claws—a single hooklike talon tipped each of the monster's legs. He bashed aside the offending limbs, but then his smashed thigh gave way with a searing, stabbing blast of pain. The agony shot through his entire body, seeming to freeze the air in his lungs as it whitened his vision. He fell heavily to the stone floor, struggling mightily just to draw a gasp of air.

One of the horax scrambled over to him, rising high, mandibles poised to strike downward into his face or chest. With a frantic effort, he swung his axe upward and felt the blade bite deep, slicing into the narrow gap between two segments of the monster's body. The horax shrieked, wrenching backward, spilling guts and gore onto the prone dwarf. The creature's flailing death throes pinched the blade of the axe between two plates of the armorlike shell, and as it twisted away, the weapon was wrenched from Brandon's hand.

The final horax pounced. The injured, bleeding dwarf, his body wracked with pain, looked up at the hideous face, its mandibles clicking and snapping with almost palpable hunger. Brand felt Gretchan beside him and wished he could do something to protect her from the hideous beast, but his strength was ebbing, his leg was broken, and as the horax lunged closer, he felt his awareness slip away, leaving only blackness.

FIFTEEN

THE HORDE

Brandon regained consciousness very gradually, which was a blessing since, for a long time, he recalled nothing of the terrifying horax, the slicing mandibles, and the cruel wounds that had scoured his flesh. He forgot about the king's League of Enforcers, the descent into the Atrium, and his and Gretchan's precarious position on a narrow ledge a thousand feet or more below the lowest levels of Garnet Thax. His pain was pushed to the fringes of his awareness, and he held his axe close to his heart, as if some benefit from the enchantment of his family's ancient talisman could seep directly into his bloodstream.

Instead of dangers, perils, and pains, his awareness suggested that he was with Gretchan in some comfortable camp on their long journey north. He could almost smell fresh trout grilling over the coals of an oak fire—possibly with a hint of wild onions! Was that the sound of geese flying overhead? He sighed and stretched out, luxuriating in the feeling of soft grass beneath his back, a mossy hummock for a pillow. Somewhere water splashed, and he imagined that Gretchan had slipped away to bathe in some forest pool. With a sly grin, he thought about sneaking through the shrubs for a peek; strangely, at the moment even that little voyeuristic excursion seemed like too much effort, so he lay back and allowed himself to rest some more.

It took him a long time to realize he was lying on something much harder than a grassy meadow. He sniffed and decided that, whatever he smelled, it wasn't fresh-grilled trout. Only when he tried to open his eyes did the memories start flowing back, and he groaned in painful recollection. His thigh was burning, and every muscle in his body seemed as though it had been stretched on a rack. Each twitch of movement was sheer agony.

Only after taking stock of his many pains did it occur to him that he should probably be surprised and grateful to be alive. He recalled the blackness creeping over him as he fell under the charge of the last horax and wondered how it was that the monster hadn't killed him and Gretchan as well.

Gretchan!

He grunted, coughed, and tried to open his eyes. They were shut tightly, apparently sealed with some kind of crusty glue—like dried blood. He called her name, but his throat was dry, his voice an inarticulate croak. He could hardly part his lips.

But he felt her soft hand against his face, then the merciful relief of cool water, trickling slowly through his lips, bringing blessed wetness to his mouth, throat, and flesh. He sucked greedily until the bottle was pulled away—and just in time as he coughed and choked.

Finally, he forced his eyes open, breaking the brittle crust that tried to blind him. All of the terrible memories that had come flooding back proved to be accurate. He was lying on the same shelf of rock where the two fugitives had alighted after their glide down into the Atrium. The long shaft rose into the mountain right beside him, and high above he could barely make out the glimmering lanterns of Garnet Thax, the lights that dangled from so many of the plazas at the edge of the deep shaft. How far down were they? A thousand feet? Two thousand? A mile or more? He had no way of knowing, but they might as well have been stars in the sky for all the help they offered right then.

His view was blocked, then, by the welcome image of Gretchan's face, rosy cheeked and free from wounds, her nose and eyes crinkled upward into an expression of deep concern that he found vaguely comical. He couldn't help it; he laughed.

"What's so funny?" she demanded. "You could have been killed!"

"I thought I *was* killed," he replied. "And I'm happy to find out I was wrong!"

"Don't try to talk," she urged. "You were hurt pretty bad. Your leg was broken, and you lost a lot of blood."

"Tell me about it," he said with a grimace. Being the stubborn dwarf that he was, he flexed his "broken" leg. The muscles protested with a stab of pain, but he found he could move the limb. He reached across his chest to touch his wrist where the horax claw had torn his flesh and found that, beneath the crusted blood, his skin was whole, unbroken.

"Did you . . . ?" He left the question unasked.

She smiled gently and touched the miniature anvil on top of the staff that lay across her knees. "I prayed for you, and Reorx granted his blessing. The worst of your wounds—the broken bone, the deepest cuts—are healed. He also granted my plea for sustenance since we didn't have time to pack a lunch before jumping down here."

She offered him the waterskin again, and he drank greedily without coughing or choking. Next she handed him a small piece of bread and a wedge of cheese, food magically conjured by her cleric spell. Feeling more like himself, he sat up and took a bite of each. The food was not exceptionally tasty, but it seemed as though he could feel the nourishment seeping right into his bloodstream. He looked around, not surprised to see the bodies of five or six dead horax lying in a heap at the mouth of the cave.

"What about the last one?" Brandon asked abruptly, feeling strength return to his voice as well. "I thought it was going to have me for dinner . . . and you for dessert!"

"That's it lying there," she replied, pointing to the nearest of the dead monsters. "You hurt it, badly, with your axe, before it knocked you out. I hit it over the head with my staff, and then Reorx struck it down."

"Reorx again, eh? Seems like I should probably get to a temple more often," Brandon said wryly. "And, um, thanks. I guess I'd be in the hands of the Enforcers right now if it wasn't for you. When I was fighting these damned bugs, I felt something—you touched me and were chanting. Whatever you were doing helped. It was like my strength had doubled; I didn't feel a lick of fear. Was that Reorx too?"

She nodded. "It was my battle prayer, a blessing upon warriors who fight in Reorx's name." Suddenly she leaned over and put her arms around him, and he held her fiercely, feeling her shaking from the emotion of barely contained sobs. "Oh, Brand—I was afraid I was going to lose you!"

"I guess we were both in a bit of a pickle," he admitted gruffly, enjoying the embrace. "Still, it seems like we don't do so badly when we work together."

"Yes," she admitted. "But what are we going to do now?"

"Well, I don't suppose Reorx would agree to fly us out of here?" Brand asked with a grin.

"Oh, you!" She pushed away from him and glared for a moment, softening when she saw he was joking. "My magic doesn't work like that!" she pointedly informed him.

"Frankly, I'm glad," he replied. "That was a nice escape you arranged, but I'm happy to have some solid rock underfoot. Let's have a look in this cave. There's a lot of connecting passages through this mountain, and my people have been working to expand them and map them out for more than a thousand years. With any luck at all, we'll be able to find our way into the lower mines, and from there we might be able to sneak back to the city."

He grimaced then, remembering what awaited them in Garnet Thax. His stomach tightened with worry as he pictured his parents in the hands of Heelspur's Enforcers. "It's my fault they have taken my parents!" he growled, shaking his head, suddenly guilty over the time they were wasting sitting on the ledge. "My father warned me not to come home, but I didn't listen, and now look what it's happened!"

His muscles creaked and strained in protest as he stiffly rose to his feet, but he found that his body responded to its instructions with complete obedience, if not the supple quickness he was used to. The kinks, he told himself, would work themselves out.

And so, stepping around the gory remnants of their battle, they entered the cavern, which proved to be a natural cave with swooping turns, some narrow channels, and a few large chambers replete with shimmering stone curtains, stalagmites, and stalactites. Using the pale illumination emanating from the head of Gretchan's staff, they could see clearly enough to identify obstacles and to pick a path through the winding tunnels. Water trickled in places, sometimes spilling through gaps in the walls, sometimes seeping down from sandy beds or trickling through gaps in the floor.

After passing the slain horax at the cave mouth, they didn't encounter any more of the creatures nor any indications the bugs had taken up permanent residence in that cave. The slope of the ground tended to gradually carry them downward, which was the opposite of what they wanted, so the dwarves kept their eyes open for any promising options. After several hours, Brandon located a chimney—a narrow shaft where water had eroded a vertical passage through the rock. Bracing themselves against the steep sides, the two dwarves were able to climb several dozen feet, emerging into a cavern larger than any they had previously encountered. Reaching down, Brand assisted the priestess onto the level floor, and they took stock of their new surroundings.

It, too, was a natural cave, high ceilinged and, in that stretch at least, quite dry. With Gretchan's staff still glowing, the pair started along the wide cavern, only to stop almost at once when they reached a pile of square rocks, bricklike boulders scattered all over.

Brandon studied the walls and the strewn stones. "This was a wall, here," he said, pointing to the chisel marks and dried mortar where the stones had been anchored to the cave walls. He examined the blocks, recognizing the sharp edges, the regular size. In some places stones had been carefully carved to match tightly to the irregularly shaped cavern wall. "It was built by good masons, dwarves no doubt." He swiped at the barren wall and looked at some of the dried mortar. "They put it up a long time ago, but it was knocked down fairly recently. See, there's no dust collected on the faces of the rocks where they lay on the floor."

"Who would build a wall here?" asked Gretchan. "And why?"

"Well, my ancestors did it, most likely," Brandon speculated. "There were lots of these kind of plugs down here in the old days. Because of the horax, Kayolin dwarves invested a lot of energy into blocking any possible places where they could make their way into the kingdom. Horax don't do any digging themselves—at least, not through solid rock or sturdy stone walls. So it was probably built to keep them at bay."

"Well, who would knock it down, then?" the priestess wondered, coming up with the next logical question. "Not the horax?"

Brandon had been thinking about that same mystery. He studied the loose stones carefully before answering. "No, I don't think so. Look: they've been struck with hammers and picks," he said, identifying some of the scrapes and dents. "Tools applied with a lot of force. I'd say dwarves knocked it down, though I have no idea why."

"Well, let's see where it leads," Gretchan said, tilting her staff forward.

They continued on for a hundred or more paces, working their way steadily upward. Abruptly the priestess stopped, standing still, listening or searching for something.

"What's that smell?" was the first thing she said.

Brandon sniffed then winced; he hadn't noticed the odor before then, but it was a not-unfamiliar mixture of filth, refuse, and unwashed bodies, a miasma that might be encountered in the underbelly of just about any dwarven community.

"I'd say gully dwarves," he guessed.

"Well, that can only be a good sign, then," Gretchan said with a chuckle. "It means we're getting out of horax territory and closer to Garnet Thax."

"I guess you're right. It seems to be stronger in this direction, up ahead. Should we go have a look?"

"Sure."

They continued on and soon approached a large, airy cavern, where the stench of gully dwarves seemed to come into sharper—or stinkier—focus. But as they entered, they both felt a more oppressive, sinister presence as well. Three distinct tunnels connected to that cavern. In the center was a deep, clear pool of water, while a number of niches and alcoves around the walls contained dirty mats, well-gnawed bones, and, in one, a ragged, stuffed doll.

"Look—they lived in those little holes," Gretchan guessed, pointing.

"And here's a fire pit," Brandon observed, kneeling to look at a small pile of ashes in a depression beside the pool.

"But where are the Aghar, then?" the cleric wondered aloud.

Brandon made no reply as he stared at several brownish stains that were pretty clearly dried blood. It had been a thriving village of gully dwarves once, but it was a dead village now. They found more of the spilled blood, including telltale trails leading back toward the way they had come, but no living Aghar. Nor, despite the signs of battle, were there any bodies there.

"The horax took them," Brandon said grimly.

Gretchan, her expression equally serious, could only nod in agreement.

They were just starting to look through the pathetic little hovels, many of them blood-spattered, all of them empty, when they heard the sinister clicking of horax mandibles.

—DH—

"Did you *see* them?" demanded Sadie Guilder, clocking Peat over the head with her bony fist. "They were gully dwarves! Right in our shop, big as life and bold as you please!" She lowered her voice to hiss accusingly, "You let them come through the dimension door!"

"*I* let them?" Peat retorted, raising his arms and shielding himself as best he could. "It was *your* spell! *You* copied it; *you* cast it! Why didn't you think of the danger? Where did they come from?"

"They came from Pax Tharkas, of course. And don't you dare talk to me like that!" she spat. "I'll turn your tongue into a lizard!"

"Oh, you'd like that, wouldn't you?" he shot back, straightening up when he sensed that she was through hitting him, for the time being at least. "Well, I'd turn you into a shrew, but that would be redundant!"

"How *dare* you—"

She stopped at a loud knocking coming from the front door. Glaring at each other's pale, disheveled faces, they immediately nodded with businesslike efficiency. Sadie adjusted her thin white hair while Peat patted down his beard and made his way over to the door. Bracing himself, he pulled it open as if he had nothing in the world to hide.

Why wasn't he surprised to see Abercrumb standing there? Peat forced himself to adopt a confident, beaming facade.

"Abercrumb!" he declared heartily with a big smile. "What can I do for you?"

His neighbor and fellow merchant didn't reply. Peat noticed the fellow was standing almost on his tiptoes, trying to see over the Theiwar's shoulder as if determined to examine the interior of the shop. Peat heard Sadie come out of the back room, closing the door behind herself, so he stepped out of the way to graciously usher the Hylar into the shop.

"Sadie, look who's come calling," he announced—perhaps a little too cheerfully, he thought, as he drew a sharp, disapproving glance from his wife.

"What does he want?" she demanded tartly.

"Well, just stopped by to ask how business has been," said their neighbor with a cheerful tone that matched Peat's own. "I mean, since I've noticed some folks coming and going. Which is more than I can say for myself!" His voice dropped to a conspiratorial whisper. "Though I can't say I like the sight of all of 'em. Those last two that came out of here—forgive me for saying so, but they looked like gully dwarves!"

Peat felt his stomach turn into knots. He groped for a clever or dismissive reply, but all he could come up with were variations on the confession he'd soon be giving to the king's interrogators. Or, even worse, to the Master. Willim the Black didn't mind his agents making a small profit from their shop, but Peat felt certain that the black-robed mage would take a dim view of their new, and very lucrative, side business.

Fortunately, as usual, Sadie was thinking a little faster than he was. "Filthy scum, they were!" Sadie spit.

"Don't think we let 'em through our door! Why, I heard them slip the lock somehow—probably thought we'd left the neighborhood, as so many have around here—but when I caught them in the act, I kicked them six ways from Gods' Day, don't you know! You should have seen them scurrying down the street."

"Well, as a matter of fact, I did see them," Abercrumb explained. "And they were certainly beating a hasty retreat. But, the thing is, I could have sworn that your door opened without any help from you, and that they came *out* of your shop on their own legs. Mind you, I don't think Two Guilders, for a moment, would entertain those filthy wretches as customers. But, well, a fellow has to know what's going on in his own neighborhood, doesn't he? I mean, with the king's proclamation and all . . . was it number seventy-seven or seventy-nine? You know, the one where Aghar are banned from the kingdom?"

"Of course we know the gully dwarves are banned!" Sadie declared. "You don't think we're familiar with the law of the land?"

"No, of course not. That is, I mean, everybody knows about the gully dwarves," Abercrumb stammered hastily, retreating a step from the angry, old crone.

"Why, certainly!" Peat agreed. "And surely you're mistaken." He turned to Sadie with a puzzled expression. "You didn't let those rascals into the shop, did you?" he asked innocently.

"Most certainly not!" she replied. "Why, they would have bothered the paying customers!"

"Paying customers? You had paying customers?" Abercrumb said breathlessly. "Why, yes, I thought I spotted a happy couple. A Daergar fellow, I do believe, and a lass who was, well, rather much younger, I thought."

"Yes. The old fellow wanted a charm for . . . well, for personal reasons," Sadie said with a knowing wink. "And in fact, yes, the, er, lady was quite a bit younger."

"I should like to meet them!" Abercrumb declared, beaming. "They're still here, aren't they? I mean, I saw them come in, but I feel certain I didn't see them leave again."

"Oh, they left, all right. Right after I shooed off those Aghar. You must have been distracted by the little gullies—not that I blame you one bit. Why, they'll steal the very belt off your waist if you're not paying attention."

"But I'm certain—" Abercrumb started to object, but Sadie cut him off.

"Peat, we have that stink potion brewing in the back room! Get me some newt powder . . . right now." She turned to their neighbor apologetically. "I'm so sorry, but we have to finish this. If we don't, well, there could be an accident. A very *bad* accident. It would make the neighborhood unpleasant for, oh, I don't know how many years."

Abercrumb, like most dwarves, was terribly suspicious and fearful of magic. Eyes wide, he quickly made his excuses and was out the door before Peat even knew what was happening. By the time he realized there was no stink potion brewing in the back of the shop, Sadie had him by the arm and was dragging him into their private room.

The expression on her face told him she had something very important that she wanted to discuss.

—DH—

The monsters attacked with only minimal warning: the clicking sound indicated their presence for several seconds before the buglike creatures scrambled into the village from two different directions. They spilled out of the cavern from which Gretchan and Brandon had just exited, and they charged from another, smaller tunnel mouth. The two groups blocked the dwarves from reaching the third passage, the only other escape from that miserable hole in the ground where the Aghar had been hiding and, for a time, surviving.

Gretchan screamed and swung her staff, smashing it over the head of one fast-approaching horax. The monster dropped, stunned or killed, but another one scrambled over that one and snapped its mandibles around the priestess's arm. Crying out in pain, Gretchan clutched her staff tightly before losing her balance and falling. Two more horax pounced, quivering and snapping, trying to pinch her legs in their cruel jaws.

Brandon, meanwhile, met the first two horax with crushing blows of his axe, swinging from left to right and back again, splitting their armored heads, then twisting his grip to pull his weapon free as the creatures fell dead. Two more closed in, and he swung the weapon wildly, forcing them to retreat. It was then he saw the dwarf maid fall onto her back, desperately swinging her staff to hold off the attack of two of the horrid monsters.

She knocked them aside long enough to allow her to climb to her feet and retreat. But Brandon saw another horax, looming behind the segmented bodies of its fellows. Unlike the other grayish bugs, it was a crimson red and was further distinguished by a bulging growth on the underside of its head. The monster reared back, and something shot out from that pulsing lump, like a long stream of rope, and Gretchan screamed again as she was tangled in the strands of a tough, sticky web. She dropped her staff and fought against the tangling lines, but her struggles only seemed to wrap her more tautly in the webbing. The red horax reared up and pulled, and the strands entangling the cleric tightened, pulling her inexorably toward the monster.

"Gretchan!" Brandon cried, lunging after her and chopping right through the body of a horax that blocked his path. By then the monster dragged the still-struggling priestess out of the cavern and back into the tunnel the two dwarves had used. Still more horax were creeping forward from the passageway, adding their numbers to the half dozen already swarming the ruined village. All of them closed in on the axe-wielding dwarf, their eyes glittering, segmented bodies rearing, hook-tipped forelegs waving in the air.

They formed a barrier, a wall of armored, arachnoid bodies lined up before him, but Brandon hurled himself against that barricade like a dwarf possessed by the devil. The Bluestone Axe struck and struck again, seeking out any weaknesses in the horax carapaces, plunging into the soft flesh between the armored joints, lopping off legs, and gouging eyes.

In seconds he had dispatched three of the beasts, but two other horax materialized with snakelike speed to occupy the breach and re-create the wall of armored bodies. Cursing, all but spitting in rage and frustration, Brandon chopped at the two, cutting the heads from both of the hideous creatures. Somehow the wall blocking him formed again.

"Gretchan!" he called again, his voice cracking from the strain.

By then the priestess had vanished, borne into the darkness in the clutches of the grotesque monsters. He strained to hear a scream, some sound of distress, and his heart sank when he could discern nothing beyond the incessant clacking of the horax who seethed and reared, blocking his pursuit as if they were tactical-minded rearguard soldiers.

Outnumbered at least six to one, Brandon didn't hesitate, didn't even pause to consider the odds. Raising his axe over his head, the blade still dripping with the guts and ichor of horax innards, he hurled himself at the monsters in a frenzy of battle rage. But instead of plunging into the center of the formation, where he would have been swiftly overcome, he dodged to the side, swinging a roundhouse blow that cut the head and the first two body sections from a rearing horax. As that monster fell, Brandon tried to skip past.

As he did, he swung a sideways blow, his axe again biting deeply into an arachnoid body. The stricken horax fell, hissing and wriggling, but the dwarf already had moved on to his next target, bringing a hard blow down on one of the bug monsters that, unfortunately, only glanced off it hard skull, though it did cut through one of the two jutting mandibles and sent the monster recoiling in something that resembled fear.

Still the bugs rose and snapped and swayed, blocking him from pursuing Gretchan. Brandon, feeling acutely aware of each passing second, ignored the badly injured bug wriggling on the floor and took stock of the three horax that continued to block his path.

The one with the cracked mandible held back from its two fellows, rearing in the center of the tunnel mouth. The others advanced slightly, jerking forward with four legs supporting each of them, while the forward half of their bodies, four legs waving menacingly in the air, reared and bobbed, weaving back and forth like snakes looking for an opponent.

"You want a target?" Brandon growled, addressing the horax to his left. "How about *this?*"

He sprang forward, axe held high, and just as quickly bounced back. His apparent target reared farther back, rising so high that two more of its legs came off the floor. All six of the taloned limbs spread wide, ready to grab him in a lethal embrace. The other two horax, reacting in concert with their companion, struck viciously in his direction.

Only he had dodged the other way. He brought the axe down savagely on the back of one horax's head, lopping it off at the neck. The second horax was still exposed, and the dwarf pulled his weapon around on the backswing, driving the sharp, gore-slicked blade right between the monster's eyes. Suddenly, the odds had shifted. Only one more horax stood between him and the rescue of his cherished companion.

The remaining horax surprised him, however, by seeming to sense his intent and acting to counter him. The creature scuttled away, backing into the tunnel where Gretchan had disappeared and taking up a position at a bottleneck where the cave was only five or six feet wide. Brandon lunged toward it, swinging wildly, but the monster feinted and bobbed away like a boxer. It spun to the side, leaving the path into the tunnel relatively free, but the dwarf was quickly beginning to understand that the monsters were smarter than he had thought. Far more than instinct drove them, and he knew that he was being dared to try to charge past the remaining horax. Even if he succeeded in a mad dash, he would have left an implacable enemy following him to his rear.

So Brand raised the Bluestone Axe and attacked again, chopping from the left and the right, as if he were chopping away at the trunk of a large tree. He sliced one foreleg from the horax's left side and two more from the right. The beast's multifaceted eyes glittered with some angry emotion—whether fear or hatred, the dwarf couldn't tell—but when he drove in for the last attack, swinging the axe forward and slicing through the chitinous plates of the rearing monster's belly, the gleam in those eyes swiftly faded to the universal blackness of death.

But Brandon didn't wait to see the creature die. He was already sprinting down the tunnel, chasing along the path where Gretchan had been taken, hoping desperately that, by some miracle, he could catch up to her while she was still alive.

He had gone a dozen steps when he skidded to a stop, remembering the staff that she had dropped when the red horax had tangled her in its web. Running back into the ruined village, he snatched up the shaft of wood and returned past the bleeding bodies of the slain horax. As he headed deep into the cavern, he noticed that the anvil at the head of the cleric's shaft was glowing slightly, adding just enough light to allow him to run as fast as he could.

SIXTEEN

PANICKED PURSUIT

The miniature silver anvil on the head of Gretchan's staff, which was Brandon's only light source, bobbed and weaved crazily as he sprinted down the uneven bed of the cavern. He descended rapidly, following the slope as he pursued the retreating horax. All thoughts of reaching Garnet Thax, of escaping from that underground nightmare, were forgotten in the desperation and fear he felt for his captive companion.

"Gretchan!" he called again and again, only to hear the echoes of his terrified cry fading into the darkness before him. Was she still alive? He had no solid reason for believing that she was except for his own desire for that possibility. But he refused to surrender hope, so he kept running, heedless of ambush or treacherous footing.

He tripped over a protruding rock and flew headlong onto a pile of boulders. The staff flew from his hand as he tried to protect his face and his axe, absorbing the blow with his body. Ignoring his new bruises, he stumbled to his feet, realizing that the light on the staff had been extinguished when he dropped it. After a panicky minute spent feeling around in the lightless cave, he again wrapped his hands around the smooth wooden shaft, and was rewarded by a godly glow emanating from the anvil icon of the dwarves' patron god.

"Reorx, please let me find her, save her," he prayed, his words a rasping whisper in the darkness. "I'll offer you anything—my own life! My axe! Just let me reach her!"

Though there was no answer, not even any change in the anvil's glowing illumination, Brandon forced himself to believe that the Master of the Forge had heard his prayer and would take pity on him.

He proceeded as quickly as he could, slowing down from his headlong sprint only when the dry rasping of his lungs forced him to collect his breath. He knew that he would need his strength if—when!—he found Gretchan, so he slowed to a steady jog, marshalling his energy and staring intently into the subterranean darkness before him. Belatedly he realized that the horax, having already displayed surprising battlefield cunning and tactical sense, might be waiting for him in ambush. Remembering the way the creatures could climb the walls and even walk on the ceiling of an enclosed tunnel, he made a point of studying the passageway in all its parts and corners as he moved forward.

But still he trotted with reckless speed. The staff in his left hand, with its glowing tip, led his quest through the darkness. His axe he carried at his right, elbow cocked, blade poised for a quick chop forward or a parry to the side and back. For long minutes he ran thus, his alertness at fever pitch, his imagination conjuring wicked mandibles and bulging eyes in each shifting shadow, every imminent bend in the winding cave.

Every so often he came to a brown stain on the floor, and even a cursory glance confirmed that the stains were dried blood. Each spot of blood made his stomach lurch with fear, and his only consolation was the knowledge that Gretchan had been carried through there not long before. If she were wounded, her blood would still be bright, wet crimson. He guessed that the blood spots he'd found were grisly reminders of the fate that had met the gully dwarves who had once dwelled in the dead village.

He came to a place where the descending floor dropped away, as if the stream that had once carved the channel had spilled over a subterranean waterfall. Extending the light, he saw that the drop was barely six or eight feet, so he wasted no time in scrambling over the edge, dropping toward a rock at the base. His left foot slipped from the curving rock as he landed, and he tumbled, bruising his knee and wrenching a shoulder. Despite the pain, he bit back any exclamation and worried more about the clatter of his fall.

Only then did he notice that the drop had placed him in the middle of a new type of passage, one that was not a natural cave, but instead seemed to be a relic, a roadway or hall, from some ancient civilization. He blinked in surprise, holding the light up.

The winding cave had dumped him through the side wall of a precise, straight passage that had obviously been excavated under the ground there some unknown but long time earlier. The ceiling was twice his height, and the hall was at least six or seven paces wide. Columns, round as pillars and unadorned, lined the walls at twenty-foot intervals, and the space extended to the right and left as far as Brandon could see.

The horax—which way had they gone?

Once again the stains of Aghar blood gave him proof; he spotted a brown smear a dozen feet to his right. Immediately he started that way, jogging again, warily examining the walls, ceiling, and floor in his path. He came to more bloodstains and reminded himself that Gretchan had been caught in a web—the monsters wouldn't have had to clamp her in their jaws to carry her. He thought of Gus Fishbiter, an annoying fellow but a friend of Gretchan's, and felt a stab of pity for the miserable Aghar that had been carried away by the horax. Even gully dwarves didn't deserve such a fate.

At the same time, he was relieved to see that there were no signs of fresh blood. He quickened his pace as the wide, smooth floor seemed to offer an open route ahead.

Abruptly he emerged from a tunnel mouth into a much larger space. Still standing on a smooth, carved floor, he raised the staff to see that he was in an expansive chamber, one where the ceiling dome rose so far overhead, it was out of the reach of his magical light.

He stepped forward slowly, staring around with frustration. At any other time, in any other delving, such an experience would have filled him with awe: in one corner of his brain, he realized he was exploring a relic of some civilization more than a thousand years old, perhaps predating even the dwarven colony of Kayolin. He saw suggestions of wide columns ornamented with hieroglyphics. Beyond the last column was even a stone chair in the commanding position of a large throne. The rest of the chamber was hidden in the darkness, but clearly very huge, very solidly constructed.

Brandon looked around in vain for some sign of Gretchan. He saw scratches and scuffs in the dust, marks that looked as if they could have been made by horax claws, but they seemed to go in every direction in the great hall; none stood out as a particular path.

He started to search along the near wall, going around the large columns, holding up the glowing staff head so he could see the throne. That, too, was covered with dust, though apparently undisturbed by the bug monsters' footsteps. He was about to move on when something drew his attention back to the throne: a spark or a blink of sudden light.

Going over to the throne, he discerned a circular shape, a ring more than a foot in diameter, outlined underneath the dust. When he picked it up and blew it off, he was nearly blinded by the reflections of sapphire and silver. The blue stones, a dozen in number, were arranged in a perfect circle around the ring of metal. Then the anvil on the head of Gretchan's staff blazed with an invigorated light, a brilliance that suddenly cast the whole subterranean throne room into an illumination nearly equal to daylight.

That circlet was hinged at one side and secured by a clasp opposite the ring. It could be opened to be placed around something like a column . . .

Or a dwarf's neck.

"The Torc of the Forge!" Brandon gasped out loud.

As if acknowledging his statement, the glow of Gretchan's staff settled back to its more normal dimness. Oddly, Brandon's dark-vision hadn't been destroyed by the brilliant glare; it was as if his pupils absorbed the brightness of Reorx's blessing and adjusted.

His mind churned. If the artifact really was the Torc of the Forge, than Regar Smashfingers was using a fake in the construction of his crown. His coronation was based on a forgery—

Gretchan! At once his thoughts returned to the priestess, his lost companion. He thrust the torc into one of the pouches at his belt and hoisted his axe and the cleric's staff again as he continued to search the large room.

Two minutes later he found a crack in the wall, opening into a tunnel marked with many horax tracks. Just a few steps inside the opening, he saw another telltale bloodstain, proof that the captured Aghar had been carried that way once, reasonable enough evidence to support his hope that Gretchan had been taken the same way.

He checked the ceiling and walls—clear—and started into the new tunnel. He wanted to shout Gretchan's name again, to offer her some hope if she could hear him. But caution forced him to bite his tongue.

And fear made him hurry.

—DH—

"Ouch!" Gus declared as a shard of pottery bounced off of his head. He kept running with Berta, her bare feet slapping on the cobblestones of the road, trotting behind him. Another piece of crockery flew over the heads of the two Aghar to shatter in the street, leading Gus to veer sideways into a narrow alley. With his lady friend beside him, he collapsed against a wall and sagged down to sit on the ground.

"Ow!" he repeated, rubbing his skull where a lump was already forming. "Why those bluphsplunging Hylar got to be so rude?" he groused.

"Prolly cuz we was stealing they bread," Berta said sagely. She proudly held up a heel of crusty rye, from which a large bite had been torn off. "Look! Berta steal bread while highbulp Gus make Hylar mad."

"Give me!" declared Gus, greedily snatching the piece out of her hand. He had to admit, she had some skills, Berta did. "Hey! Who bite this?" he demanded, looking at the generously sized, tooth-marked crescent that had been removed from the corner of the slice.

"Me!" Berta declared, unabashed. "Otherwise, highbulp eat whole thing. Berta go hungry!"

Gus glared ominously at her but couldn't decide upon an appropriate response. So he took a bite of the bread himself, chewed, swallowed, and took another bite. The food felt good in his belly, which had been rumbling and empty for the past several days. In short order he polished off the rest of the piece, smacking his lips.

"You say lotsa food in Thorbardin," Berta declared irritably, watching him finish off the last bite. "So far we not find lotsa food. Only little food. But lotsa big, mean dwarves."

"Yep," Gus agreed. So far Thorbardin certainly wasn't as exciting, or bountiful, as he remembered it to be. "Maybe this only bad part of Thorbardin. We go look for big lake. There be cave carp—and Agharhome!"

"Like Agharhome Pax Tharkas?" Berta said, intrigued. At least in a town of gully dwarves they weren't always getting smacked around by the big dwarves.

"Yep, only bigger. Two times big," Gus said, remembering the tangled web of sewer tunnels, ruined caves, and steeply sloping lakeshore where he had been born and raised. His family probably still lived there, but he decided that wasn't reason enough for him to stay away.

"Come!" he said, standing up, feeling the full authority of his highbulp status running through his diminutive stature. "We go find Agharhome!"

Berta was willing enough, so the two gully dwarves made their way carefully down the street, toward the big plaza that seemed to lie in the center of the big city, which they had heard called Norbardin. Fortunately, the street and the plaza were virtually empty, except for a bunch of dead bodies lying around. The Aghar ignored those and made their way to one of the large gates leading out of the city and down toward the Urkhan Sea—the body of water Gus remembered as the Big Lake.

There were some guards at the gatehouse, but they were gambling and talking, not paying much attention to the wide plaza. The gates themselves had been smashed, with no attempt having been made to repair them, so Gus and Berta simply skulked along the edge of the wall, staying low, darting from the cover of one chunk of rock to another. Soon they had passed under the city's portal and were striding boldly down the long, subterranean road.

After two hours, or two miles, of walking, Gus estimated, they came around a gradual bend, and the whole of the Urkhan Sea spread out before them. Though they were underground, the vast cavern was illuminated, very faintly, by lanterns and fires dotting around the long, winding shoreline: the camps and dwellings of feral Klar, Theiwar hunters, and those few hardy survivors who still lived in the ruined cities that had been ravaged by the forces of Chaos.

Berta gasped audibly at the wondrous sight, and even Gus felt an unfamiliar tug of emotion. It was a majestic vision and, since no one was trying to kill them at the moment, they stopped and gawked for two full minutes. Finally they started walking again, striding along with real bounce in their steps. They heard a party of Daergar warriors coming, tromping boots and clanking armor, and quickly hid in a ditch beside the road. When the soldiers had passed, the two little dwarves resumed their trot toward the shore.

Several stone piers extended into the lake, and a couple of boats were moored there. Crewmen—more Daergar, though not heavily armored like the soldiers—lounged around.

"We not go there!" Berta hissed, grabbing Gus's arm.

"No, this way," he said, in complete agreement with her.

The place where the road met the lake was a wide cave mouth, some one hundred feet across and more than thirty feet high. To the right and left, the edge of the tunnel merged into a steep stone slope where the side of the great cavern plunged into the water. The wall of the vast cavern was not a sheer cliff, however. Instead, the lower side of the Urkhan cavern was a sloping grade, a series of ridges separated by equally steep ravines. The footing was precarious but not too treacherous, and Gus confidently led Berta out of the tunnel and onto the steep lakeshore. The ground dropped away to their right and climbed steeply to their left, but they traversed the first ridge, scrambled through the ravine beyond it, and made their way up the next elevated crest.

"Agharhome up here," Gus realized, rather surprised to see that they had come to the lakeshore very near the place where he had lived most of his life.

They were coming down the next ridge when they discovered several fellow Aghar hunkered in the ravine some distance above the water. There were three of them, and they all stood up and watched curiously as Gus and Berta approached. Two of the strangers were males, but the other was a female, and she looked strangely familiar.

"Gus?" she asked. "Gus Fishbiter? Who died in the water?"

"Slooshy!" he cried, immediately recognizing her. "No! *You* died! In the water!" he said, rushing forward to embrace his old friend, remembering that the two of them had been trapped in a drainpipe and carried by a rush of water deep into the bowels of Thorbardin. Gus had escaped—only to be captured by the black wizard—but he had taken it for granted that Slooshy had drowned.

"Me not die! You not die!" Slooshy squealed, giving Gus a sloppy kiss.

Suddenly he was kicked, hard, from behind. He turned to look at Berta, who had delivered the blow.

"Who Slooshy?" Berta demanded with her arms folded across her skinny chest. She was glaring at the other female.

And, for some reason, she did not look pleased.

—DH—

Brandon ran and ran through the darkened passages until it seemed as though his lungs and heart were ready to explode in his chest. Blindly keeping up the pursuit, almost sobbing with grief and fear, he could think of nothing except the sight of Gretchan being carried away in the terrible web of her buglike captors. Had they killed his dwarf maid already? Were they feeding on her warm flesh? By Reorx, he would kill them all! He would wipe them from Krynn, banish their spawn to the depths of the Abyss, where they could suffer forever in the fundamental flames of existence.

Angrily he shook his head, just before he suddenly tripped over an irregularity on the floor and went sprawling, clutching his axe but once again losing his grip on Gretchan's staff. The wooden shaft went clattering into the darkness, the glowing anvil fading immediately. Pure instinct pushed the weary Brandon back to his feet, but he was breathing so hard, his heart pounding so violently, that he realized that he could barely stand.

"What good am I to her if I can't even draw a breath?" he asked himself, panting out the whispered words. He knew that he had to rest. Carefully, he felt around in the darkness, relieved when he found the staff after only a minute of searching. He took a seat upon a boulder, holding the shaft across his lap, grateful for the mild glimmer of illumination that again started to shine from the anvil head of Gretchan's talisman.

Gradually his breathing returned to normal. As soon as he could do so without panting, he rose to his feet and continued on, at first merely walking. Taking stock of his resources, he realized he was pretty much limited to his axe and the cleric's staff. No, he was also carrying his small dagger, as well as a piece of flint that might be useful for striking a spark.

He was trying to think if he had any other useful resources when he entered a circular chamber, like a large room in the tunnel of the cave. He started across then came up short when he realized that at least three different passages led out the other side of the cave. His heart sank. How was he to choose which way Gretchan had been taken?

Wondering if he might find a trace of blood or some other sign, he raised the staff, extending the faint light into the first passage. Seeing nothing other than bare stone, he inspected the second tunnel with much the same result. When he turned to the third passageway, however, the anvil—Reorx's symbol—at the tip of the staff flickered with brighter light. He didn't hesitate, immediately starting down the third cave.

That one descended rather sharply, and he found himself having to slow his pace just to keep himself from skidding downward. Treading carefully, he tried to avoid patches of loose stone, knowing that a trickle of debris preceding him could only attract the monsters' unwanted attention. Despite his fear, he felt himself drawing closer and closer.

But would be find Gretchan alive?

Abruptly the floor dropped away, leaving a shaft plummeting into darkness. Brandon halted just before he stepped off the brink, and for a moment he froze in panic. Had Gretchan been taken down that hole?

He was about to thrust the staff and its glowing symbol into the darkness when he caught the sound of a faint moan. He looked past the hole, and there, to his astonishment and pleasure, he spotted the sought-after priestess. She was alive, though from her pale skin and weak, twitching movements, it seemed she was in a feeble state, and she had been fastened to the cavern wall with a network of pasty, thick webbing.

There was a small ledge allowing passage around the hole in the floor, and Brandon wasted no time in skirting the gap, finally reaching the large, flat section of wall where Gretchan was imprisoned. His stomach lurched as he caught sight of many skeletal frames nearby, also entrapped in the webbing. Some were dwarf-sized, while others were small enough that they must have been gully dwarves. Bones and clothing were still there, behind the gauzy web, but the corpses looked as if all the flesh and blood had been drained away.

Desperately, Brandon used his knife to slice away at the strands imprisoning Gretchan. Her eyelids flickered and opened, brightening when they saw him. Then they widened in horror.

"Look out!" she croaked. "The queen is coming!"

SEVENTEEN

THE THIRD QUEEN OF THE HIVE

Brandon's axe, still gummy with the residue of the webbing he'd shredded, slashed around in a wide arc as he spun. He almost gagged at the sight of a massive head, bulging eyes glittering, huge mandibles poised to crush. The obscene shape loomed out of the hole he had almost tumbled into. His reaction was instinctive: the Bluestone Axe smashed into one of those vicious jaws—a crushing blade the size of a large sickle—and chopped a deep nick into the hornlike material.

The monstrous horax fell back, avoiding a second blow aimed at its foreleg.

"That's the queen?" he gasped, turning back to the priestess. Even as he asked, he knew the answer.

"Yep, that's her," Gretchan replied, shivering in disgust. "She came up to have a look at me when the tangler tied me up."

"Tangler?"

"The red ones. They cast the webs." She pushed and twisted, working one arm free from the sticky strands, tearing the silk of her blue tunic in the process.

He chopped away at more of the webbing, and she

pulled her other arm free while he lowered his aim, hacking at the strands imprisoning her lower body, taking care to cut away only the web while avoiding her skin. She wriggled one of her legs out of the tangled mess. He glanced back, saw no sign of the queen at the dark hole, and with a wrenching tug, pulled Gretchan free from the rest of her bonds. He braced his knees, ready to catch her as she fell, but was startled to see that she was standing on her own.

"You seem all right!" he exclaimed. "By Reorx, I was praying they hadn't hurt you!"

"Maybe he was listening," she replied, gratefully taking the staff of her god from his free hand and leaning on it. "They had me tied up tight—it was damned hard to breathe—and I was dizzy by the time those bugs brought me down here." She flashed him a sharp look, tinged with an incongruous iota of amusement. "But did you think I was going to let them have me without a fight? I knew you'd be along to get me out of here."

"I—I'm glad I made it," he stammered, immensely relieved. "Now come with me!"

He turned, ready to retrace his steps up the steeply angled tunnel he had descended, then stopped in horror as he saw a swarm of horax making their way down toward them. The ceiling, walls, and floor of the tunnel were covered with the many monsters, dozens of them forming a solid barrier against their escape. He looked hopefully in the other direction, but beyond where Gretchan and the other victims had been imprisoned, the passageway terminated in a solid rock wall.

"Any chance we can escape down there?" he asked, leaning with trepidation over the deep hole, the gap from which the queen's head had emerged. Gretchan extended the glowing head of her staff over the aperture, and

Brandon saw a massive pile of what looked like round, white stones, each bigger than a dwarf's head. The queen, her massive jaw clacking, sat upon that mound, glowering upward with bulging eyes that seemed to boast a hundred facets each.

"How can we get out of here?" he asked despairingly. The horax blocking the exit tunnel clicked and seethed, apparently content to obstruct the passage—at least, they didn't try to close in.

"Did you see all those eggs?" Gretchan asked as Brandon hoisted his axe and stepped around the hole, warily watching the swarm of bug monsters in the upper cavern.

"Eggs? Oh, sure. So that's what they were," he replied, remembering the big pile of what he thought were rocks.

"Well, I wonder if that bloated bitch has any maternal instincts," the priestess replied. "Keep an eye on those soldiers. I'll see if I can make their boss understand me."

"What are you talking about?" he protested.

"Don't worry—just do it!" she snapped.

Willing to grasp at any straw, Brandon glared at the swarm of horax blocking their path, trying to look intimidating. He heard Gretchan chanting something, a harsh, aggressive sound very different from any spell he had heard her cast before. Abruptly he heard a sharp crack of sound, followed by a screaming wail rising from the depths of the egg chamber.

"Look out!" Gretchan shouted, and Brandon sprang away from the hole as the queen swelled upward. Her head and jaws emerged through the opening, thrashing and clacking aggressively. The priestess smacked her staff against the monstrous horax, the blow producing a bright flash of light, and the queen tumbled back down to perch atop her egg pile, warily staring upward with those buglike, multifaceted eyes.

Brandon looked down for a moment and saw that one of the eggs on the top of the pile was shattered. At the same time, Gretchan repeated the harsh incantation of her spell and pointed her staff. The dwarf felt a jolt of energy, though he didn't see any corresponding flash, but in the light of the enchanted anvil, he saw another egg quiver and explode, hurling its gory contents across the queen and the rest of the pile.

Once more that grotesque matriarch shrieked her outrage, but instead of leaping toward the hole over her head, she seemed to spread out across the top of the great clutch of spheres. Her abdomen was massive and distended, very different from the segmented, chitinous bodies of her warriors, and she splayed it as wide as she could.

"Call off your soldiers!" Gretchan shouted, raising her staff and aiming it toward the mound of eggs. "Or I'll destroy all of them!"

"Do you really think she can understand you?" demanded Brandon incredulously, glancing over his shoulder as he brandished the axe to hold the swarm of horax at bay.

"I know she can," the cleric replied. "I'm speaking aloud for your benefit; I'm connecting to her with my mind. She understands full well that I have the power to destroy all those eggs, or at least a lot of them, before her soldiers can drag us down."

To prove the point, Gretchan raised her staff again, shook it menacingly, and shouted in that harsh, guttural language Brandon didn't understand. The horax soldiers started to advance, clacking menacingly, and the axe-wielding dwarf feinted a charge that caused them to halt uncertainly. They hunched, twitching and snapping, creeping closer until the queen shrieked deafeningly. The sound was a piercing whistle that left the dwarves' ears ringing, but it clearly brought the swarm of her followers to a halt.

"Call them down there to you! All of them!" Gretchan ordered. Again she brandished the staff, and the queen squawked and clacked.

The sounds were loud but nonsensical to Brandon until he saw the effect they had on the horax blocking their escape route. Hissing and shifting nervously, snapping and glaring, the monsters slowly began to back away. He advanced, holding his axe at the ready, and saw they were withdrawing through a narrow gap in the floor, a shadowy crack. One after the next, the horax wedged themselves through the opening and dropped out of sight.

"They're clearing out," he called back to the cleric. "I don't see any more in front of us."

"Stay there!" Gretchan called, her voice stern, even menacing, as she again waved her staff into the pit. With once last glance, she sprinted after Brandon, who was already leading the way upward to safety.

"Do you really think she's going to obey you?" he asked, still amazed by her negotiation with the queen of the horax. "She's just a giant insect, for Reorx's sake!"

"She's a lot more than an insect," the cleric retorted. "I would think you've seen proof of that. And now that I can't menace her eggs, I don't think she'll hold them back for a minute!"

"Then," he said, taking her hand and pulling her up an unusually steep stretch of the cavern. "We'd better make some tracks."

Once again Brandon ran until his lungs ached, with Gretchan rushing along right behind him. After half an hour of frantic climbing, they stopped to catch their breath, drawing deep and ragged lungfuls of air. Brandon was about to point out that they couldn't afford to rest for long when his companion murmured a brief incantation, and the dwarves' fatigue melted away, her words infusing them with a shot of pure, intangible energy.

So they started upward again.

When several pathways presented themselves, Gretchan raised her staff, and the brightened light on the head of the shaft continued to select their route. Always they climbed, and they never encountered a bottleneck that forced them to backtrack, nor did they see any sign of any horax in the first hour of their flight. Several times, however, they passed the wreckage of the ancient stone walls that had been erected to prevent the bug monsters from approaching the dwarven city. The barrier stones were solid and perfectly chiseled, but in every case some unknown force had wrenched them down.

Inevitably the rejuvenating effects of Gretchan's spell wore off, and the two dwarves paused once again to catch their breath.

"Why would those walls be knocked down?" the cleric asked again, shaking her head in confusion and dismay. "It was clearly done intentionally. But what purpose can it serve?"

Brandon frowned. "I've been thinking about that," he said. "I have an idea, but I'd need some proof before I could take my claim to the people of Kayolin."

"What's your idea?" Gretchan asked, intrigued.

"Well, we saw in Regar's proclamation that one of the

arguments he used to support his elevation to the kingship, and his creation of a national army and League of Enforcers, was the menace presented by the horax. My parents repeated the same thing; it's a primary foundation of his claim to kingship. He says that the horax are expanding their range, attacking the lower levels of Garnet Thax, and as we have seen, he's right."

"So the king's men might have knocked the walls down to make the horax more dangerous," she conclude. "And then he's using that as an excuse to justify his increased power?" The priestess shook her head, incredulous. "That's crazy—not to mention terribly dangerous!"

Brandon merely shrugged. "It's especially dangerous to the dwarves who live down in the lowest parts of the city—the poorest and weakest of the population. If Smashfingers is as ruthless as I think he is—and my brother's fate suggests he's all that and worse—what would he care about a few dozen, or hundred, or even a thousand of his most wretched citizens perishing? And if the horax appear in the bottom levels of the city, I'm sure he's confident his army will be able to defeat them. They're only giant bugs, after all."

At that moment the steady sound of clicking mandibles rose from the tunnel behind them. None of the monsters were in sight yet, but the sound clearly proved that they were being pursued. Even as they climbed to their feet, the volume of noise grew louder.

"Run!" Brandon cried. He pulled out the axe that had been strapped to his belt for most of their flight. "I'll hold them off!"

"Don't be an idiot!" she snapped, bringing a flush of anger to his cheeks. "If you stay here, then I'll stay here with you, and we'll both go down to death! Is that what you want?"

"What? No! That's ridiculous! Run, I tell you!" His voice rose to a roar. "Get going!"

She glared at him with her chin jutting out aggressively, her own cheeks flushed with emotion—fear, no doubt, but also excitement or anger. Then, right in front of Brandon's disbelieving eyes, her lips twisted into a slight, mocking smile.

"Make me!" she taunted.

"You're crazy! Do you know that?" he bellowed, giving her a shove on the shoulder to spin her around. "I'll be right behind you—now *go!*"

Naturally, she looked over her shoulder to make sure that he was following her closely, and he did as both ran for their lives. They raced up the gently curving floor of the cave, panic-stricken at the thought of the bug monsters chasing them. They knew, though, that there was not likely to be any timely rescue, no miraculous escape.

The cavern grew steeper and straightened out. Glancing back, still seeing no sign of the clattering pursuers, Brandon slung his axe from its strap again so he could use his hands to help pull himself up the rough, ascending cavern floor. Gretchan carried her staff in her right hand and used it as an extra limb, pushing against outcrops and irregularities in an effort to climb more quickly.

The sounds of the horax grew louder, and Brandon risked a glance over his shoulder. The creatures were in sight now, spilling along the cavern in great numbers, dozens of them crawling all over each other, clawing and scratching to climb after the fleeing dwarves. Some of the bugs used their hooked talons to claw their way up the walls, even climbing on the ceiling, so the whole shaft of the cavern looked like some arachnid-infested nightmare.

"Come on!" Gretchan gasped. He scrambled after her, surprised by how fast she was able to climb. In fact, he reflected wryly as he hastened to catch up, it almost looked as though he were dawdling. To make up some distance, he flexed his legs and sprang upward, grabbing knobs of rock with his hands and quickly drawing closer to her.

The steeply climbing tunnel turned into a larger chamber with a flat, albeit irregular, floor. Two different corridors darkened the far wall, each leading into a narrow cavern that seemed to continue upward. Once more Gretchan raised her staff and extended the anvil tip; it immediately sparkled into light when turned toward the right-hand passage.

With the priestess still in the lead, they barged toward the path and found themselves facing a series of stone ledges, leading steeply upward like some natural stairway—albeit, one formed of giant steps. Each ledge was about waist high to the fleeing dwarves, but Gretchan used her staff to vault up one after the other. Brandon hurled himself after, flinging his leg up as he approached each step and almost keeping pace with her. He glanced back again and saw, with a sinking heart, that the horax still clattered relentlessly after them. The monstrous bugs were also having a hard time climbing, however.

"How far up . . . to Garnet Thax?" Gretchan asked through gasping breaths.

"Don't know," he replied. "We've got to be getting close," he added encouragingly, not at all certain that he knew what he was talking about.

Then Gretchan scrambled over the last step and darted forward, but froze. "Uh-oh," she said grimly.

He scrambled up beside her and immediately understood. The tunnel ended in a ledge, a perch on the side of the Atrium similar to where they had landed on their initial, gliding descent. They were much farther up than that place, but there was no pathway, not even handholds, that would let them climb up the cliff away from there.

Above, tantalizing them from no more than a hundred feet away, lanterns gleamed and the dwarves of Kayolin chattered and laughed at the lowest of the city's cliff-side inns.

But for all the help they could offer, they might have been a thousand miles away.

—DH—

"Will you two be quiet!" Gus demanded. "Bunty hunters hears us and cuts off heads!"

"Shut you bluphsplunging mouth, doofar!" Slooshy snapped at him. "You nots me boss! We talkin'!"

"Yeah, we talking! And you not highbulp, neither!" Berta added, stomping her foot for emphasis.

Gus clapped his hands to his ears, ducked his head, and continued jogging down the dark alley they had been following through one of Norbardin's dingier neighborhoods, the slum known as Anvil's Echo. He hoped that, if he ran fast enough, his two companions might get left behind. But no, they simply trotted along closely behind him, yakking even louder than ever about his many failings and inadequacies.

The Aghar sighed, wondering how it had come to that. After all, having a dwarf maid attending to his every need had been a pleasant experience for Highbulp Gus. Indeed, the weeks and months and years—two, at least, of each, according to his arithmetic—that he had spent with Berta had been the best weeks and months and years of his life. She'd brought him food, rubbed his feet, and provided comfort and affection in ways that had never ceased to delight him. It seemed only logical, since he had two dwarf maids willing to attend to his needs, his life would get twice as good as it had been before.

However, it wasn't working out quite as he would have hoped. It had been a long time since either of the females had offered anything even vaguely resembling comfort and affection. Instead, they seemed to be engaged in a constant contest to unearth new faults of their male companion.

In fact, having Berta and Slooshy both accompany him seemed to make things more complicated than ever before. Instead of having two women catering to his every need, it seemed the pair was concerned only with each other, bickering and arguing and fighting so continually that Gus himself seemed to get lost in all the confusion. Instead of *two* girls, it seemed he had *no* girls!

Exasperated, he had marched his way back to Norbardin, with Slooshy and Berta trailing after him, bickering endlessly. When they had approached the city, the highbulp broke into a run, thinking that perhaps he might sneak away from them. But when he sprinted through the gatehouse, into the wide plaza, there they were—right behind him.

Since then they had been hiding in the great city, looking for food as always, and dodging the crafty Theiwar, who were only too likely to chop off a gully dwarf's head to collect the bunty. No, Thorbardin wasn't the nice place Gus had remembered it to be.

And that was before he found out that there was a war going on.

"All right," said Brandon, thinking furiously despite the evident helplessness of their position. "You stay behind me!" He turned to face the tunnel and the swarm of pursuing horax. He expected Gretchan to step up to his side, to offer to fight—and to die—with him as a comrade, not someone under his protection. That anticipated reaction, even against the backdrop of his despair, was vaguely comforting.

Her reaction, however, was not what he expected, and with the horax already clattering into view, he didn't dare turn and look at her.

"Help!" cried Gretchan, leaning out to shout upward from the ledge. Her voice echoed upward through the Atrium. Brandon knew that she would be plainly audible to the dwarves at the Deepshelf Inn, which looked to be about a hundred feet overhead.

"We're being attacked by the horax!" she cried in a loud voice. "Can you throw us a rope, drop a ladder? Anything? They're almost here!"

"Yes, a rope!" Brandon shouted over his shoulder. "I can hold the bugs for a few minutes, but that's all!"

As he spoke, the first of the pursuing bug monsters clattered near to the terminus of the steeply climbing tunnel. Four of the creatures eyed him hungrily but halted. The dwarf brandished his weapon and they hesitated. He feinted a charge, raising the axe over his head as he lunged back down the cavern.

The monsters hissed, clicked, and reared but showed no inclination to retreat, and Brandon hastily backpedaled to the ledge. He glanced up and saw that Gretchan had attracted the attention of a number of dwarves at the Deepshelf Inn. Several were shouting encouragement, waving, pledging that other dwarves were going to seek a rope or ladder. "Hold on!" one burly fellow called.

The horax stayed back, perhaps thirty feet down the cavern, warily watching the two dwarves. Brandon kept his eye on them, holding his axe at the ready. He didn't know how long they would linger there, but he got an idea of what was next when he saw the teeming mass of bug monsters part, allowing a large, red-plated horax to advance toward the front of the file. He remembered the gooey webbing that creature had expelled at Gretchan, allowing the monsters to drag her off.

"Uh-oh. They're bringing up a tangler," he shouted over his shoulder. "Hurry up!"

The crimson horax skittered forward, rearing onto its rear legs. The tubelike protrusion on its chin came into view, and immediately the creature spit a thick strand of webbing straight at Brandon. He raised his axe and sliced at it, cutting the web into ribbons before the beast could pull him back. But the mass of bugs crept steadily closer.

"Here's a ladder; they're dropping a rope ladder," Gretchan cried.

"Climb it!" Brandon urged frantically. He parried another blast of webbing then looked back to see Gretchan's boots disappear as she climbed up the set of rungs attached between two supple lines. He darted out of the cavern and jumped to grab a rung with his left hand while still holding his axe with the right. Quickly his feet found another rung, and he climbed upward as quickly as he could while still keeping an eye out below.

Seconds later horax started spilling out of the cave, scrambling onto the narrow ledge. Above them, dwarves screamed and started shouting and pointing at the creatures. Looking up, Brand saw that Gretchan was climbing swiftly, her staff strapped to her back.

The whole rim of the Deepshelf Inn was lined with gawking dwarves, and farther up, along the walls of the whole vast chimney of the Atrium, other dwarves were gathering on the balconies and perches, looking down at the daring escape and pointing. The horde of horrible monsters attacking them was in plain view of the whole city.

"Behind you!" shouted one of the dwarves in the Deepshelf, and Brandon looked down again, startled to see a horax scrambling right up the ladder behind him. The monster ascended faster than the dwarf, but thinking fast, Brandon reached down to chop through the ropes of the ladder with his axe. He severed the first one, and the lower stretch of the ladder sagged, forcing the monster to hang on with many of its legs. When he cut the other rope, the bottom of the ladder fell, carrying three horax down into the depths of the bottomless shaft.

But the horax didn't need a ladder to climb rock walls. Some of those that emerged from the cavern were scrambling right up the cliff face of the Atrium walls. They weren't moving as fast as those that had hitched onto the ladder, but their steady upward progress was undeniable. Even worse, the great red shape of the tangler emerged onto the ledge. Lifting its head, it arrowed a strand of webbing straight up, sending the sticky ropes all the way up to Brandon's boot and ensnaring it.

The monster pulled, and the dwarf was almost jerked from the ladder. Clinging for his life, he reached down and sliced away the web before it pulled him down. By then, Gretchan had reached the inn, where willing hands pulled her off the ladder and onto the balcony. She turned and shouted encouragement to Brand, who continued to climb as fast as he could.

By then more than a thousand dwarves were watching from dozens of different vantages, rising through most of the city's stacked levels. They shouted encouragement to Brandon while calling others to come and witness the thrilling chase. Every balcony, shelf, and plaza was lined with onlookers. From the opposite side of the Atrium, a few intrepid crossbowmen fired shots at the horax pursuing Brandon. Several of the bolts struck home, and one horax shrieked and writhed, losing its grip on the cliff to tumble into the depths of the Atrium. But such deadly missile weapons were not common among the folk of Garnet Thax, and only a few of their wielders were in position to shoot.

Another strand of web snagged Brandon's foot, and that one pulled his boot off before he could cut himself free. A second web shot past his shoulder, flying all the way to the railing of the Deepshelf Inn, where it snagged onto the stone parapet. By then sturdy dwarves were pulling the ladder up, hand over hand, doubling the speed of Brandon's ascent. Moments later he was grabbed and helped over the railing, collapsing into the willing embrace of Gretchan, as a dozen hearty miners clapped them both on the backs and offered congratulations.

The celebration was short-lived, however, as other witnesses, looking down, reported that the horax were still climbing. Several were sawing at the web that had attached to the stone railing, but their knives and swords seemed unable to slice through the gooey strand.

"Here, let me at that!" Brandon declared, breaking free of the throng and striding to the web with his axe upraised. He looked down to see no less than a dozen horax slithering quickly up the ropey strand, which apparently did not stick to their claws. With one swing of his Reorx-blessed axe, he cut the web free, and a loud cheer rang out as all of the bugs on the strand tumbled, writhing and clicking, into the depths of the Atrium.

Again and again the tangler sent its web shooting upward, latching onto the parapet, providing a path for the horax to quickly slither upward. Each time, Brandon waited until a number of the creatures were suspended by the web, then cut it free to send them plummeting.

A few of the horax climbed directly up the walls, but that was harder going, and when they reached the edge of the Deepshelf Inn, the monsters were invariably met by a half dozen burly, ill-tempered dwarves. The commotion had drawn enough attention that many of the dwarves had come running with their picks, hammers, and shovels, and those weapons were sufficient to batter the precariously clinging monsters free from the edge.

Finally, the monsters seemed to recognize, if not defeat, at least a stalemate. Those that were still in view, including the tangler, disappeared back into the tunnel. The deep shaft of the Atrium was silent for several seconds as the great throng of watching dwarves seemed to hold its breath.

Then the whole space erupted with cheers, nearby dwarves clapping Brandon and Gretchan on the shoulders, others, from higher vantages, shouting and whooping their congratulations on their victory in the public battle and very narrow escape from death.

"Bluestone!" Gretchan shouted, wrapping Brandon in a firm embrace. "This is Brandon Bluestone!" she repeated loudly. "You know," she said in a lower voice, winking at Brandon, "famous for his Bluestone Luck!"

He was about to ask her what she was doing when he heard the chant picked up by the dwarves in the Deepshelf Inn. It rose like smoke through the chimney of the Atrium, borne higher by a thousand voices:

"Bluestone! Bluestone! Bluestone!"

He looked at her in amazement, knowing that their return to the city could not escape the notice of the Enforcers. He glowered and was surprised to see her beaming at him.

"You do realize we were going to try and sneak back into the city?" he demanded.

She kissed him and nodded. "But just let the king try to arrest you now!"

Part III

The Heir

EIGHTEEN

NORBARDIN'S NIGHT

King Jungor Stonespringer, wrapped in his shabby robe, with his golden artificial eye gleaming, studied General Ragat carefully. The military commander did not flinch under the scrutiny but stood at attention and waited for his monarch to speak. The great square of Norbardin was silent, as it had been for the several days since the battle had ended. Though there were many dwarves throughout the city, those that dwelled there were in their homes, hiding, while those that belonged to the two armies remained in their camps, healing and resting and awaiting the future with a universal sense of foreboding.

The two dwarves stood on the summit of the prayer tower, which had, miraculously, survived the ground-shaking tremors that had rocked Norbardin and brought the civil war to an abrupt halt. It was the same place where the black minion had been obliterated by its collision with the Kingsaver Shield, the place where Willim the Black and his female apprentice had flown to confront the king directly—and from which they had toppled when the ground shook and the stone-lined cavern began to crack and crumble.

Ragat still held the Kingsaver Shield, the metal disk burnished to a high gleam, even after the dissolution of Willim's flying minion. The city of Norbardin, sadly, was not so untarnished. Even then, several days after the fighting had ceased, smoke lingered like a miasma of gloom. The convulsion of the brief earthquake had smashed buildings and brought large pieces of rock tumbling from the ceiling. Bodies were rotting all across the vast square, still lying where they had fallen during the battle as their comrades, blinded by the explosion of god's light, cowered in their camps, barely able to feed themselves or bandage their own wounds. As to the citizens of the once-great city, they remained hiding in their homes, terrified even to venture onto the streets.

"The will of Reorx was made real!" the king declared forcefully. "You were here; you saw it!"

"Yes, my king. His will was a blinding light, and when it seized the bedrock of our nation, he shook the world and brought the battle to a stop in the same instant," Ragat agreed, even as he studied his king warily. The shield had blocked the loyal general from the flash of light, so he hadn't been blinded, but the king had suffered along with the rest.

"And he drove the wizard and his wench away!" the king exulted. "The will of Reorx rendered the rebel army weak kneed. Even now they cower under archways and stout columns; they fear to venture on to the attack!"

"Yes, Reorx's display did all those things, my liege," agreed the general noncommittally.

"Then why can you not muster a counterattack?" the king demanded. "The black wizard's army is scattered, ill prepared. You could sweep them from the gates and reclaim the city's outer defenses!" Stonespringer blinked, his good eye shifting wildly across the war-torn city until finally, again, settling on his general.

"The men refuse to fight, my liege," Ragat declared bluntly. "They took the message from our god as an immortal command, an expression of Reorx's displeasure with the war. Many are still blinded or can see only a little. Even those who had their eyes averted, who were unaffected by the light, will not fight. It seems that neither the enemy's nor our own soldiers will agree to recommence the attack."

"The fools!" snapped Stonespringer, turning to stalk to the edge of the parapet. "The god was showing his pleasure with *me,* his favored prophet and spokesman! I demanded his action, and he acted. His blow struck at our enemies when they stood at the verge of triumph—Reorx brought their attack to a halt so that we could prevail! Do the men not see that?"

"I regret to say, sire, that they do not. Those who saw the blast of light sweep from the tower at the middle of the battlefield still are blinded. The priestly healers tell me it will be days, if not weeks, before their vision begins to return. And even those who were not blinded felt the tremor that threatened to bring the mountain down on our heads, and they took that to mean that they should no longer fight their kinsmen."

"But those arrogant rebels are still there! They cling to the gate fortresses. They could strike the city again at any moment." The king waved his arms, gesturing at the plaza, to the gatehouses, and to the many places where the enemy forces crouched in their camps.

"Begging your majesty's pardon, but my spies suggest that the rebel troops are no more anxious to fight than are your own soldiers," Ragat reported, repeating the assurance he had been giving the king over and over since the battle had been interrupted several days earlier. He spoke calmly, patiently, though his heart broke to reject his king's orders.

"Spies can be wrong!" Jungor hissed. He trembled, clenched his fists, and made a visible effort to restrain himself from striking the loyal general in the face. Instead, he turned abruptly toward the door into the palace. "We need to know Willim's plans, to understand his resources and what actions he might take next. Where did he go after he fell from this tower?"

"It is impossible to say, my liege. All who might have witnessed his flight were still suffering from the blindness of Reorx's light. But it is certain that neither his body nor that of the female are anywhere below the tower. We must conclude that he was able to escape Norbardin." Ragat himself had led that search, and he, too, had at first refused to believe that their enemies could have escaped. But an exhaustive investigation of all the grounds around the palace had confirmed beyond any doubt that Willim the Black and his female lackey were gone.

"We must know more!" the king declared. "What does the black wizard intend next? How many of his troops survive? When might they be ready to attack?"

"Begging my king's pardon, but I have a spy who has been very accurate in his reports to me," the general reported. "He came to me even during the battle for the palace. He says he has identified some of the wizard's agents, here in Norbardin. It may be that, if we take those spies, they will be able to tell us something about their master's intentions."

"Go to him, then," ordered the king. "Seek out your agent and have him take you to these enemy spies. Be sure to take them quickly, and with surprise; remember, our enemies possess arcane magic, obscene power that we cannot fully understand. Arrest them, and bring them to me!"

—DH—

"Bluestone! Bluestone! Bluestone!"

The cry echoed through the tunnels of the deep-levels, up and down the Atrium, rising into the city of Garnet Thax on a cresting wave of triumph and celebration. Brandon held on to Gretchan's hand and let the swelling shouts, the pats on the back, the cheers, and the congratulations sweep him along. They had just emerged from the Deepshelf Inn and made their way along a street suddenly crowded with boisterous revelers. It was only then dawning on Brandon that they were celebrating because of *him.*

In the midst of the fight with the horax, he'd been only vaguely aware of the rest of Kayolin—at least, beyond those dwarves in the Deepshelf Inn who had helped rescue them by throwing them the rope ladder—but he realized that his battle and almost single-handed defeat of a swarm of the bug monsters had been observed by a significant portion of the population. They had watched in horror as the clicking, hungry monsters had swarmed up the walls of the Atrium like some nightmare from the ancient past. And they had seen the wielder of the Bluestone Axe fight them back, slashing through the webs of the tanglers and sending dozens of the horax tumbling to their doom.

Clearly, from the adulation he and Gretchan received as they strode proudly along, with more and more citizens of Kayolin streaming out of houses, shops, and inns, the word had spread rapidly among the city's dwarves about their amazing fight.

"You're quite the hero," the cleric said, pressing his hand and impulsively leaning over to kiss him. That gesture drew another round of cheering as well as some hoots and whistles from the crowd, mainly male, for there were many miners and smith-workers who thronged the lower levels.

Brandon couldn't hide his grin until he remembered the reason they had plunged down the Atrium in the first place. "I imagine the League of Enforcers are going to hear about this," he said grimly, glancing around for a glimpse of the dread shiny black leather uniforms.

"Do you think they'd dare to arrest you now?" Gretchan asked, shaking her head vigorously. "Even a king has to pay a certain amount of attention to the peoples' wishes. I would say, right now, the people would like to see you rewarded, not arrested. And remember, he isn't even the blasphemous king yet; he won't be until they clap that sapphire-studded crown on his head, the one he's having made from the Torc of the Forge."

Brandon wasn't so sure, but Gretchan's words reminded him of the treasure he had claimed from the horax lair—the torc encrusted with blue stones that he hadn't had a chance to show to Gretchan yet. He wasn't going to pull it out from his belt pouch there on that crowded street, so he leaned over and told her, "As soon as we can get some privacy, I have something to show you."

"You rascal!" she teased.

He blushed and lowered his voice. "Not that!" he growled. "Can't you be serious for a moment?"

"Serious? When I'm in a parade with the greatest hero of Garnet Thax? I don't think so!" she replied teasingly.

She took his arm and hugged it close, beaming at the cheering dwarves surrounding them.

They turned onto the nearest spiraling ramp—no more darkened stairways for the Horax Hero, Gretchan declared—and started the trek upward. At each landing they met crowds of friendly, congratulatory dwarves, many of whom joined the march along behind them, whooping and shouting in the impromptu victory parade. More and more dwarves thronged the plazas and streets around the landings as they climbed, and Brandon had to decline multiple invitations to sit down for a beer or share a bottle of dwarf spirits. The name "Bluestone" echoed from the walls, down the streets, into the houses and inns.

As the accolades continued and grew, he noticed the utter absence of the king's Enforcers in the crowd. He was further surprised to note several members of the Garnet Guards, veteran professional soldiers distinguished by their bright red cloaks. They seemed to be off duty but were good-naturedly following along the procession, joining in the cheers and hoisting overflowing mugs with the rest of the citizenry.

"Who are they?" Gretchan asked when he pointed them out.

"They're the oldest regiment in Kayolin," he explained. "Their leader, General Watchler, was a protégé of my grandfather, in fact, back during the War of the Lance. When I left here they were in charge of watching the city gates and patrolling the streets—not that there was ever much trouble. Seems like a lot of their work has been taken over by the League of Enforcers, now."

The outpouring of affection continued, with the celebration steadily growing, spilling onto side streets and different levels. Yet suddenly, Brandon wanted nothing more than to get away from all the hubbub. He felt a cold stab of shame and fear when he remembered the raid on his parents' house and the panic of his and Gretchan's flight from the royal agents.

"I have to get home!" he protested forcefully as a pair of strapping young millworkers tried to bodily haul him into a tavern. They released him, agreeably enough, and went on their way, but Brandon pushed ahead with increased urgency, tugging Gretchan at his side.

They continued rapidly up the long flights of stairs from the lower deep-level to the upper middle part of Garnet Thax, steadily approaching the Bluestone manor. Everywhere it seemed as though a national holiday had been declared, with boisterous drinking and cheering of the "Horax Hero" as they passed through the city.

By the time they reached the fourth midlevel and emerged from the ramp, the street was thronged with cheering dwarves, his name having been shouted upward and the news traveling before them faster than the two dwarves could climb.

Outside the Cracked Mug, Bondall met them with two full mugs of chilled ale, handing them over then impulsively kissing Brandon on the cheek.

"My hero!" she declared, smiling broadly. "And the hero of all Garnet Thax!"

The hero of Garnet Thax could only blush, as Bondall gave Gretchan a congratulatory hug. "You're a lucky gal!" she said.

"I know," replied the priestess, amused. She winked at Brandon. "I'm rather proud of him myself. You know, he saved my life down there."

Only as they made their way down the street to the

Bluestone house did the crowds thin a bit and grow more solemn and watchful. Many dwarves, friends and neighbors he'd known for years, clapped Brandon on the back and offered a hearty "well done." But they knew he risked his life by coming back home, and their knowledge filled him with dread.

His mood lightened somewhat when he saw his mother waiting for him. But there was no sign of his father, and when he embraced Karine Bluestone and she started to sob in his arms, he could only fear the worst.

—DH—

Willim the Black was alone in his laboratory. His terror at Facet's frightening plunge, coupled with his fury at his own army's cowardice, had driven him back to his laboratory—to work, to scheme, to prepare. He had left the blinded female with the healers who were tending the rebel army's infirmary, ordering that she receive the best care, before teleporting by himself back to his laboratory.

He still remembered the gagging fear that had gripped him when his beloved female acolyte toppled over the edge of the king's prayer tower. Blinded by the god's light, flailing in terror, she had plunged toward the stone paving a hundred feet below. She hadn't been enchanted with the flying spell herself since she had been borne through the air by her master, and when she had toppled from the rampart, gravity had swept her toward certain doom.

It had taken all of the wizard's skills—along with the good fortune that he himself was still enchanted by the spell of flying—to muster the power to swoop down and catch her in his arms just before she crashed into the ground. She had sobbed, clutching him in her terror, and her emotions had touched him deeply. The confrontation with the king forgotten, he had flown away from the palace, toward the safety of his own army.

After finding General Darkstone blinded on the gatehouse parapet, groping for the stairway leading down to the plaza, Willim had demanded that the attack be resumed at once. The veteran commander had stood firm in the face of the wizard's rage and argued, irrefutably, that blind troops could not very well be expected to wage war.

"I desire vengeance against the king as much as anyone, Master," Darkstone declared. "But I cannot even see the blasted foe! How can I or anyone attack?"

The black wizard's most frenetic commands, dire threats, and hysterical exhortations had been unable to sway more than a handful of his troops—those that had been inside buildings or otherwise screened from the brilliant flash—to organize for another attack. Even those stalwarts had simply advanced a few hundred feet, until they were away from their commander's influence. Shaken and pale, looking around as if they were afraid that Reorx would smite them directly, they had quickly gone to ground.

After railing against even his most veteran commanders and loyal troops, mocking their refusal to fight in the face of what they considered to be clear proof of Reorx's displeasure, Willim departed Norbardin in disgust. The wizard had returned to his lab, seeking a solitary place to brood, to plan, to marshal his power, and to scheme.

His enemies would pay.

He continued to believe that he was alone, but then his spell of true-seeing detected the glimmer of magic very nearby. He straightened, summoning the words to powerful spells of death and destruction. If it was an enemy arriving, his foe would be killed instantly.

But it was not an enemy. Instead, Willim recognized his apprentice Facet. She was wearing a black robe, but it was not the thick material of her wizardly garb. Instead, it was a silken outfit, gauzy and transparent—seductively transparent, and would have been so even without the benefit of the black wizard's gift of true sight. The female apprentice was alluring in her shapeliness, beguiling in her expression. Her lips glowed like fresh blood, and her hair shimmered and flowed like liquid with each step she took. She came up to her master and bowed deeply, lowering her head in supplication. She no longer seemed to be suffering ill effects from her near-death experience.

"Why did you come here?" he asked, surprised at the unusual catch in his voice. "I left you with the army in Norbardin. But let me ask you: How are your eyes?"

"The healers were good to me, Master. In you, I can see all that I need to see."

He felt himself stirred by her words as well as her presence. She took a step closer, and his blood pulsed in a way both frightening and thrilling. He reached out, touched her smooth, black hair, lifted the pale face with the lips painted so shockingly, so appealingly crimson.

"I am worried about you, Master," she stated softly. "I sense your keen disappointment. I detest those who pledged you their loyalty but now fail you in your hour of opportunity . . . and of need."

She understood! Willim felt a stab of powerful desire, an almost breathtaking awareness that the dwarf maid was the only one who could see into his soul, could sense that the wonderful prize, which had lurked so close, had seemed so attainable, was disastrously, tantalizingly out of reach.

"You are precious to me, a rare treasure," he said, reaching for her, casting his scarred, eyeless face down upon her own image of rare beauty. If she was repulsed by his appearance—for the first time ever, he actually worried that his visage might be upsetting to another dwarf—she gave no outward sign. She melted into his embrace, and he held her, kissed her, pulled her close.

"You are suffering, my master," she whispered to him. "I will do anything in my power to ease your distress."

An hour later, he knew that she spoke the truth.

NINETEEN

FACTIONS AND FLIGHT

"Another Theiwar came to talk to me. He's a diamond merchant, one of the wealthiest in all Norbardin. And he's willing to pay an even greater fortune to get out of Thorbardin!" Peat informed Sadie as they sipped bitter spirits in the back room of the Two Guilders shop. "I think we should do the dimension door spell again."

"Well, *I* think it's time we thought about getting out of here ourselves," she snapped testily. "We're lucky the ceiling didn't come down on our heads when the Master and the king faced each other." She glanced meaningfully around the shop. Always crowded, it was at that time a tangled mess as several shelves had toppled, smashing jars of potions and ingredients onto the floor, during the short but violent earthquake. "And that flash of light! It seems half of the city has been blinded. Everyone's saying it was the will of Reorx himself! I'm not sure I want to hang around to find out."

"Surely you don't believe that superstitious nonsense?" Peat scoffed. "Why, it was just ten days ago when we went out into the square and dropped that stone on the king's man. You know very well who exercised the will of Reorx on that occasion!"

"I remember," she retorted. Still, she looked hesitant, glancing around nervously as if she suspected someone, or something, was lurking in the shadowy corners of the room.

"What is it?" her husband asked in exasperation.

"I'm not kidding. I'm worried," she admitted. "What if the Master suddenly decides he needs us? What if one of his messengers shows up at an inopportune time, just when we're hosting one of our dimension-door customers?"

"I think he's too busy with the war to need our kind of help at the moment."

"What if he finds out I stole the dimension door spell from him?" Sadie asked bluntly.

Peat could feel his face going pale. "What? *That's* where you got the scroll?" he gasped. "You stole it from Willim the Black? Why didn't you tell me this before?"

She waved his objection away with a gesture of contempt. "Where did you think I got it? Where else would I find something like that, in Thorbardin? Of *course* I took it from the Master. And he hasn't missed it for twenty years. I don't think he'll be missing it now all of a sudden. But I do think he'd recognize the spell as one of his own."

"Oh, that's just great," Peat muttered. "Maybe you're right. Maybe we should use the dimension door ourselves, while we are still alive to enjoy the fruits of our labors."

"Yes. Maybe we should. This Theiwar you're talking about. What kind of payment could he make? Maybe we could risk it just one more time, so we have a real fortune to take with us wherever we end up."

Peat reached into his pouch and pulled out a stone that nearly filled his palm. Even his weak eyes could discern the multiple facets, the crystalline clarity of the gem. "That diamond merchant gave me this as proof of his good faith. He said he has eleven more like it and will spend them all of 'em just to have a one-time use of our dimension door."

Sadie's eyes flashed with greed at the sight of the massive diamond. She snatched it out of his hand and held it up to the light of the eternal candle flickering magically over the worktable. "It's fabulous," she allowed after a moment's study. "I've never seen its equal. And eleven more, he said?"

"Eleven more . . . for us," Peat declared.

"Well, all right, then. One more time, we'll do the spell. But then, after that, it's time for you and I to get out. Before the king, or the Master, learns about what we've been doing."

"Right, good plan," Peat agreed.

"But there's one more thing," his wife reminded him.

"What's that?"

"I'm not about to bring more gully dwarves into Thorbardin!" Sadie replied. "I just about had a heart attack when those two little runts came strolling into our store! And who knows where they dashed off to!"

"Right, those gully dwarves," Peat agreed, shuddering at the nasty memory. "But surely we can pick a different place to anchor the spell! I mean, what are the odds of opening a dimension door into another gully dwarf lair!"

"Odds, shmodds! Magic isn't always so controllable. I can't decide if it's worth the risk. After all, we've got plenty of treasure already!" Sadie retorted. Even as she spoke, her eyes drifted back to the magnificent diamond that she still held in her crooked fingers.

"No—how can you even say that?" Peat argued. "Remember, there's eleven more of them, a fortune, available for the taking just for casting that same simple spell."

"It's *not* a simple spell!" she reminded him haughtily. "Or do you want to try and cast it?"

"No. You know I could never do it. But you can!" pleaded her husband. "You can get this Theiwar diamond merchant out of here and get his diamonds into our strongbox, and then we can escape from this awful place!"

"But where would I send him?" she asked almost plaintively.

"Well, we can't just open a dimension door into the wilds of the Kharolis," Peat agreed. "Why, these dwarves would step through and get eaten by a bear or smashed by a giant. Or buried under a blizzard or an avalanche."

"True . . ." Sadie said, deep in thought. "Of course, no one would necessarily know that result," she observed.

"No!" Peat said, startling them both by standing up to his wife. "I don't mind taking steel, lots of steel, to let these refugees get away from Thorbardin. But I won't send them to certain deaths!"

"Well, I'm not saying we should send them to *certain* deaths!" Sadie protested. "But we know that for some reason the dimension door into Pax Tharkas leads into some squalid nest of gully dwarves. So I'm not using that one again!"

"There must be other places that're safe—at least, that we can presume are safe," Peat suggested. "You know, another place where there are . . . many, many dwarves."

"Are you thinking of Kayolin?" Sadie asked. "That's a long way away, but it doesn't really matter for the spell. I mean, we have the maps and charts. We could pick a place in that nation and let our refugees go there."

"Kayolin! That's a splendid idea," Peat, who hadn't really had any specific destination in mind, agreed. "You get out the map and figure the coordinates. I'll wait by the door and let the customer in when he gets here."

The decision made, the two Guilders plunged into activity. Sadie had just a little bit of work remaining to prepare another scroll, but she would have to hurry. She got out an ancient tome and blew the dust off the cover so she could read the title: *The Dwarven Nations of Krynn.* Flipping it open to the section on Kayolin, she began to seek an appropriate destination.

The book included a detailed schematic of the northern nation, and she immediately found some likely locations. "Hmm. Garnet Thax would be the right place," she mused to herself. "Not too high up—don't want to have him falling into the governor's lap first thing. But not deep down in the mines either."

Her nearly deaf ears picked up a sound, and she looked up, irritated at the interruption. What could Peat be doing to raise such a racket?

She was about to shout out to him when the door to the back room opened. She blinked in surprise: it wasn't Peat there at all, but their neighbor Abercrumb. The Hylar stepped out of the way as two burly soldiers burst in, charging over to Sadie. One of them clapped a hand over her mouth before she could even think to cast a spell.

Only then did she see Peat, already bound and gagged. The old Theiwar was pushed into the back room by a silver-armored Hylar she recognized as one of the king's generals.

"There she is!" declared Abercrumb, his face creased by a smug smile. "I tell you, they're both working for the black wizard!" He pointed at the scroll on the table. "Look there—that's some kind of dark magic they're fussing with, you can mark my words!"

None of the soldiers seemed any too willing to examine the scroll or anything else in the shop. Instead, the two who held Sadie bound her hands behind her back, and one stuffed a dirty gag into her mouth. The general stalked over and looked her right in the face.

"Sadie Guilder!" he barked. "I arrest you and your husband in the name of the king!"

—DH—

"So you haven't heard from Father since Baracan Heelspur forced him to confess?" Brandon confirmed, gently prodding his mother for answers.

They were seated in the great room, the same room where they had been when the Enforcers had turned their lives upside down only a few days earlier. Brandon was so angry that he clutched the haft of the Bluestone Axe with white-knuckled intensity, almost hoping that a mess of officials would barge in again. He was all but certain that none of them would have gotten out of there with his life.

Gretchan put a hand on his shoulder. Her touch, as always, soothed and calmed him, and he shook off the dark, violent impulse that had been taking over his thoughts. His hands relaxed, though he still kept his weapon in his lap, ready and willing to use it.

"No. There has been no public report. The standard procedure in a case like this, with a signed confession of wrongdoing, is for the king to determine the sentence.

When he does so, that sentence will be posted at the gate of the palace. I have been going there every day, and there has been no public announcement yet."

She glanced from Gretchan to Brandon, her face a tight mask of fear. "It was Baracan Heelspur himself who interrogated him. He said they would do terrible things to me if your father didn't confess. So, of course, he did."

"What did they charge him with?" Brandon asked.

"Well, with harboring a fugitive, first of all," said Karine, frowning. "But Heelspur was talking crazy. He spoke of something called the Bluestone Faction, as if your father was some kind of revolutionary. There's nothing to it, but the Heelspurs—and the king, too, I'm sure—are terribly worried about our clan. He already had to deal with a mutiny in the Garnet Guards."

"What happened there?" Brandon said. "I noticed a few of the redcoats as we wended our way here. They seemed to be permanently off duty."

"Yes. They've been relieved of their official tasks since a couple of them got into a fight with some of Heelspur's Enforcers. The Enforcers took kind of a beating, even though they had the advantage of numbers. Of course, Smashfingers took his friend Lord Heelspur's side. The guards have been furloughed for the season without pay. I understand they've taken to wearing their uniforms as a point of pride, and the Enforcers haven't been able to muster the gumption to order them to take off those red jackets."

"That could be useful to us," Brandon said, glad to hear that all was not well in the ranks of Regar Smashfingers's men-at-arms.

"I have an idea," Gretchan suggested. "Let's not wait for the king's public pronouncement. We should do whatever we can to spread word through the city about Garren's plight and contrast it with Brandon's heroism. From the reception we have been getting, just climbing from the deep-levels up to here, it's clear that many dwarves will be sympathetic. You're the Horax Hero, after all."

Brandon frowned and his mother shot him a sympathetic look. They had told her all about what happened, but she knew that Brandon didn't like to play the national hero. "I'm not about to go bragging about fighting for our lives!" Brandon objected. "And we wouldn't even have been down there if not for the League of Enforcers chasing us!"

"And that's a point that the dwarves of Kayolin would do well to remember. As to you bragging: no, of course you shouldn't do that," Gretchan said, her eyes twinkling. "Your mother and I will do that job better than you! And we'll enlist your friends. I'd bet that Bondall would do a good job of spreading the news. This story is already taking on a life of its own."

"What should I do, then?" Brand asked, intrigued by the idea even as he was frustrated at the thought of handing over the initiative to Gretchan and his mother. "Just sit around and look heroic while my father rots in the Enforcers' dungeon?"

Only then did he remember his discovery in the subterranean throne room, when he had been racing after Gretchan and the horax that had captured her. He pulled the torc out of his belt pouch.

"Wait, I forgot to tell you! I found this in the horax lair," he said excitedly. "Do you think it could be real? I mean, *the* Torc of the Forge?" He held the silvery circle up, and the blue stones flashed in the firelight, brightening the room as if they possessed an internal source of brilliance.

Gretchan froze with a little gasp of awe. Then she reached forward and touched the artifact, and as she did so, the miniature anvil on the top of her staff pulsed with a dazzling light. She swayed dizzily, and he caught her as she almost swooned onto her side.

"It is, isn't it?" he said fiercely. "It's the real torc!"

She nodded, awestruck. "I believe so. It's the power of Reorx, more concentrated than anything I have ever seen before. An artifact, lost for centuries far below the civilized depths of Kayolin. And you just found it when you were coming after me?"

"That's it! I found you—*you* led me to it, even though I suppose you didn't do it on purpose." He described the ancient hall with its dusty floor and the solid stone throne. "I got the feeling that the place was even older than Kayolin. I don't know if it was even inhabited by dwarves; it might have been those ancient ogres or some other culture that's now lost to history. The whole place has been overrun by the horax for a thousand years, and this torc was just sitting there as if it had been waiting for me to pick it up."

"That is exactly right; Reorx wanted it found," Gretchan said reverently.

Brandon was quickly struck by a new thought. "Then the torc the king—the governor!"—he spat the lesser title triumphantly—"is having made into his crown . . . it's a fake!"

"It has to be!" Gretchan agreed. "His authority is built on a false claim." She frowned thoughtfully. "But what do you plan to do about that? Are you going to take this up to the palace?"

"Yes!" crowed Brandon. "I'll brandish it in his face, right in front of the entire court, so the whole nation will know his falseness."

"That might work," Gretchan allowed. "But I wonder if it might not be prudent to wait a little bit before you do that. You know, to let word of your triumph filter through the city. To let the people hear that you were called a fugitive by the League of Enforcers. Before you, you know, saved the city from a swarm of horax. Let the word spread."

"But I can't just sit here on my hands and wait for rumors and stories to spread."

A rap on the door sounded before either of the dwarf maids could answer. Brandon crossed the room and, still carrying his axe, opened the door to find two dwarves standing there. They wore the black leather tunics of the secret police, with gold braid on their shoulders suggesting they held some sort of exalted rank. Unlike the last occasion, they weren't bashing the door down, but rather stood there respectfully. One even bowed, almost sheepishly, as Brandon appeared before them.

"What do you want?" he demanded curtly.

"We bring a message from King Smashfingers," said the second dwarf, the one who hadn't bowed. He was holding a piece of parchment in his hand, and he didn't exactly look happy to be there.

"What is it?"

The dwarf read from the page he was holding. "King Smashfingers has been apprised of your heroism in single-handedly defeating a horax infestation that nearly reached the city's deep-levels. While he has dispatched some more troops to deal with any remaining threat, he would very much like to honor you with a medal of valor and to learn of your experiences with the monsters. This message is an invitation to attend to him in his court at your earliest convenience."

Brandon, surprised, looked back at Gretchan. "Should I go?" he silently mouthed.

The priestess came over to him and took his hand. "Yes, your mother and I have plenty to do," she said conspiratorially. "As for you, I suggest you go and see the king."

—DH—

Willim the Black was sweating and breathing hard, elated in a way he had never been before. Carefully, almost tenderly, he laid his whip on the worktable of his laboratory and stepped to Facet's side. The female apprentice was sobbing quietly as he released the straps that had attached her wrists to the rack. She fell into his arms, still crying, and he held her tenderly, avoiding the bloody welts that marked her back.

"I'm sorry, Master," she said, shivering. "I tried so hard not to cry out—"

"Shh, my little one," he said. "Your courage was so inspiring to me. You have given me a great gift, one I dare not squander."

"Oh, thank you, Master!" she exclaimed, pulling him tight. But then she leaned back and looked at him in puzzlement. "But what gift could I possibly have given you?"

"The gift of resolve, my brave apprentice. You have shown me the way, showed me that I must stand true to my goals, my beliefs, yes, even my desires."

Her eyes flashed at his words, and his vision, the magical enchantment of true sight, showed him that she really did understand. He released his female apprentice, and she gently pulled away, standing. She did not cover herself, and he was pleased.

"Take a sip of potion," he said gently. "Some of those cuts are deep; you must take care they do not become infected."

She went over to the potion cabinet and quickly took out a bottle of healing elixir as well as a jug of strong red wine. He watched her affectionately as she mixed the two and took a sip. Behind her, the cabinet was neat and orderly, a hundred bottles all polished and lined up. She had done that for him, cataloguing and organizing all of his potions as well as many of his other components.

She smiled as the healing began to ease her pain, and he sighed, wondering how he had ever gotten along without her. Without his even asking, she poured a second glass of wine and brought it over to him.

"What do you plan to do now, Master?" she asked as he sipped. She put her robe on, much to his disappointment, but he knew she couldn't go unclothed forever.

The wizard felt a new resolve. "I have one more weapon, one I have yet to use. But I think it is time," he declared.

Willim stood up and crossed the laboratory, stopping near the edge of the great chasm in the floor. As always, Gorathian seethed and burned down there, yearning for release, craving the destruction and chaos that, up until that moment, Willim had prevented the monster from attaining.

"Awaken, my beast!" he barked. The wizard snapped his fingers, breaking the first spell of confinement, the enchantment that held the fire dragon at bay, deep within its rock-walled lair.

Immediately flames surged upward, brightening the vast laboratory and warming the skin of the two dwarves. The heat increased, until their silken robes started to smolder, and Willim cast a spell of protection, a shielding globe that surrounded them both, insulating them from the fire dragon's infernal temperatures. The monster rose from the depths, gouging the stone walls of the chasm with its fiery claws, pressing upward until the burning head and serpentine neck twisted from the narrow gap, its great maw open and roaring.

"Now, rise!" commanded Willim, clapping his hands and breaking the second spell of confinement.

Gorathian roared again, jaws spread wide, fire spuming outward to surround the two dwarves. Only the enchantment of the powerful wizard's spell protected them from certain and instant immolation. The beast's large head loomed above them, rearing back on its strong, sinuous neck. The fire dragon's skin was like liquid lava, shiny and flowing. Its eyes were black, utterly soulless, but every bit of the rest of it was blazing orange and white, as bright as an infernal blaze. The jaws spread wide again, and a massive cloud of flame billowed forth, igniting the air just over the two magic-users' heads.

"Do not attack me! Do not attack my apprentice!" snarled the wizard.

He raised his hand, palm outward, then pressed downward. The dragon writhed and howled, unable to resist the powerful magic that pressed it, against its will, back down into the chasm. The creature roared more loudly than ever, the sound rattling the potion jars on their shelves. Massive forefeet, each tipped with talons as hard as steel, clawed at the stone floor, leaving smoking, blackened gouges in the hard stone.

Abruptly, Willim pulled his hand away, and the dragon surged upward, wings of fire spreading wide and carrying it into the air, high above the floor of the vast, domed chamber. The wizard smiled tightly, knowing that the monster would not dare to attack him or the female under his protection again.

Gorathian roared again and flew in a tight spiral, constrained by the size of the laboratory.

"Have you ever seen such terrible magnificence?" the black wizard demanded, gloating.

Facet took his arm and shook her head, staring upward, shivering in terror and awe.

"Now!" cried the eyeless Theiwar, addressing the fire dragon and pointing at the stone wall that barricaded the chamber, which blocked it from access to all the rest of Thorbardin. "Go! Find my enemy, the king! Smite him!" he shouted.

With a bellow so loud it shivered the very bedrock of the laboratory, the fire dragon flew straight at the wall. Solid stone was no barrier to that creature of Chaos—kin of those that had ruined so many of Thorbardin's cities during the Chaos War, more than a half century earlier. As it struck the wall, it immediately gouged a hole into the rock, forcing its way through the barrier, soon bursting explosively into the wide chamber beyond.

Facet stared at the flaming wake of the monster, her eyes wide, her mouth open with awe and excitement. She stared at the large hole in the face of stone, the gap smoldering and molten with crimson fingers of fire around the fringes. She turned back to her master, evincing adoration and exultation in her expression. "What will we do now?" she asked breathlessly, her hand taking Willim's and squeezing his scarred and stubby fingers.

"Why," he said, with a dry chuckle. "We follow it, of course. And we watch our enemy's destruction."

And he cast the spell of flying upon them both, and the two wizards, master and apprentice, took to the air.

TWENTY

EMPTY THRONES

Unlike his last appearance at Regar Smashfingers's court, when he and his father had quietly entered amid a large group of casual observers, Brandon strode forward at the head of a retinue of noisy well-wishers. Some were neighbors who'd been with him since he'd passed the Cracked Mug, while others were those who had joined as he'd climbed the long ramps to the noble level. The Enforcers who had brought him the invitation, interestingly enough, had melted away during the climb. Once again, however, he spotted some of the redcoats of the Garnet Guards. One burly veteran hoisted a mug to Brandon and winked broadly as he strode past.

The governor's palace occupied the highest level of Garnet Thax. Two stout gates, standing open, greeted those who climbed to that lofty height. The entry led directly into the throne room, a long, rectangular chamber with the ruler's seat at the far end. Both sides and the far end of the room were crowned with balconies, which rose twenty feet higher than the floor. They were galleries for citizens and observers, and Brandon's first glance into the huge chamber showed him that those vantages were lined two or three deep with interested dwarves who had rushed there at the rumors of a confrontation between Brandon Bluestone and Regar Smashfingers.

As he stepped into the palace, he was greeted by saluting guards in black capes who stepped back, forming an aisle that directed him down a ramp toward the floor of the throne room. The last time he had looked at that room, he was an observer watching from the balcony that surrounded the large chamber. As he glanced at all those dwarves who reminded him of his previous experience with the room, he walked proudly toward the great seat upon which sat the dwarf who had the temerity to call himself king.

Brandon wore his axe slung over his back. He still carried the Torc of the Forge in his belt pouch, having decided over Gretchan's objections that he might need it. The royal guards didn't ask him to hand over his weapon anyway, though a pair of big spear carriers walked forward with him. They looked like an honor guard, but he knew they'd be ready to act against him if he made some aggressive action toward the king.

They didn't need to worry. Brandon was there to learn and evaluate, not to do anything foolhardy. He looked around, noticed lots of smiling faces, and recognized some of the attending dwarves—including one young noblewoman, Rona Darkwater, who had been one of Brand's lovers, once upon a time. She blew him a kiss, and he blushed.

Still looking around, Brandon was surprised but not displeased to see that neither Lord Alakar Heelspur nor his son was present. That was good; he wasn't sure he could have controlled his temper in the presence of the dwarves who had arranged his brother's murder and his father's imprisonment and coerced confession.

Several well-dressed courtiers stood flanking the throne, their silk shirts and colorful cravats at odds with the more common, workmanlike garb typical of Kayolin's citizenry.

Regar Smashfingers sat up straight in his great stone chair then leaned forward as Brandon advanced. The king had a broad face and an unusually large nose, with a tip that hooked downward, not unlike the beak of a hawk.

"Presenting Brandon Bluestone, sire!" declared one of the guards, thumping the butt of his spear against the floor.

"So you are the hero who warned us about the horax attack—and then, apparently single-handedly, sent a hundred of the bugs tumbling into the Atrium?" said Smashfingers with every appearance of graciousness. He looked Brandon up and down, smiling with a broad display of white teeth.

"I don't know about the hero stuff," Brandon said with genuine modesty. "And it was certainly less than a hundred of them that fell to my attack. I was fighting for my life and the life of my companion. I did what any other Kayolin dwarf would have done."

The king's eyes narrowed—probably because Brand had intentionally avoided using any honorific title—but he merely nodded thoughtfully, as if digesting the information.

"Unusual, isn't it, to find the scum so high in the mountain—right up to the deep-levels, aren't they?"

"I've never heard of them there in my lifetime," Brandon admitted, thinking: Was it you who ordered the walls knocked down? He wanted to ask the question aloud, but—acting on Gretchan's wise counsel—decided it was not the time to confront the king on that issue. "They seem to have found some new ways out of their hives," he settled for saying.

Smashfingers sat up straight again and spoke in a loud, clear voice to all the dwarves in the throne room as well as those on the ring of the surrounding gallery. "Let it be known to all that Brandon Bluestone is a true hero of the realm! He is to be treated with the honor appropriate to his deeds, and I hereby award him a bounty of a thousand platinum pieces for his service to Kayolin!"

The gathered dwarves cheered wildly. Brandon felt a little stunned by the turn of events. The bounty, he was pretty certain, more than doubled his family's net worth, but it wasn't coin he was after. As the applause and shouting faded down, he bowed and decided to speak boldly.

"Thank you, sir," he said. "That is a generous reward. I hope you don't find it inappropriate for me to ask an additional favor at this time."

Once again the king's eyes narrowed almost imperceptibly, but he concealed his displeasure with a broad smile, leaning back in his throne and waving expansively. "Ask away!" he declared.

"My father has been taken into custody by the League of Enforcers. The charges against him are false, but a confession was extracted from him when Baracan Heelspur threatened to harm my mother if my father would not sign a false document. He signed the false confession to spare her, of course, as any honorable dwarf would do. I ask, my lord, that the confession be discarded and my father released."

"This is most unfortunate!" Regar Smashfingers declared with every appearance of sympathy. His eyes were wide, his expression guileless, though his hands gripped the arms of his throne so firmly that his knuckles whitened. "What is his name, your father?" he added innocently.

You know very well! Brandon's mind screamed. Once again, he bit back the words he wanted to say. Instead, he replied. "His name is Garren Bluestone. He's the patriarch of House Bluestone—all that's left of us, in any event."

Brandon watched the ruler carefully, certain that he recalled every detail of their confrontation less than two years before, when the younger Bluestone had accused the king's strongest support, Alakar Heelspur, of murder and thievery. Yet somehow Regar Smashfingers masked any sign of recognizing the past.

"The name is not familiar to me," said the king with breathtaking effrontery, managing to look puzzled. He gestured to a scribe, a young dwarf seated behind the throne who had been taking notes. "Write that name down. I shall check on the prisoner's status."

Puzzled, Brandon nodded his thanks, bowed stiffly, and backed away from the king's throne. Thinking it over, he was not surprised that he hadn't immediately obtained his father's release. In fact, he was reasonably satisfied with the course of the interview. He understood that he and Regar Smashfingers had taken each other's measure, and Brandon Bluestone sensed—to his astonishment—that the ruler of Kayolin was afraid of him.

—DH—

"These are the spies, my lord," General Ragat reported, saluting King Stonespringer in his throne room. The monarch had been pacing back and forth in agitation, but he stopped to stare at the new, pathetic arrivals with his one intense, shining eye. "Peat and Sadie Guilder, sire. They operate a shop that sells components for magic-users, with potions and elixirs, that sort of thing, for sale."

King Stonespringer regarded the two Theiwar. With their arms thoroughly bound and mouths gagged, they were not terribly impressive. Both were elderly, the male stooped and thin-haired, the female wrinkled and even smaller than her mate. Each was closely trailed by a strapping guard, a Hylar, who held tightly to a rope lashed around the prisoners' wrists. The two Theiwar stared at him with eyes that bulged almost comically over their tight gags.

"I see you have taken precautions so that they cannot wield magic," Stonespringer said approvingly.

Ragat nodded. "We took them by surprise, sire. I considered cutting out their tongues and amputating their fingers, for more permanent hindrance, but I decided such actions should be your decision, not mine. So the gags and bonds will suffice, for now."

"Indeed," Jungor said with a bark of laughter. "Tongueless spies might be difficult to interrogate." The king waved toward the door, where another dwarf, a Hylar, stood watching the proceedings with interest. "Who is this other one?" demanded the monarch.

Ragat gestured to the other dwarf, who stepped proudly forward from the shadows of the doorway. "This is Abercrumb, the silversmith who discovered the Theiwar spy ring. He has been one of my trusted agents for a number of years. He observed suspicious activity around the Guilders' shop and came to inform me of his findings during the midst of the recent battle. I can testify he is brave and loyal, sire."

Jungor looked him over with an expression of distaste. "I don't care for silver," he said, waving his fingers. "Send him away!"

Abercrumb's eyes widened—he clearly hadn't been expecting such a curt dismissal—but a hands-down gesture from Ragat caused him to hold his tongue. Instead, he merely bowed and swiftly backed out of the room, leaving Ragat, the king, the two Theiwar prisoners, and their brace of guards.

General Ragat turned back, watching his king nervously. Stonespringer paced around the throne room, bobbing up and down on the balls of his feet, swiftly turning to one side, taking a few steps, then spinning back to move the other way. He glanced at Ragat, looked over the spies, but didn't seem capable of studying anyone or anything. His golden eye glowed with an unnatural gleam, while his other eyelid blinked repeatedly.

Ragat cleared his throat and stepped up to the king, gently ushering him to the far side of the large room, out of earshot of the captives and the guards.

"Do you wish to speak to the prisoners separately, sire?" Ragat asked quietly. "By all accounts and appearances, they are a devoted couple. We could use one to leverage information from the other."

"Send them to the dungeon!" Stonespringer said suddenly, waving the spies away. "I have more important matters to attend!"

Ragat hesitated, surprised. But the king's intense expression did not invite disagreement, so the general nodded and turned to his guards. "Put them in the first cell, where they can he heard from the ward room if they try any mischief. Make sure that they remain gagged. And I want a man posted outside the door at all times."

"Aye, General," replied one of the Hylar. Tugging

none too gently on the ropes, they led the two hapless prisoners away.

"Come with me!" the king ordered his general as soon as the door closed behind the departing captives and their escorting guards.

Ragat followed the monarch through the great throne room and into an adjacent hall. Several dwarves in shiny armor snapped to attention as the king and the general came through the door; the two leaders ignored them as Stonespringer ushered the general into a private receiving room and stopped at a sturdy, locked door. One guard, bearing a long-hafted axe, stood at attention.

"You are dismissed," the king told him. "Leave the palace now, and do not return until tomorrow."

"Yes, sire!" the dwarf replied, clapping his fist to his chest in salute before marching stiffly away, the long pole of the axe perched stiffly on his shoulder.

Jungor watched the fellow go. After he had departed, the king went over to the outer door, opened it to peek out, then closed and locked it. "I have something to show you," he told the general. He laughed, almost giggling, and Ragat felt a growing prickle of alarm.

Stonespringer produced from beneath his robe a key that dangled from a leather thong around the king's neck. Once again he looked around, as if afraid that someone might have magically teleported into the room with them. Finally satisfied, he inserted the key into the lock on the small, stout door.

"Take the lantern off the desk," he ordered.

Ragat took up the oil lamp and touched a spark to the wick while Jungor pushed the portal open with a creaking of rusty hinges. The king gestured for the general to follow him into the darkened room. The chamber was small and contained several chests secured with chains and heavy locks. Ragat had not known the place existed and found himself wondering what sorts of treasures his ruler had been concealing there.

Stonespringer went over to the smallest chest, knelt, and used a second key to open the lid. He pulled out an apparently heavy object wrapped in a small leather cloth. Clutching it to his chest, he led the general back into the office, where he placed the treasure on the desk with obvious reverence and care.

Ragat found himself holding his breath, waiting to see what his monarch was going to reveal. Slowly, drawing out the drama, Jungor Stonespringer unfolded first one corner, then another, from the wrapping. Finally he revealed a wedge of stone, perhaps a foot long, four inches wide at one end, tapering to a moderately sharp edge at the other. The piece of rock was red in color—not translucent and sparkling like ruby, but more like it had somehow been painted with fresh blood.

"Look!" said the king. "It has been glowing like this, since I prayed to the Master of the Forge!"

Ragat leaned in closer and saw that, indeed, the stone bore a faint aura of phosphorescence. Still, it was barely noticeable, certainly not the sort of thing that should have inspired the reverence and awe with which the king regarded the red stone.

"What is it?" asked the general hesitantly.

"It is the treasure of Thorbardin's kings," said Stonespringer. His one eye was glowing with much more brightness than the stone. "It has been locked up and secured for generations, for centuries. But when it began to glow, I recognized it for what it truly is!"

Ragat waited for his king to expound. He looked more closely at the wedge of rock, not at all certain that he could discern any kind of glow emanating there.

"Can you not see? It is the eye of Reorx!" crowed the king. "And through it he makes known his love for me and his desire for my triumph. Look!" He pointed gleefully, his eye flashing, his mouth locked into a twisted grin.

"He loves me!" he crowed. Again he laughed, the sound a shrill, even giddy, cackle.

The general nodded solemnly, not trusting himself to speak. How, in any event, did a loyal soldier such as himself speak the truth that was apparent. For Ragat knew, beyond any doubt, that Jungor Stonespringer was utterly, completely insane.

—DH—

Brandon made his way back down the midlevels, lost in contemplation. He was moderately relieved by the fact that, finally, he was not accompanied by a parade of well-wishers. He needed some time alone to gather his thoughts.

However, he was surprised to hear someone with a heavy footstep come hurrying up beside him. He looked up to see one of the strapping members of the Garnet Guards who had winked at him on his way up to see Regar Smashfingers.

"Hello," he said, taken in by the fellow's broad grin.

"Hello yourself," said the redcoat. "I wonder if you'd do me the honor of letting me buy you a drink."

"Well, thanks," said Brandon, thinking of Gretchan and his mother waiting back at home for his report. "But I'd really best be getting back—"

"Ah, the womenfolk are keeping themselves busy, mark my words," said the soldier. "And trust me, this might be the most important drink you have all day."

Intrigued, Brandon agreed, and the redcoat—who introduced himself as Maxxer Dare, ushered him through an unmarked door that turned out to reveal a cozy inn. A dozen more redcoats sat around the room, enjoying the radiance from a fireplace overflowing with ashes and glowing coals. A one-armed bartender, white haired and cheerful, stood behind a dark wooden counter.

"Garry, a draught of your best for the Horax Hero here," Maxxer said with no trace of irony. He led Brandon to a table where, moments later, Garry brought them two tall mugs overflowing with creamy foam.

"Well, thanks, friend," Brandon said as they touched mugs and proceeded to soak their mustaches in the cool, bitter ale.

No sooner had he set the heavy mug down than another redcoat, older and stouter than Maxxer, pulled up a chair to sit with them. The newcomer looked somewhat familiar to Brandon, and he chuckled at young Bluestone's quizzical expression.

"Yep, lad. I knew your grandfather quite well." The fellow nodded at Brandon's shiny-bladed weapon. "He bore that axe with pride and honor. I know it'd warm his heart to learn that you're doing the same."

"Well, thank you . . . General Watchler, right?"

"The same," replied the old commander. His tunic was clean and bright red like those of his men, though it was not distinguished by any mark of rank. Maxxer Dare grinned, looking at both the other two dwarves with obvious affection.

"Thanks for the drink," Brandon said. "Um, to what do I owe the pleasure?"

"Just think of it as a friendly chance to get acquainted," said the general. "I think we both have something very important in common."

"And that would be . . . ?" Brandon let the question linger in the air.

"Well, I think we share a rather powerful enemy," said General Watchler. "And in my experience—and your grandfather's—I would guess that that fact makes us friends."

Brandon nodded and lifted his mug again. "I'll drink to that," he agreed.

—DH—

Gretchan Pax and Karine Bluestone were finding plenty to keep them busy while Brandon was away to see Regar Smashfingers. The pair met up with Bondall in the back room at the Cracked Mug. Brandon had spoken to his old friend before heading up to the palace, and she had arranged for a number of other dwarf maids, many of whom remembered Brandon fondly, to join them for a little meeting.

They were all interested in the pair's experience down in the horax den and reacted with surprise and horror when Gretchan told them that the walls protecting Kayolin from the bug monsters had been destroyed, obviously by dwarves.

"Who would do such a thing?" asked one breathless dwarf maid, the bartender who worked with Bondall. Gretchan had learned that her name was Fiona Shaveblade.

The priestess shrugged. "Who has anything to gain?" she asked. "You tell me. Is anyone using the menace of the horax to further their own position?"

The females exchanged knowing glances. "Smashfingers!" exclaimed one older matron. "That was one of his excuses for putting himself on the throne."

"Would he really expose the people of his own nation to a threat like that?" asked another, shaking her head in dismay.

"Who lives and works in the deep-levels?" Gretchan said firmly. "Those are the ones who are placed in danger. And I'd wager they're not the friends and associates of Regar Smashfingers."

"No, they're not," Bondall said. "And I think this makes it pretty clear how much—or how little—he cares about them."

The other women exchanged looks of horror and disgust, and Gretchan was satisfied that the news, as well as gossip and speculation about its cause, would soon be percolating throughout Garnet Thax. She was about to proceed with a more important discussion when a knock sounded at the door and another dwarf maid entered. She was cloaked and hooded so that only a shadowy glimpse of her face was visible, but she removed the outer garment to reveal herself as light-haired beauty dressed in a long gown of red satin. Jeweled rings sparkled on her fingers.

"Ah, Rona, I'm glad you could make it," Karine Bluestone said, quickly rising and ushering the newcomer to a seat at the crowded table. "This is Rona Darkwater," she added to the others. "I knew she was an old, um, friend of my son's. Her clan is one of nobility, but she was most concerned when Brandon had to leave the city last year. I thought she might be interested in joining our discussion today. It turns out that she has been fending off some unwanted attentions from Baracan Heelspur."

"Glad to meet you," Gretchan said. "We have that in common; we're all trying to avoid attention from the Heelspurs."

Rona laughed wryly at that and quickly joined in the conversation. "Well, his attention has its advantages.

The young lord is quite the boaster, and he seems to think he can impress me by bragging about the trouble he and his Enforcers cause. I was able to warn a couple members of the Garnet Guards that they were going to be arrested. My warning gave them enough notice to go into hiding, for the time being."

They spent some time talking about the League of Enforcers, who were universally despised. "What did you learn when you were in their headquarters?" the priestess asked Karine Bluestone.

"They were very happy to have an excuse to arrest Garren. Baracan Heelspur accused him of leading the 'Bluestone Faction,' which neither my husband nor myself have ever heard of. But the Enforcers seemed to be very worried about it."

"The Bluestone Faction?" Gretchan mused. "Did he say what he thinks the Bluestone Faction is?"

"Not specifically," Karine said. "But he has reason to remember our name. My son Nailer was killed on Lord Heelspur's orders, to enrich his clan, and Regar Smashfingers benefited as well. Perhaps he fears that our resistance is more organized than it really is."

"Well, that's about to change, isn't it?" Gretchan said staunchly. "From this moment forward, I suggest that the Bluestone Faction is real."

With a clinking of mugs, they toasted the inauguration of the movement.

"But what can we do, really?" asked Fiona worriedly.

"We can tell the truth," the priestess replied firmly. "Tell it loudly and often. Make sure that the dwarves of Kayolin know what kind of leader is trying to set himself up as their king."

"Yes!" Rona echoed. "The kind of dwarf who would disband a loyal regiment like the Garnet Guards. Who would knowingly let the horax loose upon his citizens. And who would try to frame a good man like Garren Bluestone just to shut him up. Not to mention, chasing his son and Gretchan down into the depths of the Atrium."

"How did you and Brandon find yourselves down in the horax hive in the first place?" asked a young woman.

Gretchan told them all about her and Brandon's return to Kayolin and made sure that the women knew about the role the League of Enforcers had played in forcing them to flee down into the Atrium in the first place. By the time she was finished, she could see the expressions of outrage and determination on the faces of all the dwarf maids.

As a last order of business, she talked a bit about the history of the dwarven nations, leaving them with the reminder that, for all of dwarfkind, the only historic throne had been in Thorbardin.

"The throne is in Thorbardin," Bondall repeated, nodding. "And that's the way it should remain."

TWENTY-ONE

THE SECOND CHAOS WAR

Willim and Facet flew after the fire dragon, twin flying spells carrying them through the tunnel carved by Gorathian as the monster sliced its way through the rock walls enclosing the wizard's laboratory. The wizard had cast his spell upon himself but also upon the female, so she could fly on her own and did not depend on his touch to stay in the air. Facet sensed that her master was focused on something besides herself, and she fought against the fear that that knowledge provoked.

Onward they went, wind slashing their faces as they used the enchantment to fly with the utmost speed and balance. The flaming serpent had burned through the solid stone wall that had long before sealed the chamber from the rest of Thorbardin. When the two wizards flew through the hole created by the dragon, Facet winced against the lingering heat that would have blistered her skin had she not been moving so fast.

The female dwarf at her master and saw his eyeless, scarred face creased with concentration. Was it possible that he could lose control of the monster, the beast he had tended and protected—and imprisoned—for so long? She couldn't believe that. To her, Willim the Black was capable of anything but error and defeat. His great power had lured her to him, made certain she would continue to serve him as an apprentice, as a female, even as a slave if that was what he desired. He was her key to power, to that which she craved above all else, and she would do everything she could to learn that power.

Did he even suspect how much initiative she had taken? She didn't think so, but she couldn't be sure. So many times she had taken liberties, done things that the wizard did not suspect, and that secret knowledge thrilled her even as it terrified her. She had arranged Gypsum's death, of course; she'd really had no choice since until that moment Gypsum had been her master's favorite apprentice. That was a situation Facet could no longer tolerate. She herself was growing closer to the black wizard, to her source of power and influence. But she had to be careful!

The magic of the flying spell buoyed them and propelled them along, though the powerful wizard seemed to be moving faster than his apprentice. Facet applied every ounce of her strength and ability to the task, but even so, she was dropping behind the speeding black-robed mage. She wanted to call out but, knowing his temper and his impatience, dared not. Instead, she focused her energy and flew. Magic pulsed in her veins, and she held her hands before her to steer, exulting in the wind sweeping past, tearing at her robe, coursing through her hair. She strained for speed, but his dark form still pulled away from her.

They soared up the great tunnel that had once been intended to connect the new council of thanes to the great city of Norbardin. That road was unused since the chamber that had been excavated for the council had been sealed off completely once the menace of Gorathian had been discovered there. Willim had always cherished the joke: that the work of the king's own excavators had created for him the perfect lair. Then the royal masons had secured the privacy of his laboratory by building the supposedly-impermeable wall to seal it off from the city proper.

Impermeable, that was, until the fire dragon had torn through it as though it were smoke. That barrier was far behind the wizards as they flew over the gatehouse and into Norbardin itself. Facet was awestruck by the scene of violence and chaos that met her eyes. The battles of the civil war had been one thing, with all the killing and the destruction, the magical and mortal devastation wrought upon the city.

But the assault of the fire dragon, commencing just minutes earlier, was something else entirely. Gorathian swept low over the plaza, the heat of its passage igniting the corpses still strewn there and burning the rubble and debris left from the wrecked stalls and shops of the once-thriving market. Hundreds of dwarves still survived in that place, the remnants of two armies. They no longer did battle but had been hunkering in their camps, nursing wounded and waiting for the blinded to recover their sight.

When Gorathian burst into the city and flew above the great square, dwarves of both armies fled from the fiery serpent, and those who moved too slowly were incinerated as the monster passed. The remaining dwarves took shelter in holes and craters, trembled within buildings, or fled down the adjacent streets leading into Norbardin's maze. Some of the blinded cowered in the open, unable to see, sensing doom swirling around them. The luckiest of those were led to safety by sighted companions; others could only quail and huddle, hopeless in the face of flaming death.

Willim soared ahead of his apprentice, raising his hands, casting spells to try to restrain, control, and guide the flight of the fire dragon. But Facet could see that the creature was attacking dwarves of both the king's and the wizard's armies, appearing to make no distinction as it burned and killed.

Willim screamed, his words barely intelligible above all the commotion:

"To the palace! Go, my pet! Strike the palace of the king!"

The fire dragon seemed at last to hear. The monster spread its wings, each trailing sparks that tumbled to the ground and incinerated anything flammable below. It soared up to the lofty ceiling that spread its dome over the whole of the great city.

Finally, it veered to one side, banking through a spiraling turn to dive at the palace of King Jungor Stonespringer.

—DH—

Gus and his two lady friends had been hiding in Norbardin for many days. Every time they came around a corner, they encountered more soldiers, and it didn't matter to which army they belonged: the soldiers invariably struck out at the miserable Aghar with curses, kicks, and blows of sharp weapons, even loosing an arrow or crossbow bolt in their direction if the gully dwarves were too slow to run away.

They had made their way across the great square, skulking through the ruins of the stalls and shops that had been destroyed in the waves of battle. Here and there they found enough crumbs and morsels of food—once, even, a whole loaf of bread pinned underneath a broken countertop!—for them to survive. But every moment was fraught with danger, and to make matters even worse, the two females couldn't seem to decide if they were jealous of Gus's affections and, thus, angry at each other or if both of them were angry at Gus and, therefore, united in their contempt and disdain. Either way, they weren't making his life any easier!

Currently the three gully dwarves were sidling along the shattered wall of one of the terraces near the king's palace, staying in the shadowy niche at the base of the rampart. One by one they scuttled over the loose rocks, ducking into first one hole then the next. Nervously, Gus peeked over the rim of the crater and saw that they faced a good distance—at least two steps—before they could reach the next potential hiding place.

"Go first," he said to Berta hopefully, gesturing toward a darkened doorway that was their next objective.

"You no boss!" Berta told him. "*You* go first!"

"Yeah! Bluphsplunging doofar *Gus* go first!" Slooshy chimed in. In a remarkable display of coordination, the two females reached down, each taking one of Gus's feet, and hoisted him bodily out of their hidey-hole.

Sprawled unceremoniously on the open flagstones of the square, he clapped his hands over his head and waited for the blow that might come from any direction. Only after counting two heartbeats with no attack forthcoming did he risk peering through his fingers for a look around.

He yelped at the sight of a big soldier dwarf sitting against the base of the wall nearby then gulped in relief as he saw the arrow jutting from the fellow's breastplate.

He noted the lack of any movement or any other sign of vitality. A careful sniff confirmed that the soldier was indeed dead and had, in fact, been so for a long time—two days at least.

Seeing no sign of any living dwarf, Gus stood up and dusted himself off. Sneering back at the two females, who peered nervously up at him from their hiding place, he did his best impression of a swagger as he started toward the next dark shelter in their haphazard course across the square.

But then he felt the ground shake under his feet and heard a booming *crash* of sound explode through the city. So he dived right back into the hole, knocking the two dwarf maids down.

"Look out!" squawked Berta, hauling back a grubby fist.

The blow never landed. Instead, she gaped in horror at something behind Gus, who quickly scrambled around to get a look for himself.

They saw a fiery explosion tear through a rampart in the middle of the square, sending stones and dwarves flying in all directions. Noise roared through the vast cavern, forcing the Aghar to clap their hands over their ears. Fire and smoke churned in the middle of the wreckage, while screaming dwarves tumbled through the air, slamming into the ground with brutal finality. Gus gaped in slack-jawed horror, staring at the immense force, the shocking destruction all around them. Black smoke swirled, thick and choking, and at first they couldn't even see what was causing the damaging violence.

Then a massive, burning dragon swept out of the murk, wings spreading as it soared overhead. Gus felt his guts turn to water, and when he tried to talk, he could only gibber incoherently. Helpless, paralyzed, he stared upward at the nightmarish image. The dragon swept high above them then dived, right toward the wall of the king's palace. The monster smashed into that barrier, and a great tumble of rocks and bricks pounded the ground, many bouncing into the hole where the three Aghar huddled. One big stone conked Gus right on the head, knocking him down and leaving him groggy. He came to and found two pairs of hands tugging him, one set on each of his arms.

"*I* help highbulp!" Berta was declaring, pulling Gus to the right. "Go 'way, you bluphsplunging tramp!"

"No! I saw first! *I* help him!" Slooshy challenged, pulling Gus to the left.

With a wrenching tug, the highbulp pulled his hands free, sending both of the females tumbling into the rubble. Groggily, Gus stood, looking around to see what had clobbered him. Smoke swirled thickly, but through that black murk, he could see shimmering patches of liquid, fiery skin, and he caught a glimpse of the cavernous maw of the terrible creature, looming far above, opening to spew a great column of flame, fire so hot that it melted the stones of the palace wall as though they were made of butter.

"Help!" he squawked. "Run! Hide!"

He tried to follow his own advice but found that his limbs still wouldn't respond. Instead, he could only sway, supported by his companions, as he stared up and saw that the fiery monster had smashed a hole right through the wall of the royal palace.

Then, even worse, he saw the black wizard, with his unforgettable stitched, eyeless sockets, flying right toward him. The same wizard who had tried to kill him so long ago. His dread nemesis. A worse nemesis, even, than the dragon.

In that moment of sheer panic, Gus found his strength. He hopped out of the hole and sprinted after the dragon, through the hole in the palace wall—and away from the wizard.

—DH—

"It's the eye of Reorx! Can't you see that?" demanded the king, holding the wedge of red stone over his head, admiring the smooth block with madness gleaming in his eye.

"But . . . but, my liege, how can that be an eye?" Ragat asked, finally unable to mask his alarm at the king's deranged behavior. "It looks like a hammerhead, or perhaps a wedge. But an eye?"

Even as his question lingered in the air, unanswered, Jungor Stonespringer and Ragat Kingsaver heard screams of terror and alarm from within the castle. The general started toward the door but fell hard when the room, the whole palace, was jarred by a powerful shock. Debris rained down upon him as the ceiling collapsed, heavy stones and beams slamming down to block his path. A massive slab of rock bounced just inches from his head.

It felt as though the end of the world were upon them. Fire blossomed through the room, and King Stonespringer screamed, dropping the red stone and throwing his arms over his head. The outer square echoed with screams as smoke clogged Ragat's nose and masked his vision.

"My king! Where are you?" he called out.

"Here!" Stonespringer replied weakly. Ragat crawled to the monarch, found both of his hands, and pulled him to his feet.

"Follow me!" he said, forgetting formality as he tugged his ruler toward the gap that had opened in the wall of the room.

Jungor Stonespringer and General Ragat clawed through the wreckage of the fallen ceiling, emerging onto the palace rampart in time to see a blazing, serpentine image sweep through the air. One infernal wing touched the tower of the king's prayer tower, and it seemed to slice through the stone like a feather. The upper portion of the tower swayed and tumbled, carrying a dozen dwarves to their deaths, while the lower portion stood like a tree stump, an irregular gash marking the place where it had been sliced asunder.

Everywhere in the city, fires burned, and the air thickened with smoke. Hundreds of dwarves coughed and choked, struggling to see. When they did regain their sight, the appearance of the fire dragon was so terrible that most simply turned and fled, dropping their weapons in fright.

"Open the gates!" cried one terrified centurion. "Open the kingdom! Let us flee Thorbardin!"

The cry grew to a swelling chorus as more and more fighters, on both sides of the civil war, gathered around the palace, begging and pleading for the king to allow them to leave.

"Open the North Gate!" wailed many in the crowd. "Let us get out of here!"

"Cowards!" Stonespringer screamed at them from the smoldering wreckage of his medium-high rampart. "Stay and fight! You shall not leave Thorbardin; no one leaves Thorbardin! Stay and do the bidding of your king! Stay, or die!"

But his words had little effect on the frenzied mob. The fire dragon, after searing past the palace, had flown on, plunging into the bedrock that formed the city's wall, moving vaguely in the direction of the Urkhan Sea.

"Your majesty!" The words were repeated, again and again, but so intense was the king's focus that it took him a long time to realize that someone was speaking to him, was even tugging on his robe.

He spun in fury, his good eye flashing as he saw a dwarf recoil in terror. The fellow was wearing the uniform of a general, Jungor saw, but only gradually did he recognize Ragat, the commander of his most elite troops and of the entire castle garrison.

"What do you want?" snarled the monarch.

Ragat, surprisingly enough, stood boldly in the face of his ruler's fury. "You command the troops to fight the monster," he declared. "But you offer them no hope! Our weapons are useless against the fire dragon. Our defenses crumble in its presence. We are brave, O king, but we are not fools. *How* are we to fight that which cannot be fought?"

"Faith!" cried the king, his voice a howl. "Fight with our faith, with the courage of our righteous god!"

His eye flashed again, and his mouth curled into a wicked grin. "The eye of Reorx!" he crowed. "The red stone will give us the means to defeat the monster!"

Ragat could only watch impotently as the monarch hastened back into his quarters on the high palace level. Moments later Stonespringer returned, clutching the wedge of red rock that he called the eye of Reorx. The general watched skeptically as the king strode to the edge of the rampart and held the stone up for all of the teeming, panicked dwarves to see.

"Behold!" the king cried, his voice shrill and cracking. He held up the Redstone. "Behold the eye of Reorx. The Master of the Forge is watching us! He will protect us!

"Witness the power of our god!" he continued shouting. "Here is the talisman of his own self! Here is the means to defeat the fire dragon! Have faith, my people—"

He did not finish, for at that moment the fire dragon returned, dropping right through the ceiling of the vast cavern of Norbardin. Ragat felt the searing heat of the monster's approach and saw blisters rising on the skin of his hands as he held them up in a futile attempt to defend himself.

Then those crushing wings came down, and the fire enveloped him. The high rampart of the palace collapsed, sending the king, the general, and the vaunted Redstone tumbling into the smoldering ruins of the palace's courtyard.

—DH—

Gorathian flew on, a being of pure Chaos. The fire dragon had no goal, no objective, no destination. It exulted in its flight, relished the sweep of destruction, reveled in killing, inflicting pain, and causing terror among the pathetic dwarves.

But it also understood that it had a very powerful enemy. For long years it had languished in the chasm below the wizard's laboratory, imprisoned and taunted by Willim the Black. The mage had exerted powerful controls through his sorcery, occasionally rewarding the fire dragon with morsels of flesh or promises of imminent freedom. Yet always, when Gorathian strained to rise, the wizard's magic had forced it back. A powerful barrier of sorcery had pressed the serpent down, and the bedrock of the cavern—a strata of ore heavily infused with iron—had prevented the creature of Chaos from burrowing to either side, effectively blocking it from any potential path of escape.

Gorathian had been trapped since the Chaos War, when, as one of the great legion of destructive beings, it had roared through Thorbardin, laying waste to cities and lives and everything else in its path. It had dived into the chasm, deep within the mountain, and found itself confined by the heavily metallic rock. By the time Gorathian had twisted around to seek an escape, its fellows, the whole army of Chaos, had been borne away from Krynn by the intervention of the gods.

Only Gorathian remained, sealed away in the depths of the mountain's footings.

But the dwarves, ever industrious, had excavated great blocks of stone away from the fire dragon's prison, carving out the chamber that was to be the new council hall for the ruling thanes. Fortunately, just before Gorathian would have been freed, the dwarves had realized it was the prison of the lethal and destructive beast. They had hastily resealed the chamber and withdrawn, leaving the monster to languish for the rest of eternity.

Then the wizard had come.

Willim the Black had been drawn to the lair in part because of the deadly monster, and he had used spells of powerful sorcery to tantalize the fire dragon, allowing it to sense freedom even as he tamped it down and kept it imprisoned in the deep crevasse.

For that the dragon feared and hated the black wizard, even as it sensed that Willim was the reason the creature had been, at long last, released from its entrapping chasm. As Gorathian felt the containing magic ease, the beast understood that the wizard was relaxing his control and aiming the fire dragon at the dwarf's enemies. Since it had gained flight, it would never, ever, return to that stone-walled prison. Gorathian embraced the release but remained vigilant against the wizard's control.

The dragon flew on, wings spread as it soared higher. The great dwarf nation of Thorbardin beckoned: thousands of lives, all quailing in terror at Gorathian's approach. The fire dragon roared in exultation, fiery breath engulfing a whole block of small houses. The monster sliced through the rock, causing an entire section of Anvil's Echo to collapse, crushing a hundred dwarves under many tons of rubble.

The fire dragon flew and it slew. It roared in the pure joy of destruction. And it knew that, for the first time in countless ages, it was free.

TWENTY-TWO

THE REDSTONE

Shrieking in terror, Gus ran from the eyeless wizard who was flying so swiftly through the air, seemingly straight toward him. The magic-user's black robe flapped around his skinny legs, and he swooped like a bird toward the palace wall, very near to where the three gully dwarves had been cowering. Too many terrifying memories surged through the little gully dwarf's brain, and he was desperate to get away.

Gus well remembered that horrible, eyeless face from his first encounter, a long time—two months, or two years, at least—ago. Gus had been a quivering, terrified captive in a small cage in the laboratory deep underneath Thorbardin. He could still hear the wicked laughter as the black-robed Theiwar had ordered him to drink an obviously lethal potion. The wizard had used a magic spell to compel Gus to drink the potion. It was only good luck that had given the gully dwarf a life-saving option: the magic-user had failed to notice that he had left a second bottle on the table, near the poison, and he failed to tell Gus *which* potion he was supposed to drink.

So the gully dwarf prisoner had drunk the wrong potion and—much to his surprise—had magically teleported himself out of Thorbardin instead of dying a prolonged and agonizing death as the wizard had intended. His lucky escape had gotten even luckier when he had met—and fallen madly in love with—the priestess of Reorx Gretchan Pax. He had shared fascinating adventures with her, strolling along beside her and her mighty dog, Kondike. He saw wonders he had never imagined, went to places he didn't even know existed. In a way, that was why and how he became a highbulp.

As he recalled all of those dizzying events, Gus couldn't really remember why he'd been so eager to get back to Thorbardin. Sure, it was maybe a little more interesting than Pax Tharkas, but it was also a lot more dangerous! It seemed like every time he turned around, the place was finding a new way to try to kill him.

He ducked again as he heard a large crash and spotted the fiery dragon smashing through the high wall of the king's fortress. The wizard, he was relieved to see, flew after the dragon; he had not been pursuing the gully dwarf after all. Still, that was little consolation for Gus as another avalanche of rubble plunged down from the heights, stones smashing and bouncing all around him in a pounding, destructive barrage.

Gus heard shouts of terror and saw two dwarves tumble down with the breaking wall. One was dressed in silver armor; the other wore a robe, and when his face momentarily turned toward the gully dwarf, Gus saw that the other dwarf had a bright golden eye in one of his sockets. The two plunged to the ground and vanished into the cloud of dust, still shouting and cursing.

More flames trailed through the air, sparks falling like rain across the plaza as the dragon flew past again. Gus screamed and ducked, covering his scalp with his arms. He saw Berta crouching nearby and tried to pull her over his head for added protection, but she bopped him on the skull with a fist that was as hard as stone. Feeling miserable, forlorn, and friendless, the Aghar pressed his face downward, burrowing into the pile of rubble that had tumbled from the palace tower. He could still hear the two dwarves who had fallen there, one of them shrieking hysterically, the other trying to calm his frantic companion.

In the darkness of the piled boulders, Gus spotted the gleam of something red on the ground amid all the gray and black stones. It looked vaguely familiar, and when he reached down between two blocks of the fallen wall to pick it up, he recognized it—at least, recognized it as resembling wedges of stone he had seen before.

In that instant the dragon, the wizard, and the chaotic destruction surrounding him were all forgotten.

"Hey!" he cried, sitting back and hoisting the stone, which was smooth and heavy. "This Redstone! Matches Bluestone and Greenstone!"

"So what?" huffed Slooshy, huddled nearby. Still, she looked up, glaring crossly, to study the wedge of rock he held to his chest. "Who care 'bout stupid bluph-splunging rock?"

"My friend do!" Gus retorted. "In Pax Tharkas. Got two stones, blue one and green one. Her want this stone!"

He well remembered Gretchan Pax's delight when the dwarves had produced the two stones, matching them together to make . . . well, something interesting, anyway. He remembered that it was, or at least had *seemed* to be, very important. He also recalled them talking about another stone that was also important, and he guessed—with some uncharacteristically shrewd intuition—that he had just discovered that other stone.

And in that flash of insight, he got another idea.

—DH—

Peat and Sadie, still bound and gagged, had been dumped unceremoniously into a tiny, windowless room. The door slammed behind them, a sturdy lock clicked, and they were stuck in the darkness. Through the uncounted hours since then, Peat had finally managed to work his gag free and began to work on his wife's. After great effort, he had just bitten through the last of the strings tying Sadie's cloth tightly against her mouth.

And he was already regretting the accomplishment.

"Why did you have to be so damned greedy?" she hissed at him quietly, apparently still concerned about not attracting the attention of the guards they could hear pacing back and forth in the outer hall.

"Me?" he whispered back indignantly. "I wanted to get out of Thorbardin a week ago!"

"Don't lie to me!" she spat, her voice cracking as it grew louder in spite of herself. "Why, if I could only—"

The rest of her threat was drowned in a chaotic explosion of sound coming from beyond their cell. They heard stones crashing to the ground and felt the vibrations of massive destruction. An eerie red glow flared in the corridor beyond the dungeon door, and they heard guards screaming in terror. The voice of one quickly faded into the distance as he fled, while the other's cries, right outside the door, grew weaker and weaker.

Another violent convulsion shook the palace,

knocking stones loose from the ceiling. A large beam snapped, swinging perilously close to Peat's head and smashing into the side of the cell near the door. Peat cursed as a rock struck a glancing blow against his shoulder. He tried to roll away, to shelter under the narrow bunk along the wall, but there was too much rubble for him to move. They were surrounded by heat, a radiance so intense that Peat could only imagine they had been tossed into some kind of oven.

He was surprised to see that Sadie was sitting up. Somehow she had wriggled her hands free of the bonds, and was using them to pull the coils of rope off of her arms. Once she was done, she knelt beside her husband and worked on his ropes with her stiff, arthritic fingers. After a second she gave up, pointed one of those fingers, and snapped out a word of magic.

Peat yelped as the magic missile shot past his skin, ricocheting from the floor into the wall, trailing sparks. He was about to shout his objections when he noticed that the spell, in addition to burning him, had ripped through the ropes that had been binding his hands together.

"Um, thanks," he said, blinking in astonishment before looking blurrily around.

He noticed the red glow still brightening the corridor behind the dungeon, but only when Sadie started toward that firelight did he realize he was seeing a lot more illumination than he should have been able to observe through the narrow dungeon window.

"The door's gone!" he exclaimed.

Sadie shot him an exasperated look as she passed through that empty doorway with Peat hastening after her. They saw one of the guards, a stout Hylar warrior, gesturing weakly to them from the floor. He was pinned under a large flat rock; the weight of that stone was obviously crushing the life from him.

The two Theiwar wasted no time on mercy, however, instead hobbling away from the dungeon cell as fast as their bony legs could carry them. The room beyond was full of smoke, the floor coated with rubble. It had been staffed by a dozen guards when they had been brought to their cell; it was empty when they entered again. They started up the stairs toward the palace's main floor, pushing small stones out of the way and scrambling over the rocks that were too large to move.

A minute later they had reached the top of the long stairway and found, once again, that a stout door had been torn from its hinges. And not just the door: when they stepped into the great hall, they saw that half of one wall was simply gone, smashed away by some unspeakable force, leaving an outline of smoking blocks, charred timbers, and dangling arches. There were dwarves in the great hall, covered with soot, all of them looking dazed and shocked. Some helped others who had been buried in the collapse, while many simply fled toward the doorways or leaped out through the hole that had been knocked in the wall. No one seemed to pay any attention to the two elderly Theiwar hobbling up from the dungeons.

"Come on!" Sadie urged, gesturing as her nearsighted husband hesitated. He couldn't see any place that looked safer than any place else, so he simply followed her, trusting her better eyes—and sharp instincts—to lead him to safety.

The old crone clawed her way up a sloping rock to the edge of the gap that had been torn in the wall. Peat scrambled up behind her, just in time to see her slip through that opening and tumble onto the stones of the courtyard beyond. Wincing, he tumbled after, landing hard on an irregular chunk and knocking the breath from his lungs.

Wheezing, he slowly drew a painful breath, forcing himself to hands and knees and, gradually, to his feet. He was moderately surprised to see that his wife, hands on her hips, was still standing nearby, waiting for him.

Together the two Guilders made their way across the smoking, rubble-strewn courtyard. They heard dwarves shouting in terror and pain, saw soldiers and citizens alike running this way and that, and once Peat even caught a glimpse of a burning shape gliding overhead, like a massive, soaring fireball with flaming wings. His knees turned to jelly and he almost fell, but when Sadie determinedly kept plodding ahead, he put down his head and followed her.

"What's going on?" he asked plaintively, catching up to her and trying unsuccessfully to reach her hand or to catch the hem of her robe.

Whether or not she heard his question, Sadie didn't deign to answer. Instead, she continued to press forward, finally reaching back to grasp his hand when Peat staggered and hesitated at a particularly broken stretch of ground.

If any palace guards were present, they apparently had more pressing matters to concern them than the escape of two elderly prisoners. In any event, no one even spoke to the pair as they dodged around the larger piles of debris and crawled through the holes and trenches that seemed strategically placed to block their path. The palace wall loomed here and there, but in many places deep notches cut into that barrier, some extending all the way to the ground.

Soon they were across the courtyard and out of the palace, using one of the gaps in the outer wall to make good their escape. The great square of Norbardin was obscured by smoke, apparently coming from dozens of individual fires, but they knew where they were going.

Still, they had to skirt many obstacles: a spear-lined battlement stretched across their path, manned by only the dead, but they had to climb over the treacherous debris. Beyond, more debris smoldered as the wreckage from the shattered shops and stalls continued to burn. It took them a half an hour to make their way to First Street. Once they were there, however, they found the path clear of rubble, the few dwarves on the streets all scurrying, like them, away from the plaza. The two Guilders skulked down the road, ducking behind the piles of rubble whenever they came upon a detachment of soldiers. Both the rebel and royal troops had abandoned any pretense of making war and had started simply to loot and plunder.

They halted for a moment, warily watching Abercrumb's shop, which was dark with no sign of the occupant. "I'd like to go in there and feed that weasel a few spells!" Sadie muttered.

"No!" Peat said in panic. "There's no time! Come on!"

A few minutes later, gasping for breath and trembling in fear, they reached the door of the Two Guilders Emporium. They were relieved to find that the shop had been spared by looters—no doubt because of the fear of curses and magical traps. Sadie touched the locked door and uttered a word of magic, and a second later, the pair of Theiwar tumbled through the door, slamming it behind themselves and still shaking in fright.

"You watch for trouble," Sadie said when her breathing had settled down slightly. "I'll go and start casting the spell."

"Hurry!" Peat said, holding his palms against the door as if he intended to stop an army with a battering ram.

"I'll work as fast as I can," Sadie snapped as she disappeared into the back room.

—DH—

"There's the king!" Willim the Black crowed in elation, watching as the fire dragon swept toward the monarch atop the palace wall. He flew quickly, soaring fifty feet above the plaza and weaving around the pillars of thick smoke. As an added bonus, Ragat Kingsaver stood behind the monarch, and the wizard allowed himself a thrill of hope: both of his enemies could be struck down at the very same time!

Only then did he turn and look around for Facet, surprised to see that she was some distance behind him. The spell of flying allowed him to hover, so he waited in the air, watching her as she swept closer. He rejoiced at the sight of her black hair whipping in the wind, and at the light of passion and excitement in her eyes when she swept up to her master and swirled through a little pirouette that brought her right to his side.

"Come, pretty one," Willim said. He pointed at the tower, watching as the fire dragon swept past the rampart and brought a cascade of debris showering into the courtyard. "There is our enemy!"

The black wizard swooped down, ignoring the fire dragon, the dwarves of the two armies fleeing in panic across the great square, and the smoking destruction already wreathing the great city. His spell of trueseeing allowed him to scry through the murk, identifying his target in the tangle of debris.

He found Jungor Stonespringer groping around among the stones at the base of his palace wall. General Ragat, silver shield slung over his shoulder, was trying to get the king to flee to safety, but the monarch seemed intent on searching for something in the rubble. The king pushed himself up to his hands and knees, clawing and digging through the mess of broken rock.

The nature of his quest became apparent as the two wizards swooped in.

"The eye of Reorx!" King Stonespringer screeched. "I must find it!"

Willim settled onto the crest of a large rock, standing firmly and looming over the frantic king, who was still rooting around in the rubble and stones below. Facet alighted beside the wizard, and his heart thrilled to her touch as she wrapped both of her arms around one of his. Her breasts felt soft against him, and the sensation made his blood pulse with vitality and heat.

"Perhaps you seek an eye to replace the one you have lost?" sneered the wizard, addressing the king.

Jungor Stonespringer didn't even look up or react. Instead, he dropped flat on his belly and clawed at a large stone. "Help me!" he called to Ragat.

The general, however, did look up, ignoring the king's command. He stared coldly at the wizard, holding his shield before his chest.

"Will you kill him now, Master?" Facet asked breathlessly, licking her crimson lips.

Willim smiled tightly. "I haven't decided yet, my pet."

Only then did the one-eyed king take note of his enemy and glance up from the pile of rocks. Still kneeling, he shook a fist at the wizard then gestured wildly with both hands.

"Look what you have wrought!" he cried. "This destruction! You bring ruin to all Thorbardin! And for what?"

"I bring ruin to you and your reign," the wizard retorted. "It is you yourself who have done so much to destroy this proud nation."

"Kill me if you dare! Reorx will have his vengeance!" declared the king, stumbling to his feet. In a dramatic gesture, he tore his robe away, baring his chest to his enemy's attack.

"Death shall be your reward. But it will not come quickly," the wizard declared.

He raised his finger, pointing at the king's single good eye. He grinned, a cruel grimace of triumph, and fired a carefully aimed magic missile. The blast of searing magic tore into Jungor Stonespringer's face, and the king tumbled back to the ground, screaming, hands clasped to the gory wound.

"Now they match!" Facet declared, laughing wildly and squeezing Willim's arm even more tightly. "A blind king and his fool!"

General Ragat didn't so much as blink. He stared defiantly and with hatred at Willim.

"How pathetic you look, grubbing around in the stones," the black wizard said to the king. "And to think you once fancied yourself a ruler of dwarves!"

"You may destroy!" Jungor cried, gasping out the words despite his great pain. "You may bring ruin and death. But your army is doomed. You shall never win this war. I see the truth of your being. I have your spies in my dungeon!"

Willim blinked and scowled. "Enough prattle," he snapped. His voice dropped menacingly. "It's a shame, in a way, that you won't see this next spell coming, for it will be your death," Willim said calmly. Again he pointed his finger, growling out the deep sound of his most lethal dark magic spell.

But he had paid too little attention to the general, crouching near his king and watching the wizard with narrowed, calculating eyes. Willim chanted the guttural sounds of the lethal spell, feeling the killing magic well within, pulsing through his blood, yearning for release. He spit the last word, a sound of death and triumph, yet just as Willim finished casting the spell, Ragat leaped forward, the Kingsaver Shield in his hand.

The general sprang to the ground before the blinded, hysterical king, holding his shield at the ready. The death spell tore into the shield, rending the metal disk, shattering it and driving Ragat back to the ground. The enchanted barrier split down the middle, the two halves falling away as the searing blast of the spell tore into the general's breast.

But the Kingsaver Shield, one last time, performed its duty. As the lethal spell ripped through Ragat's flesh, a ricochet of magic surrounded the king, momentarily outlining him in golden light. Perhaps it was the power of the god or maybe the enchanted shield, which had been cast to protect the life of Jungor Stonespringer; either or both of those summoned one more miracle at the moment of the shield's final destruction.

The explosive light snuffed out, and the king was gone.

"Where did he go?" shouted Willim, stepping forward and looming over the gashed, bleeding general. Ragat merely looked up and laughed, coughing blood from his mouth and his nose.

The wizard leaned close, trembling in rage. He took the dying dwarf by his throat, cruel fingers tightening.

Ragat laughed again, knowing he was beyond hurt.

"What did he mean, he has my spies?" demanded Willim, twisting his grip on the general's throat. More blood spilled from his mouth, but Ragat somehow managed a bubbling laugh.

"Two Theiwar . . . the Guilders," the general croaked out. "They betrayed you!" he gloated before his eyes closed and he died.

TWENTY-THREE

A DWARF'S BEST FRIEND

"I need to find out where they're keeping Father," Brandon declared, pounding his fist into his palm. "The king was lying; that much is for sure."

"Yes, certainly," his mother agreed, wringing her hands.

"How can you find out?" Gretchan asked.

The three of them were sitting in the kitchen of Brandon's home, discussing what they had learned and what they needed to do.

"What can you tell me about the League of Enforcers' headquarters?" he asked his mother.

"There are guards at the front door, of course. When I was taken there by a pair of Enforcers, the guards didn't ask questions; they just opened the door as my captors marched up with me." She went on to describe a ward room in the front of the building with multiple corridors leading deeper into the complex. "They took me through the first door to the left. There were a number of rooms down there, and your father was in one of them with Baracan Heelspur. The corridor turned deeper into the headquarters after that, and from the look of the heavy door down there, that's where the dungeon cells are likely to be."

"But you can't just go charging in there," Gretchan warned.

"No, of course not. I need to make a plan. But I do think it's likely that's where they're keeping him."

"All right, that's a start," the priestess agreed. "We know where he probably is, but you have to be careful. This is not the time to get yourself in trouble with Regar Smashfingers. Meanwhile we've got people all over the city who are telling the truth about Regar and the horax—and what happened to your brother and your father. You need to stay above the fray while the word continues to spread. I'll keep moving around, meeting people, get people thinking. We're already making progress."

"All right, good."

Brandon had told the women about his meeting with General Watchler and the Garnet Guards. They had taken comfort from the fact that there were other influential citizens in Kayolin who viewed Regar Smashfingers suspiciously. Though events were moving too slowly for Brandon, he had to admit that at least they were moving.

Gretchan had spent the past two days walking around Garnet Thax, mingling with dwarves in the inns and public places of the city, chatting with them, helping to spread the story of the Horax Hero. She had explained to anyone who would listen that she was collecting notes for a comprehensive history of the dwarves, and that it was the first time she had visited the great city, known as the jewel in Kayolin's crown.

Because of the infamous horax attack, the people were shaken and much concerned with the campaign being waged by the king's troops against the bug monsters. She added to those concerns by mentioning, at every opportunity, the fact that the stone barricades that had long protected Kayolin from the horax had been mysteriously destroyed, and that the Garnet Guards—the city's traditional first line of defense—had been disbanded upon Smashfingers's orders. She let her listeners reach their own conclusions, and public opinion was growing in support of the notion that the king had ordered the destruction to heighten the sense of emergency and justify his imminent coronation.

Some people had mentioned the Bluestone Faction to her, asking about the alleged conspiracy, wondering if there really was a movement afoot that would cause Regar Smashfingers some discomfort. She did nothing to disabuse them of that notion.

The cleric also did what she could to plant doubts about the authenticity of the Torc of the Forge that Smashfingers claimed to have found. It turned out no one had given the matter much thought, but that issue, too, began to percolate through the restive population. The fact that the ruler had not publicly displayed the torc further aroused suspicions.

At the same time, Karine, Bondall, and the other dwarves who had met at the Cracked Mug were speaking to their friends and acquaintances, talking about what they'd learned about the legacy of their people south of the Newsea. Many people were not aware that the kingship claimed by Regar was a relatively new concept to Kayolin.

Soon "The throne is in Thorbardin" was being whispered through all the streets of Garnet Thax and became a whispered greeting on all levels of the great city of Kayolin.

And thus the Bluestone Faction was born and grew.

—DH—

Regar Smashfingers sat upon his small throne, the seat in his private council chambers, and glowered at his chief ally and supporter. "I saw another one of those slogans marked on the wall, right outside the palace gate! Who is writing them?" he demanded testily. "Surely your agents can spot these miscreants in action?"

"Begging your majesty's pardon," Lord Alakar Heelspur said. "But the perpetrators are devilishly clever. The phrases are clearly seditious, but the dwarves who write them are careful not to be discovered."

His son, Baracan, stood behind him, listening silently.

The king snorted. "First it was 'Our Throne is in Thorbardin!' " he quoted. "Now they're writing 'Who killed Nailer?' Clearly it's the work of the Bluestone Faction!"

"That would seem logical, sire," replied the lord with a deep bow. "We've had the son and the wife watched carefully and discreetly. It's quite clear they're not the ones writing the slogans all over the city. But we haven't been able to find out who *is* doing it."

"You overreached with the Nailer Bluestone affair," the ruler declared bluntly. "You were too greedy!"

"Sire, I must remind you that the vein of gold discovered by the Bluestone brothers was the wealthiest find in recent memory. If they had retained control of that wealth, you would have found one of your staunchest foes among the city's powerful merchant clans."

"Perhaps they would not be my staunch enemies if their son had not been murdered by your own family," Regar declared sternly.

Heelspur waved away the objection with a look of irritation. "Why do you insist on rehashing old arguments? Simply know that the Bluestones are now your most dangerous enemy."

Smashfingers hunched in his seat, glowering, and did not reply.

Lord Heelspur glanced up slyly. "You do recall we have the patriarch of the Bluestone clan prisoner in the royal dungeon?"

"Yes, yes. I haven't made up my mind what to do about him," snapped the king.

"May I suggest . . . perhaps you do not need to do anything," the lord said. "Perhaps the prisoner could try to escape . . . there might be an accident. A fatal accident?"

"I don't like the sound of that!" Regar said. Still, he stroked his beard, eyes narrowed in thought. "What would be the point?"

Only then did the king notice the female, a dwarf maid wearing a shimmering gown with a jeweled necklace around her neck. She stood just to the side of and behind Baracan Heelspur.

"Who are you?" Smashfingers demanded, startled.

"Ah, forgive me, Majesty," said Lord Heelspur. "I invited my son here with his betrothed. This is Rona Darkwater, of House Darkwater. I had hoped you would do us the honor of announcing their engagement to the rest of the city."

"Ah, of course," said the beaming king, all too willing to set aside the previous disagreeable discussion. The Darkwaters were one of the wealthiest and most influential clans in the city, and a marriage alliance between them and the Heelspurs would only help to solidify Regar Smashfingers's hold upon the throne. "Please, my dear. Come forward. Tell me, when may we look forward to the happy event?"

—DH—

Peat had been too grateful for his and Sadie's miraculous escape to think much about the strange events that were transpiring in the kingdom. The more he thought about it, however, the more worried he became. Fire raging in the stone-walled palace! Destruction raining down upon the city! What was going on? And more important, would it prevent the two Guilders from making their escape from Thorbardin?

While Sadie busied herself in the back of the shop, finishing the last markings on the scroll that would allow the two of them to escape Thorbardin once and for all, Peat went to the front door of the shop and cracked it open. He could still see the glow of massive fires burning in the great plaza, which began a quarter mile down the street. Screams and cries, more sporadic than when they had escaped from the palace, still rang out. Several dwarves, gasping and out of breath, came running down the road from that direction.

"What is it?" demanded the shopkeeper, accosting a terrified Theiwar whose beard and hair had been badly singed. "What's going on?"

"A fire dragon!" the man gasped. "It's like the Chaos War is starting all over again! It burst up from the ground, burning a tunnel right up through the rock. It flew through Norbardin and then returned to the square. Now it's attacking the king's palace again."

Feeling sick to his stomach, Peat released the dwarf's arm and let him resume his escape. The Chaos War! He and Sadie had been much younger during that awful time, just starting out in business, in fact, tending a small shop in Theibardin, right on the shore of the Urkhan Sea. Already they had started to prosper with a loyal and steadily growing group of customers when the creatures of Chaos had exploded into the kingdom of Thorbardin. Peat well remembered the shadow wights sweeping across whole neighborhoods, wiping out not just the residents, but any memories of those dwarves in the minds of the survivors. He had seen the powerful daemon warrior, striding like an avenging giant, smiting buildings, boats, and dwarf soldiers with his crushing fists.

But worst of all had been the fire dragons. Driven purely by rage and the lust to destroy, they had flown through the city, gouging tunnels in the rock that seemed no more substantial than smoke to their flaming advance. It was the fire dragons that had destroyed the great cities of Thorbardin, carving away at the supporting bedrock, gouging through palaces, manors, and slums with equal callousness. When the forces of Chaos had finally withdrawn—they had not been defeated by dwarves, but rather compelled to depart because of factors in the greater war between the gods—they had left Theibardin and the other great cities of the underground nation so badly damaged that the surviving population had migrated, excavating the new city of Norbardin, to begin life anew.

And he watched as that new city was being terrorized by the same menace. Peat could hardly bear the fear, the anguish, that threatened to overwhelm him. He was quaking and on the verge of tears as he closed the door, feeling a fresh sense of urgency. Hastening into the back room, he saw that Sadie was still scratching symbols on the scroll.

"Hurry!" he whispered, knowing she wouldn't be able to hear him. He had to do something to occupy his mind, so Peat went to the strongbox wherein the two Guilders had stored their treasures, the vast wealth they had amassed from those dwarves who had used the dimension door to escape Thorbardin. He was so nervous, he fumbled with the lock twice before he finally inserted the tiny key and pulled it open.

He found a bag of holding on a nearby shelf and carried it back to the chest. With one trembling hand, he scooped out diamonds, rubies, platinum coins, emeralds, and all the other trinkets they had collected. The treasures tumbled into the sack, ten or twenty pounds worth of them. But because of the enchantment on the bag of holding, the little sack weighed only a few ounces and took up only the space of a small belt purse.

"Where are we going to go?" he asked Sadie.

So intent was her concentration—and her deafness—that he had to repeat the question three times, each more loudly than the last, before she answered.

"The same place as I was going to send that last dwarf," she finally replied. "Kayolin. I don't want to take the time to work out a new destination." She gestured to the empty strongbox. "And now, at least, we'll have enough wealth to be comfortable."

"Hurry!" he pressed.

"Well, if you wouldn't keep chattering . . ." she replied ominously.

Finally she jotted down the last symbol and capped the ink bottle. "Do you have everything?" she demanded.

"I'm ready to cast the spell."

"Yes, right here," he said, holding up the bag. "This should be all we need."

She nodded curtly and turned toward the lone blank spot on the shelf-lined walls. Reading carefully, she chanted the words to the powerful spell. Peat watched anxiously, almost fearing to breathe, as the enchantment slowly took form.

First the blue circle began to glow on the wall. Gradually, the hole in the middle of the circle—the dark wormhole that was the actual pathway of the spell—took shape. With each word, more of the scroll on the desk before her burned away until there remained nothing but ashes.

Finally Sadie finished, sighing with exhaustion, but quickly pushing back her stool and standing up. The blue circle glowed firmly, the dark tunnel of the magical passage beckoning to them, promising escape, freedom, riches—and safety.

Peat finally began to relax. He wondered about Kayolin. One thing he knew was that it lay hundreds of miles away from their shop, far to the north. It seemed highly unlikely that the king of Thorbardin, or their wizardly Master, would be able to track them down there. And they would be fabulously wealthy; they would have every comfort that their nearly bottomless hoard of treasure would be able to purchase.

Sadie looked at her husband and started to speak. "Time to—"

She halted with an audible gasp. Peat blinked, perceiving that she was looking at something beyond him, just over his shoulder.

In a panic, the elderly Theiwar turned around, eyes bulging as he spotted a black-robed figure that had silently, suddenly, come through the door into the back room of the two Guilders' shop.

In that same instant, Peat recognized their master.

It was the wizard Willim the Black, standing there calmly, his scarred, eyeless face expressionless as he gestured toward the blue circle on the wall. Finally, a small smile parted his beard and creased his ghastly lips.

"Going somewhere?" asked the most powerful magic-user in all Thorbardin.

—DH—

"I wanna go Pax Tharkas!" Slooshy whined as soon as the three gully dwarves made their way through the palace wall and back into the tangled, debris-filled cover of the plaza. "No big mess there alla time!" She had no firsthand experience with the city, but she imagined it from what Berta had said to her.

"Yep, Pax Tharkas *nice* place!" Berta retorted. "Not like stoopie burnrock Thorbardin, alla time hot and hungry!"

"Girls be quiet!" snapped Gus. "Highbulp gotta think!"

Gus reflected. Berta and Slooshy had a point. Pax Tharkas was a rather nice place, especially compared to the terrible mess that Thorbardin seemed to be in. It was reasonably safe and very quiet. Sure, it was small and didn't have a lake. But what was so great about the lake, anyway?

Then there was the other thing, he abruptly remembered, as he almost stumbled because of the heavy red rock he was carrying. That rock matched the blue and green rocks in Pax Tharkas. Gus could take the red one there and make the king pretty happy. A happy king meant, at the very least, some good food for Gus. Suddenly he wanted to go back there very much.

And just as suddenly, he knew how to do that!

"Come on!" he said. "Girls follow highbulp, plenty fast!"

"Hey! You no highbulp!" Berta reminded him.

"Yeah! No boss me neither!" Slooshy declared.

"Stay, then, bluphsplunging wenches!" he shouted, startling them both. "Gus go Pax Tharkas by himself!"

Carrying the Redstone, he started running from the plaza, back toward the street where they had arrived in Norbardin.

"Hey! Wait for me!" Berta called.

"You no go so fast!" Slooshy objected. Two sets of feet pounded behind him, and he felt surprisingly happy that they were coming along with him. Sure, they could be disobedient and argumentative pests, but all in all, he was glad to have their company.

Finding the right street was not easy in the midst of all the chaos and destruction that had marred so much of the city, but he finally picked it out and started down the way, leaving the dragon-wracked plaza behind. After running for two minutes, he guessed he was getting close and slowed down. He paused, thinking and looking around, and he finally recognized the shop where he and Berta had arrived there via the magic blue hole in the wall. It looked different because the front door was standing wide open.

He darted through the open doorway with the two females in close pursuit. He strode through the shop, barely noticing the wreckage of tables and shelves. The back door was closed, but it opened when he turned the latch.

Immediately he saw what he was searching for: the blue magic door, swirling on the wall. The same two old

Theiwar were there also, but fortunately their backs were turned away from him; he well remembered the old crone's skillful aim when she was shooting her magic missiles at him. Then he froze to notice there was a third person in the room—the eyeless wizard!

Panic nearly choked Gus, and he wanted to run away. But then he saw that the frightening figure was glaring at the elderly Theiwar, and the two of them looked so terrified at the wizard's presence that they didn't even notice the gully dwarves creeping into their back room. The opportunity was there, and Gus wasted no time.

"This way!" he whispered as best he could, leading his girlfriends in a sudden forward rush.

But the old Theiwar crone must have heard him; her eyes turned toward him, and she opened her mouth to scream, which was when the wizard slapped her before the scream could come out. And the wizard didn't even turn around or glance over his shoulder.

Gus reacted instinctively, breaking into a sprint. He dived through the blue door as her scream echoed after him. Gus tumbled onto a hard stone surface and looked up to see, with relief, that Berta and Slooshy had followed him through, sprawling beside him on the other side of the magic door.

Even as he watched, the blue circle shimmered and faded and disappeared.

—DH—

Kondike paced down a quiet street in Garnet Thax. The dog had been roaming through the dwarf city for a long time, and though he'd never forgotten his mistress, nor his new master, he had not been able to locate any scent of them. He'd drawn significant attention from the city's dwarves, most of whom had never seen a dog anywhere near his size, and thus, considered him a wild and dangerous animal. After a few unpleasant encounters, such as being hit by clubs and rocks and narrowly avoiding a hurled spear, the dog had learned to stick to the less inhabited byways of the vast, labyrinthine city.

For the first few days of his wanderings, he had gone back to the house where Gretchan had taken him when they first arrived in the city. But there had been no sign of her there, and the crowded streets of that neighborhood had been too dangerous for the dog to find a safe hiding place. So he had wandered off and not gone back there for quite a few days.

He was prowling the alley behind a flourishing food market. He'd had success stealing cheese and even some cuts of meat from several of the vendors, and his gnawing, empty belly had compelled him to go back there. But the food-sellers seemed to be watching for him, and he was met with a barrage of well-aimed stones, missiles that bruised his flesh and forced him to flee back into the shadows.

He whimpered quietly and limped into a shadowy alcove where he had found some discarded burlap to serve as a slightly-softer-than-stone bed. He lapped up some stagnant water from a pool in the floor. His stomach growled, but there was nothing to be done about that at the moment.

Instead, he lay down and went to sleep.

Abruptly he started awake, sniffed, and raised his head. A deep growl emanated from his chest as he stood, ears upraised, looking around. He couldn't see anyone and didn't smell anything. But some unknown sense prickled his awareness. The alley was empty; there was nobody in the alcove with him. Yet he felt certain that someone was approaching.

The dog's attention was drawn to the nearby wall. He growled more loudly, staring, as the stone surface began to shimmer. In another second he saw a raggedy-dressed gully dwarf there, stepping right out of the shimmering place on the wall. The big dog barked, startling the gully dwarf, who yelped and leaped to the side. Then a second and a third gully dwarf materialized, tumbling through to sprawl onto the floor, startling the dog so much that he jumped backward, barking again.

Kondike barked once more, but something in the little dwarf's scent was vaguely familiar. He wagged his tail tentatively.

The little dwarf, whose nose was bleeding from the impact of the fall, looked up and grinned.

"Kondike?" he said cheerfully. "Is that you?"

TWENTY-FOUR

MURDER THWARTED, TRAP SPRUNG

Brandon awakened with a start, instinctively reaching for his axe before he realized it was his mother who had nudged his shoulder and was urgently speaking to him.

"I'm awake," he said, sitting up in bed and shaking his head to clear the cobwebs. "What is it?"

"Rona Darkwater is here, and she says she needs to speak to you right away!"

"Rona Darkwater?" asked Brandon, quickly rising and donning a light tunic. "What does she want?"

"Ask her yourself," came the reply over her shoulder as Karine bustled back to the front room.

Brandon followed after his mother quickly and nodded politely to the glamorous dwarf maid who was sitting in the lamp-lit chamber. He noted that Gretchan wasn't there; she was probably still whispering her way through the city's neighborhoods, reminding people that "the throne is in Thorbardin."

"Hi, Rona," he said. "To what do I owe the pleasure?"

Only then did he notice that Rona's face was drawn and taut, and she glanced nervously at the door as if half afraid they'd be interrupted. Karine brought her a mug of steaming tea, and the young female clutched it as though it were the nectar of life itself.

"It—it's your father," she said abruptly. "I've just come from the palace. I overheard the king—the governor—order Lord Heelspur to have him executed! They plan to make it look like an accident, to claim he was trying to escape!"

Karine gasped, and Brandon's fists clenched involuntarily. "Do you know when he plans to do this?" he growled.

She shook her head and blinked her tear-filled eyes. "No. But I'm afraid it will be very soon!"

Brandon crossed to her and knelt at her side, taking her hands. "Thanks, Rona. You took a great risk coming here; it means a lot to me."

She smiled wanly and squeezed his fingers. "I had to do it," she said. "You know, for old time's sake. And because the whole League of Enforcers business, the way they are bullying all of Kayolin, it's just wrong."

"Maybe it won't be that way much longer," Brandon said grimly. "Thanks to you, we have a chance to stop them. Damn Heelspur!"

"I know," Rona said with a shudder. "I've spent too much time with Baracan already. He scares me!"

"I'm just grateful you were there—and that you came here," Brandon said sincerely.

With that, she kissed him on the cheek, pulled a hooded cloak over her head, and vanished through the front door, leaving the portal open just as Gretchan was coming in.

"Who was that?" asked the priestess, watching the cloaked noblewoman hurry up the street.

"An old friend—Rona Darkwater," Brandon replied.

"Oh, yes, she was at our meeting at the Mug. She had some good information about the Heelspurs and the League of Enforcers," Gretchan said. She suddenly seemed to sense the somber mood in the room. "Well, what did she have to say?"

"They're even more ruthless than I thought," Brandon replied curtly. He was already shucking his leather outer shirt over his shoulders and picking up his axe. "My mother will explain things; I have to go out for a while. There's something I have to do."

"Wait!" Gretchan declared. She nodded at his weapon. "Is this about your father?" she asked shrewdly.

"Yes!" he replied curtly.

"All right. I know you have to go," the cleric said, "but just talk to me for a minute first. All right?"

In a rush, Brandon told her the news that Rona Darkwater had brought to him. "I have to go look for him, find him—try to stop this!" he said desperately.

"I know," the cleric said calmly. "You have to. But listen to me for just another few minutes. I think I can help you."

—DH—

"So, Kondike," Gus said, leaning contentedly against the wall and stretching his feet. He scratched the big dog's head and sighed with satisfaction. Ever since the blue magic circle had disappeared from the wall, he'd felt relaxed and confident again. After all, he was back in his own domain, Pax Tharkas, where—whether Berta liked it or not—he was highbulp.

Or *was* it Pax Tharkas? He looked around and scratched his round-topped head, surprised he had never seen that part of the fortress before. Pax Tharkas was a big place, but it wasn't *that* big. In fact, he was looking at a tangled maze of streets and alleys, more like a city in Thorbardin than the interior of the fortress of Pax Tharkas. He had never seen anything remotely like that neighborhood in all his time in Berta's home.

Berta and Slooshy had gone off to explore, while he sat there with the dog who, after all, had been the first creature he had met after his initial escape from Thorbardin.

"Hey," he said to Kondike, suddenly remembering something. "You went away from Pax Tharkas! With Gretchan!" Indeed, the departure of his beloved priestess from Pax Tharkas had left a distinct void in the little Aghar's life. Though, living in the sewers and dungeons as he and his fellow gully dwarves had done, he hadn't seen a lot of her. But she had come down to visit him every now and then, and he had missed her after she left. "When you come back here to Pax Tharkas?" he asked, wishing the dog could do more than look at him and pant with that long pink tongue hanging out.

"Psst! Hey, Gus! Look here!"

It was Berta, jogging back into the little alcove with Slooshy following close behind. "Not now," he barked. "Me talkin' to Kondike!"

"You come look!" she insisted. "Now!"

Groaning at the heavy burden of responsibility, reflecting that the illustrious role of highbulp wasn't all just foot rubs and free food, Gus pushed himself to his feet. "What now?" he demanded. "Me and Kondike just restin' . . . nice."

"Come see!" she insisted again, and he plodded along behind, knowing she'd never stop pestering him until he did as she asked. Slooshy, too, was all agog, and took his hand to pull him forcefully along.

They led him down a street, fortunately deserted, and around a corner, pointing triumphantly before them. Gus could only gape as he found himself standing on a balcony at the edge of a deep, wide shaft. He looked down and swayed dizzily, discerning only a vague, reddish glow very, very far below. He leaned back to peer upward and saw that the big space extended above them as far as he could see.

"Hey?" he asked. "Where in Pax Tharkas are we?"

"Not Pax Tharkas at all!" Berta declared, triumphantly crossing her arms over her skinny chest. "We go somewhere new!"

Gus could only gawk in awe, trying to absorb the astonishing idea. He had to admit it seemed like Berta was right. He looked from Berta to Slooshy to Kondike. All three stared blankly at him, and he pulled at his hair, wondering what to do.

"We come through blue hole," he argued. "Blue hole go Thorbardin, from Pax Tharkas. Blue hole go Pax Tharkas, from Thorbardin!"

"New blue hole go somewhere new!" Berta insisted.

It was the dog who spoke next, woofing curiously and tilting his head to the side as he looked at the frustrated gully dwarf. It was that soft bark that gave him the idea.

"Hey!" he said. "Maybe you come this place with Gretchan! Where Gretchan? You take us her?"

Kondike's ears pricked up at the familiar name. He looked around as if he expected to see the cleric standing right behind Gus, though, of course, she wasn't there. But the name had clearly triggered something deep inside Kondike, for with another woof, the dog took off at a trot, moving easily down the street of the new dwarf city. The three gully dwarves, running as fast as their stubby legs could carry them, followed him, trying to keep up. Gus held the Redstone in both hands, his feet slapping against the stones as he jogged along. Somewhere up ahead, he was almost certain, he would find Gretchan.

She would know the answers to his questions—questions that were piling up so heavily that his head was starting to hurt.

—DH—

Meanwhile Willim the Black faced the two terrified Theiwar, his once and disgraced spies.

"Where did you get the scroll that allowed you to cast a dimension door?" Willim the Black said, casually pulling out a spare stool and sitting down very, very close to Sadie and Peat, peering at them with intimidation clear on his eyeless face.

Sadie looked at Peat, who could only shrug helplessly.

"Perhaps you stole it from your master," the black wizard suggested. "From he who established you in your store here in Norbardin, who cared for you and trained you, provided for your needs . . . all the while asking for so little in return."

"Please, Master . . ." Sadie's voice was a croaking whisper.

"Silence!" barked Willim the Black. He snapped his fingers, and even though Sadie's nearly toothless mouth continued to flex, no sound came from her. Peat yelped, or tried to yelp, but his own voice was also swallowed within the cloak of the wizard's muzzling spell.

"Ah, that's better," said Willim, leaning back and propping his feet on one of the workbenches. "It's so much better when one doesn't have to listen to lies. Especially the lies of formerly trusted, lowly underlings.

I'm sure you'd agree, wouldn't you? That is, if I allowed either of you to talk."

The wizard made a show of emitting an elaborate sigh. Leaning back his head, he called out. "Facet, my dear. Won't you come in here now?"

The two Guilders stared in apprehension as the shapely young magic-user, her black robe swirling easily as she moved with uncanny grace, strolled through the door into the back room of the shop. "Tell me, has there been any change in the plaza?" Willim asked.

"No, Master," she replied. "The fire dragon seems to have departed. I have not been able to learn anything about the whereabouts of the king."

"No matter, that," the wizard replied with a shrug. "He is blinded now, and I don't believe his god will bless him with the gift of sight—not in the way my magic does. I will find him in good time. But first, there is this little matter to attend."

He gestured to the pair of elderly Theiwar, who were gawking at him with slack jaws, faces gone white with terror. "Do you know?" Willim said casually. "Once I trusted them. Once I would have rewarded them. Once they might have attained power that most dwarves could only dream of."

"I understand, Master. But now what?" Facet said. She looked at the two Guilders, licking her crimson lips. "Shall I kill them for you? It would be an honor—and a pleasure."

The wizard, almost reluctantly, shook his head. "No. Killing them would be pleasurable, of course. But it would of necessity be quick, even merciful. And this is not the time for mercy. No, I would like them to contemplate their treachery, to reflect upon their greed and their failures."

Abruptly he sat up and snarled a quick phrase, the command to a short, powerful spell.

Immediately Peat and Sadie Guilder screamed—soundlessly as they remained in the grip of the wizard's spell of silence—and began to writhe. Facet watched, fascinated, her eyes shining as the two dwarves shrank and shriveled before their eyes. In seconds they had diminished a foot in height, then two, then even more. They were the size of young children by then and still growing smaller.

"Catch them, my dear, before they scuttle away to some mouse hole," Willim directed gleefully, and his female apprentice swept forward to snatch up the small Theiwar by the scruffs of their necks. Holding one in each hand, she lifted them up for her master's inspection.

Only then did Willim the Black rise. He crossed the room to the place where a clear bell jar rested atop a marble burner. Lifting the glass jar, he held it expectantly while Facet placed the two shrunken dwarves on the burner. Peat collapsed to his knees, while Sadie glared upward, barking something soundless at them as she shook a tiny fist.

The wizard quickly placed the jar down on the marble circle again, trapping the two miniaturized dwarves underneath it. His face twisted into a wicked grin as he looked at his beautiful apprentice. He gestured to the little oil pot underneath the marble burner.

"Now," he said with uncharacteristic cheerfulness, "light the stove."

—DH—

Brandon approached the doors leading into the headquarters of the League of Enforcers. Two burly guardsmen flanked that entrance, each dressed in the shiny black leather tunic of their order and holding a long-hafted axe with the butt braced on the floor and the blades held upright, as high as their heads. It took all of Brandon's willpower to remind himself that, courtesy of a little priestess magic, he, too, wore a shiny black leather tunic and bore an axe that had been magically enhanced to exactly match the weapons of the two Enforcers.

The one difference in their uniforms was the silver bar that decorated each of his shoulders. It was that insignia that caught the eyes of the two guards, bringing each to attention. They clapped their fists to their chests in salute, one standing aside while the other reached out to open the door for the "captain."

Brandon nodded a curt thanks, remembering to maintain the haughty air that Gretchan had coached him into adopting. He strode into the headquarters as if he owned the place, hoping that his confusion—and his desperation—didn't show on his face. Apparently it did not, for the guards let him pass then closed the door behind him.

Fortunately, his mother had accurately described some of the details of the interior of the headquarters, based on her own memories. First he entered the ward room. The interrogation rooms lay to the left beyond that, and Brandon remembered his mother's suspicions that the dungeon cells lay farther back in that direction. Several Enforcers were seated around a table in the main room, but he ignored them and they ignored him as he turned and went through the door leading to the left.

That led into the hall his mother had described, with a series of doors on either side, currently shut. At least one led into the interrogation room where she had last seen Garren Bluestone. He burned with anger as he pictured that confrontation: the Enforcers threatening his mother, using her terror to coerce Garren into signing his false confession.

Operating only on his hunch and his mother's best guess, Brandon continued down to the end of the corridor, which made a turn to the right and led deeper into the complex of rooms. Again there were doors to either side, but his attention was centered on the door at the very end of the hall. Unlike the other plain plank barriers, it was bracketed with iron straps and clasped with a heavy lock, latched on the side from which he was approaching. He couldn't stop himself from glancing over his shoulder and was relieved to see no one was in the corridor with him. Reaching out, he lifted the latch and released the clasp, pushing the door open.

He found himself in a darkened corridor, a place that smelled of damp stones, stale air, and urine. Blinking against the darkness, he hesitated a moment, letting his keen eyes adjust to the lack of light, and he listened.

The place was as silent as any tomb, but Brandon refused to be discouraged. Step by step, he advanced cautiously along the darkened hall, trying to set each foot down as soundlessly as possible. Pace by pace he moved into the dungeon, past doors that were marked with small iron grates, confirming his hunch it was indeed where the League of Enforcers kept its prisoners. The doors were closed, secured with stout-looking locks. He couldn't hear any noise in any of the cells.

Unfortunately, he couldn't think of any silent means of finding out what, or who, lurked behind any of those closed doors. Acutely conscious of time passing, fearing that, at any moment, the executioners might come looking for Garren Bluestone, he finally decided on a bold course.

"Dad?" he asked, his tone at a conversational level. "Are you here?"

He heard a scuffle of movement from one of the rooms halfway down, to the left, and took a few steps closer until he was right outside that door. "Dad?" he probed again.

"Brandon?" came the incredulous, whispered reply.

His heart soaring, Brand reached for the door, not surprised to find that it was locked. "Yes, it's me!" he whispered back. "I've got to get you out of here!"

"How?" demanded Garren. "You can't take the chance! Get out of here. I can take care of myself!"

"Stand back," Brandon growled, hefting the Bluestone Axe. "This door is coming down!"

His father had the sense to stop arguing, and Brandon leaned back, gathering his strength for a single blow. The enchanted blade smashed into the wooden door with a loud crash, sending a shower of splinters into the cell and cracking the sturdy barrier right down the middle.

Immediately Garren pulled on the wrecked door, dragging the biggest piece of it into the cell. A portion still swung from the solid hinges, but there was enough space for the dwarf to slip out through the gap. For just a moment, father and son embraced, the clasp of their strong arms saying more than any words could have done.

"Now come on, hurry," Brandon said, taking Garren's arm and starting back toward the entrance.

But that door swung open before him, and he raised his hands to screen his eyes against the torchlight flaring there. Two brands burned, held high in strong hands, but the Bluestones could see a host of Enforcers crowding there, completely blocking the exit.

"What excellent timing," came the words in Baracan Heelspur's voice. "I come to execute one Bluestone, and I catch two of them in my net!"

At the same time, the doors to several of the cells burst open, fully revealing the trap. In another second the dungeon corridor was full of dwarves, all of them dressed in the black leather of the Enforcers' agents, closing in around the two Bluestones.

In the next breath, father and son were disarmed, and both were prisoners.

—DH—

"Whoa there, Kondike!" puffed Gus, red faced and sweating as he chased the big black dog down another street in the strange city. He could barely see his waving tail as the animal coursed around a corner.

Berta and Slooshy, as doughty as their male companion, jogged steadfastly along. All three Aghar, as well as the dog, had climbed many, many stairs, but the gully dwarves were too focused on their guide even to consider to where in the world they had traveled. Kondike seemed to have a destination in mind. From the moment Gus had mentioned Gretchan's name, the dog hadn't wavered in his determined course.

They hurried down a street with houses and taverns to both sides. Many dwarves were walking about there. They gaped in surprise at the big dog and moved out of his way—and stayed out of the way of the three Aghar who scurried behind. Gus did take the time to reflect that it was very different from Thorbardin, where their appearance in such a crowded locale could have only ended in disaster—probably with their heads chopped off by Theiwar bunty hunters.

They passed one more tavern, marked by a sign picturing a large mug with a jagged crack running down the side, and turned down a narrower, quiet street, with Kondike taking off at a run. The three gully dwarves had just turned the corner when the dog came to a halt in front of the doorway to a dwarf house. The dog barked once, loudly, then repeated the sound with growing urgency.

The door flew open a few seconds later, just as Gus was drawing close. His heart flipped happily in his chest as he saw Gretchan rush out, kneeling down to embrace her dog as Kondike yelped and licked and generally wiggled in ecstasy.

Still panting, Gus slowed to a walk, stumbling slightly in his weariness. Still, he pictured himself as the pinnacle of dwarfish style as he sauntered up to her and offered a big, cheery smile.

"Hi . . . Gretchan," he said between gasps for breath. "Sure is nice . . . to see you!"

"Gus?" she gasped, staring at him in shock. "What are you doing here?"

"Well, I don't know," he replied honestly enough. "First, tell where 'here' is."

"You don't know?" she asked then laughed ruefully. "I guess I shouldn't be surprised. You certainly do have a way of getting around. Somehow you've gotten yourself to Kayolin; I can't even begin to imagine how."

He was about to ask what Kayolin was when they were interrupted by a breathless dwarf running down the street. Gretchan stood up quickly, her face creased by an expression of concern.

"What is it?" she asked.

"The League of Enforcers," explained the puffing dwarf. "They've got Brandon and Garren in chains—they're taking them both up to the palace!"

TWENTY-FIVE

THE BLUESTONE FACTION

Brandon and Garren, hands shackled and the Bluestone Axe snatched away, were being marched side by side up the stairs from the Enforcers' headquarters to the highest level of Garnet Thax, the palace of Regar Smashfingers. Baracan Heelspur led the detachment of Enforcers, more than two dozen, who escorted the prisoners up to the palace.

"Never trust a woman," Baracan said with a chuckle, walking along behind Brandon. "Rona Darkwater thought she was good enough for me! Imagine—as if I'd accept one of your castoffs. But she served as the perfect pawn, didn't she?"

"What have you done with her?" Brandon growled, appalled at the way the noble dwarf maid had been used.

"Oh, she'll be fine once the bruises heal," Lord Heelspur's son assured him breezily. "I didn't even break any of her bones when I beat her."

Brandon thrashed, trying to turn, but he was cuffed harshly on the ear by one of the guards. Glowering at the floor, he kept moving, his mind churning with schemes of the vengeful violence he'd like to inflict upon Baracan Heelspur. He didn't know how or when, but he'd make the smug bully, the murderer who had killed his brother, pay for his villainy.

They marched right in to the great throne room with the two shackled prisoners prodded forward by the sword points of several grinning Enforcers. As usual, the galleries above and to either side of the throne were lined with spectators. The whole room was wrapped in a strange pall of silence, though, and Brandon couldn't help but take encouragement from that. He was also encouraged to spot several scarlet jackets in the crowd; he could only hope the members of the Garnet Guard would be ready to help.

Even more heartening, he heard a series of whispers—"Bluestone, Bluestone!"—coming from the gallery until Lord Heelspur, who stood behind the throne, gestured irritably. Numerous black-garbed Enforcers began to move through the crowd, and the rebellious muttering died away. The procession advanced at a steady march and came to a halt before the throne. Baracan Heelspur saluted stiffly.

"I recognize these dwarves," Regar Smashfingers proclaimed, lounging casually back in his throne. "But why do you bring them to me in chains?" he asked innocently.

"Sire, they are rebels, plotting the overthrow of your reign!" Baracan Heelspur proclaimed, his voice loud enough to ring through the gallery. "The father has already been charged, and at your command was secured by the League of Enforcers in a cell. The son entered the League headquarters through subterfuge—a magical disguise—and attempted to free the father by smashing down the door to his cell."

The one word, magic, seemed to echo by itself through the cavernous throne room, provoking a volley of mutters and prayers among the superstitious dwarves. The king's eyes widened in a mocking display of surprise.

"Can this be true?" he asked of Brandon. Before the prisoner could answer, he addressed his captain of Enforcers. "What was the nature of this magic?"

"I know not, sire, except that it cloaked his appearance in deception. He was made to look like a captain of Enforcers. Even his axe"—Baracan produced and brandished the Bluestone Axe, the legendary artifact known to all Kayolin dwarves—"was concealed to resemble the halberds of the League's guards."

"These are serious charges!" the king declared. "And to think, barely six days ago I welcomed this criminal into my court, acknowledged him as a hero! The Horax Hero indeed! This is a sad day in the noble history of Kayolin!"

Regar Smashfingers actually managed to sound distressed as he recounted the distressing facts, though Brandon could plainly see the delight flashing in the old scoundrel's eyes. That delight quickly focused on the two prisoners, changing into a glower of cruel cunning. The king spoke again, and though his tone conveyed regret, his expression belied the sadness of his voice.

"I had hoped my coronation would signal a new dawn in Kayolin's days, an era of peace and prosperity of benefit to us all. And still, it is my hope that this will be the case. It had been my intention, in fact, to promote the legendary Bluestones back into Kayolin's nobility, to the rank they held so long, so *very* long, ago.

"But I shall not have the Bluestones in my court when I finally don my crown. There will be no place for rebels amid my loyal nobles."

Smashfingers stood suddenly and, with a flourish of his right hand, gestured to Lord Heelspur. "Bring me my crown, that I may wear it now, as I pronounce sentence upon these criminals!"

Immediately the loyal follower advanced, bearing a velvet pillow upon which rested an object covered by a silken cloth. A courtier whipped the cloth away to reveal a stunning crown, a circlet of silver bejeweled with startlingly blue stones, each blinking and sparkling in the reflected light of a hundred torches.

Regar Smashfingers stepped down from his throne, descending the three steps to the chamber floor. He came to stand beside Alakar Heelspur, where all could see.

"Behold the new crown of Kayolin!" he declared. "Molded from the Torc of the Forge itself, the blessed talisman of Reorx. These blue stones are proof of his blessing, proof of his favor, proof of the rightness of my rule—"

"They are proof of nothing!"

An audible gasp rushed through the vast chamber as the words, spoken in Gretchan's voice, resounded through the assemblage.

"Who speaks?" demanded Lord Heelspur. "Who dares to challenge the true king?"

"I speak," Gretchan declared, stepping to the edge of the gallery. She was wearing a white bearskin cloak, and her staff was held firmly in her hands. She banged the wooden post against the floor, and it struck a blow that reverberated through the huge room, seeming to vibrate the stones under every dwarf's feet.

"And just who *are* you?" demanded the king, genuinely puzzled. At the same time, Baracan Heelspur gestured to his Enforcers, many of whom began to filter through the crowd, closing in on Gretchan.

Brandon, watching her, desperately hoped she had more of a plan than simply to challenge the king.

She did. With her free hand, she pulled a gleaming circlet of silver from her purse and held it high. Twelve blue stones, as bright as those in the king's new crown, glittered from the ring of brilliant metal. The gathered dwarves gasped in awe, some of them sidling away from her, others pressing close. Some of the latter included the redcoats of the Garnet Guard. The latter formed enough of a barrier, Brandon saw with relief, that the Enforcers would not be able to reach the priestess without passing through the obstacle of several dozen sturdy dwarves.

"I am a priestess of Reorx," Gretchan Pax declared calmly. "And I tell you all that this, in my hand, is the real Torc of the Forge. It is the talisman of our god, and until Brandon Bluestone, the Horax Hero, found it in the hive of those foul creatures, it was lost to our people for many ages."

"Lies!" cried Lord Heelspur. He raised the crown. "These are the gems from the torc!"

Gretchan looked at him with an almost palpable glare of contempt. She beat the butt of her staff on the floor again, and the anvil atop the shaft began to glow, far brighter than all the torches in the great hall.

"If you are certain you speak the truth," she said coldly. "Then I suggest that you place that crown upon the false king's head. Let the people of Kayolin see the proof of their god's displeasure."

Regar Smashfingers glanced at Heelspur, and Brandon could see real fear in his eyes. He stared at the crown as if it were some kind of poisonous spider, while Alakar Heelspur's face twisted into a glare of fury.

"Here, my king!" he said boldly. "Let me place the crown upon your brow!"

Caught in his own bluster, the king nodded. Heelspur stepped up onto the short stairway before the throne, so he was a little above the king, who still stood upon the floor. With a grand flourish, he set the circlet of silver on Regar Smashfingers's head.

The king almost winced as the metal touched his scalp. Then he relaxed as, for the moment, nothing happened.

"Dwarves of Kayolin!" Lord Heelspur declared forcefully. "Behold the power and the glory of your king!"

There were a few cheers, mostly from the Enforcers and the men of the king's personal attendants and loyal courtiers. The majority of the spectators watched warily, casting glances between Gretchan and Smashfingers.

She timed her challenge perfectly, as the tension built to an almost explosive level.

"Dwarves of Kayolin!" she cried. "Behold the power and glory of your god!"

Again she smacked the staff on the floor. The torc in her hand began to glow with a brilliant light. At the same time, the king shrieked in pain and pulled the crown off of his head. His hair was smoking, and he dropped the metal circlet with a curse. It struck the floor, and all twelve of the sapphires popped out of their mounts to roll crazily across the throne room floor.

A bolt of light shot from Gretchan's staff, touching the shackles around Brandon's and his father's wrists. In the searing blast of that beam, both sets of manacles sprang open, falling to the floor with clangs of iron. Brandon wasted no time lunging forward and snatching his axe from the startled Baracan Heelspur. At the same time, Garren pulled a sword from the sheath of a nearby guard—a dwarf who was frozen in place, staring at his monarch with a horror-stricken expression.

"Stop this treason!" Alakar Heelspur shouted. "Stop, I command you! In the name of the king!"

"No! Our king is in Thorbardin!" roared General Watchler.

The commander of the Garnet Guard, resplendent in his red uniform, had stepped forward to stand beside Gretchan at the edge of the balcony. "You are the treasonous one—feeding us your lies, working your murders, using your Enforcers to terrorize your own citizens. Tell us, Lord Heelspur: Who killed Nailer Bluestone?"

"Take him!" cried the chief of the Enforcers, frantically gesturing at the general. But there were too many redcoats surrounding him, and the League's agents, in their shiny black leather, were clearly reluctant to charge the veteran troops.

The two Bluestones, father and son, advanced side by side upon Baracan and Alakar Heelspur. From somewhere that seemed very far away, Brandon heard the chant pick up again: "Bluestone, Bluestone, Bluestone . . ." And with each recitation of their name, it picked up in volume and force, rumbling like a distant drum approaching quickly.

Regar Smashfingers dropped to his knees, scrambling around the floor and snatching up a sapphire here, another winking gem there. "My crown!" he wailed, his voice spiking to a shrill, high pitch. His courtiers and guards stepped back, staring at the ruler as if desperate to get out of the way of his clutching fingers. One fawning nobleman dropped down to help, but Regar slapped his hand away as he reached for one of the rolling gems.

"Mine!" shouted Smashfingers, his voice cracking.

"I tell you, this is treason!" cried Alakar Heelspur, stepping around the king, ignoring his ruler as he pointed at the two advancing dwarves. "How dare you challenge the rightful law of this place! The rightful government, your new king?"

He waved at the rank of Enforcers who stared aghast at the figure of their ruler crawling around on the floor.

"The rightful law, the one that killed my brother, Nailer Bluestone?" Brandon roared, taking another step forward. "The lawful government that allowed that murder, that practices treachery and theft, giving to House Heelspur the treasure rightly won by House Bluestone?"

He raised the Bluestone Axe in his right hand, pointing at Baracan with his left. "I call you murderer! I name you thief! And Nailer Bluestone will be avenged."

He advanced at a rush, as Baracan drew his sword and circled away from the throne to give himself fighting room.

"Stop him!" shouted Lord Heelspur. "Enforcers, take him down!"

The agents of the League finally reacted as the command snapped them from their shock. Swords slid from sheaths; mighty halberds were raised high; and the black-garbed dwarves started toward Brandon from both sides and from behind.

"Murderer!" the younger Bluestone repeated, sprinting toward Baracan before the Enforcers could interfere. He raised his axe, haft held in both of his hands, over his head.

"Bluestone! Bluestone! Bluestone!" The chant resounded through the throne room, echoing from the ceiling and thumping through the very bedrock itself. The Enforcers hesitated, glancing at each other nervously. Several swordsmen of the Garnet Guards stepped forward, weapons sheathed, to interpose themselves between the black-clad agents of Heelspur's League and the duel taking shape before them.

Brandon brought his axe down in a short, controlled chop. Baracan, expecting a more forceful blow, parried the attack and retreated, circling around behind the throne. With his axe dancing right, left, high, and low, Brandon followed. A part of his mind reminded him to be cautious, but cold fury doused his attempts at restraint. He made a sudden rush again, slashing back and forth, while his enemy jabbed, carving a cut on his wrist before he could push out of the way.

The two battlers came around the other side of the throne. Brandon glanced up, looking for danger, but he saw that the Garnet Guards, while not taking part in the fight, had formed enough of a barrier that the Enforcers were effectively held back. At the very least, they would have had to push aside the stalwart members of that ancient regiment in order to get to Brandon. Garren Bluestone, too, was holding back, though he held his sword at the ready, his eyes shifting from Regar to Alakar to Baracan.

Even the ruler had ceased his hunt for the scattered gems. He rested upon his knees, looking up at the duel raging before him, wincing every time steel clashed against steel.

Brandon's mind flashed a picture of Nailer, his older brother hoisting a mug, toasting his friends, his face full of youth, beaming with pleasure. Then he saw that same face, lifeless and bloody, on the floor of a lonely cave. Nailer had died because Lord Heelspur craved the vein of gold the Bluestone brothers had just discovered, and Lord Heelspur's son had led the assassins. That murder would finally be avenged!

With a grimace, the axe-wielding dwarf flew at his opponent, launching another flurry of blows, forcing Baracan into a rapid retreat. The other dwarf's sword flashed back and forth, each time knocking away the Bluestone Axe, but always that keen blade pressed a little closer to the noble scion's pale skin.

The throne room had fallen silent—even the "Bluestone" chant fading away—as the witnesses stared at the do-or-die battle enacted before them.

"Look out!"

Brandon heard the shrill cry of alarm, recognized it as Gretchan's voice, and tried to spin away. But Baracan, eyes alight with impending triumph, thrust once, then again, forcing the axe-wielding Bluestone to parry his blows or suffer death. Then Baracan's eyes, looking past Brandon's shoulder, widened in shock and dismay. A groaning sigh, mingled with cheers, erupted from the crowd. As Brandon finally broke away from the fight, he saw Lord Heelspur fall on his face. Garren Bluestone stood behind the dying nobleman, holding a bloodied sword.

"He tried to take you from behind," the senior Bluestone said almost apologetically.

"Thanks, Dad," Brandon replied sincerely.

Setting his axe at the ready, he again advanced toward Baracan, who retreated with fear in his eyes. "This isn't the way it was with my brother, is it?" demanded Brandon, smashing the axe down in a series of measured, controlled hacks, forcing Baracan's retreat. "You had four of your assassins with you when you killed him, didn't you? You'd never take on someone in a fair fight—at least, not someone like Nailer, who knew how to use a weapon." He taunted Baracan loudly, shaming his foe, instinctively feeling the mood of the city swing over to his side.

Baracan screamed and charged, overreaching as Brandon skipped out of the way of the thrust blade. The Bluestone Axe swung through a full half-circle—measured and controlled no longer, but like a living thing bent on blood and vengeance. The keen edge bit into Baracan Heelspur's neck, slicing all the way to his spine before Brandon finally pulled it free.

His enemy's head flopped backward, barely connected to the torso, as a geyser of blood erupted from the slashing wound. Already dead, Baracan's body swayed like a drunk; his knees collapsed, and he fell heavily to the floor.

For a moment, all was silent. Regar Smashfingers stared in dumbfounded horror. The Enforcers looked about nervously, slowly edging away from the dwarves of the Garnet Guards and the two Bluestones. The murmurs started softly, quickly swelling.

"Hail to House Bluestone!" General Watchler said. "And shame to Regar Smashfingers and his legacy of greed!"

"Spare me!" Regar cried. Already on his knees, he threw himself face-first onto the floor, hands groping for Garren's feet. "Don't kill me!" he pleaded, nearly blubbering. "You can have the kingship! The throne is yours!"

"Throne? No, you speak of the governor's chair," Garren Bluestone said, drawing a deep breath and speaking so that all could hear. "The throne is in Thorbardin!"

Then the cheers began, the cry of "Bluestone, Bluestone, Bluestone!" rose to the domed ceiling, echoed through the shaft of the Atrium, and thrummed in all the many levels of Garnet Thax. Dwarves embraced each other, cheering and sobbing with relief. The Enforcers beat a hasty retreat, and in moments there were none of the black-clad bullies to be seen.

Gretchan and Karine made their way down to the floor, and Brandon embraced the priestess, reveling in the feel of her soft skin against his face, her kisses finding his lips in the midst of his bristling beard. He pulled her close, almost weeping in relief, and spotted his mother as she ran up to embrace his father.

"Here—you should take this spot," said General Watchler, escorting Garren Bluestone up the steps before the great throne. "You would do it honor!"

The citizens of Kayolin cheered as Garren Bluestone sat on the great seat and was appointed, by acclamation, to be the new governor. The shouts and accolades thundered through the throne room, lasting for a very long time. The Bluestone chant changed to the new cry: "The throne is in Thorbardin!"

Brandon watched his father accept the acclaim, and he felt a burst of pride, accompanied by a lump in his throat. Nailer should be there, seeing that, he knew. But that would never be. Still, when he saw the pride, the pure happiness, on his mother's face, he was able to feel his own sense of accomplishment and joy.

"Hey, where did he come from?" Brandon asked in surprise, staring open mouthed at Gus and two other filthy gully dwarves mingling with the crowd and moving toward them. The little females to either side of him clutched his arms desperately, while Gus looked around in amazement, unsure of himself but clearly rather proud.

Gretchan nodded toward the little Aghar tenderly, smiling at Brandon. "Oh, I meant to tell you. Gus and his friends are here. I think the Master of the Forge was looking out for him and them—and for us. He came here through a magic spell; he's not sure exactly how. But the big news is that he brought us something important."

She pulled a crimson wedge of rock from her sagging pouch, and Brandon's eyes widened. "It's the same size and shape as the Bluestone . . ." he began, understanding slowing sinking in.

"And the Greenstone," she said. "Both of which are in Tarn Bellowgranite's hands, in Pax Tharkas."

"What are you talking about?" asked Garren, rising from the seat and stepping close. "This stone matches the Bluestone of our clan; I can see that much."

"It's part of an ancient artifact," Gretchan explained. "It's called the Tricolor Hammerhead, and it can smash any fortification—including, according to the legends, the Gates of Thorbardin itself. But it can only be forged with all three stones."

"And we thought the Redstone was locked away in Thorbardin," Brandon added. "So it didn't help much that Tarn Bellowgranite has the blue and the green parts." He blinked and looked at Gretchan. "Where did this come from anyway?"

"I brought it!" Gus said, stepping forward proudly. "Out of Thorbardin, when whole place burnin' up and stinkin'."

Brandon raised an eyebrow, exchanging a glance with Gretchan. She gave him a "we'll talk about it later" look.

Then she smiled and put an affectionate hand on Gus's stringy-haired head—which she quickly removed when she caught a glimpse of the dour glares on Berta's and Slooshy's faces. The two Aghar females continued to hug Gus's arms, each pulling so firmly that they seemed about ready to dislocate his shoulders. The male gully dwarf, meanwhile, gazed blissfully up at the priestess.

"Gus said we could have this stone on one condition," the cleric explained seriously to Brandon and his father.

"What condition?" asked Governor Bluestone, already assuming an air of authority.

"He tells me that one of King Jungor Stonespringer's acts, as ruler of Thorbardin, was to outlaw the very presence of the Aghar. He killed their highbulp and had his chair removed from Thorbardin's Council of Thanes. The rest of his people are being hunted and killed. I told Gus that if we use this stone to complete the hammer and if we are able to liberate the kingdom, I promised him the gully dwarves would be restored to their traditional chair at the council."

"That's fair enough," Garren said. "You have done all dwarfkind a great service," he solemnly told Gus, who beamed so brightly, his face turned red.

General Watchler came forward to join the discussion. "What is this about Thorbardin burning?"

Gretchan did her best to summarize the Aghar's extensive descriptions of the chaos in that ancient nation, with Gus chirping in every now and then with added detail.

"It sounds like the whole place is being torn apart by civil war," she finished at last, looking around at everyone's grim expressions. "The dwarves there need help, but since the king sealed the gates, a whole army could march against the place without any prospect of success. There has never been any way to reach them . . . until now."

"But with the Tricolor Hammerhead, we could enter Thorbardin!" Brandon exclaimed, seized by the grandness of the idea. "Tarn Bellowgranite would help, I'm sure. But we'd need a bigger army, more than just his refugees in Pax Tharkas—"

"A force like the Kayolin Army?" General Watchler suggested.

"Yes!" Brandon said. "With that, and Tarn Bellowgranite's support, we could restore him to his rightful throne, and bring Thorbardin's nightmare to an end!"

"That would be a mission worthy of our steel," the general noted. "But we have the horax to deal with."

"The horax are an engineering problem, not a combat enemy," Brandon explained. He described the fallen barriers, which upon interrogation, Regar Smashfingers had readily admitted were destroyed by his and Alakar Heelspur's orders. Regar had one of his courtiers retrieve a map of the deep caverns, on which the Heelspurs had marked every place where they had removed the barriers to horax exploration.

"We'll have to hold them back toward their hive," Brandon explained. "And that'll take some time and effort. But once we do that and rebuild those walls, they'll be no more of a menace than they've been for the last thousand years."

"And in the meantime . . . ?" Watcher said, eyeing Brandon shrewdly.

"In the meantime," the younger Bluestone said confidently. "I'd like to plan with you to lead an army of Kayolin dwarves to the south, where we'll join with the Pax Tharkas refugees, smash the North Gate, and liberate Thorbardin from the grip of the mad king."

"Bluestone! Bluestone!" echoed the chant from the gallery.

And in that same instant, the army that would liberate Thorbardin began to take shape.

EPILOGUE

With his treacherous agents suitably punished, Willim the Black and Facet teleported back to the comfort and security of his laboratory.

"But what about the fire dragon, Master?" asked the female. "Can it not seek us, find us, here?"

They both knew that Gorathian still flew wildly through Norbardin, but the wizard was not ready to face the creature of Chaos in open combat. "Perhaps it has doubled back into the city," he suggested. "I suspect that it is intent upon seeking out and slaying me. But it will not find me until I am ready to face it, and that time has not yet come."

Instead, Willim chose to return to his laboratory and make a new plan. He had his mistress by his side, and all other concerns seemed to fade in the face of that truth. He stretched, sighed, and was pleased.

"How can we fight that beast?" Facet asked, clinging to her master's arm.

"Powerful magic, my sweet," the wizard told her reassuringly. Even so, he turned his face, stitched eyelids squinting in concern, toward the lofty wall of the lair. He murmured the words to a spell, a powerful protection, even as he held her close and felt the warmth of her flesh soothing, invigorating, and empowering him.

Moments later he broke the embrace and gestured toward the black-rimmed gap through that wall, the place where Gorathian seared through the thick divider. "Already I have a barrier on that hole, one I think even the fire dragon would find daunting."

"Yes, Master," Facet replied, eyes downcast. She was well aware that the monster, capable of melting a hole through any density of rock, would have no need of using its point of egress as a route of attack. But she did not give voice to her fear.

Instead, she turned toward the large, central work-table in the laboratory. A sturdy bell jar rested there on a circle of marble. Within that jar, two shimmering shapes writhed and drifted. They were devoid of dwarf features, more like wispy scraps of pale blue silk or even smoke, yet they were clearly alive. The two imprisoned beings circled and swooped and intertwined with each other in a manner that could have signaled affection or anger—or both.

"I see that your spies have found a new home," Facet said, stroking her white-fingered hand across the surface of the jar.

Willim hacked out a dry chuckle. "Yes. They will have much time—forever, in fact—to contemplate the consequences of treachery."

The black wizard sighed and ran a hand through his beard. The hairs were bristling and tangled, and he could feel the grit of smoke and grime on his fingers. With a quick magical word, he groomed himself, instantly combing his hair and beard, vanishing the grit and grime right off his skin. Only then did he turn to his apprentice—though it was getting harder and harder to think of her as a student; in many ways, she seemed to be teaching *him*—with a grimace that was his best approximation of a smile.

"But I am weary, my pet. Come with me to our chambers . . . where we might rest. Or find ourselves reinvigorated," he added with a throaty chuckle.

"Certainly, Master," Facet said with a low rasp that set Willim's blood to tingling. "But first, can we share a sip of wine?"

"A splendid idea," the wizard said. "Please, pour us both refreshment."

Facet shifted against the counter as she poured the wine. Her gown slipped to the side, exposing her curving leg all the way to the hip. Willim's attention, the full force of his true sight, focused on that white skin; it was all he could do to keep his tongue from licking his lips. His pulse pounded in his head, and his breathing grew short. How could she be so beautiful, so compelling, so irresistible?

And he never saw the bottle of potion, the charm that had been serving her so well, that Facet tipped over his glass. A few drops splashed into the surface of the wizard's wine, but the bottle was stoppered and shelved a moment later, when she turned to offer him his glass.

She smiled and his attention was swallowed by her eyes—so soft, so yielding . . . so impenetrable.

—DH—

King Jungor Stonespringer sat in the darkness of his ruined palace. He touched the golden eye that filled his old, empty socket. The fresh wound where the wizard had destroyed his other eye was a gory gash, but he didn't feel any pain. Even as his fingers probed at the scab, he felt a liberating joy. Reorx was his master, his comfort, his protection. He did not need to see!

Instead, he would feel, and right then he felt heat. There was a mighty warmth before him, a roasting presence that was greater than any normal fire. He turned his face toward that radiance and knew that the fresh blood on his face was crusting and drying under the baking heat. His skin reddened, his robe smoldered, but still he relished the power of that great fire.

"It is you, my master," he said, sighing in pleasure. Finally, the heat grew too intense, and he fell back, uncaring that he lay on a floor covered with broken stones.

"I feel the power of the forge," he said, ecstasy filling his head. "Immortal Reorx, warm your humble servant!" He turned his empty eye sockets upward, embracing the presence.

Above him, the source of the heat looked down. Great nostrils flared, while a tongue of flame licked forth from a hellish maw.

It almost seemed as if Gorathian was smiling.

TRACY HICKMAN
PRESENTS
THE ANVIL OF TIME

With the power of the Anvil of Time, the Journeyman can travel the river of time as simply as walking upstream, visiting the ancient past of Krynn with ease.

VOLUME ONE
THE SELLSWORD
Cam Banks

Vanderjack, a mercenary with a price on his head, agrees out of desperation to retrieve a priceless treasure for a displaced noble. The treasure is deep within enemy territory, and he must survive an army of old foes, a chorus of unhappy ghosts, and the questionable assistance of a mad gnome to find it.

VOLUME TWO
THE SURVIVORS
Dan Willis

A goodhearted dwarf is warned of an apocalyptic flood by the god Reorx, and he and his motley followers must decide whether the warning is real—and then survive the disaster that sweeps through their part of Krynn.

November 2008

RICHARD A. KNAAK

THE OGRE TITANS

The Grand Lord Golgren has been savagely crushing all opposition to his control of the harsh ogre lands of Kern and Blöde, first sweeping away rival chieftains, then rebuilding the capital in his image. For this he has had to deal with the ogre titans, dark, sorcerous giants who have contempt for his leadership.

VOLUME ONE

THE BLACK TALON

Among the ogres, where every ritual demands blood and every ally can become a deadly foe, Golgren seeks whatever advantage he can obtain, even if it means a possible alliance with the Knights of Solamnia, a questionable pact with a mysterious wizard, and trusting an elven slave who might wish him dead.

VOLUME TWO

THE FIRE ROSE

Attacked by enemies on all sides, Golgren must abandon his throne to undertake the quest for the Fire Rose before Safrag, master of the Ogre Titans can locate it and claim supremacy over all ogres—and perhaps all of Krynn.

December 2008

VOLUME THREE

THE GARGOYLE KING

Forced from the throne he has so long coveted, Golgren makes a final stand for control of the ogre lands against the Titans . . . against an enemy as ancient and powerful as a god.

December 2009